LOVE
IN THE
CLOISTERS

Love in the Cloisters

Published by The Conrad Press Ltd. in the United Kingdom 2023

Tel: +44(0)1227 472 874
www.theconradpress.com
info@theconradpress.com

ISBN 978-1-915494-37-5

Copyright © Irene Devereux, 2023

Disclaimer:
This is a work of fiction and any resemblance to any person living or dead is purely coincidental. The place names mentioned are real but have no connection with the events in this book.

Typesetting and Cover Design by:
Charlotte Mouncey, www.bookstyle.co.uk

The Conrad Press logo was designed by Maria Priestley.

Printed and bound in Great Britain by Clays Ltd, Elcograf S.p.A.

LOVE
IN THE
CLOISTERS

IRENE DEVEREUX

I dedicate my novel to my mum and dad,
Frank, Clare, Brian, John and
Gemma-Leah, for all their support
and love through the years.

I can resist everything except temptation.

Oscar Wilde

CHAPTER 1

Forbidden fruit

As Cameron led the way along the dimly lit hallway he whispered:

'Be careful you don't fall over something, Georgia, the light is dim in here and pray to Christ we don't bump into anyone.'

In an irritated voice Georgia heard herself say, 'Why all this cloak and dagger, Cameron? We're only walking along a hallway.'

His comments had made Georgia feel a little anxious. Now the reality of the situation began to hit home, her heart started to beat a little faster, as she began to understand the implications. This wasn't just any hallway, this was the hallway in a monastery. She thought to herself, maybe coming in here wasn't such a good idea. I had an uneasy feeling the moment I stepped in through that big old heavy wooden door, I Just knew I had made one of my many bad decisions.

As they approached the stairs, Cameron began to explain:

'Honestly, Georgia, even before guests have time to allow their eyes to gaze in the direction of this stairway they are ushered into the parlour. They are never allowed to venture one step past the parlour, anything further than that is considered forbidden terri-tory. The place the deacons call the inner sanctum, the private area up those stairs includes the deacons' and priests' rooms or cells as they are called.' He continued, 'The housekeeper, Miss Maisie Coyne wouldn't take too kindly to me, a young deacon escorting you, Georgia, a beautiful young lady along this out-of-bounds hallway, towards that winding staircase.'

She smiled. In that moment Georgia realised the impact it

would have on Cameron if they bumped into the housekeeper. Maybe he was afraid Miss Maisie Coyne would tell his mentor and that would spell trouble for Deacon Cameron.

Georgia had never met that lady but the name Miss Maisie Coyne had a sternness to it that conjured up in Georgia's mind different versions of what the lady looked and acted like. It was as if Miss Maisie Coyne was being presented, the introduction was almost theatrical. Georgia repeated to herself *Miss Maisie Coyne* and again her mind painted a picture of Maisie. In it Maisie looked like a true artist and like a lot of artists had several different personas... A happy Maisie Coyne, a sad Maisie Coyne, a judgemental Maisie Coyne, a stern Maisie Coyne. Stern Maisie Coyne, this was the one her mind settled on. Georgia also wondered if deep down in Maisie's soul, there was a sensitive Miss Maisie Coyne. She had no idea if there was or not but she was determined to find out.

'So far so good,' said Cameron, 'no Maisie Coyne, no Audian.'

'Who in God's name is Audian?' asked Georgia, trying to catch her breath.

'He's someone from my neck of the woods, we entered the monastery on the very same day.'

Luck was on their side, no Maisie, no Audian, in fact not a living soul in sight. How lucky were they? There it stood, their biggest obstacle, the large, shadowy, dimly lit stairway. Every stair was visible to anyone passing by. Every stair climbed without hearing a creak or seeing a soul was a relief.

Up and up they climbed. The banisters felt slippery on the never-ending stairway probably from all the vigorous polishing poor Maisie Coyne must have done through the years. In Georgia's mind she imagined Maisie cleaning the stairs, being ever so thorough polishing and shining the bannisters, the steps and every rung of the staircase, with her chamois cloth and mansion floor polish making sure the bannisters, steps and every rung of the stairway gleamed, after all it was her masterpiece, if it shone, she shone. She guessed Maisie knew every nook and cranny. They reached the top exhausted. Cameron stopped for a moment, looked back down into all the corners of the dimly lit, shadowy stairway to ensure there were no spying eyes. Once happy, he began to fumble in his trouser pocket until a large set of keys, on a circular piece of metal, emerged. Into the lock went the big long brass key, he turned the key, a loud clinking sound echoed all around the large space. Thank God, the door opened quickly, they ran in. Bang… that hollow sound, the door closed, in went the long brass key, another clink and the door was locked. They were safely inside. Georgia couldn't believe her eyes when she looked around the room, it was so small, only big enough to fit a single bed, a bookcase and a tiny table with a lamp, talk about bijou!

They had walked through the huge expansive gardens, through that big wooden door, along that vast hallway, and then the two passionate humans had taken their lives in their hands as they sneaked up those wide shiny stairs. Now here they were at last, alone together. It was hard to believe there was so little room behind that big heavy door. Georgia in her innocence had imagined a large palatial room. Surely grown men would need a lot more space than this she thought. Surprisingly, the single bed looked big and inviting in such a small space or was it that Georgia's mind was focussing on the bed! Her yearning body had waited long enough for this moment.

For the last couple of months Georgia had tried to focus on her well-being and changing her career. Now, after a lot of studying she was part of the beauty industry - beauty, makeup, massage and all that goes with it. A big change from auctioneering, a career she'd spent quite a few years perfecting. That was her past. Now looking towards her future, and for the good of her health, she surrounded herself with as many beautiful things and calm spaces as possible - lovely scented candles, bouquets of dried flowers and soft music playing from her speakers, anything to take her mind off her deviousness. Yes, Georgia had to be surrounded by all these things. They made her feel calm in her world of mayhem. She, Georgia Brown, who only a few months earlier had taken vows at the sacred altar when she married Ross, the love of her life, was now cheating on him and wrestling with her emotions. *Would she stay or would she go?* They were the words of an old song. He was the best husband any girl could wish for, a man who would do anything for her. He had been her complete world. The guilt of her stupid actions made her tummy feel jittery. Ross, her gorgeous husband didn't deserve to be left alone, he was guilty of no crime. She was guilty of contemplating desertion, yes deserting her marriage and a young husband who she had promised to love for the rest of her life. Now she was making a complete 360 turn. It was the guilt that consumed her, that had created this mayhem in Georgia's being and made her feel lost, alone and very sad. The only way she could cope now was to focus on the present and future, Not the Past.

CHAPTER 2

Distraction

Now she was back in the moment, she could feel the heat from her skin and her heart beating faster and faster. What a feeling, a pure adrenaline rush. Cameron wasted no time at all on small talk, all the control he had exercised earlier on that dimly lit stairway, was gone with a bang, just like the bang of the closing door in his small cell.

Clothes landed everywhere, floor, bedpost, lamp shade, to hell with control, loyalty and tidiness. Georgia and Cameron forgot all that as they indulged in the best sex ever, passion past boiling point. The song – *Son of a Preacher Man* – sprang to mind as Georgia enjoyed the sins of the flesh. Tears streamed down her face, tears of ecstasy, she didn't care if Cameron felt them on his skin, it only made the moment better. His skin felt moist and silky all at the same time and the exotic aroma of his Tom Ford aftershave made the moment even more sensual, it was an almost out of body experience. Where did he learn to make love like this? Was it out in an exotic land among all those exotic people who let their bodies move like the branches of a beautiful tree? Who cares, Georgia certainly didn't. She now realised that while the room was very small there was plenty of room for manoeuvre, after all they had touched almost every centimetre of the teeny tiny room. They had tried desperately not to make too much noise, after all a seminary full of budding priests surely wasn't the place to make love in. Maybe that added to the excitement, forbidden fruit is always the most delicious. It seemed as if hours had passed by before the two lovers returned to earth. In all that time there had been no talk of love, lots of signs of lust but no talk of love.

The two sexually charged human beings regained their composure and retrieved their clothing from places like the lamp shade - where her top had a great effect by darkening the room, the telephone - that was now occupied by her bra, the floor - that had a mixture of Cameron's bits and bobs and her skirt. Guess where her fancy pants had landed - on the handle of the big brown door. She couldn't remember throwing them. Every garment lay in a mess somewhere in this little teeny tiny room and to think Georgia had ironed every bit of her clothing to make sure there were no creases, before she left home. One thing was for certain, all her clothes would be a bag of creases when she left. Shame on you Georgia Brown, she thought. Then very quickly dismissed that thought as her mind drifted back to earlier – pure ecstasy. Now back down to Earth, would she do the walk of shame or would she brazen it out as she left and passed by the wonderful Maisie Coyne? (if she was there) How could Georgia appear in public in clothes that resembled articles purchased from a very bad second hand stall? How could she leave this place when anyone who saw her would surely see stamped on her forehead:

We had great sex. Forbidden fruit tastes the best.

She placed her top on the bed, and proceeded to smooth it out with her bare hands while Cameron donned his trousers and pulled up the zip of his fly. The zip of Ross's trousers never sounded like that, it must be the echo in this small space, this was a first. Georgia looked up as Cameron pulled his T-shirt over his head. Wow, she thought, how can men return back to normal so fast, while women have to straighten out their clothes, fix their makeup and tidy their hair? She watched as Cameron just put his fingers through his hair. He looked strikingly handsome and judging by the look in his eyes ready for another romp beneath the sheets or wherever. Ever Ready should be his name instead of Cameron, (he must have been sex starved) yes Cameron was too serene a name for a wild bull like him.

Turning the key in the door sounded even louder on the way out, Cameron was nervous, he fumbled, the bunch of keys fell onto the wooden floor with a loud thud all because he was panicking. Now Georgia realised the stark reality had sunk into his head. If he was caught red-handed with a pretty young lady up there, where no one except invited guests with permission were allowed to be, it would be looked on very seriously indeed. There's no doubt, if he was caught, Cameron would be frog marched right out through the front door, never to return again. His mother would not be too pleased to know her son had left the seminary under a grey cloud, bringing shame on his family. Every noisy step they took on that never ending stairway was terrifying. At last they were almost down on terra firma, the last rung of the stairway, relief, the toes of their shoes landed on the hallway to a huge sigh of relief. Then they bumped straight into Maisie Coyne who stopped dead in her tracks and announced:

'Cameron, Father Sebastian is waiting, he says you have an appointment with him.'

'Oh, Maisie, I completely forgot that appointment.'

Georgia looked at Cameron, he looked like a little schoolboy knowing he had been caught out. With one look Maisie summed Cameron up, she felt sorry for him. She blurted out:

'I'll tell you what, if you like, you go ahead because Father Sebastian is very agitated and I'll take this young lady down to the parlour. You can catch up with us in a while.'

Cameron dared not even resist, he awkwardly kissed Georgia

on the cheek in front of Maisie and whispered in her ear, 'I'll catch you later' then hurried on trying to catch up on time. The deacon took a nervous look back at Georgia and vanished into the distance. There was an eerie silence as Georgia and Maisie walked along. Georgia knew that Maisie knew what they'd been up to. Maybe Maisie had walked this road before? She turned to Georgia, looked deeply into her eyes, shook her head, twitched her nose and tut tutted. That look, that tutting and that twitching of Maisie's nose made Georgia very nervous. She couldn't help but wonder what that look or twitch or tut was trying to say. As their shoes thudded their way along the hallway, Maisie erupted into conversation.

'Believe me you're wasting your time, young lady, break that spell, move on.'

Georgia was lost for words but in her mind she wondered what stories Maisie had stored in her head of all her adventures inside these high walls. She became very curious about Maisie's experiences in the seminary and wondered if she had tasted the forbidden fruit. And if she had tasted it, Georgia wondered had she ever managed to break the spell?

Just as they reached the parlour Maisie did some more serious talking to Georgia. The two ladies walked to the big shiny mahogany table. Maisie continued to rant as Georgia pulled out a Chippendale chair, complete with armrests and sat down.

'I hope you don't mind me saying miss and please don't think I'm being impertinent to say, you should think long and hard before you get too involved with a man of the cloth. He'll always be torn between you and God. Do you know if he leaves he'll regret it and do you know if he stays he'll regret it? There are some men like that, especially here. It's the usual thing girl, the forbidden fruit. Sure didn't I fall for one of them myself a long, long time ago.'

Georgia looked in Maisie's direction, astonished. There stood Maisie, with rosy cheeks and a frowning forehead holding her apron in her hand and rubbing the sweat from her brow. Little did Maisie know Georgia had her own set of problems. She also had decisions to make, not that unlike Cameron's. Question was if she left Ross would she regret it? If she stayed with Ross would her body yearn for Cameron for the rest of her life, also giving her regrets? Decisions, decisions.

'You see I used to be the priests' housekeeper,'

Maisie pointed in the direction of the chief priests' house, it wasn't visible through the parlour window. Maisie didn't waste a minute or take a breath as she filled Georgia in on some of the things that happened in her life. She continued breathlessly knowing she only had a few minutes, it was make or break time for this gal Maisie, so she was determined to get every word in.

'Sure didn't I fall for one of the priests… puff… and he led me up the garden path… puff.' She puffed as she was trying to catch her breath.

The only way Georgia could explain that breath in between words, was that puff of air. While Maisie was taking in a puff of air, Georgia was beginning to wonder if she left Ross for Cameron, would her life also become unfulfilled if Cameron left her, to remain in the monastery. She came back down to earth with a bang when she heard Maisie saying,

'Look at me, I have no family, no life, sure I'm an unclaimed treasure.'

Georgia couldn't help herself, she'd never heard that saying before, she just laughed out loud, nervously, at the thought of her being left an unclaimed treasure, all because of her crazy wants and desires.

'Maisie, I think that's the funniest saying I've ever heard.'

Maisie stood up straight, she had that stern look on her face, this was the stern Maisie Coyne, the one Georgia feared.

'It may be funny to you, missy, but every word I say is true. All I ever did was pine for him and look at me now, I'm lonely. Girl, just stop dreaming of a future with him, forget him, instead, grab your own future with both hands and don't remain hypnotised by a man of the cloth. Break away now while there's still time.'

Georgia's mind was working overtime. It's hard to put an old head on young shoulders but I'm beginning to think Maisie might be right.

Now Maisie's face was roaring red and her breath was almost gone but she was a determined lady. She was going to tell the end of this story if it killed her. And Georgia feared it just might kill her.

'Did you hear me, girl? Will you heed me, girl?'

Calm down please Miss Maisie Coyne or you might have a heart attack. Georgia couldn't stay still, she fiddled with her hands. She was now nervously giddy. She wanted to know this woman's story. She already imagined it in her head but she needed to hear it from Maisie's lips. Perhaps this was the antidote she needed to quell the desires she felt for Cameron.

'Well as I said he led me up the garden path, he wasted years of my life. When he finished with me I felt too old, too sad and too disillusioned to look at another man.'

Georgia thought to herself, I have never been disillusioned with my life and I never want to be disillusioned with my life. Years from now, I couldn't bear Maisie's Coyne's story becoming my story.

Maisie continued, 'So now when the choir girls get together and if some of them fancy one of the deacons, I tell any of them who will listen, to be careful. Sometimes you know, young lady, your dreams can turn into nightmares, mine did and I hope yours don't.'

'I don't need nightmares' said Georgia 'I need my beauty sleep unaffected.'

Maisie looked at Georgia sternly then took out a tissue from her apron pocket and dried her eyes. The tears continued to flow, poor thing, beads of perspiration rolled from her forehead, poor, poor Maisie. Georgia could see that the memories came back to haunt her every day.

It's not fair what some people can do to each other. They shatter all their dreams and are left with nothing.

Georgia didn't know why but she blurted out,

'Maisie, would you like to meet me someday in the village for a cup of tea and a chat?'

Maisie's face brightened up instantly and a weak smile that she really pushed herself to give, turned into a real big beaming smile that lit up her face.

'I would love to,' she said with her voice up about three octaves. 'I'll tell you where I often go for tea, Apple Pie down in the village, I just love it.'

'OK' said Georgia 'The sooner the better we meet. I think both of us need time to chat. What time do you finish in the evening, Maisie?'

'I finish at around 4.30.'

'OK, I can be in the Apple Pie café from 5 o'clock next Thursday evening. If that suits you, we can have a chat, a cuppa and a slice of apple pie.'

Now beginning to feel very uneasy, Georgia sat there waiting for Cameron to return. She occupied her time imagining Maisie divulging secrets of the monastery one week from now, over a cup of tea and a slice of apple pie. She would just have to wait in anticipation. Maybe there was a lot more to this woman than meets the eye. It's funny how you can take people for granted, sometimes you can forget that ladies like Maisie, have had a full life too, and maybe an interesting one, if only we had the time to listen and if only they took the time to tell their story, Georgia thought.

Georgia's train of thought was broken when she heard Cameron returning.

'Sorry to keep you waiting, Georgia,' he said as he walked into the room. Georgia glanced at Maisie, her face had transformed. Now, not a tear on view, her back was straight and that determined look was back on her face, that big new warm smile, probably dreaming of Thursday evening sharing her thoughts and memories with Georgia, a real trip down memory lane for her. As she left the room, she whispered in Georgia's ear 'See you Thursday evening,' Maisie was ok. She confidently walked to the door, opened it, then quietly closed it behind her, leaving Georgia and Cameron together.

Georgia and Cameron walked side by side through the building and out into the gardens filled with rows of wild flowers swaying gently in the breeze, a sight to behold. Georgia could feel someone's eyes looking out at her. She didn't have to look back, she knew it was Maisie. When Maisie was a young housekeeper, she must have walked this walk and talked this talk and like Georgia, she probably felt very privileged tasting some of the forbidden fruit, (in this den of iniquity) behind those closed doors, so different from the outside world, from the hustle and bustle of normal life. Maybe Georgia liked the dream, maybe Maisie cherished the memories. Georgia hoped hers wouldn't end in sadness with her marriage over and her dreams for the future ending up in smithereens.

No holding hands between Georgia and Cameron, it wouldn't be fitting in a place like this. With so many windows you could never tell who was watching as you walked in this large square shaped garden surrounded by grey buildings. They walked right to the other side and stopped at a tall brown grained door. Out came the keys again, the large ones on the circular piece of metal, into the lock went the big key, clink, that loud sound. They strolled through and walked to Georgia's car, where there was a restrained goodbye. She drove home filled with uncertainties of what was to come next and happy memories of the day. She wondered why a man so sexually charged would have entered a Roman Catholic seminary, knowing sex and marriage were forbidden, a complete contradiction. How could Cameron vow to deny all pleasures of the flesh and content himself with celibacy (true he was only a Deacon now, not a priest, for now he had choices) when he had spent an afternoon making mad, passionate love in his room, with Georgia the witness and accessory to the crime? Was he just torturing himself by staying in the seminary, maybe because of something he did in his past life, or was he trying to make someone else happy like his mother or his father, by having a son a priest, or was he just confused, or mad, or was he all of the above? Maybe he preferred loving everyone (as his congregation) and not just loving one alone (singular), except God?

CHAPTER 3

Remembering

R oss had done what he always did on late Sunday mornings and gone off to the Blackberry Market in search of some hidden treasure, like old records, oil lamps and old musty books. She was alone with her thoughts. Her mind drifted back to the night that she knew had changed her life forever. That night, in The Trocadero, when her friend Heidi hurried to a candlelit table, occupied by only one man. After a short conversation, he stood up and then Heidi practically dragged him towards their table. Obviously she had decided he was going to meet the gang whether he liked it or not. He had arrived at their table complete with a large umbrella hanging over his arm, his book and holding a pint of Guinness that fitted in very well with the drinks Georgia had already ordered for her friends. After that Georgia's evening had certainly turned out a lot different from the one she had imagined. In her innocence, she'd thought her friends and herself would have spent the evening enjoying the meal, telling girlie stories about their love lives (or lack of them) and viewing her Wedding Photos, including the photos of all three of them. Her three best friends from all the way back in kindergarten, her three bridesmaids. Heidi introduced the man to her friends.

'This is Cameron, he used to be a work colleague of mine.'

The name Cameron had flowed from Heidi's lips, it definitely suited him. Georgia reminisced on that electric shock shooting up through her arm when he stretched across the table and shook her hand. His eyes! Georgia always truly believed your eyes are the mirror to your soul and if her theory was correct then, she thought, his soul must be very pure because his eyes were beautifully mysterious, hazel in colour, deep like a nut caressed by a squirrel, surrounded by long black eyelashes. As he sat back down on the rich burgundy, padded, velvet bench, Cameron had seemed a little uneasy with all the happy chattering girls in a circle surrounding him.

She remembered feeling lucky and honoured to have such a vision of beauty sitting directly opposite her. She also remembered thinking how handsome he was. If only I was single, she thought. In all the time she'd been with Ross that was the first time that thought had ever crossed her mind. She remembered feeling like a young teenager falling in love for the very first time, the more she had looked at Cameron the better he looked. She had asked herself is there such a thing as love at first sight? You might be excused for thinking Georgia should know the answer to her own question and in this moment Georgia did know, because in the time it would take to flick a switch she knew she had now fallen in love with Cameron, this charismatic man, at first sight.

With Ross it had just happened. From day one she had had no doubts, he was the one for her, strong, reliable and predictable, the qualities every woman should look for in a man or a future husband, but of course not a lot do. Georgia realised there was a part of her that liked the uncertainty, the animal magnetism and sexual attraction she felt for Cameron.

Georgia said to herself, 'There's a lot to be said for being at one with each other, feeling comfortable together, always feeling happy together and the one thing I love with Ross is our ability to read each other's thoughts.' Georgia vividly remembered feeling very happy that she could keep staring at Cameron, he stood out on his own in that restaurant, he seemed oblivious and she had been glad for that. She had continued to feast her eyes quietly, until a sudden jolt had taken her back to reality when she touched the little gold band on the ring finger of her left hand, she had dropped back down to earth with a bang and became painfully aware that in fact the man she loved was waiting at home, but her feelings had been so strong for Cameron she couldn't resist him. In that instant she just knew she had fallen madly, passionately in love with him at first sight. She imagined how everyone's life would be turned upside down if she left Ross and walked away from her marriage for Cameron.

Their meal and desserts were delicious. Georgia remembered standing up and with her very own hands scattering the photos right across the table so each girl could pick their favourites for their personalised bridesmaids' albums. Georgia just had to show all her wedding photos to all her friends. She wanted them to see every single, solitary wedding photograph clearly, after all the photographer needed to know exactly which photos everyone wanted, so they could prepare the albums. She also wanted Cameron to know exactly what was going on in her life, she felt a great need to be up front with him but she didn't quite know why. In fairness it turned out to be fantastic, viewing the faces of all their friends and families, aunties and uncles, dressed in their best, smiling up from the photos. Up to that moment the little group just didn't seem to get around to looking at any photos of the wedding, mostly because they needed space on the table and that was only made possible when all the cutlery, plates and leftovers had vanished. They would have much more fun once they could see all the photos clearly without cups, saucers and flowers obstructing their view. The four friends had relived the happy wedding day and gossiped about all the guests they'd met at the reception, and a lively lot they all were. They'd laughed as they caught their expressions in the various shots.

In between laughing and joking, a camera was passed around between the four friends and Cameron. Expressions of joy and amusement were captured from various angles. They always took lots of photos of every special occasion. Some of these photos would end up in their personal bridesmaids' wedding albums. Georgia was lucky enough to stand beside Cameron for one such shot. This was one shot she was looking forward to seeing when developed, especially as she and Cameron had beaming, getting to know you, smiles on their faces. The girls had liked some wedding photos and some they didn't like but in the end it all made up the complete picture of happiness on that day, even down to the groomsmen, who just like her girlfriends had all grown up together.

Ever since Ross had been introduced to Georgia's mum, Nellie, she had seen a different side to it all. Right through the romance Georgia always felt that her mum didn't feel that Ross was the one for her, even if he did have his own car and a house, plus an apartment in Spain, which showed at least he was ambitious. Maybe it wasn't that Georgia's mum disliked Ross - It might have been that she knew in their heart it was Georgia, who in actual fact was not ready for marriage or settling down, she felt Georgia needed to go out into the wide world and just live but that didn't stop Georgia, she just forged ahead with her plans and married the man she loved anyway. Maybe her mum was right after all, she could see the flirty side of Georgia and realised she needed a few more years to mature and explore life. Georgia remembered her mum meeting her to discuss her pending marriage. Nellie was honest when she said 'Georgia it's pretty easy to get into it but it's very hard to get out of it.

As they used to say, you can get carried away with the dress and the Tiara.' Yes, Nellie was a wise woman.

Ross was so happy with himself when he returned home clutching his prized new, old records and an old bockety lamp and of course, he had a story to tell over dinner. He said, so many people wanted to buy the records he bought but, of course, he was there early and as they say the early bird catches the worm. As they sat down and listened to Elvis and Frank Sinatra singing along with the odd scrape here and there on the vinyl records adding that quaintness. Ross was so tired after dinner he fell asleep on the chair by the fire.

Georgia was alone with her thoughts again. She drifted back to that wonderful night, the one she had wished would never end, but end it did and as the other girls' taxis arrived and they vanished into the cool night air, Georgia paid the bill for the fabulous meal. Instead of running home to her beloved, Georgia wanted to run off with Cameron, that night was crazy. The Trocadero had been planned before her wedding for all her bridesmaids. It was her way to say a big thank you for all their work and to decide which photographs they would like in their very own personalised bridesmaids albums. Georgia remembered making small talk with Cameron, just trying to hold onto the moment. She was glad he wasn't in any hurry to leave and even though now he knew she was only married a short time and had studied the photos of her dressed in her wedding gowns, he wasn't put off. He had seemed very happy to view the photos and even happier to remain in her company. Georgia had hoped she was reading the situation correctly as she continued to make small talk. As they were leaving, without any warning, she had stumbled on God knows what and was only saved from pure embarrassment when Cameron caught her hand, stood her back up on her feet and escorted her out into the street. Georgia's head had spun, was it Cameron's hand holding hers that had sent that electric shock through her body? The feeling was good but was it all too fast? Why was she embracing the feeling and letting herself fall too fast for a perfect stranger?

She remembered not wanting to rush home that night, so she was happy when Cameron suggested a late night drink at The Four Seasons Hotel in Ballsbridge. Georgia was always the impulsive type and judged things on their strength at that moment in time, and that moment felt just right. Georgia and Cameron were happy to jump into the first taxi that came along. He still carried his umbrella but thankfully he didn't need to use it. The taxi sped straight to the hotel where they headed for the Ice Bar to join the bustling crowd of Yuppies who posed with glasses of wine in hand, knowing it was the place to be. The world was changing, it seemed everything was either frivolous or disposable. While she didn't like the idea of everything being frivolous and disposable, she began to realise here she was living proof of that… frivolous, disposable, was her marriage just that?

Georgia remembered feeling just a little bit uncomfortable as she prayed to God nobody would recognise her, after all she was only a few months married, she kept on repeating that to herself over and over again in her head but it still didn't seem to sink in. The feelings she was feeling were too good to miss out on but she still surveyed the crowd searching for that one spoilsport who could spill the beans to her new hubby and make her life miserable. If she had really cared about all that she shouldn't have been there in the first place but life is about taking chances and Georgia was taking the biggest chance of all. Nevertheless, she looked poised and totally in control as she sipped a Bloody Mary to give her false courage and help her relax.

As Ross continued to sleep quietly in his favourite comfortable chair, Georgia tried to engross herself in a book, she even turned the pages but inside her head was spinning. Her mind drifted back again, this time to Cameron's eyes as he looked straight at her in the Ice Bar and said, *I know this sounds really silly, Georgia but right here, right now, I know my prayers have been answered.*

Georgia remembered a little voice inside her head had shouted, you're married, you're married, but outside her head Georgia remembered just one thing, a feeling like she had never felt before with Ross or indeed any other man. But how could she make a decision based on one chance meeting, one long conversation, and one look into someone's eyes? And yet that was exactly what she had done, imagined a life with Cameron. Georgia had known this was a big turning point in her life and in reality there'd be no turning back. Almost like Cinderella, she had also realised if she waited any longer there would be no point in crawling back into her marital bed that night because in just a little while a new day would start to dawn, so Georgia, in a very weak voice, had announced, *it's time I went home. Really Cameron, I really must go home.*

He hadn't pushed the issue, they had just finished their drinks, ordered their taxis, exchanged mobile numbers and kissed tenderly. Georgia had felt electricity like a bolt of lightning sweeping through her being, she wondered had he felt it too. As they went their separate ways Georgia remembered still feeling that tender kiss that lingered on her lips. Her body had begun to recover very slowly from that bolt of lightning.

She remembered her heart was beating like a drum as she paid her fare and slipped out of the taxi a block away from her home. With the key of her front door in hand, she had closed the taxi door as gently as she could, and as the taxi vanished along the street, Georgia had removed her killer heels and walked barefoot to her house where she gently placed the key in the lock, turned it slowly, then crept into the hall and ever so gently closed the door behind her. Thank God there were no creaking doors, nothing that needed an oiling even the stairs didn't creak. She was in luck, Ross had gently purred, a sound that was like music to her ears. She didn't even dare clean her teeth, which was something she hated doing but this was all in a good cause she had thought as she slid beneath the covers and kissed Ross very softly before getting into a comfortable position. Sleep just wouldn't come. She remembered just lying there restless, wondering had he an inkling of her deceit but as he put his strong arms around her she knew there was nothing to worry about, for now.

Her feet were freezing cold from walking without shoes that night. She remembered being tempted to put her cold feet on Ross's warm body to thaw them out but she daren't, she also remembered she wanted to toss and turn but knew she must stay still, not to draw attention to her uneasiness. It had seemed like hours, then she heard the alarm buzzing away and saw Ross's sleepy body heading towards the shower room. She just lay there pretending to be asleep, going over and over again all the events and again she had wondered would her life ever be the same again. Now she knew it would never be the same again.

CHAPTER 4

THE RENDEZVOUS

Monday morning, work as usual, nothing too eventful happening, she would just have to go with the flow and take the time to come to grips with all her life's confusion. Ross was busy as usual, his work certainly needed dedication, which was good news for Georgia, at least when he came home most nights, the poor fellow was too tired to notice Georgia's uneasiness, as usual he focused on work and keeping his pretty wife happy.

Tuesday evening would have to be dedicated to plucking, shaving and moisturising, to be prepared for the girly night with Coco on Wednesday and since Ross was far too busy to come home for dinner Georgia picked up a little quickie dinner from M & S. *(It wasn't just food it was M & S food as the voice over (Dervla Kirwin) announced so eloquently. Those words made her voice known throughout the land. Dervla said the words so smoothly it almost sounded like a kitten purring.)* Georgia couldn't resist mimicking the advertisement for Marks & Spencer's. Gratin potatoes and salmon, nice and light, then she put on her favourite CD and proceeded to organise all the little things she needed, to make the tasks in hand as painless as possible. Unfortunately even the lavender scented candles, relaxing as they were, did nothing to numb the pain. She wasn't quite sure which end of her was suffering more, her eyebrows or her legs, still it was all in a good cause. Every now and then a little voice in her head told her to stop! Think! And remain in the happy world she belonged to right now. It told her this was as good as it gets! Georgia tried to block out the voice but it just kept on returning.

Her phone rang. Without thinking she answered the call to discover it came from Cameron.

'Hi Georgia" His voice sounded a little nervous, he cleared his throat, 'Georgia I hope it's ok to ring, I'm sorry I just can't stop thinking about you. Georgia, please say something!'

Georgia felt her knees weak, how could a man, any man, have this effect on her?

'I'm here Cameron, sorry, I feel stuck for words, but I miss you too.'

'Georgia when can we meet?'

Pause...

'How about tomorrow, Wednesday at 10pm.' She sounded far too eager.

'Brilliant! The Westin Hotel, just on the corner across from Trinity College.'

Then they said goodbye. She was determined to go down the road of adventure at any cost, and at last, after a restless night Wednesday finally arrived, Ross and Georgia sat down to breakfast, just orange juice, cornflakes, toast and tea. Ross remarked how well Georgia looked, she smiled and gave a flirty flutter of her long dark eyelashes, he always fell for all the teasing, a promise of things to come. Unfortunately for him, the only person who would benefit was not him but Cameron. She kept busy all day trying to push her liaison with Cameron to the back of her mind, anyway first she was meeting with Coco at 7pm. (Her alibi for the night)

Once work was finished for the day she set off to her favourite changing place, the Westbury Hotel, where the ladies room was just the right size to lay out her clothes on the back of the chair supplied. Then she donned the little red dress she had purchased in Kookai, just because it was beautiful, classy, sexy, not too expensive and the chiffon fell so softly on her slender body. The thin shoulder straps felt just right and the accordion pleats that fell from just under her bust and finished just above her knee were complimented by her silver, strappy, killer heeled, Gina shoes. She liked the all-round view the long mirrors gave. Yes, overall she didn't look too bad, well as good as she was ever going to look.

A minute's walk across the road and Georgia was there, McDaid's, her first stop of the evening. She glanced at her watch. It was exactly 7pm, just bang on time to meet Coco and there she was waving frantically across the crowded room. Georgia could only see the head of shiny hair and an arm outstretched but it definitely was Coco. That busy little wave, it could only be her but who did the other outstretched arm belong to? None other than Tanya. (Surprise)

Georgia managed to reach the table and there it was a large glass of pure orange juice, just what was needed to completely restore life into her tired body, all that Vitamin C, instant energy. The first drama story concerned their fond friend Tanya who was usually casual about most things including love, but this time had fallen head over heels both in and out of love in a matter of months, and it was sad, because Tanya, usually bright and breezy, was now dull and dismal. The whole experience seemed too much for this tall lean lady. This time was different because she had fallen hard and the feelings seemed mutual. Coco explained she had witnessed with her own eyes, the flowers and chocolates Tanya had been presented with in an array of colours.

One week: Cream,
Then: Yellow,
Followed by: Pale Pink, Shocking Pink, Purple.

And having mixed and matched the colours through the months and coming up with some great displays, he finally came to the grand finale, red, all little buds blossoming into voluptuous, full, lustrous, perfumed roses. She thought this was it especially when he arrived with a Zara bag containing a little teeny weeny midnight blue, petite, beautiful dress and red roses, complimenting the midnight blue dress, this was all too good to be true.

Tanya, butted in,

'I felt secure, comfortable and safe (in that order). Girls, I now realise that was a very dangerous feeling.'

Her guard was down, and then like a bolt out of the blue he ended it. The love affair of a lifetime was over, he gave no explanation, just the usual line, and wouldn't you imagine he would have come up with something more original, but no, out it came 'It's me and not you, all my fault' he had said in a squeaky voice and there it was most men's excuse for that quick retreat. An old song her gran used to sing had returned to haunt her, Red Roses for a Blue Lady. Well the roses were red and her dress was blue, sure the song must have been written just for her all those years ago, she had confided in her old friend Coco (in her very own words). She was finding it very hard to shift the solitary lonely feeling within her and the only people she could turn to in her hour of need were her old faithful buddies.

Georgia did her best to concentrate as the girls continued this epic story.

Tanya had accepted all the reasons, you know:

It's not you, it's me!

It's not where I am right now!

I'm not ready for a serious relationship!

I'm afraid of commitment!

Georgia wondered? Why do some men take you under their spell, almost like a fish on a hook being reeled in and then when it's too late and you're completely spellbound, they drop you, just like a bomb into the big blue ocean. Her conclusion was they liked the chase. (That seemed to be a reasonable explanation.)

For whatever reason Tanya was alone and it didn't feel good. Her heart was broken, how could anyone hurt her so much? She wasn't one for revenge, instead she usually just got on with life thinking only good and positive thoughts to encourage good Karma. This time she found it hard not to let herself be pulled down by the rejection. She already knew that feeling, she'd felt it so many times while at college, that feeling of isolation, rejection and worthlessness, when you look around you and everyone seems to be happy, that is, everyone but you. Georgia felt very sorry for her poor lonely friend and made a promise with herself to ring her every day for the next week or so and just in case she would forget, she fumbled in her hand bag until she found the little red book, and once she had her pen in hand she wrote, Urgent, ring Tanya tomorrow and for the next seven days, just to see how she's coping.

It was time to change the subject to an equally uncomfortable one. A few photos had surfaced in the evening bag Coco wore on Georgia's wedding day, of course Coco had them now ready to show, but Georgia really didn't want to look at even one more photo of herself and Ross together, such a constant reminder that she was two timing her brand new husband. It was hard enough to cope without being constantly reminded she was a married lady, especially as in less than 2 hours she would meet someone who was a real threat to everything the photos represented and stood for and even though Ross's face peered from each one of them as if to say Georgia, stop, think, she just didn't care, her

34

mind was set. Georgia didn't concentrate very well that evening, in fact she knew she wasn't good company, just like her friend Tanya, but luckily for them Coco was so brim full of energy and had another great story to pass on to her friends who smiled when required.

Coco explained she was attending French classes in the Alliance Francaise. She had a good knowledge of the French language but needed more conversational skills. Her teacher was patient and very helpful so Coco felt she was coming on in leaps and bounds. He had taken a little group of students to visit Paris where they could try all their newly acquired skills and it was there Coco met a Parisian who requested an invitation to come to Ireland to visit her. It seems everyone wants to visit Ireland, maybe because it's just a little island with a fabulous shape and so many light-hearted inhabitants or maybe it's for the craic! Well for whatever reason he was coming to Ireland, Coco was thrilled. Just one more drink, some more chat and it was time to make a move.

'Girls, I'm so tired tonight.' Georgia announced (giving her best impression of an actress in one of those old silent movies) 'Would you mind if I go just a little early?'

'Not at all,' her friends declared. 'Sure we'll meet again soon and catch up a little more.'

Georgia was pleased with her friends' reactions. In fairness this was the very first time she had told even a white lie to any friend but what was she supposed to say? *Coco, Tanya, actually I'm meeting Cameron in less than half an hour! I know I'm married, but frankly (in the words of Bette Davis) I don't give a damn, I just lust after Cameron.* No, Georgia thought that kind of honesty would not go down well especially with Tanya, who right now couldn't hold onto one boyfriend and here was Georgia with a husband and a lover. She loved her friend Tanya, so the best thing to do was take her leave quietly. She did the usual kiss, kiss on both cheeks, making sure to pout the lips and then she walked towards the door only looking back for that final wave. To be honest Georgia wanted to run towards the taxi but no, she paced herself and walked slowly, gracefully, heart beating like a drum, then she was sitting in the back of the little grubby taxi. It headed towards College Green just a few minutes away and pulled up right outside the main door of The Westin Hotel. She could feel all the butterflies in her tummy but to hell with them. Outwardly she appeared quietly confident as she stepped out of the taxi, paid the fare and made her way cautiously (just in case she'd fall and ruin the look she'd spent ages perfecting) up the steps and into the foyer of this beautiful hotel.

CHAPTER 5

Issey Miyake

She was lucky to be early, all of 15 minutes, so there was a little while to unwind and where better than sitting beside the lovely open fire, in fact there were two open fires in the room but Georgia preferred the smaller cosy one. She sat down on the plush fireside chair making sure her presentation was perfect and tried to clear her head. It was easy, easy to stare into the colourful flames and feel her body going right into relaxed mode. What is it about flames? They just make you use up all your imagination conjuring up remarkable images as the flames red, blue and orange dance up towards the chimney stack. Georgia stared and stared right into the fire trying to ignore her butterfly tummy and beating heart. It seemed like ages and then he was there. She didn't need to turn around, she just knew the hand touching her shoulder was his, that hand that sent electric shocks running up her spine. He moved slowly around to face her, she was speechless. How could one human being have this effect on another? Oh what a feeling! She felt so alive. Cameron sat down beside her and held her hand. Not a word was spoken for what seemed like hours. The silence was only broken when the sound of glass hitting the ground brought them back to earth with a bang (so to speak).

Had their moment been shattered? No.

Did they want to come down to Earth with a bang? No.

They were both so bewitched by each other, nothing could break the magic spell.

The poor waiter who had let a tray full of glasses fall to the ground was now on the floor picking up the pieces of broken glass, hurriedly putting them on his tray. He stood up and scurried into the kitchen with a big red face and a tray of broken glass. He returned a few minutes later to their table holding a clean tray, and enquired if they would like to order something to eat? (His face was still roaring red) They ordered tea for Georgia and coffee for Cameron. It seemed as if it had only been ordered when it arrived along with chocolate biscuits, so the cheating love birds tucked in and began to exchange loving words and their life stories.

Cameron seemed anxious to spill out his life story, he wanted Georgia to know every little bit of his life BG (before Georgia). He came from a quiet farming background right down in the heart of Mayo. Having gone to a religious school, he learned through his school years about all the good deeds the priests had done in Ireland, Sierra Leone, and so many different parts in this big wide world. He thought it might be a good idea to join up and add to this great Christian cause. She listened as his life story unfolded. He had joined the priesthood at eighteen, having completed his second level education, without giving it another thought. He headed straight into a new world of theology, psychology and philosophy.

'The priests gave me the opportunity to visit Sierra Leone. It was a magical experience. Back then people thought priests were gods. Villagers would sit at the foot of the steps waiting for them to arrive home, eager to make their dinner and wash their clothes. When I came back to Ireland, Georgia, my mind was in turmoil, I was unable to make a decision as to whether I wanted to be ordained and become a Catholic Priest or leave the monastery and start a new career and a new life. I decided the safest thing to do was to stand back, take a deep breath and take time away from the seminary. I took office work, that's where I met your friend Heidi. That decision has had a profound effect on my life because now I've met you. The parting words from the priests were, we will pray for you, Cameron, here in the monastery. May God give you guidance' Georgia laughed out loud with nerves and instead of thinking in her head, she blurted out the words,

'Do you think God is answering your prayers, Cameron? Do you really believe being here in The Westin having tea and biscuits with me, amidst all the yuppies drinking their glasses of wine and talking nonsense, is making anything clearer?'

Then she thought, have I really said that? She knew she had when there was a deafening silence. She felt herself withering inside. Cameron looked up and straight into her eyes, but he didn't utter a word.

Georgia had to admit to herself this situation didn't seem right. She felt uncomfortable, she was a good girl at heart but like most human beings had the odd temptation now and then. Unfortunately for her, she had succumbed to the ultimate temptation, Cameron's charms and the question kept arising inside her head, why? After all Ross was a fantastic partner but somehow he just didn't light her fire, ring her bells or make her go weak at the knees. Cameron had perfect ticks for all three, fire, bells and knees. Was it his cool attitude? Was it his teddy bear build, or just the whole package? Yes, Georgia knew the last one was right but knowing all these things didn't necessarily make things right. So there it was, Georgia's problem, out in the open, everything now was crystal clear, isn't it amazing how for months, sometimes even years, your life can seem mundane, even fuzzy, then like the click of a switch in your head, it feels as if a huge cloud has been lifted, well that was exactly how Georgia felt and although the evening wasn't all plain sailing, she knew everything would be all right in the end. Tea and coffee were continuously poured through the evening as the conversation went on and on and then it was 2am. How was Georgia going to get back into bed beside Ross? How was she to explain this late homecoming?

The Maître d' ordered a taxi. It took only a few minutes to arrive. Cameron held her hand and as they left the hotel he kissed her goodnight. Georgia found it hard to drag herself away from the heavenly aroma of his Issey Miyake aftershave that was too good to say goodnight to, still they must. Cameron went his way, Georgia went hers knowing they wouldn't continue this pattern for long, there was an unspoken plan that would unfold soon.

Taxi fare paid, Georgia found herself at her front door, with key in hand. She opened the lock oh so gently and tiptoed through the hallway that now seemed endless and on up the stairs into the bedroom. She silently prayed Ross wouldn't hear her. Now, once more she prayed he would stay asleep long enough to let her slip into bed and defrost her frozen feet. The thing was, Ross trusted her emphatically, he could sleep silently in the knowledge his new bride was out with her friends, the ones he trusted and loved, the horrible truth would soon unfold. She had left her shoes downstairs just in case the noisy leather soles would be heard as she climbed the stairs and now she was paying the price, her feet felt like icicles. First, teeth had to be cleaned, make up taken off, clothes removed and then the big task in hand began, and Georgia slipped back the covers and gently, very gently slid in. She didn't move either way, instead she just lay there motionless. Her frozen feet began to thaw, life was returning to them. Centimetre by centimetre she edged closer to

Ross, the manoeuvre took some time then she mooched her tiny feet onto his legs and settled. He felt warm and cosy, she kept quite still. Then he turned to her, wrapped his arm around her slender body and smelt her hair, 'lovely perfume' he murmured, then he continued to sleep... She was grateful.

CHAPTER 6

Getting to know you better (in the cloisters)

A ringing sound in her ear woke her from her turbulent sleep. Georgia sat up and rummaged around her bed until she found her phone. It was too late the ringing had stopped. There was a dead silence and a little pinging sound to indicate someone had left her a message and there she was flicking through the phone until she realised it was a voice message and not a text message. Urgently she pressed 171 and waited... 'Ahem.' She heard that sound. That was all she needed to hear to know it was him. He always cleared his throat before he spoke

'Hello Georgia, Cameron here. I won't beat around the bush, I'll come straight to the point. Do you have any spare time in your busy schedule to meet up with me?'

Georgia wracked her brain trying to find a free space and then it all came together. She had clients up until 12pm. She would ring the salon and ask the receptionist to mark her out for the rest of the day, relief, she could see Cameron. Swiftly she sent him a text. 'Could you meet me in that little French coffee shop at 2.30pm?'

She was nervous and a little apprehensive as she drove there. Maybe she'd feel nothing when she saw him, she convinced herself that would be the best thing that could happen. It would be nice just to retreat back into Ross's arms and continue the comfy life they had built together... Maybe.

The car came to an abrupt halt and kind of jolted forward as she pulled on the hand brake too hard, that's how tense she was. Georgia opened the car window and inhaled a lot of fresh air into her lungs, then she took her little black bag and held it tightly, she slipped out of the car and walked into his arms (well not exactly his arms - the coffee shop) He was already there waiting. The two lovers sat facing each other, listening to French songs on the music system while they politely drank hot chocolate and ate French pastries, barely able to swallow with nervousness, excitement and anticipation. Then they were out of there, away from any prying eyes that might recognise Cameron as a server of Communion on Sundays or Georgia as the wife of Ross. Into the lovely little car they sat, feeling safe. On went the engine, off went the hand brake out of Dublin and up through the Dublin Mountains the pretty little mini took them, on that beautiful sunny afternoon. They pulled in at Glencree, at a lovely stone building with lots of history attached. During the war, back in the day it used to be a German camp, now in real time it had a happier life as a gorgeous little museum and coffee shop, perfect for enquiring, hungry travellers. They went in and enjoyed hot wholesome food, lots of tea and the best thing of all a real big chat, a sort of getting to know each other better, chat. Georgia spoke of her friends, Coco, Tanya and Heidi, all of the lovely times they'd shared from kindergarten, then their First Holy Communion, Confirmation, chasing boys, secondary school and of course the big debs, on and on together, through good times and bad. They were Georgia's core go to people, the people she trusted with her heart and soul. The funny thing was she hadn't mentioned anything of Cameron to them which she felt was strange. This was indeed the first time in her life since kindergarten she hadn't shared her story with them.

Cameron spoke of his indecision and of his one close friend in the Seminary, Audian, who was going through exactly the same as him. Would he stay? Would he leave? There was no one else in his life, but there was something telling him he must walk away from the life he was living and begin a new one. Now Cameron had just returned to the seminary but he knew the next time he would leave, it would be for good and it would happen soon. They had parked the car around at the back of the building and by the time they left, the restaurant was just closing. All the guests had already moved on to higher ground. Nothing was planned, not the mad love making in the back of the mini that exceeded Georgia's expectations. This time there were no lamp shades, no door handles, only the floor of the mini, the wheel, the mirror and the perfect padded seats. Every time she made love with Cameron it just got better, they seemed to reach dizzier heights… What a way to spend a sunny afternoon. Before the long goodbye, before the last kiss, before the can't live without you, Cameron made sure Georgia had the telephone number for the monastery and the extension number for his room and a promise from her to call him the next day, just to say hello.

CHAPTER 7

Game, Set and Match

Maisie Coyne answered the telephone, that kind voice. Georgia just loved her friendly way. She could imagine the scene, shiny gleaming furniture all cleaned and polished earlier by Maisie, polished floors and those echoes, the whole thing. Maisie connected Georgia to his room, it was that simple. She imagined the room, his cell, really holy with the echo of prayer surrounding him as he knelt on the cold floor praying for inspiration. His two poor knees must have been red from kneeling, trying to keep his mind off Georgia and the sins of the flesh. Sure if he was a housekeeper his poor sore knees would have been called housekeepers' knees, all red and rough caused by kneeling down to scrub floors. Yes! Georgia had a vivid imagination. She knew the sound of her voice would echo right around the quiet, peaceful, holy room.

'Sorry to distract you.'

Georgia heard herself mutter. She could hear that little clearing of the throat she was becoming accustomed to. She waited for a response. Once he started to talk there was no stopping him, it was as if all his thoughts just came pouring out. Georgia tried to sum it up, maybe he had been spending too much time alone, immersed in prayer (or maybe the other priests had a pain in their faces listening to him).

'Georgia, I'm already distracted by you. Never feel you are intruding on me.'

Then before she could utter another shaky word Cameron invited the poor lusting Georgia to visit him again. How could she refuse the sexiest, creamiest, most seductive voice she had ever heard? What could a girl say but YES, YES, YES? She couldn't wait to visit the squeaky clean seminary again but this time she wouldn't feel nervous, shaky or anything else, in the long dark hallway. Her mind was clear, she felt like a young soldier going into battle with only one thing in mind, conquering Cameron. She would see him and lay to rest the madness, the uncertainty of having her heart torn in two.

Georgia had left her day completely clear, nothing to do in the way of work. As Cameron had a lecture he only had 2 hours free (if she was lucky), if not a 10 minute quickie then exit. The sun shone right into Georgia's eyes making her squint and feel uncomfortable as she made her way to the monastery. And, guess what, she'd forgotten her sunglasses. She took a quick glance into the wing mirror, her worst fears were realised, yes it was a sorry sight that looked back at her through that mirror and it was her, with her mascara running down her face. Typical! Just when she wanted to look her best she looked her worst! What would she do when Cameron looked into her bloodshot eyes with all those black blobs of mascara here, there and everywhere, a little bit like a panda bear? Still, there was no going back, it was onward and upward.

She continued to drive her little mini onto a slip road to save a few minutes driving time and found a little place where she could stop along the way to sort out her black eyes. Using a little Vaseline on a tissue Georgia removed all the black dots of Mascara, leaving her eyes clear and ready for fresh make up to be applied. Yes, she loved that MAC foundation, a dab of Cheeky by Benefit and fresh mascara and this panda bear was once more restored to as perfect as she would ever be. Just a little tossing of the hair and it was back into the car, indicating and then taking her lane once more she gently guided the little red mini, complete with white roof to its destination. Georgia's car almost glided along the last miles until she pulled in and came to a stop right at the front door of the seminary. This time she didn't bother to look in the rear view mirror instead, she convinced herself if it's not broken don't fix it. Stepping out into the open air she felt a light breeze, her senses awoke and she felt the heat of the sun kissing her face. She even noticed the leaves on the trees gently swaying and caught a glimpse of wild flowers in a field nearby. They swayed to and fro on their little fragile stems trying to hold themselves together. It was a perfect day.

Oh, it's such a perfect day
I'm glad I spent it with you
Oh, such a perfect day
You just keep me hanging on
You just keep me hanging on

Were the sun and the light breeze an indication of what was to come? She checked, just to make sure her tan courtesy of Coty, in medium mat, had not streaked. No, her legs were still a divine brown, what would a girl do without cosmetics, especially false tan in an Irish climate. All Irish girls prayed it wouldn't rain just in case the tan would be streaky on their legs, streaky on their faces and streaky on their arms.

CHAPTER 8

Tea served by Maisie Coyne in the cloisters

Georgia rang the doorbell. Maisie opened the door, now she was inside in the big airy hall. Without a word Maisie held her head up, looked straight ahead and led the way into the big reception room. Just before she left the room Maisie gave Georgia that look, the look that says, girl you're wasting your time, run, leave him to his ways and you to yours. Without saying a word she had said it all. The sun shone through the windows, brightened up the flowers on the polished table and put that extra sparkle on the gleaming floors... then Him. She was alone, no other voice to fill the gaps, only hers and she was saying nothing, she was dumb struck. Cameron sat beside her, they stared into each other's eyes, she thanked God she had fixed her makeup. There were no words, no cuddles, nothing, Nada. Georgia didn't know what to do, this reaction certainly wasn't expected. Maisie came to the rescue with a tray full of nice things to eat. As she laid the tray down beside Georgia, she smiled a sweet calm smile as if to say, I know what you're feeling, I had many awkward moments in this room with Fergus. I used to feel someone was looking out at us from the dark corners (spooky). It used to make me feel uncomfortable.

There she goes again, thought Georgia, thinking things in her mind that I actually understand.

Georgia was taken away from her thoughts as she watched Cameron standing, pouring, with such precision, the bloody tea. Why was it some of the little things he did could irritate her so much and yet she was spellbound by this charismatic man? If Ross had poured tea at this slow pace she would have possibly taken the pot of tea from his hand and poured it herself, or worse still hit him with it. Cameron continued to pour the tea as Maisie made her exit. The clinking of the spoon stirring the sugar in this echoing room brought Georgia back to earth. Cameron sat down beside her, leaving the expanse of mahogany table behind. They ate sandwiches followed by fruit scones with butter and jam. Cameron reached out and held her hand, Georgia felt a lump in her throat and she fought to hold back the tears.

When she had arrived at the seminary she was happy but somehow Maisie's coldness towards her had changed how she felt. It's funny how someone else's mood can change yours, she thought. How could I let Maisie upset me and have my emotions running away with me so easily? Maisie's story isn't my story. She remembered when she was a little girl her friends used to tease her and say you're just a little cry-baby, so maybe now that she was a fully-fledged grown up, she was just one big cry-baby. Damn, she thought as her mascara mixed with tears burnt her eyes, I just have to control my emotions. I can't believe how vulnerable I feel. Ross never made me feel like this, I always felt equal, I must be mad to let all this be happening to me. Sometimes when I'm with Cameron I feel like a bumbling idiot, now I have to slow down my breathing. Take lots of deep breaths. She had heard from someone who seemed to be an authority on the subject, that breathing into a paper bag does wonders to completely calm a frantic heart, but all that didn't really matter because there was no brown paper bag, she would have to stick to controlling each breath, so in slowly, out even slower, inhale – exhale. She listened to herself breathing. She could feel her body beginning to relax, more and more. At last calmness returned. She took a paper napkin from the table, dipped it in tea and patted her burning eyes. Luckily she had a little powder compact in her bag, so out it came and on went the make-up. Through all this Cameron sat speechless, was he too upset to say anything or was it the training in psychology that kept him so controlled? If Georgia wasn't married she could have joined the nunnery, then she too could be cool, calm and sophisticated instead of a mumbling, bumbling idiot, perish the thought! Georgia hated taking orders, she'd never make a nun. She would just have to live with herself, an emotional wreck.

Miss Maisie Coyne knocked gently on the door and announced to Cameron he was needed outside by one of the priests. He excused himself from the table and left Georgia in the company of Maisie (still quiet). She tidied the table and stacked the plates, cups and saucers onto the tray. As she dusted the crumbs from the table Maisie began to chat to Georgia. She continued to dust the table, even though now it was already spotless. Maybe Maisie thought the table was like Aladdin's lamp and if she kept rubbing it Aladdin himself might appear and grant her wish. What would it be? Now she was beginning to clumsily get down on her hands and knees to vigorously brush the crumbs up off the floor with a little brown brush in one hand and a scoop in the other. Sure the room was like something out of a five star hotel when she was finished. Maisie dragged herself back up on her feet with the aid of a sturdy Chippendale mahogany chair and sat down beside Georgia, out came one of her magical statements from her lipsticked lips.

'There were many other girls like you. Most of them belonged to the local choir, that's why they were here in the first place. The Deacons and sub-deacons used to join them in the choir when they needed tenors or baritones. Then that crush would start, most times it didn't amount to anything but for the ones who fell hard and had a dream of making a life with one of the deacons or sub-deacons, like with a lot of dreams, they left with all of them shattered.'

'Ahem!' And he was back, the lone ranger.

In the time Georgia had spent talking to Maisie she had pulled herself together and decided three things:

1. If she felt this romance was going nowhere, then it was over.

2. Georgia decided if at all possible, she would make love to Cameron this afternoon.

3. Georgia would call the shots this time, the way she wanted it and on her terms.

Oh, there was another decision, the 4th one, not to let Maisie ruin her romance. It seemed to her Maisie had a lot of bitterness in her heart. She would have to talk to Maisie and find out the nitty gritty bits that Maisie left out when she tut tut tutted and made statements that were all to do with her and not Georgia. In her head Georgia said these words, Feck off Maisie, you're just jealous because I'm having a living, breathing romp in his cell/room while all you have are memories. (Now who's being bitchy?) Today she felt empowered.

Cameron led the way from the parlour all along the corridor, up the winding, dark stairway into his cell. He began to remove his clothes.

'Stop right there, Cameron. I'm sick of this wham, bam, thank you mam kind of love making. Yes it's amazing, Yes it's exciting, Yes sometimes it's an out of body experience, all of those wonderful ingredients but most times I'm left feeling there's a lot of lust but not a lot of love. So for today Cameron we're going to take it slow, it's my turn to guide you.'

Poor Cameron, he didn't know what to do. He was used to rushing into his room, removing Georgia's clothes at the speed of Superman. Taking it slow for him was really a hard task, almost like asking a Formula 1 racing driver to drive slowly when the adrenaline rush was phenomenal and he was driving at full speed. He did slow down, every touch meant something, every caress, every butterfly kiss, wow! It felt more loving, exactly what she had wanted and when it came to a grand crescendo, Georgia realised she had felt the crashing of the cymbals, the rhythm of the drums, the romance of the violins, the soft sound of the waves, yes the whole ensemble. Now calmness had returned to Georgia's being and it was time to leave Cameron's room. As they almost flew down the stairs the thought of being caught was the only thing on their minds. It was only as they ran towards the door and out into the open air the panic began to subside. Georgia jumped into her car, gave him a kiss on the cheek and left with a smile on her face. On her terms it was good. Love in the cloisters can be a beautiful thing.

Answering her questions to herself:

1. Yes, this romance could go somewhere but it needed nurturing.

2. Yes, slowing things down and enjoying the moment and being on her terms was an out of body experience.

3. At this moment, if Cameron decided to leave the Seminary… for him.

   She would be prepared to see what the future would hold… for them.

CHAPTER 9

Tea and chat

How this week has flown by, she thought, as she glanced at her watch. It was ten minutes to five, almost time to meet Miss Maisie Coyne. Time would move fast enough, first she would have to park the car. In a small village like this it would take time to find a parking space and then she was there, sitting in the window seat on the most well-padded, comfy bench. Maisie knew how to pick her cafes, this one was so pretty, all done out in turquoise and pink with little baskets of roses decorating each window. Even the table had a small vase with a fresh flower encased within. The vases on the tables were all different colours, altogether a gorgeous, pretty space.

Promptly at 5.00pm Maisie arrived. Wearing a little hat on her head and a very prim and proper grey coat, a pair of leather gloves and a nice dusty pink handbag held over her arm. She dressed exactly the way Georgia pictured she would, after all she did have a status she had to live up to. She was Miss Maisie Coyne, housekeeper at the beautiful monastery. Everyone knew her, she had to be presented in that lady of the house type of way. One of the waitresses came over, took her coat and hung it up, leaving Maisie looking absolutely beautiful in her pale pink skater dress. Maisie's hat was still in place, it looked lovely. The girls in the café knew what Maisie liked and almost before she had perched her round bottom on the chair, her tea and a slice of apple pie, heated to a medium temperature, perfectly perfect for Maisie, sat in front of her.

'Can I be bold Georgia, and say something a lady like me

shouldn't say? Did you have a good time in Cameron's cell?'

Georgia was happy Maisie asked her this question instead of giving her a lecture. Georgia said nothing but blushed bright red, lowered her eyes and concentrated on the toasted cheese, ham and tomato sandwich she'd ordered and was now relishing. When she composed herself she looked back up.

'Maisie' she said 'You're like myself, you come straight to the point. I shouldn't talk about it, Maisie, but I just have to tell you, the time I spent with him was amazing.'

'Do you know Georgia that very room you were in is the very room I was in all those years ago with the love of my life?'

(Georgia knew she was right, Maisie did have a sour taste in her mouth from Fergus) They catch a glance between them. Georgia imagined Maisie was thinking, did she have as much fun as me?

'I just loved that room. I think looking back on myself as a young woman, I felt freer inside those four walls than I'd felt anywhere else in the world and when you think of it, Georgia, those four walls are completely forbidden. If you believe what the Catholic Church says, priests must be celibate but to be honest I don't agree with that.'

'But, Cameron's not a priest yet, Maisie. He's a deacon and he's not sure if he really wants to take the final step and be ordained a priest.'

'I know, Georgia, I know I cried when I spoke to you last time, I was feeling a little emotional. You might have thought I'm not happy in my work but I love working in the monastery. When I came here first, I was a young girl from a country village. I started work in the kitchen, cleaning and polishing the furniture and then moved up to be the housekeeper. Once my relationship with Fergus was over, I felt so betrayed, unfulfilled and for a while very bitter. I just couldn't find a new path to my life. I should have left there and then but I liked my job so I soldiered on. He went to a parish in a different country and we lost touch. I often wonder did he leave the priesthood and marry someone. Although I wonder about these things, I don't want to know the answer because my heart would truly break if he'd picked someone else instead of me. All I've done all these years is think about him day and night.'

Georgia's imagination was running wild.

'What if he'd left the monastery and didn't marry anyone at all? Maybe somewhere out there there's an ex priest hoping that Maisie Coyne would find out where he is and come looking for him.'

Maisie burst out laughing.

'That sounds like him Georgia, he was always a bit lazy, he would never look for me and he would expect me to look for him.'

Georgia gazed around the café to see if anyone noticed them but people seemed oblivious, deep in their own conversations.

'Mmm' said Maisie as she tipped her lips with her index finger. 'Maybe I'll follow up and see if I can locate my Fergus, my story could have a happy ending after all.'

'Maybe both of us will end up with men of the cloth. We could compare notes.'

That was such a funny thought, the two of them laughed. Georgia was delighted to see that Maisie had a twinkle in her eyes, maybe she'd given her back that ray of hope.

'Maybe someday my story will have a happy ending.' Maisie said as the last morsels of food disappeared from their plates.

Georgia was thinking, I'm beginning to have doubts as to what my future will hold.

These two women had something very special in common, that only they understood. It had been nice to take this space and time to talk openly of their feelings. Well Georgia wasn't completely open, first she wasn't wearing her wedding or engagement rings and she hadn't told Maisie she already had a husband. She was living a lie. She wondered if she had told her would Maisie have got up and left, after all she was a staunch woman. Georgia doubted she would have approved. There was nothing really left to say, the tea and chat was complete… both women left feeling happy, having found in each other someone to confide in. It's funny how a little chat with someone outside your circle can make you see the world a lot clearer.

CHAPTER 10

New direction

The days drifted on, it was Sunday again, when she awoke she felt as if she hadn't slept at all, her neck creaked and her head ached, the only solution was to take two Nurofen and drink lots of cold water. She really wanted to enjoy the big fattening, tasty Irish, fried breakfast Ross was cooking downstairs. The delicious aroma floated up to the bedroom. When Georgia walked into the kitchen in her dressing gown, the vision of the beautiful table set out so nicely, complete with a single rose was sensational. The newlyweds sat down and enjoyed a lovely morning chat as they feasted on the crispy bacon, the succulent sausages, tomatoes and mushrooms, black and white pudding and of course the big mortal sin - fried bread. What a cosy feeling… their normal Sunday morning.

With the chatting and eating, time flew by and before you could say Speedy Gonzales it was time for Ross to do the thing he liked to do best on a Sunday morning, rummage through the vinyl LPs and single records in the Blackberry Market in Rathmines, one of those places where time seemed to stand still. As he left on his way to explore the stalls, Ross planted a kiss on Georgia's cheek. She smiled to herself as she remembered how excited he always was when he arrived back home holding two or three new records. He would immediately play them on his old record player and the two of them would laugh out loud as they danced around the sitting room.

Georgia turned on the TV and tried to settle down but memories of Cameron kept flooding back. As she browsed through the channels she realised that exercise was a waste of her time. She wondered how she would pass the next few hours trying in vain to concentrate on reading magazines, manicuring her nails, plucking her eyebrows, anything to stop her remembering but nothing worked. She felt uneasy, if only Ross had stayed in she would have been occupied but instead she was alone with thoughts of Cameron running through her head. Would she be tempted to ring him? You bet. Just as she was about to reach for the phone and commit the deadliest sin called Cameron, it rang and saved her from her fate.

'Hi Georgia, it's Tanya here. I'm at the Departures lounge in Dublin Airport and guess where I'm going?' Before Georgia got a chance to answer, Tanya continued 'Over to Granny's house.'

Of course Georgia knew who Tanya's granny was, in fact all the four friends from kindergarten, had visited Tanya's Granny's house quite a few times through their adolescent years and arrived back with some amazing and memorable stories.

'Georgia I'm sipping the most delicious Smirnoff Ice while eyeing up all the men around, including the cabin crew.'

Yes, Georgia's beautiful friend Tanya was single and free to eye up every man in sight including the cabin crew that Georgia knew Tanya was praying would be the cabin crew on her flight. Things were looking very rosy for Georgia's friend, Tanya. How Georgia would have loved to confide in her friend right now. If only Tanya knew Georgia now had two men in her life but she daren't say a word. For now she would dream along with Tanya and see where it would take her, while in her mind she would sift through her options to try to make some sense of them.

'Birdie must literally fly Georgia. Soon all will be revealed.' Moments later Tanya yelped 'Georgia the cabin crew are going through, he is on my flight. I'll keep you posted. Bye for now.'

Tanya was gone.

The silence was back, Georgia was alone again. Thank God the key in the door turned, her hubby was present and correct. As usual happy as a lark, completely elated, keeping with tradition he played his new vintage vinyl records on that old record player that he cherished while they ate dinner and later as they crunched on the chocolate dessert, they danced around the sitting room to the sound of *She Loves You, Yeah, Yeah, Yeah* by the Beatles. Everything seemed perfect.

Surely the eagle has landed. Tanya was already, hopefully, in London City Centre Airport and surely at this very moment would be pressing buttons on her phone to reach her fond friend and relate every moment of her flight and true to form she was. Would you believe if this girl fell into cow dung she'd come up smelling of roses! Mr Cabin Crew (steward) yes, the guy she'd been eyeing up as she sipped her Smirnoff Ice, was indeed on this flight and would you believe he had to give the demonstration on what to do with the seat belt and how to blow into a whistle for a good result. Tanya had Georgia in fits of laughter as she explained to her how she had sat there and stared straight into his face, making him go crimson with embarrassment. She didn't care, as far as she was concerned it was all part of the fun. He could blush, she could watch and later on at the rendezvous, (she hoped would happen) discussing his moves would break the ice between them. Georgia looked across at Ross, he was asking ever so quietly,

'What is all this laughing about? I can't wait to hear the story.'

'I'll fill you in later Ross, when you finish reading that book you bought at the Blackberry Market.'

Georgia returned to her phone call with Tanya. Tears of laughter flooded down both girls' faces as they continued their phone conversation. Georgia's imagination ran riot. She could imagine the steward blushing and feeling like he wanted to fade into oblivion but she knew Tanya, and Tanya was not going to let this guy get off lightly. He was smitten, she was thrilled.

'Would you believe it, Georgia' she said 'he actually moved me, Miss Sexy Pants up to first class.'

The class she assured Georgia she was born to be in. She also confirmed there was ample leg room in first class, enough to stretch her long legs while she waited to be served hot chocolate or whatever was on offer. By the time everything was served and tidied up Tanya had already exchanged phone numbers with Frederick, the Aer Lingus steward, promising to be his guest at a show and dinner afterwards. Now, Tanya was happy and if it got boring with Granny Twinkle, there would be someone in the background to amuse her. She had put his number in a very safe place, her cleavage where there was no chance of it escaping. Now she was off to Granny's house.

Georgia began to wonder if she was starting to live her life through other peoples' stories. She'd better get a life, wake up from this dream. If only it was me who had just arrived in London, just been chatted up by the steward and had his number down my cleavage. Now that wouldn't have worked for Georgia, her bra was padded and still there was lots of room. If Georgia had placed the cabin guy's number in her bosom, that wasn't oosum, she would have lost it and there would be no flirty nights, no sexy fun, just disappointment. Where was all the fun gone? All the fun she used to be part of? She had wasted too much time and energy and had become too serious as she chased after Cameron, that forbidden fruit. That forbidden fruit was too much of a temptation to ignore.

Down on the carpet after dinner the couple rummaged

through the old albums. The songs were wonderful, sung by old artists such as Ella Fitzgerald, Billie Holiday and Satchmo (Louis Armstrong). All that brass and smouldering voices was enough to put Ross and Georgia into a romantic mood that came to a grand crescendo as the firelight flickered images onto the ceiling. They couldn't get enough of each other, it seemed like old passions were aroused. Georgia felt with Ross a grounded love and a love that had been built up over time, a lasting love. So why was Georgia betraying this love?

Bank Holiday Monday, 12 noon, Georgia awoke to the sound of her mobile phone. Another episode in the life of Tanya was only moments away. Mr French Steward had made a date with Tanya. He was taking her to a fabulous night club in Leicester Square and afterwards for dinner at the Marylebone Hotel. She assured Georgia he was fun to be with and knew exactly how to treat a lady. At this point in the conversation Georgia wanted and longed to tell Tanya all about Cameron, the expert on how to treat a lady (and she was living proof).

'As you know, Georgia, I'm a firm believer in make hay while the sun shines and if Granny Twinkle has her way this could be my last chance saloon, my last chance of a date for the next seven days. Granny Twinkle (she was given the name because of her bright, shiny twinkly eyes) hasn't warmed so kindly to his smouldering charms and feels hard done by having waited so long to see me, her favourite grandchild, to be upstaged by an air steward.'

CHAPTER 11

Taking a break

Georgia had enjoyed her day and night with Ross so much she had taken the decision not to ring Cameron for the foreseeable future. Instead she would wait, leave the ball in his court after all he had a lot of decisions to make and so had she. They both needed space and time. Maisie Coyne had made so much sense and made a huge impression on Georgia when she made that statement, *you should think long and hard before you get too involved with a man of the cloth, he'll always be torn between you and God. Do you know if he leaves he'll regret it and do you know if he stays he'll regret it? Girl, just stop dreaming of a future with him, forget him, grab your future with both hands, don't remain hypnotised by a man of the cloth. Break away now while there's still time.*

With Maisie Coyne's words ringing in her ears Georgia decided to take the bull by the horns and rekindle her love affair with Ross by setting up, our new first date. She rang him at his office and asked him out. Although a little bewildered he agreed to the cinema date on Friday evening after work and to a special our new first dinner date that very evening. He could make up his mind later over dinner as to what film she would take him to on Friday night. It could be good fun to meet up after work. Ross was so excited when his lovely wife asked him out for a date. He seemed to love the idea and asked:

'Have you any instructions for me, Georgia?'

Her instructions to Ross were:

'Pretend it's our first date, dress accordingly, we'll meet at the

Savoy Cinema and have a new first date in 2 days' time. We'll have great fun.'

Ross butted in 'I'll buy the Maltesers, popcorn, orange drinks and ice cream.'

Georgia stopped him right there.

'No Ross, it's me who will be buying the Maltesers, ice cream, the popcorn and the orange drinks. We can pretend we're just two teenagers on our very first date. Oh! and by the way when you come home later please go upstairs shower and dress up for our, new first dinner date tonight. Love you.'

'Oh,' said Ross repeating the words out loud 'our new first dinner date.'

Georgia was doing far too much daydreaming and not enough of the things she should be doing. Now she was feeling guilty. What is it about women? They take a few hours to themselves and then the guilt comes along crushing their spirits. Why did I waste my day? I should have done this, I should have done that. Stop! You didn't waste your day. Georgia continued to talk in her head to herself. You took a few hours off from work to cook dinner for your husband and get ready for your, new first dinner date.

Georgia was not feeling well, nothing to worry about, just a dizzy head and a nauseous feeling in her tummy. Maybe I'm just feeling sick because of all the guilt I'm carrying around inside and worrying about what I'm doing to Ross. It's all just eating me up. I'll have to stop blaming myself. I fell in love with Cameron, I was not out flirting with men, our paths crossed but now I'm really trying to get my marriage back on track. Maybe all Ross and I need is to take more interest in each other's lives then everything might fall back into place. When I look back on what I've accomplished in the past few years, Georgia continued to talk to herself, I've got married, I've said goodbye to an old boss, I've changed my career and now I'm in a transition period of my life. Maybe this very day is the day when I finally find my path. Here's to the future.

When the old song came on the radio, *I've never been to me*, Georgia remembered those words and sang every word out loud. Her mum used to play that song quite a lot and taught her all the words. Back then she didn't understand what the words of that song meant but now she understood every word.

It's half past 4, I'd better get a move on. Georgia thought as she checked the dinner cooking in the oven. It was practically ready. The time had come to stick some Velcro rollers into her hair. Georgia rummaged through her wardrobe, looking for the perfect dresses to wear for her two new first dates with her husband Ross, dinner at home tonight and the cinema in two days. There were so many dresses in her wardrobe, most of them old so she flicked them to one side and began to sift through dresses for occasions, you know the ones with a bit of sparkle or vibrancy. Wow, she picked the one she wanted for tonight's dinner date, in on the waist, full on the skirt, it was one she bought on a vintage web site just recently, mint green with a little white collar. She stepped into her underskirt, buttoned it up, it felt a little tight around her waist, then she put the dress on over her head, she had a little bit of pulling on the zip to get it started, then it was there. She would have to pull her tummy in tonight. She'd wear her white kitten heels but underneath all this prim and proper dress would lie the secret, a white net, full under-skirt, the skimpiest pants she could find from Victoria's Secrets, suspender belt and silky mesh stockings. For the Cinema date Georgia decided on a similarly shaped dress with a lighter underskirt, all in baby pink, with darker pink shoes.

Even before Ross turned the key in the front door Georgia already had the first course on the table. The main course was already baked and ready on plates covered with tin foil they would only take a few minutes to reheat. She loved the aroma of the meal she had prepared and loved the idea of spending time with her Ross even more.

When he arrived home she could tell he was happy by the tone of his voice.

'Hello, Georgia, I'm home, I'm going upstairs to shower and change clothes for our new first dinner date.'

She shouted; 'Hi Ross, see you in a few mins.'

Georgia's cue to remove the Velcro rollers from her hair, take down the champagne glasses and put them beside the bottle of bubbly. Everything was ready and waiting. She heard the sound of Ross's feet sprinting down the stairs. Her heart skipped a beat, Champagne Popped, glasses filled, Georgia looking beautiful, Ross looking handsome, happy and hungry. They both enjoyed every morsel of food. That night Ross told his wife how proud he was of her going to the trouble of making a lovely meal for him and how all his colleagues were jealous, wishing their wives or girlfriends went to that much trouble to make them a gorgeous meal and organise a new first date for them.

As they listened to old fashioned music on the radio and spent time just happy in each other's company, Georgia realized how stupid she really was to ever let anyone come between them. The awful thing was she still felt she was under Cameron's magical spell and wondered if she could ever break that magic spell. Yes, it was good that Cameron hadn't called. He had probably given up on her and realised it was one big bad idea and he would be much better off starting all over again on his own, Young, Free and Single.

Ross kissed Georgia then took the slide from her hair, it fell down loose around her shoulders. Georgia was getting in the mood. Ross vanished upstairs. When he came back into the room he said,

'This is our new first date but with a difference. I just lit some candles and ran a gorge bubble bath for you. Come with me.'

Up the stairs they went, Georgia couldn't believe her eyes when she saw all the different coloured candles, decorated around the bathroom and a bottle of Bollinger Champagne sitting there with two real champagne flutes and strawberries in a dish. Ross unzipped her dress, it fell to the ground, looking quite pretty surrounding her, then he proceeded to unbutton her under-skirt, it fell down. Everything looked voluptuous on the floor.

'Oh My God' said Ross 'I feel as if I'm unwrapping a box of the most delicious chocolates.' Ross continued 'I think we should savour this moment, Georgia, I've never felt like this in all the time we've been together. To celebrate let's pop the cork and take a sip of that champagne.'

'Ross, you have gone overboard tonight.'

'That's because it's a new first date, Georgia, I aim to make a good impression.'

'Well you certainly have, especially with that bottle of Bollinger, It's delicious.'

It was true they had both gone all out for this special new first date. The last few garments Georgia had decided to remove herself, in keeping with that thought she pressed the button on her small tape recorder, she'd sneaked into the bathroom, out came the words of the song, sung by Chris DeBurgh, and what better song than *Patricia The Stripper* a light hearted sexy little song that always made herself and Ross smile. There was one line they really loved, that was *To tremendous applause she took off her drawers.* Georgia gave the performance of a lifetime, (forgetting her nausea) she thought it was so good she could become a Burlesque Dancer, this could be her new calling.

Ross took her hand, helped her into the tub and then she was in there, lying beneath the bubbles while he gave her a beautiful neck massage. Her eyes remained closed as she lay there peacefully with the candle lights flickering around her. She could feel Ross stepping gently into the tub. That gave her a fit of the giggles because the bathtub was not a very large one but somehow it worked, as they say where there's a will there's a way. She opened her eyes and he was there holding two more glasses of champagne, she thought this was the funniest sight she ever saw. Sip, sip on the champagne followed by the most awkward, funniest love making ever. After lots of suds, splashing and fumbling the bathroom floor looked like Lake Garda, leaving a lot of water to be dried up but as they say, live for the moment.

Ross and Georgia sat down on the carpet beside the lovely fire watching one of those old romantic movies, Casablanca, a great film, easy to watch, relaxing, calm and once they heard the words *Of all the gin joints in all the towns in all the world, she walks into mine,* they lifted their two glasses and tipped them together in a toast to two lovers in love. Georgia was amused when she heard Ross, with the best American accent he could conjure up, say those magic words:

'Here's looking at you kid.'

Such a perfect evening, except for one thing, that feeling of nausea and lightness in her head had returned. Hopefully after a good night's rest she'd feel back to her old self in the morning.

Two days had passed, the new first cinema date had arrived. Georgia worked until 3pm then she was free to prepare for her date beginning soon at the Savoy Cinema. Showered, washed and dressed in all pink with a cream coat and a pale pink tiny bag. Georgia jumped into her little car and before she knew it she was driving down the road in her little mini all set for the 6 o'clock showing. She hoped Ross's eyes would light up when he'd see her. She'd know by the look on his face that her new Husband had not grown tired of her and still fancied her madly. Was she going mad? Acting like a child needing adulation and excitement all the time to keep her happy. She wasn't feeling very well and her emotions were all over the place? Luckily she found a parking space and in moments she was walking towards the Savoy Cinema doing her best Marilyn Munroe impression as her dress swayed in the breeze. All she needed now was that grating over that shore and the breeze coming up from it to give the desired effect of Marilyn Munroe's dress almost blowing over her head in the film *Seven Year Itch*.

There Ross stood with the fab sign of the Savoy Cinema shining down on him like a star, she just had to stop and stare. Yes, he had gone to a lot of trouble for their new first cinema date. He must have packed all the clothes he was wearing when she was busy last night talking to friends on the phone and put them into his car. She could see he was holding a single red rose. Had she been delusional, thinking of leaving this man for a man of the cloth who didn't really know what he wanted, a total contrast to Ross, who from day one had been straight forward with her, always focussed and sure of himself. She had been prepared earlier, to put her life on hold for Cameron, now she wondered could she ever leave her marriage or was it too important to her?

Ross caught her gaze and smiled, that quietly amused smile. She hoped it was saying I never know what to expect from you Georgia. He always seemed fascinated by his lovely Wife. She hoped he was thinking I find you fascinating, funny and I love you. She would never know what he was thinking but she was thinking, was this handsome man standing there before her, the only man she could ever truly love, they had history between them. He presented her with the perfectly formed crimson rose and kissed her cheek. They strolled into the Savoy Cinema. She insisted Ross decide which movie he would like to see but Ross didn't go for his type of movie instead he picked one for her *Eat, Pray, Love*. Georgia hadn't a clue what it was about but from the moment it began she completely lost herself in it, the way Julie Roberts' character's life evolved. Julie's character had taken several journeys, each one fabulous, from Italy for food, then to India to pray. Her final journey was to Bali. She had gone on these journeys to find herself but she found more than that, she found the love of her life. Maybe it's true what they say, sometimes we have to go away, take a step back from our lives to realise our futures are already set out for us, written in the stars.

Now home drinking champagne and contrasting with that, they were also eating an easy Chinese take away meal, already ordered, delivered and now being devoured. Georgia and Ross agreed everyone should have a new first date at least once every six months in their married life to remind them of how they fell in love in the first place. While Ross went ahead to shower and prepare for the next working day Georgia remained in the sitting room, thinking to herself how happy she felt all because she'd organised that cinema date earlier and the meal two nights ago. Now she was happy in the knowledge she had a few days off work because she was feeling very tired. It was nice to just sit there and stare into space while she played one of David Bowie's records on Ross's prized record player. The hands of the clock were at precisely 10.45pm, the music was so gorgeous, she just loved the beat of David Bowie's music. His voice was so distinctive and so powerful it engulfed her.

Apart from the music there was no other sound, that was until her phone rang, and guess whose name was sitting there looking back at her... Cameron's. She shouldn't have taken that call but of course, she did. As Oscar Wild said *I Can Resist Anything But Temptation,* unfortunately for Georgia this particular temptation was too powerful.

'Hello Georgia.' Down the line came that gorgeous, silky, chocolaty voice, the one she couldn't resist, the forbidden fruit.

'Jesus, Cameron. Maybe that's the last name I should say to you, religious Cameron. After all it is Jesus and Ross who are coming between the two of us. Why the hell are you calling me at this hour of the night? Ross could have easily been here and noticed your name coming up on my phone' Georgia continued to rant. 'He doesn't deserve all this Cameron, he's such a good man and we've had a new first date today and it went really well.'

She was breathless. Up to this moment, Cameron hadn't spoken a word.

'I'm sorry Cameron, I'm sorry, I'm just trying to live my life one day at a time, keep living in the moment. So what's happening to you?'

'Well' said Cameron 'The words you said when you answered the phone have made it crystal clear to me that my first thought was the right one... not to ring you. I just wanted to tell you how much I love you. Audian is the only one I trust to pour my heart out to and he trusts me but we're both walking on eggshells right now, trying to make decisions and I felt you were the only one to make me feel at least not as mad as I'm feeling.'

'I know how you're feeling Cameron. There hasn't been a moment when you haven't been on my mind and in my heart, but unless I move out of here and you move out of there and we make a life together there's just no point in torturing each other the way we have been. Your decision to leave the monastery is a huge one but after all you're just leaving a place and people you like but you don't love. You haven't got a house with someone, a marriage with someone, a real life full of love, mortgages, shopping, real things, with no housekeeper like Maisie Coyne to look after you, with no one fixing the garden or mending the fence because Cameron that would be the reality. We'd have to do that ourselves, all the mundane things as well as the happy things, if you and I set up home together. Do you feel ready to take this huge big step and leave the comforts of the monastery to be with me? And my question to me is do I value you more than I value Ross. Do I love you more than I love Ross and the biggest question of all, am I capable of turning my back on my home, my marriage and all the love I built up with Ross to step into the unknown with you, who one minute wants to leave the monastery and the next you're not too sure?'

'My mind is in turmoil'…

'Please just stop right there, Cameron, this is not the time to talk about your life, I'm sick listening to your wants, your needs. I've heard it all, seen it all, don't want to know it all, not right now. I've gone along with you. You have to do what's right for your life, God gave you a life, He also gave me one, Cameron, sometimes you know you can waste time and spend too long wondering what you should do with your life and miss out on your present and future opportunities.'

Cameron knew what Georgia was saying, as the song says *You say it best when you say nothing at all.* (so he said nothing at all)

'Once I leave my marriage I doubt if there would be any way back, so please Cameron can you think things through tonight and meet me when you are ready to do some straight talking and see where the future can take us, whether it's to be together or to be apart, we both need clarification and closure?'

'OK, Georgia, I will call you real soon.'

'Thank you, Cameron. I'll make sure I'm not treading the light fantastic.' Georgia nervously laughed. 'I will be available.'

'Thank you for taking my call, Georgia. Can't wait to see you.'

The phone went silent. Now Georgia was still sitting there but in a completely different mood, not only did she feel sick, she felt agitated and irritated. There was so much of her that really wanted to share Cameron's life but the little practical part of her kept shouting to her soul, stay, you made the decision to be with Ross because you loved him and what's wrong with the marriage? Nothing. Anything that's wrong is wrong with you, Georgia. Just get a grip on yourself and sort things out for better or for worse. Georgia crept up the stairs into the bathroom, cleaned her teeth and slipped into bed beside her lovely husband. He turned around, put his arm around her, kissed her on the forehead and in the sleepiest voice ever, said the words 'I love you' hard to understand but lovely to hear.

Georgia lay wide awake in bed thinking, he's such a good husband, I should wrap him up in cotton wool and throw sugar at him.

CHAPTER 12

Awkward moments

It was so nice to have the place all to herself, for one particular reason, Georgia was feeling so nauseous she spent most of the morning kneeling down beside the toilet being violently ill, but for some reason or other at about midday those feelings subsided. Her phone rang… clearing of the throat,

'Hello Georgia. Have you got a moment to talk?'

'Yes, Cameron, go ahead, what do you want to tell me?'

'I know you're tired listening to me talking about the seminary, as you call it blah, blah, blah but it was a big decision I had to make and I've made it. There's no turning back for me, I want to be with you if you want to be with me. Before you say a word Georgia I just want to say sorry for saying all of this to you over the phone. I have just come out of a meeting with my mentor and I've told him I'm leaving. There're a few loose ends to be sorted out but I will be out of the seminary in two weeks.'

Georgia felt dumb struck but at the same time she had things she needed to say and since he had said all this over the phone, she had to continue.

'Cameron, please don't leave the seminary for me. I can't promise to be with you forever. I'm going through a lot in my own head but just to say I really do love you and I am in love with you. It's just that I cannot have any of this falling on my shoulders. You have to be leaving because you've decided the religious path is not the one for you, if you do that I'm happy to see where the future leads us but if there's a lot of pressure on me I have to say here and now, it's over. If you want to continue with me, take your time and let us build things up together. I'm happy to do that but if you think you're going to move in with me when you leave the seminary I have to tell you it's not going to happen. I apologise for being so blunt and so straight but the last few weeks have torn me apart and now all I can do is look after me for a while.'

There was a silence on the phone, Georgia actually thought he was gone, she knew he hadn't put the phone down but she thought he had just walked away from it, unable to handle her honesty and then she heard that clearing of the throat...

'Georgia, I am leaving because I don't want this life. Earlier when I spoke to my mentor I was very scared, asking myself if I was making the right decision. After all I've spent six years here and in a few months from now a different life would be there for me. I would be a priest in a parish, I could help people and I could look after the community. It's something I've always loved doing, even when I was in college we used to visit the elderly in their homes. My mentor was beyond amazing, he helped me sift through my fears, pointing out if I did leave I could do most of the things I want to do anyway, outside the monastery. He even thought I should go into teaching. I was delighted he said that, as I had sent my CV to one of the schools I used to work in.

As he explained everything, it became clearer and clearer to me. My life could no longer continue here and to be honest Georgia, it's not because of you I'm going, it's because I've grown up and faced myself and realised what I want out of life. I want to be married, I want to have children, I want a house with a little back garden, a holiday once a year and Christmas with my own Christmas tree and children around it. Georgia, there's no pressure, believe it or not, I'm just happy that my mind is freed. I'm a free man for the first time in my life. Oh and by the way,

I've already told my parents and Georgia they're happy for me. I think they've grown up too and realised having their son in the priesthood is not the only way, all they ever really wanted was for me to be happy.

As I said earlier, I sent my CV into a school, one I visited through my work here and it's looking like I just might get a job there. I would be teaching Religion and English which would suit me down to the ground. I know I'm choosing the right path in going into teaching.'

'Cameron, I'm so happy for you and I can't wait to see you. Would it be OK if I came to the seminary and helped you pack?'

'That would be marvellous Georgia, I'm brutal at packing but I don't have a lot to take with me. Why don't you come over tonight? There's a retreat going on for the deacons who are being ordained soon, there will just be myself and Audian here. As you know he has also decided he's not moving forward in the seminary. He's applied for and has been accepted as a trainee policeman. He'll be heading off down to Templemore. We're going to take a small flat together until it's time for him to leave. We will share the bills and that will help both of us. It'll be very quiet here tonight. If you come up at about five, Maisie Coyne will let you in. Looking forward to seeing you then.'

The phone went dead. Georgia sat down and said to herself, remember, Georgia, don't take all his problems on yourself. He's got to deal with his problems the same way you have to deal with yours and no one can help him just like no one can help you. In the end the truest saying ever said is, you come into the world on your own, you go out of the world on your own. If you're lucky you'll meet good people along the way but the buck stops with you.

Georgia went into her shower room, ran the shower, took off

her clothes, opened the door and stepped in. As the water, the suds, the conditioner and the comb touched her, Georgia felt cleansed. Out she stepped onto a nice fresh mat, dried herself and then scrunched her hair. It was a nice day outside so she decided to wear something nice and light, a very pale lilac silky dress. No bra and her prettiest pants. On went a new pair of runners, all white with a little bit of lilac and then added a touch of make-up, fresh lipstick and a quick spray of Gabrielle by Chanel. She went like the wind in her little mini with the white roof all the way to the seminary.

This time she didn't feel like she was trespassing, awkward or out of place as she rang that doorbell possibly for the last time and there stood Maisie Coyne. She had the biggest beaming smile you could ever imagine and it was funny but Georgia was starting to look on her as a friend, (moment day dreaming). She would have her up to tea sometime. It would be good for Maisie and her. Maisie could answer anyone who asked, are you going anywhere special this evening, Maisie? Oh I'm just going to meet a friend of mine. Georgia knew Maisie would be smiling and beaming knowing she had a friend she could meet up with to brighten up her day.

'Go right ahead' said Maisie 'I assume you're going to see Cameron. I believe he's leaving here altogether.'

'Gosh!' said Georgia. 'News travels fast in this place.'

'My friend is Cameron's mentor's assistant, so I hear everything that goes on here. I shouldn't but I do.'

Georgia bounced down the corridor, no hiding in dark corners on the way. Up the stairs she pranced like a young happy puppy. He must have heard her coming, he had the door open and his arms around her and the smile on his face said it all. He lifted Georgia into the air and swung her around the room. She was afraid she would break her ankle off a chair, with the speed she was going and the size of the room. Then without further ado Cameron unzipped her dress it slid from her shoulders then he kissed her lips and guided her to the bed. She didn't put up a fight. In some ways Georgia would have loved to have lots of clothes on so like the first time they made love, they could have landed on the floor, the handle of the door, the lampshade and the telephone. Instead her light dress was now on the floor, her pants were on the chair and that was it.

This time Georgia felt completely relaxed and loved every minute of the love making. Cameron didn't have to try too hard this time, it just happened. She did cry just like that first time and it was for the very same reason but yet it was all so different. Somehow she felt freer and more accepting of everything that had happened to her. She was ready to accept anything that came her way. It felt like total abandonment and Georgia loved it. Any inhibitions she had were completely gone with the wind, out the door. It was the first time she'd made love since she came to terms with herself, her weaknesses, her strengths, her wants and most of all her needs and desires. With so much passion everywhere the two lovers completely forgot about the packing. Ah sure Cameron was very capable, he could pack his case himself and it didn't look like he had a lot. This would be her very last visit to the seminary, a place she had begun to feel very comfortable in and at the same time very happy to walk away from.

This time Georgia took her time walking down the large winding stairway, knowing this was her last time to walk down these stairs, she took everything in. She noticed the dark corners but she didn't feel like hiding in them, she wasn't nervous or worried would somebody catch her and march her by the collar and ass, out through the front door, just like in the old cowboy films when the Sheriff would grab the baddy by the collar and the seat of his pants and fling him out through the flappy doors into a mucky puddle in the middle of the road. No mucky puddles for Georgia, she was walking straight out that front door full of confidence with Cameron walking beside her. She knew he had an air of freedom about him too. She felt good knowing this decision he had made, he had made for himself not for his mother and father, not for the priest and his mentor and everyone else in the congregation and certainly not for Georgia. She could tell he felt a free man, all the shackles of the last few years were falling from his body one by one, wondering would he stay or would he go? Maybe because it was a comfortable place for him to be but now all of that was almost past.

All of a sudden something came into Georgia's mind. She felt she needed to talk to him about straight away.

'Cameron, I've had this wild notion. I feel and I hope you agree that we should take a little break from right now until you've completely left the seminary, in your heart and in your soul and settled into your new life. You'll not only be free from the seminary but free in your head and ready to move forward with your new life, with or without me. Both of our heads will be clear by then. Hopefully, we'll know instantly when we meet if we're meant to continue on this loving journey or if this was just one long romp in the seminary. Forbidden fruit - You hungry for sex, me lusting for you and only you.'

Cameron was so taken by surprise he just agreed. Now they were back in the hall. They bumped straight into Maisie Coyne, she walked with them to the parlour.

'Georgia,' she said 'I got used to your little visits here and actually looked forward to them. I'm going to miss them when you're gone.'

'Maisie, I was just thinking the same thing, I'm going to miss you. I honestly believe parting is sweet sorrow and with that in mind I would love to meet you for yet another cup of tea and a slice of apple tart in your favourite little cafe in a week or two.'

Maisie's face lit up like a chandelier, every piece of her body seemed alive. Some gal for one gal.

'Oh' said Georgia 'I nearly forgot, I have a little present here for you for being so kind and explaining everything to me and making me understand what I let myself in for. And there's another little something in that box for you so you'll remember me.'

To Georgia, Maisie was a mother figure, she wanted to get to know her more and maybe make her a bigger part of her life. It was hard to say goodbye to Cameron but sometimes a little time is needed before making a lifetime decision. Next time she'd meet up with Cameron he'd be a civilian like her. Would that take away some of the passion? She'd have to wait and see.

Georgia wondered what the next meeting would be like, or indeed would there be another meeting for them? Cameron was just starting a new beginning, leaving his past behind. Would she be just another part of his past that he would be prepared to leave in his past? The end of a very long journey for Cameron. If things worked out the way they planned their next meeting would be the beginning of a new chapter for both of them. Then she was gone driving down the driveway with only one glance back to the last piece of a past she wanted to say goodbye to. Georgia felt at one with the blue skies, the light breeze and the world.

CHAPTER 13

Putting her past on hold

She awoke to the sound of: 'Yoo Hoo! Yoo Hoo!' and the terrible sound of stiletto heels belting each stair until they arrived at the top. Knock, knock, knock on the bedroom door. This was not the way Georgia liked to come to life in the morning. The door opened and before Georgia's eyes could focus on the intruder, the intruder was hugging her poor weak body and saying those inevitable words:

'Rise and shine Georgia Browne, it's way past getting up time.' Georgia rubbed her eyes.

'Jesus Mum, it's you.'

'Darling daughter of mine who else did you expect at this hour of the morning only your wonderful, exciting, interesting mum. I noticed Ross's car was missing, I knew you were alone and that's why I walked into your bedroom unannounced, but I did knock. Do you like my dress?'

She did a twirl to show Georgia the complete picture.

'Yes, that's definitely another new dress. I like that red shade Mum, it matches your lipstick. Stand back a bit Mom, so I can see those high shoes that woke me up with a bang, bang, bang. I wish I looked as good as you.'

'Well if you got out of the bed earlier and made a bit of an effort, you could look just as hot as I do.'

'Gosh Mum, you definitely don't have a big head.'

'I'm just being funny Georgia but I've never seen you in bed this late before.'

'I couldn't sleep last night, Mum, and then when I was just

nodding off to sleep, Ross had to get up for work, and because he was going to be away for the rest of the week, I got up to say goodbye, then I went back to bed. The house was so quiet with no one here I fell back into a deep sleep.'

'I'm going to go back downstairs and make your breakfast, Georgia. Have you any little pinnies in the kitchen press just to save my gorgeous dress, since I've every intention of heading off somewhere very soon?'

Georgia could hear her mum's high shoes digging into the stairs and then there was silence. Georgia liked silence, she turned over and closed her eyes. He was back in her head, as clear as day, as if he was sitting right beside her. She didn't like this torment she was going through. Into the shower Georgia jumped and stood there with water streaming down on her hair and body. Wash, wash, wash her hair… conditioner… body wash… out… fluffy towel and dried. She dressed in a nice snugly pink dressing gown, went downstairs and sat at the breakfast table to be pampered while she listened to her mum's funny stories and enjoyed her company.

'A few nice rashers and a couple of your favourite little cherry tomatoes and I brought some nice fresh bread from the deli. It's all sliced and ready for you. There's also some real butter in the dish.'

Georgia loved that dish. It was a small dish with a pink lid shaped like a rabbit.

'You're going to enjoy this. I've just made you the hottest cup of tea you've ever had and it's in your favourite rabbit cup.'

(My mum loves spoiling me. She still thinks I'm ten years old)

'I know, Mum. I never stopped loving cuddly toys and rabbits were my favourite. You should know, Mum, we were always like two little peas in a pod, as close as Siamese twins that was you and me, you always knew what I liked, always.'

'But sure you're right, Georgia. There was only me and you once your Dad was gone. There was only me to protect you from the world. So I did my best to make it an interesting world for you. We went to all the best places, do you remember when you were small and every day we had a different adventure? Sometimes you and me and sometimes, you, me and pals from your school. Georgia I have to say, that school did wonders for you, meeting up with those gorgeous girls in kindergarten and keeping that friendship to this very day. You've been a lucky girl, in fact a very lucky girl.'

They chuckled like school kids. Georgia ate the fabulous breakfast, drank the scalding hot tea and enjoyed the crunchy fresh bread her Mom had brought. Georgia hadn't realised how hungry she was. What a woman her mum was, full of surprises, energy and enthusiasm. At this moment she had all of them in abundance. Out of the blue her mum announced,

'Surprise, Surprise…I'm going on a cruise, Georgia. It's going all around the Cote d'Azur, into little villages like Ville Franche. They say there are loads of little shops up there that sell fabulous trinkets and pretty dresses. I'm bound to find something to make me and you feel good.'

'Who are you going on the cruise with, Mum?'

There was a pause. The first pause her mum had taken since she entered Georgia's room almost an hour and a half earlier.

'I'm going alone, Georgia, and before you say, Ah! Mum take a friend along. Oh! Mum, can I come? Oh! Mum, get some love in your life, I'm here to tell you Georgia, I am going alone.'

Knock at the door, without thinking Georgia's mum ran out and opened it. Georgia didn't know who was there but it had to be someone her mum knew. She could hear the chattering as they arrived into the kitchen. Georgia turned around and there stood her lovely friend Tanya. There were the usual kisses and hugs.

'Tanya, you wouldn't believe what I'm talking to my mother about. She's going on a cruise… alone. That's the bit I don't like.'

Nellie repeated her words 'I am going alone.'

Georgia knew that wasn't a sentence that was a statement coming from her mum's lips.

'You can't be responsible for me all the time, Georgia. You need to stay here with your new husband Ross. I'll really miss you but I'll have lots of stories to tell you on my return and maybe I'll have some things I won't tell you, ha, ha, ha. I don't want some old pal telling me what I should do. You know me, I like to explore places and that's best done alone. Anyway, there're so many people on the ship you're only alone when you're in the cabin. I've got one up on the top deck with a little balcony, so I'll see what's happening outside. The cabins are small, so if I'm on my own I'll have more room and won't have to push past anyone in the small confined space.'

'I agree with your mother, who would want to share that small space? I think she is best on her own' said Tanya.

'Oh, I'll call you every day, and I'll send two photographs to you, one of me all casual (Georgia laughed, ha! you casual) and the second photograph when I'm all dressed up and looking absolutely fabulous before the big banquet. How does that sound to you Georgia and you Tanya?'

'That sounds great to us, Mum. You've sold that cruise very well, so very well. I have made a decision. It's a big birthday for you next year.'

'Every birthday is big,' said her mum.

'No Mum, next year is a big birthday for you, so I'm going

to take you on a cruise around the Greek Islands. What do you think Mum? I'm going to book it, pay for it throughout the year and all I need from you is your great company, your funny ways and that dress sense. You never cease to amaze me Mum. I will gladly be your escort next year.'

'I bet we'll have the best time ever and now that you're all fed and watered and you need some time with Tanya, I'm heading off, don't ask me where, I don't even know the answer myself, but I'll ring you later and if you're around, we could meet for dinner.'

'Not tonight Mum, I'm going to have a quiet dinner tonight, just me but you can always gate crash if you fancy sharing a meal for two from Marks and Spencer's. It comes with a bottle of wine and I know you like that, so if you're here we can share the wine.'

'Mmm, I'll see what's happening later. I won't call, if I'm not here by six you'll know I'm not coming. Is that OK, Georgia?'

The two girls walked Nellie to the door and watched as she got into her little car. Just like the princess she was, Georgia's mum waved that lovely wave as if she was the queen of Ireland. For a moment Georgia was back outside Buckingham Palace as a child, holding her mum's hand and watching in awe as the queen passed by in her carriage. Queen Elizabeth waved that wave with a glove on her hand. Georgia's mum must have practised that Royal wave, possibly in her head, and that was the wave she gave to Georgia and Tanya as she sped on her way to destination exciting.

CHAPTER 14

The goings on of Tanya

Tanya had taken along a bottle of wine and a box of Lily O'Brien's creamy chocolaty chocolates. They would live by the saying, eat, drink and be merry. Georgia just sat back, stuffed herself with chocolates and listened, as Tanya's fascinating story unfolded.

'Well Georgia, you know my Granny Twinkle, sure you remember long ago if it wasn't for my poor oul Granny we would never have got to see London. One, because our mothers trusted Granny Twinkle to look after us but sure she was away with the fairies and secondly because she let us stay there for nothing.'

'Yes' said Georgia. 'The four of us teenagers, me, Coco, Heidi and of course, your bold-self Tanya, we hadn't got a penny between us and anything we saved went on clothes in Top Shop. We had some good times over there and what a handy base in Greenwich, we should have all moved over to London.'

'I was thrilled to bits to go to Granny's but as usual just before I got too used to being pampered, Granny told me she was going to the theatre and then staying over with a friend. You know how particular she was about her place, she hasn't changed. She left a to-do list stuck on the wall for me. I had to follow all Granny's orders, as you know she was always a hard task master and if I didn't keep my side of the bargain there would be a price to be paid, so I did all the things listed. I polished the furniture with Granny's rusty, old, round tin of Mansion Polish from the press underneath the sink. No Pledge for my Granny, she believes in lots of elbow grease. First, before I started the procedure I had to battle to open the slippery tin containing the polish that must have been in that press for donkey's years. Once that was done and with one nail less, I proceeded to apply a layer of Mansion Polish to Granny's dark mahogany table. I shuddered at the thought of even putting a scratch on that work of art, knowing once Granny returned she would inspect it, almost soldier like, wearing her bifocals, to make sure there was not a blemish on that antique that she had since her first day of marriage.'

'Get on with the story' Georgia urged.

'Yes but this is a very important part of the story, I need to paint the picture for you Georgia. You need to listen to all of it to get the full gist.'

'Sorry for my lack of patience, Tanya, I just love to hear your stories unfold.'

'Then Georgia, I had to wait a few minutes for the polish to settle. Then with the yellow duster chamois I began to use that elbow grease I had been brought up to use.'

Tanya did all the actions. (She loved an audience, she should have been on the stage). Georgia almost fell off the chair laughing. Moments later with perspiration rolling down her forehead, Tanya stood up and acted out the part where she put her two hands on her hips and admired her handy work.

'Seriously Georgia, I knew my Granny Twinkle would be so proud of me polishing her favourite piece of furniture, the table that she adored, even though it was a bit wonky. I know she had stored in her head, memories of her gorgeous china cups and saucers adorning that table and the many sumptuous meals she'd made for special occasions like Christmas, Easter and Birthdays. At last, all my tasks were completed. I was thinking all my birthdays had come together especially when my gorgeous hunk of junk arrived. Without hesitation he threw me flat out on the highly polished shining, slippery mahogany table.'

Now the girls were in panics of laughter.

'I don't know why I'm laughing, Georgia, it didn't turn out very funny for me, I shouldn't have done such a good job on the table with the Mansion polish. In the heat of mad passion he lay me flat down on the highly polished, shiny, slippery mahogany table. You could see yourself in it, it was absolutely gleaming. As it happened I dressed in my best, a pale pink silky wrap over dress (easy to get on and off). My dress began to slide and I could feel myself cascading towards the floor. This tall, dark, handsome lover tried to save a damsel in distress by rushing to my side but it was all too late. I fell in a heap and landed flat on my ass.' The two girls continued to laugh. 'Even though I'm laughing, Georgia, it wasn't funny because all the passion disappeared as the pain flew down my leg.'

Georgia took a deep sigh, she felt the pain her poor friend had been in.

'In fairness, stop worrying, he pulled me right up and lifted me towards Granny's bed but Jesus, if her table was lopsided and made my sliding even worse than it should have been, her bed was creaky, it made rude noises, I could hear the noises and I could feel the springs springing and sprung sprunging. Now, Georgia that wasn't all I felt, remember he was hot he didn't let simple things like a slippery, bockety mahogany table and pinging, ponging springs of a bed put him off course. He was a real Casanova and knew how to make a girl feel excited. He did his best to make me forget about the bed with all his sexy moves. We did make love but while it was passionate it was also very funny. I couldn't forget about the bed Georgia, the noises wouldn't let me, but can I say between the laughing and the slipping off the table the moment was still not lost.

This was the best and the funniest story and every bit of it was true. I had a great time, I considered even telling my Granny twinkle the whole story but then if I did let Granny twinkle know that her granddaughter, the one she loved and adored, had begun to make mad passionate love on that very table that still had the smell of Mansion polish on it and was as slippery as an ice skating rink. If she also knew Tanya, her loving granddaughter had proceeded to jump into Granny's bed, with a guy who had been a stranger just hours earlier and continued to make mad passionate love, Granny would not only see red she would completely disown her disgraceful granddaughter. Yes me, the bold Tanya, whom, if I was a bar of chocolate would eat myself, had lost the run of myself as I enjoyed passion on the old slippery table and in the wonky and badly sprung old bed that seemed to have a mind of its own.'

Georgia giggled as Tanya continued her story.

'No matter which direction we seemed to move in we always ended up falling to one side on a mattress that was badly sprung and too old for human inhabitants. It was almost new on one side and old and decrepit on the other, a true indication that Granny had only used one side of her bed for too many years. Georgia, the bed was a storybook in its own right. The story it told was, Granny mustn't have had many men in the bed, not even the wolf from Red Riding Hood, and if she did, they must have been lightweights. Anyway, the unevenness made for a bit of excitement and a bit of fun. I think if I told her the whole truth and nothing but the truth she would never forgive me. I would have lost all of the brownie points I'd stored up with Granny.

1. Making love for most of the night in her bed.
2. Making love on Granny's prized mahogany table.

Georgia now I'm going to tell you why I lost the rest of my brownie points,

3. I kissed him goodbye the morning after the night before and left him in Granny's House, in Granny's Bed, while I went shopping.'

'Tanya just imagine if Casanova, who you really knew nothing about, had hired a man with a van and the pair of them stripped Granny's house from top to bottom including her prize mahogany table and her lopsided, banjaxed bed and headed down the road into oblivion, leaving it empty for Granny's home coming... what the outcome would have been' said Georgia.

'If what you imagine had really happened Georgia, I would most certainly be completely cast aside and written out of Granny's will, but luckily for me at 10am the bold Andy Pandy called to say he was indulging in a nice greasy breakfast while he reminisced on the amazing passionate night he'd had in Granny's. He begged for a repeat performance that night but my answer was, you can't improve on perfection, so I declined and left the memories to history.'

'Wasn't he a cheeky piece of work Tanya. If your Granny came home and found him prancing around in a pair of shorts, sipping coffee and eating breakfast, she would surely have had a massive heart attack.'

Georgia was convinced it was only someone like Tanya, with a bold cheerful cheekiness, who would be lucky enough to get away with such an act. She was so lucky that none of Granny's old age pensioner friends had passed by and noticed this cheeky chappie, as he tiptoed on his way to the Great Escape, not underground as in the film but as in modern times, out through the front door looking like the cat who got the cream. Tanya had no time to lose, she'd spent too long telling her story, work was calling and she had to leave.

Before Georgia knew it, it was 6 o'clock. Out came the food from the fridge, into the hot oven it went. While she was waiting she poured a glass of wine and began to sip it. Georgia put on an LP on Ross's record player, she didn't play it until her food was on the table and a napkin over her knees. She put her hand out, pressed play and out came the beautiful voice of Roy Orbison, *In dreams I'll walk with you*. Georgia wondered who would walk with her for the next chapter of her life. She was so deeply in thought she had forgotten completely about her mum, Nellie, until she heard 'Yoo Hoo', Nellie was back.

Although Georgia had thought she would like the peace and quietness of the evening she had to admit her mum's presence always lifted her spirits. Now that Nellie had no one to care for she had a lot of spare cash and loved to spend it on clothes but not just clothes for her, she very often bought little bits and pieces for Georgia. Today was no exception as she handed Georgia a small bag from River Island, inside lay a really pretty light weight dress, soft and flowy, white with little pale pink flowers and tiny green leaves adorning it. Of course Georgia tried it on while her mum tried on the outfit she had bought for herself. A very pretty pencil skirt, plain black and a white chiffon blouse with ruffles around the collar. Then they both stood up to admire themselves in the long mirror. They had a great evening together. When her mum left Georgia put her dress away nice and safe, this she had already decided was the dress she'd wear on the night she would meet Cameron again.

Her mum was gone and the house was very, very quiet. Georgia turned on the television. It was a night for a feel good film, one of her favourite movies, Roman Holiday, she had recorded it from the television, began to play. Georgia became completely immersed in each scene. She loved the easy pace of the film, the clothes and the scenery. It was one of those films she liked to watch alone because Ross never really got those old romantic films but she did. Her evening had turned into night and again she was feeling nauseous, she would have to go and see the doctor.

CHAPTER 15

Big news of the day

The sun shone brightly through her bedroom window, stinging her eyes. She put her hand across in the bed, Ross wasn't there and then her mind clicked back in. How could he be there when he was working in London? It seemed like there was a long stretch of a day ahead of her but as with a lot of things in Georgia's life, things were not quite as they seemed. A message had just arrived on her phone. Heidi had sent it 'Georgia I have something I really need to tell you. Can I call up for a cuppa and a chat?' And then she was there. Georgia was having breakfast so Heidi joined in. She loved the boiled eggs and the little soldiers.

'OK what is it you want to tell me? What is the big news of the day Heidi?'

'Do you remember my friend, Georgia?'

'What friend?' asked Georgia.

'Cameron. I've heard he's moving away.'

'Moving away where?'

'I think it's to London.'

Georgia tried to look nonchalant.

'I'm going to meet him. I wonder if you would come with me.'

'Yes. I'll come with you for the spin, Heidi.'

Georgia's plans for not seeing Cameron were starting to disintegrate. That's what she was thinking as Heidi's car drove smoothly along the road towards Cameron's new abode. Georgia felt sick. Unless she was driving herself, cars were just not agreeing with her. They pulled up just beside Blackrock Shopping Centre at a little block of apartments. The two girls got out.

Heidi pressed the buzzer and in they went. There were no words spoken between Cameron and Georgia. She was just the friend who came along for the ride. Now and then Cameron would glance at her across the room. Georgia just wanted to listen, she didn't want to be part of the conversation.

'I'm starting a new life, Heidi. I'm becoming a school teacher, but that's not until September, so I've decided to work in London on the building sites where I'll make lots of cash. It will bring me a few steps closer to having my own home, that's just what I need to do. I'm travelling with my friend Audian, he shares this place with me. While we're away two of our friends are taking over our apartment so we don't have to move anything out, or pay rent for 2 months.'

'How do you feel about working on building sites?' asked Georgia.

'When I was growing up I always worked on the farm with my father and brothers and I just loved it. I loved stacking up the hay in summer. I loved building, so if they were building an outhouse I always helped. Farmers always helped farmers. Sometimes when a neighbour would get permission to build a cottage beside them or a house, my cousins and I would help to lay the bricks. I loved watching the bricks turning into the walls of a house so I know I love the building game. We're going to live in Harlow, with other friends who work on building sites and make an absolute fortune. When I come back to Dublin I will be loaded, I can treat you all to a meal. Since we're staying in a big old house in Harlow with lots of rooms you're all invited to come and stay. The rent is cheap. We will be working long hours but both of you could take trips up to London and visit the shops and museums. What do you think of that?'

Georgia sat there in total shock, nodding her head. Heidi's

phone rang, she excused herself from the room, went out onto the pavement to take the call and brought her cigarettes. This would give Georgia a little time with Cameron. The door closed. Georgia heard Heidi's footsteps getting fainter as she walked away.

'What the hell are you playing at?' She screamed. 'When were you going to tell me you were going away for the summer? Do you realise how much I have been worrying about the decision whether to move in with you or not and all the time you're plotting and planning to move away to London for the summer? If Heidi hadn't told me and brought me over here today I have a feeling I would never have known.'

'I would have told you Georgia. I was going to phone you, meet up with you and explain. It makes sense if we're going to move in together. If we're going to buy a house together I want to have the biggest deposit I can have. So with the few pennies I've saved and my inheritance from my grandfather and the big wage I'll get while working in London, my calculations tell me I will have quite a substantial deposit. The bigger the deposit, the nicer the house, as you already know. I have a job as a teacher from September so I will be able to afford the repayments. Believe me, Georgia, I'm thinking of you and me right now. I'm leaving on Sunday morning and starting work on Monday morning. My friend has organised everything. Will you please meet with me before I leave? Please Georgia, will you try your best to come and see me in London? I'm going for two months, leaving me one month, when I come back, to sort out my teaching job.'

Cameron stood up, walked over to Georgia.

'You look a little tired pet. Why don't you stay with me tonight?'

Georgia began screaming again. She felt possessed. (But

inside Georgia was crying, she couldn't believe she wouldn't see Cameron for two whole months. Her emotions were all over the place.)

'Do you not realise that I'm a married woman? I can't just come and go when you feel I should.'

'Sorry Georgia.'

Georgia calmed down as she realised Ross was working away for a week.

'I can see you tonight. Do you want to come to my place?'

Now it was Cameron who looked shocked. The tables had turned. She was inviting him into her parlour, just like the spider, come into my parlour said the spider to the fly. Up to now Georgia was the one who had gone into his territory, into his den, into his monastery, now she was inviting him into her comfortable space. To say he was reluctant would be putting it mild. Cameron knew by the look on Georgia's face he had better accept or his life wouldn't be worth living. He nodded his head in agreement. The die was cast, just before Heidi came back into the room, they set the time for 7pm.

CHAPTER 16

Georgia's territory

She puffed up the cushions, hoovered the floor, lit the real coal fire, filled up the kettle and turned it on. Then Georgia took her favourite pill box red, enamel teapot down from the press and placed 2 Barry's tea bags inside and left it ready and waiting beside the box of Mr Kipling's French Fancies, that added that final touch. With all that done it was time to prepare the table. Georgia placed the knives, forks, cups, saucers and side plates beside the sandwiches ready to be toasted on Cameron's arrival. Taking a step back she admired her work. Yes it did look inviting, fit for a king. One moment she was on a high, then just in the wink of an eye all of her insecurities kicked in, I wish Cameron was here. I wouldn't have so much time to think, maybe I have been too hasty inviting him into our home.

All of a sudden she felt as if everything in her life was spiralling out of control. Panic began to engulf her spirit. Taking a look in the mirror she had to admit, visually she looked ok but inside she was crying. Not even one tear trickled from her eyes. She was looking at her house in a different way. It's funny how you can take things for granted and not appreciate the one thing that is so important, a lovely place that you call home, the house she shared with Ross. She never took the time to think about it until now when her lover was coming for tea. Soon Cameron would actually see it for the first time, her place of residence, her great escape. Georgia hoped it wouldn't make him think differently of her, maybe all of this was a mistake, at a bad time, when Cameron only had a few days left in Dublin.

She saw him as he arrived at the gate. She thought he looked a bit nervous. Georgia rushed to the door and opened it before he rang the doorbell and then he was inside looking very uncomfortable.

'Cameron, please don't be nervous.'

'Georgia, I don't know if I could sleep in the bed you share with Ross.' He blurted out.

'To be honest I don't know if I could let you sleep in the bed I sleep with Ross in. Why don't we just sit down, have a toasted cheese sandwich, a cup of tea and a Mr Kipling's cake and see where it all leads to?'

That's what they did. Cameron was so hungry, he devoured all the sandwiches. Georgia smiled, it was kind of funny watching him holding a tiny Mr Kipling's cake in his hand. To change the mood Georgia put on a slow romantic record on Ross's gorgeous record player. It was the very ingredient needed to change the tense atmosphere. This was the first time they actually sat and chatted in a friendly environment, not like in the monastery, where having walked the dim corridor, climbed the stairs and eventually locked the door behind them, to keep intruders outside Cameron's cell, they were too tired to talk, they always made mad passionate love but each time it had been Wham, Bam, Thank you Mam, now it was different. They sat in the cosy kitchen, at the little old table Georgia had for years, even before she met Ross, drinking even more tea and eating more sweet cakes. She could always see reality when she sat at this table, a lot of her decisions were made at this table.

'Georgia!' said Cameron 'This is the kind of house I'm dreaming of. I want a cosy house for you and me, where we can build memories. I want to have nice little bedrooms where, Please God, our children will sleep. When I came here tonight I was very nervous but now sitting here with you in your lovely warm cosy sitting room, the lights low, the gramophone playing lovely records and gazing at the colours coming from the fire, I know I will be the happiest man alive when I finally put a deposit down on our forever home.'

Georgia couldn't actually believe she was feeling resentful of Cameron being in her and Ross's private space.

He continued 'It's only now that I can see the importance of having a space to relax. I have never had that, Georgia. I came from a farm environment where most of the time all the doors were left open. You could find a hen pottering around the house.'

Georgia laughed out loud.

Cameron continued 'Then I went to the monastery to a tiny room, with central heating but with no central point and now I'm in a seventy's flat that's damp and cold. I can see so clearly the goal I'm striving for. Now that all the will I, won't I, should I, shouldn't I, is well behind me, I can clearly see the vision I have for our lives together and I hope that you visualise it too.'

Georgia just nodded her head in agreement. In that moment, being there with Cameron made complete sense to her. It turned out to be a blending of minds, hearts and thoughts. Now she wasn't crying inside, she was smiling inside and outside. There was a future to look forward to with Cameron, she only had to grab it with both hands… would she?

'I don't think I should stay tonight, Georgia. I feel it would spoil the time we have had together. You seem a little tired and I have to admit it would feel wrong if I lay on Ross's side of the bed.'

With great relief Georgia announced 'I'll take you back to your flat.'

'No,' said Cameron. 'I'll take the bus, it's more or less direct and I'll talk to you tomorrow.'

After another cup of tea and another Mr Kipling's cake, the two dreamers went their separate ways. Cameron home to his flat, leaving Georgia behind all cosied up beside the fire, staring into space, with her head spinning, conjuring up ways she could find to make it possible for her to visit Cameron in Harlow. Then just like that she had a really great brainwave. In order to reach her goal she would need to be up and ready next morning, with her mobile phone and Visa Card in her hand and a notepad and pen all prepared to jot down any information she might be given and have it ready to show Cameron when they meet up in a few hours' time. At nine am sharp everything was ready, that was the easy part, first things first, Georgia pressed the numbers on her phone.

'Good morning.' A lovely soft English voice, 'Mollie speaking. How can I help you?'

'Good morning my name is Georgia Brown. I would like to inquire if there are any available places on your course?'

'I've just had a cancellation for Monday the 14th, a month from now, if that would work for you.'

'Yes that would be amazing' said Georgia.

Swiftly Mollie continued 'OK. There are a few conditions I need to explain to you. Firstly, could I take your details?'

Georgia gave all the information Mollie required.

'That's great, thank you Georgia. If you'd like to attend our course it begins Monday the 14th. Firstly, your course must be paid for in advance, today, as it's a cancellation. Secondly, on Monday the 14th you must arrive here at 8.30 am for an informal chat, tea, coffee and light beverages. The course begins at 9.30am. You have a 15 minute break at 11am, a 40 minute break from 1pm. Each day you finish at 4.00pm, except on Friday when there is no lunch break and you finish at 2pm.'

'I understand,' said Georgia. 'I will pay for the course now.'

'That's OK Georgia, I have sent you an email to explain everything about the course. You should receive it now.'

'Yes I've received that. Please hold the place for me. I'll ring you back as soon as I read through the email.'

'Instead of ringing me back I'll explain all the details to you now over the phone and if you're happy you can pay now and take your time over reading the course information.'

Georgia couldn't believe it. She had paid for the course, she had a date for the course and she was going to London baby, in one month from now. She put the phone down, now for the next task. Georgia called her friend Prudence, who lived around Tower Bridge.

'Prudence, I'm going to London for a course, can I stay with you?'

'Absolutely' said Prudence.

Georgia could hear her jumping up and down with excitement.

'You know Georgia, I was feeling a bit down in the dumps for the last few days. I was praying something would come my way to lift my spirits. I can't wait to see you.'

'I'll be attending the course for most of the day' said Georgia 'and I'll have a lot of appointments in the evening time. Maybe you could come along to some of them.'

'I have to work too, Georgia but sometimes coming home here can be very lonely. My flat mate is away most of the time, so just having you here late in the evening or the morning before I go to work will be fantastic. I'll forward you on my address and how to get here.'

As Georgia finished the call she proclaimed out loud, second hurdle overcome, here's to the third.

CHAPTER 17

Surprise Surprise.

Georgia lay in bed that night tossing and turning. All of a sudden she sat up and said

'Oh My God, I completely forgot I made an appointment with my doctor for tomorrow morning at 9 o'clock. I'd better fix the alarm and make sure I'm there on time.'

'Georgia Brown. You can go ahead into the surgery now.'

Georgia went in and sat down.

'Good morning doctor.'

'Good morning, Georgia.'

'I'm actually wondering why I'm here. I have been suffering from nausea and a little dizziness.'

'Mmm' said the doctor.

'Today I actually feel very well. No nausea, no dizziness.'

'I'll check you out anyway, Georgia. Have you brought a sample with you?'

Georgia nodded her head.

'I'd like to check that. Now while that's working I'll check your blood pressure. Mmm, a little higher than normal, let me check your eyes and I'd like you to open your mouth. I'll check if you have a sore throat. That's fine, I'll just look at that test now.'

Maeve, her lovely doctor sat down and looked straight into Georgia's eyes:

'Well Georgia, there are a few things I'd like to tell you. Your blood pressure is slightly up, your throat is perfect, eyes perfect. There is just one other little thing.'

The doctor stood up from her chair and came around to where

Georgia was seated. She sat down on the side of her table and held Georgia's hand.

'Georgia, congratulations are in order.'

'Why?'

'I have a little announcement to make, Georgia. You're very healthy, you're also expecting your first baby.'

There was a silence that seemed to last for ages.

'How could I be pregnant?'

'Have you been taking precautions, Georgia, taking the pill, using condoms?'

'No.'

'Have you been having sex?'

'Yes.'

'Well, Georgia, that's how you're pregnant.'

They both laughed, Georgia realised the stupid question she had asked her doctor.

'Please come with me and lie down on the couch.'

Silence… very gently Doctor Maeve touched Georgia's tummy.

'I would think you are around three months pregnant, but to make everything crystal clear I'm sending you for a scan. The results will be sent to me and then I will discuss everything with you.'

'Oh, but doctor, I'm considering going to London for a week in a few weeks. Will it be OK for me to fly?'

'It would be better, Georgia, if you didn't but if you have to go just take it easy.'

Georgia stood up to leave. Now she was very wobbly on her feet.

'I'll send my assistant to accompany you home, Georgia. It's only a short walk to your house and she could do with a bit of fresh air. Again, congratulations and just imagine that within the next five months or so you will be a proud happy mum.'

Those words were enough to send Georgia's spirits in a downward spiral. Here she was, not knowing whether she wanted to stay married or change her life completely and now things were out of her hands. She had just learned one more of life's lessons, if you have sex take precautions, she hadn't taken precautions. Georgia had always looked forward to having a baby. It was written in the stars for her but not like this. She was pregnant, she almost screamed out loud, which one is the father?

The young assistant walked the short journey to Georgia's house, making small talk along the way. Georgia's brain didn't take in any of the conversation she had with that young lady. Everything was a blur. Anne said goodbye and went back to the surgery. Georgia put the key in the door and as she turned it she recalled all the feelings she had for the last couple of weeks. All the tell-tale signs had been there. Opening buttons on her skirt and her tiny bust increasing up a size. For about an hour Georgia just sat sipping tea and eating McVities chocolate digestives. Instead of being excited about this future she had made no plans for, all she could see was disaster facing her. Although she was confused and upset, with her brain all muzzled, something inside her told her for now, not to tell a soul. Not her mum, not her three best friends and certainly not Ross or Cameron. A little piece of her wanted to ring everyone and tell them her news but there was something holding her back. How would she find the words? What could she say?

Cameron I'm pregnant and it could be yours, Ross I'm pregnant and it could be yours. Friends, sorry I never told you I was having an affair with Cameron. I'm pregnant and I don't know who the daddy is. As for my mum, if I tell her she will tell the world and its mother. This is a defining moment in my life, one of those moments that will change the course of my life. Now I must make the right decisions for me and my baby. I'm looking back at my life up until this moment, back on the romance with Cameron and I'm thinking lustful, amazing and beautiful. I look back on the marriage with Ross and I think, why am I not just sharing this moment with him? When everything else fizzles out I can see so clearly.

Now I'm sitting here alone with no one to share my fabulous news with and the funny thing is I don't want to share this news with anyone right now. This trip to London has come at the right time. I will go to London, I will attend the course, I will meet with Cameron, I will go out for meals with Prudence and while I'm away I'll take care of myself and my baby growing inside me. When I come back home I pray I will see things clearly and know the road I must take, this is my decision.'

Ross was back home, Georgia was enjoying his company he was easy to live with, a hard worker who just liked to relax after his long day at the office and that suited Georgia. She could call her friends or just sit there and read a book and wait for the right time to tell him she was heading off to London for a beauty course for one week. When the time was right she told him. Ross was very easy about it.

'That's OK. Georgia. I'll be here and while you're away I'll catch up on my back log. Would you like me to drive you to the airport?

'Yes' said Georgia. 'My flight is at 8.30 on Sunday morning the 13th.'

'Would you like me to collect you on your return?'

'That would be fabulous, Ross. That flight is 7.30 from London. I'll give you all the details later.'

Between Working, adjusting to being pregnant, coping with her big secret and the terror inside her, Georgia had decided to keep a low profile and nobody seemed to notice. Cameron was too busy in London travelling to and from work, trying to cook food every night in the tiniest kitchen and on top of all of that, coping with exhaustion from all the climbing, pulling and dragging. For him the hardest thing was trying to get to sleep with people coming and going all the time. The only thing keeping him going now was, knowing very soon Georgia was coming over to London to brighten up his spirits. When he had decided to travel to London for work and earn good money he had immersed himself completely into it. He worked hard and took any overtime offered to him. Yes civilian Cameron still kept his eyes firmly on the prize, a cosy house.

It was a short flight to London's Heathrow airport for Georgia, with a smooth take off and an even smoother landing. She'd made friendly conversation with the passengers on each side of her and enjoyed tea and biscuits. Before she knew it the plane began its descent. Georgia gazed out into the big, white, fluffy, clouds that she viewed from high in the sky, all she wanted to do was get out there and lie her tense body on one of them and float right down to the centre of London but since she had no choice she watched as the plane glided down and went through them. The clouds were now larger like cotton wool, broken and dragged until they were fine at the edges but still beautiful. From high in the sky she could see houses and apartments below and then, ever so gracefully this beautiful plane continued its descent and glided back down to earth, to a smooth landing.

CHAPTER 18

London underground

London, Oh how she loved it, from the very moment she began the journey from arrivals at Heathrow Airport and out through the arrivals doors. She took in everything, the crowds outside waiting for loved ones to arrive, the chauffeurs holding up placards with the names of the guests they were waiting to collect printed on them. Then, she squeezed into the lift that took her down to the underground and the walk to the Train. Her heart was beating faster and faster. Now it was real, she was here. Soon she would meet with Cameron but first things first, onto the train to Bond Street tube Station, London. She had arrived. She began to walk to the escalator, this time to take her up to ground level. As she walked she could hear buskers playing their instruments.

Georgia always really enjoyed this bit of her journey. No rummaging for money, she always made sure to carry some sterling in her pocket to drop into their music cases lying open on the ground beside them, they were worth every penny. Sometimes, the sound of their music and the haunting words of their songs would remain with her as she walked along. Georgia loved all the hustle and bustle. She listened to the chatter and the cases being dragged on and off the train. She walked to the escalator listening to the beautiful sound of musicians playing their instruments along the way. She could feel the adrenalin rush as she emerged from the underground to the sound of ambulance sirens going, taxis beeping their horns, chattering people and the fabulous shop windows.

Straight to the pedestrian crossing and then across the road taking the last few steps to the front door of Selfridges. Her eyes searched for Cameron through the crowds of tourists, what would she do if he was not there? Calm down, take a breath, look again. Her eyes scanned through the crowds, there he was standing close to the main entrance looking uncomfortable, a little tousled, gorgeous. Across the crowds their eyes met. Everyone else standing outside Selfridges that day faded into oblivion. The Oxford Street vibe quietened. It was as if there was no one else there, just the two of them completely connected, in body, heart and mind, all they could do was hug and kiss. Then walk silently in through the main door of that amazing beautiful London store. Georgia led the way straight up onto the escalator to take them to the restaurant that served lovely wholesome food. There they sat for hours picking up on their stories from the last few days. Cameron admitted he had dropped down to earth with the biggest bang.

'The pressure is unbelievable and the work is harder than I could ever have imagined but it's getting easier now that I'm settling in. Georgia, this building game is perfect when you're young, I'm getting used to the pace so it's getting easier as I begin to understand the way everything works. Now I'm beginning to really love it. The pay is great, the people on site are so nice and interesting. My accommodation on the other hand is a totally different story. We're sharing rooms, with not enough bathrooms to go round but it's cheap and cheerful. I suppose that's the price I have to pay if I want to hold onto the money to buy (in a weak voice he said) our first house together. Georgia, at all times I just have to keep my eyes on the prize.'

Cameron just couldn't stop talking. He needed so badly to really talk to her, to explain what it was like to live here in the middle of London, in mid-summer when building sites were really hard places to work in.

Georgia changed the subject 'Cameron, are you pleased we have a hotel booked for Friday and Saturday?'

'Georgia, I'm so happy we have a hotel booked for Friday and Saturday night. Honestly, Georgia, my place is just not fit to take you to.'

'Cameron, please don't worry I'm very happy to stay with Prudence. It's close to where my course is and easy to commute to anywhere in London.'

'Is there any other news from back home?'

There was a long pause as in her head Georgia went through the doctor's appointment, her new pregnancy, how she was feeling about that, how she needed to move forward with her life but there was one thing she knew more than anything else, if she said all the things she wanted to say to Cameron everything would change. He would want to go back to Ireland with her and she hadn't even left Ross. He would assume this baby was his, when she knew different. It could be and it might not be. Her life was in a mess but to share what she was going through now with either of the men in her life would make it a total disaster.

Instead of pouring her heart out, she told Cameron all the different things she would learn at the new course. All about her work and her mum and her three friends who had all kept her busy in the last few weeks with phone calls. She assured Cameron she had just lived for this moment to see him in London when there was no one else there, just her and him, a building site, a beauty course and Prudence. He enjoyed all the lovely things Georgia said about him and in true loving fashion spoke of all the things they were going to do, starting with this evening. A meal and a drink in the sky bar looking over London

City. Georgia needed to drop off her luggage. Cameron needed to go back to his apartment so they made a date for 8 o'clock.

Georgia was off again on the underground up to Tower Hill and then on to Prudence's flat where the warmest welcome awaited her. It was nice to put the case on the bed and hang her bits and pieces up in the small space Prudence had allocated. What a nice friend to have! Prudence had bought ham, tomatoes, cream crackers, fresh bread, everything to keep Georgia well fed. She'd just made tea for her. Georgia loved the feast. She heard herself say:

'Prudence, would you like to come with me this evening when I meet Cameron? The sky bar is only a short distance from here. I insist you come.'

She could see Prudence was delighted to go for a night out. The fun began once they started dressing up and drinking champagne. Wow, the Sky Bar was fabulous, with great restaurants and the best view over London. Cameron, Prudence and Georgia really hit it off. They ate, drank and were merry but sadly at the end of the night Cameron had to go home alone while Georgia and Prudence jumped into a taxi that sped on its way to her apartment at Tower Bridge. Not once did Prudence ask Georgia how she was with Cameron and not Ross. This girl knew how to mind her own business so Georgia said nothing.

It's funny how you can still feel nervous when you go somewhere you've never been before. That's how Georgia felt as she walked into the academy, butterflies in her tummy that already had butterflies in it but she had no need to worry, the girl who had spoken to her when she booked the course was there with a big smile on her face and information packages to give out to all the participants. As promised they had light beverages and a discussion and then it was all systems go from 9.30 to 11.00

and from 11.15 to 1pm and from 1.40 to 4pm. There wasn't a moment lost. Georgia was absolutely delighted with her progress and this was only the first day. She had four days left, if every day was as exciting as this Georgia would have to admit this was the best course she had ever taken. Tonight she was meeting up with Cameron alone. Heading somewhere for bagels with cream cheese and all the trimmings and then to a cosy bar in Covent Garden where they had deep discussions until it was time to say goodbye, and so the days flew by. Before you could say gone with the wind, Friday had arrived. The course finished with an informal meeting, a presentation of diplomas and for Georgia an offer of a job that she couldn't accept.

CHAPTER 19

Two nights at The Hilton

They had decided to meet in the Hilton Hotel in Covent Garden, where they were staying for two nights. Georgia arrived early, complete with all her belongings re-packed into her case and ready for home. Her last two nights would be spent in the Hilton Hotel with Cameron, not with Prudence in her apartment. She Showered, washed her hair and changed into her new clothes. She looked fab when Cameron arrived in his shirt and trousers dusty from all the manual work. Nevertheless after a quick shower and a change of clothes Cameron was ready for a night on the town. He was so happy to be away from his flat and the building game for two nights.

Cote in Covent Garden, where they had previously booked their meal, was packed to capacity. The atmosphere was electric and buzzing. Georgia was delighted she was treating Cameron to this sumptuous meal. When the meal was finished they left the restaurant having enjoyed their time there. On this balmy evening they felt warm, comfortable and full as they taxied their way to the theatre to see *Chicago*, yet another treat from Georgia. What a fabulous production! A production they discussed endlessly over hot chocolate in a little cafe beside the theatre. Cameron bought the CD from *Chicago* and a fabulous mug, this mug was going straight into her kitchen. Every time she'd take it down from the press, it would remind her of the fabulous weekend in London with Cameron. Oh! What a night this was turning out to be, with drinks in the lobby of the hotel before they adjourned to their lovely room.

There were lots of things still to catch up on. Georgia listened to Cameron's stories all about his new job and his other flatmates. She gave him a back massage. Georgia always felt so comfortable and free with Cameron, she just kissed him all over. He was so relaxed in this comfy bed, a big change from the horrible bed and mattress he was sleeping on in the flat, he fell into a peaceful slumber. With all the manual work he was doing out in the air, he was over tired. That was the way Georgia wanted it to be, her mind was so focused on the baby. Mad sex just wasn't on her menu.

Saturday, the day Georgia had been really looking forward to all week when she could spend from morning to night in Cameron's company, was going to be a little different than they'd originally planned. Georgia and Cameron together had decided it would be lovely to take Prudence with them for a meal later on and a trip on the London Eye. Firstly to say thank you for being such a good friend and letting Georgia stay and secondly to celebrate her birthday that actually was on that day. Georgia had booked one of the capsules on the London Eye where they would have a champagne reception. She also took along a birthday cake. Not one of them had been on the London Eye before so this was the perfect opportunity. Georgia wondered would it make her sick as it moved around. It was nice to talk in the restaurant with Prudence and Cameron.

Prudence took them into her world as a teacher where she worked with so many teenagers, helping them with not just their studies but sometimes with their lives. She just loved her job, nothing was too big a task for her to take on. Cameron was happy to work on a building site for now, it would make him lots of money, but when the two months were up, he explained to the girls he wouldn't miss it, in fact he would be so happy to take up his teaching position in the Dublin school. Georgia explained she just needed this London trip to give her lots of memories to carry her through her topsy-turvy days without Cameron. That's what she said to them but she was really thinking of the topsy-turvy days of her pregnancy. What a great night, Georgia needn't have worried the London Eye did not make her sick, it went round so slowly. As for Prudence's birthday celebration, that was a huge success. Oh what a night!

As she kissed her friend Prudence goodbye she whispered in her ear:

'Make sure to look under my pillow when you go home. I left a card and a little present for you.'

'Oh no, you shouldn't have, Georgia.'

'Of course I should have, there's not much point in saying thank you if I don't back it up and let you know how grateful I am for your kindness and hospitality.'

'And thank you from me' said Cameron 'you've been so kind in letting Georgia stay with you and looking after her for me.'

They were just about to leave, hugs and kisses all round, lots of gratitude and a big thank you to Prudence, when Georgia heard herself say:

'Prudence if you're ever stuck for anything in the next while, Cameron will give you a hand. Cameron, is it ok if I give Prudence your telephone number?'

Very awkwardly and reluctantly Cameron wrote his number on a piece of paper and handed it to Prudence. They waved each other off. Immediately Cameron turned to Georgia and asked:

'Why Georgia?'

'Why what Cameron?'

'Why did you ask me to give Prudence my telephone number? I don't want her to get in touch with me. I'm living on the other side of London and all I do is work, how can I help her?'

'I don't know why.' said Georgia. 'She just looked so lonely and insular. Sorry Cameron I was very stupid.'

'Sure she'll probably never call me anyway. Let's just forget about it.'

Not another word was spoken about Prudence and Georgia's silliness, instead they put all that to one side and enjoyed their evening at Brown's full of fun, eating the snacks left on the bar and drinks. Georgia had pink lemonade, Cameron Guinness, not quite as good a taste as the Guinness back in Dublin but acceptable. Then back to the hotel for a night of love. Now there was no need for wham, bam, thank you mam, like the old days back in the monastery, instead it was yum, yum full of fun.

Georgia didn't want to let Sunday go without doing something touristy, so they needed to be up early to pack away all her clothes and fill themselves with the most gorgeous cooked breakfast, with all the trimmings. Having deliberated for some time they decided to visit the Victoria and Albert Museum in Knightsbridge. Georgia put her suitcase into the cloakroom. There would be so many things to see, they just had to focus on one. Georgia picked a fashion exhibition. The time they both dreaded had come. She didn't want her time in London to end, her days filled with gaining knowledge and learning about the industry that was now a big part of her life, her evenings filled with glamour, laughter and fun, but end it did. She said her tearful goodbye to Cameron and began her train journey to Heathrow airport with some new clothes in her case and a new frame of mind in her head. She was ready for anything.

On the plane journey home she thought of what she needed to do to achieve her goals. Just before the plane began its descent, Georgia's mind turned to home. It was like two separate things in her mind. Her life divided by the sea, Cameron safely tucked away in London, Ross waiting at the airport to welcome her with open arms and Georgia herself, pregnant. These were the three things Georgia needed to un-muddle in her mind.

Georgia's heart melted when the vision of Ross came before her eyes. He was truly lovely, she could say she was very lucky to meet two really lovely men in her life but this was an unworkable situation. Something she should never have allowed to happen. If she could turn back the clock right now, Ross would still be meeting her but there would only be him in her life. All of those things to look forward to, a new baby, a new nursery, even a new pram but instead there was Georgia all cloak and dagger, all dishonest, all playing mind games. Well, this had to end, she had to have a stable life to welcome her baby into. So she held onto Ross's arm tight as they walked out through the doors and down into the car park to collect the car. Ever the old fashioned gentleman, Ross carried her case, making sure Georgia walked on his inside so no car could pull out and knock his beautiful Georgia down.

She told him all about her course, the offer of a job she'd had from the academy which obviously she'd turned down and spoke highly of her friend Prudence, who Ross didn't know. She was a girl Georgia had met years ago at secondary school. Prudence had moved away early on and hadn't followed Georgia's marriage. Ross was so interested in her stories, she told him of all the new techniques she'd learned and maybe one day would use them on a film set, it was an area she wanted to work in. Georgia had so many stories to tell, going to see *Chicago* with Prudence, which was such a fabulous show and of course, the meal they had in Cote in Covent Garden accompanied by the photograph that made it relevant, the trip on London Eye and the celebration of Prudence's birthday with champagne and birthday cake and of course, a picture on her phone of Prudence and herself while they blew out the candles. Ross was suitably impressed.

Then they were home, spic and span surroundings, not a thing out of place with the table set and the slow cooker just about to turn off, all the signs of a hearty meal. A gorgeous roast duck, roast potatoes, turnips, brown gravy followed by apple and custard. Over tea and chat Georgia showed Ross the photos on her phone of Prudence and herself at *Chicago*. Then he browsed through the programme with all the leggy girls, in various dance positions, and was suitably impressed. Then of course, they crept into their comfy bed and made love. She fell off to sleep, with Ross's arms around her and dreams of London swirling around in her head.

CHAPTER 20

Leaving Ross

Bank Holiday Monday the shops were open from 12pm a nice way to spend the afternoon, herself and Ross shopping. With lots of bargains to be had, they would easily pass the next few hours. When all the doors had finally closed there was always a nice cosy pub where they could sip cognac and completely relax while they delved into their feelings for each other.

Ross admitted 'For the last few weeks I've felt uneasy with you and wondered what was really going on in your mind and are you still happy with me?' He continued, 'I hadn't intended talking about it today, Georgia, because yesterday we were so happy together when you arrived back home, but something is niggling me, something is just not right with us.'

Georgia just looked straight into his eyes, she found herself admitting her feelings, something she hadn't really planned on doing at all.

'Maybe I just need time to adjust to this marriage thing.' There was a pause, 'or maybe I'm just not cut out for it at all.'

Well, to even her astonishment the words just came out,

'Maybe I need time on my own.'

By the look on Ross's face Georgia knew this real nice guy was bewildered. She could almost hear him thinking, how come we made love last night and you lay asleep in my arms and now you're dropping this bombshell.

'This can't be true.' He almost shouted.

Georgia's feelings were now out in the open and in some strange way she felt relieved. The only question Ross asked was –

'Is there another man?'

That must be one of the main questions asked to an unhappy lady and would you believe, Georgia looked into his eyes once more and answered:

'NO.'

The line was drawn. There was nothing left to say and a day that had started out so well was certainly ending on a bad note. As Georgia lay in bed that night with the biggest void between her and her husband, she wondered had there been any point in letting Ross know her thoughts? Maybe she should have told him about the baby and continued her life with him. She could have muddled through the next few months, had her baby and continued her life with Ross. Surely once the baby would arrive she would be so busy there wouldn't be a moment to spare to think of Cameron.

Her mind was so mixed up that sometimes Georgia felt she wanted to continue down that marriage path and other times she felt like running miles and miles away. A decision had to be made, it was to leave Ross, her home and go it alone. Her mind was so clear that day she felt cold, so cold, it was impossible to keep her thoughts to herself, so having explained once more her feelings to her poor husband of only a few months, she marched back up the stairs into the bedroom. A soft breeze blew through the net curtains, she opened the door of her wardrobe and something unusual happened, one of the wedding dresses she'd worn on her precious wedding day, moved by the breeze and tipped off her leg as if to remind her of the day she felt the happiest she ever felt inside.

For a moment Georgia was back there, trying on her dresses and feeling the light fabric. That was the day before the wedding when she wondered which dress she'd wear first. Would it be the one Ross's mum had bought for her with all that love and care, the one made of lace or would it be the tulle flimsical dress, the dress she had picked herself when she was feeling almost as good as a fairy floating on air? Two completely contrasting designs and fabrics but equally beautiful. In the end she had worn the lace dress first and even though all her friends had said don't change the dress until after dinner, Georgia had been her usual self and not listened to anyone, she only wore the dress until after the drinks in the lobby, on arrival. Then she flew to her room with her entourage of friendly bridesmaids and changed into her tulle dress. For her it was always about living in the moment.

It was always the excitement of not really making her mind up until the last possible moment and of course, knowing she had options and then like a bolt of lightning out of the blue, she realised that was the way she'd always been and this was the way she was, living for the excitement, the buzz, the adrenalin rush. Maybe Cameron was like her second choice of wedding dress, that tulle, flimsical dress, maybe it was because he was so, up until now, unobtainable that she wanted him. No one had told her about the anti-climax she might feel after their wedding, no one had told her there could be temptations of the flesh and no one had warned her she could succumb to them.

Then she was back in real time. Logically she wondered if she would give the dresses away to a charity or would she pack them away in a box and put them somewhere in a corner, now that wasn't an option. Maybe she'd ask the French lady who owned the swop shop close to work to sell them for her. Yes, that seemed like a good idea. She would face it another time but for now she was happy Ross wasn't there.

In his own words:

'Georgia, I can't watch you leave, it would break my heart.'

He never asked how or who was moving her belongings out of their house. He just left very early that morning.

CHAPTER 21

Unknown territory

She packed as many of her belongings as she could, the rest she would have collected by a work colleague in an old van, belonging to his father's upholstery business, in the coming weeks. She had only really taken the bare essentials with her, that's all she needed. Wedding presents and any special pieces bought for their house were left in their rightful place. As Georgia walked out perhaps for the last time she was reminded of an old film she saw on TV some weeks earlier. It was just the last few minutes of the *Nun's Story* when Audrey Hepburn folded her nun's habit for the last time, very neatly packed her few belongings into the tiniest case and walked out through the door into the big wide world. Admittedly what Georgia was doing, to a lot of people wouldn't seem this dramatic, but to her it was final, so final. Audrey had left the convent she loved for something she believed in and Georgia was leaving the man she loved for hopefully the man she was in love with.

Georgia arrived at her friend's door and luckily for her, her first knock was answered. Lo and behold it was Tanya, grinning from ear to ear, just thrilled to see her friend, that was until she realised Georgia was carrying a case, small as it was, now Tanya needed an explanation. Did Georgia's explanation satisfy Tanya? Well having gone over all the details for some time, finally a look of resignation came on Tanya's by now, not so smiling face. She was concerned for Georgia and also worried as to how she was going to find space for her little pal while at the same time assuring her there would always be room at the inn (her little flat).

The two friends spent endless evenings going over and over the sordid details of the, by now, greatly publicised break up of Georgia and Ross's marriage and the one thing Tanya couldn't understand was why did Ross not put up a fight if he loved Georgia as much as he said. Tanya's comment made Georgia think and ask herself the question, why did he not put up a better fight for me if he really loved me? While she was thinking this in her head her answer to Tanya was, they had always promised to be totally honest with each other and had vowed to stay together as long as love was their strongest bond and right now it wasn't. Once they had exhausted all avenues the subject was dropped. To brighten her friend up Tanya booked a table for four, in the Hibernian Club, where jazz, blues, a good meal and chat would change everything. It was nice to get dressed up in a pretty dress, (even if it was a little tight) kitten heels and all that jazz, being accompanied by Tanya, Coco and Heidi this night promised to be a night to top all others.

Still living in Tanya's tiny apartment, although the two friends tried to stay out of each other's way and give space, Georgia felt she was intruding. It was nothing to do with Tanya, it was all to do with Georgia. With no time to waste Georgia did the one thing she was good at. Opened her lap top and looked up houses for letting and there it was a tiny little terraced house, just big enough for her. Her heart raced as she rang her friend Morgan, who used to be a work colleague when she was an estate agent, he was the letting agent for the property. She couldn't believe her luck, he was there right now showing it. Morgan persuaded her to come and view it before it was snapped up. She did, the rest would become history. It was vacant, she was eager and before she left that tiny, warm, good feeling house she almost had the keys in her hand. That was just a matter of procedure, she would see her bank manager, organise the direct debits, etc, then sign the lease and that would all be done with great speed. She could be moving into her very own little rented property, on Sunday with the help of some of her pals, if she was lucky.

She knew it was the right thing to do, she wasn't going back to Ross and the life she had. She definitely couldn't outstay her welcome in her good friend Tanya's flat any longer. She felt the universe was telling her to begin to let her new life flow and happen and thank God for friends like Morgan who, being fair, needed to let the house but he gave her the push she needed to take a decision which was something her head had not been able to come round to until now. If everything went to plan she could organise the bank in the morning. Morgan promised to stay back late in the office, he would have the lease sitting on his desk, so within the next twenty four hours Georgia would have the keys to the kingdom. She felt as if a cloud had lifted from her body, she could now see the light, yes it was time for another chapter of her life to begin.

Just then her phone rang, to her amazement it was Heidi, full of the joys of spring. Georgia would have to put her thoughts and dreams on the back burner until tomorrow for now she would totally concentrate on Heidi's spring mood.

CHAPTER 22

Party with a difference

'Georgia, I want to cordially invite you' Heidi said in the funniest voice 'to a night of murder and mystery, in fact, to my Pasta Pie and Handgun Night.'

At this moment in time Georgia would have gone to a 'Donald Duck Night' she was that desperate. Her friend assured her the details were already in the post. Be on time was the order of the day and be dressed to kill.

'And how are you?' Heidi enquired.

Georgia did a great impression of her old happy go lucky self. All the things she wanted to share with her friends she must keep to herself until she had worked through them. She fell into bed exhausted with so many things going through her mind but next morning woke up as bright as a button and ready for an exciting day.

Georgia squeezed past Tanya at the door having picked up the post, which contained as promised by Heidi, instructions for the night of murder, mystery and mayhem. Satchel across her shoulder, holding a banana in one hand, a natural yoghurt in the other and of course the invitation from Heidi clenched between her teeth, she raced into her happy car, there was no time to waste. All the things she had to do must be done and dusted just before lunch, after lunch her time would be dedicated to signing the lease. Once that was done she could let Tanya know the great news because she knew Tanya was looking forward to the day when she could have her little home sweet home back all to herself. Yes, Tanya had enjoyed getting a rent from her friend, yes, it had helped her buy a few things for her tiny abode but the long and the short of it was Tanya liked living alone and couldn't wait for the day when she could walk around naked or have her music blaring again, just the way she liked it. Never once had Tanya made Georgia feel like a burden, she'd always been chirpy, happy, welcoming and never nosy. She was always there if Georgia needed a shoulder to cry on. Yes, Georgia thought to herself as she drove down the road, Tanya was definitely a true friend and maybe someday she could return the favour.

There were only three days to get the script right for the Pasta Pie and Handgun Night, get the clothes right and get her head around the night, but right now that wasn't her priority. Her day raced along as she completed every task in hand,

- The bank – done,
- Banana disappeared,
- Yoghurt enjoyed,
- 4pm heading off to meet Morgan.

He had:

- Lease on table, pen in hand, signed, sealed and delivered.
- Keys transferred over from one hand to another.
- Drink in the nearby pub with Morgan to celebrate his conquest and her new chapter and to catch up on the gossip from her old office.
- Then back to Tanya's house.

Oddly enough it was like déjà vu, arriving at the door together, a repeat performance of the morning, only this time there was no banana in sight, no yoghurt, just a bottle of milk, a fresh sliced pan, a Tesco bag on her arm and a set of keys, which Georgia dangled from her teeth, just like the carrot in front of her great friend. Tanya seemed bemused until she followed Georgia into her tiny kitchen. Georgia put her head down and let the keys fall from her mouth onto the table. Tanya picked them up and scrutinised the address.

'Are you moving, my dearest friend?'

Tanya's voice had gone up an octave and her smile was from ear to ear. Georgia ran over and pressed on the kettle.

'Sit down and I'll tell you all' she said.

Over hot cups of Rosie Lee Georgia filled her friend in on her day's escapades.

Tanya being Tanya was honest to a fault.

'Do you know dear friend, I'm going to miss you, lots and lots, like jelly tots but I won't mind in the least having my little space back. I know you'll be happier when you have your own space where, Georgia, you can close the door and it's yours. You can think through all your problems and all your achievements and emerge in the bright light of day a free spirit.'

The two friends hugged, they always understood each other. Two new chapters in the lives of old friends, one life would return to normal with all the perks of living alone, and for the other, Georgia, living on her own for the first time. (A daunting feeling, especially being pregnant but nevertheless necessary)

'I wish I had a bottle of something to celebrate this new beginning.' Tanya said.

'Don't worry, Tanya, I have just what you need. Da Dum' and out came a bottle of bubbly from the little Tesco bag and 'da da dum, a packet of your favourite dark chocolate biscuits.'

Tanya grabbed two champagne glasses from the shelf, (these were only taken down for very special occasions) Georgia popped the cork on the champagne. Tanya pulled open the packet of her favourite chocolate biscuits and placed them on a plate already on the table and there it was, two of the best friends who came through a hard time sharing with each other and getting through it. They tipped their glasses together, kissed each other on the side of the cheek and with all that mmmmm they were very happy to be still best friends because as they say 'if you want to know me come and live with me'. Tanya had figured out why living together had worked out so well, she shared the conclusion she had come to with Georgia.

'It was because we had respect for each other's privacy.'

The two friends nodded their heads in agreement. Subject closed.

'Tanya there's an old saying, 'Saturday flitting is short sitting'. So, if you don't mind, I won't be moving until Sunday.'

As they sipped champagne and felt the bubbles tipping their noses they laughed heartily. What a lovely way to get to know each other even better.

CHAPTER 23

Murder mystery

Georgia felt honoured to play Mama Rosa, widow of the 'VICTIM'. The invitation and the preparation kept her busy and before she knew it she was arriving at the party complete with a black and grey long wig half hidden beneath a black lace veil, accompanied by a black dress and a solemn face, which wasn't much of an effort for her to put on, in fact she felt sympathy for the widow. She was greeted by the host Heidi, whose character for the night was Angel, dressed in sparkling flowing yellow. Tanya and friend Amy, arrived in character, Tanya as 'Tutti Frutti', girlfriend of 'Beaujolais' (BeJasus), who was already seated in the lounge, sipping on his first cocktail of the night and chatting away to 'Rocco Scarfazzi', the victim's brother, dressed immaculately in a black pinstripe suit, white shirt and tie, black hat, cane and red slip on shoes. He was 'Clair Voyant's' (Amy's) boyfriend, just for one night. (If Georgia took up selling shoes she'd definitely change his mind on this fashion statement.) 'ClairVoyant' was dressed in a turquoise flowing skirt, gypsy top, bandana and silver earrings hanging from her ears. A work friend of Coco's had a bit part as the second 'ClairVoyant' dressed gypsy like, little plaits added to her hair, a bandana and gypsy dress and for the grand finale as Georgia entered the dining room, there he stood, dressed as a priest, Cameron or 'Car Dinalli'.

Georgia almost collapsed when she realised Car Dinalli was none other than the man she loved, who was supposed to be in London. He was now standing right before her, looking damn sexy. Her body began to heat up, her face felt red and flushed. She was all of a dither. To Cameron this must have felt like a good plan, to take a weekend break, come home to be with his friends and also give Georgia the biggest surprise of her life. He didn't know she was pregnant and surprises weren't exactly what she needed right now. Georgia had learned to detach herself from situations like this and so with that thought in her mind she moved to the next room where she bumped into the last two remaining guests. They had just arrived and thank God they did, their funny costumes changed Georgia's mind set and made her think a bit straighter, stopping her from running back into the room where Cameron was and covering him in kisses (she could do that later). Anthony or 'Marco', friend of Heidi, was dressed in a shirt, bow tie, a pair of shorts, red football socks, and football boots. He was a man of many talents who had the best personality ever and once behind the bar went shaking cocktails with the best – Sex on the Beach, Down Under Fizz, Hawaiian Vodka, Gin Tropical, Screwdriver and Moscow Mule.

'Tara Misu' was last but not least of the guests, quite prim and proper. She seemed to have studied her lines very well because once the story began to unfold she fitted in like a glove. The perfect accent, the perfect gestures, in fact very believable and so the night went on, one cocktail after the other, (for Georgia pink lemonade) one course after the other, one look across the table to Cameron from Georgia. The candles were starting to burn down when at last all the lines had been read and the murder was about to be solved, just one more tape to go. At this point, it usually goes around the table asking each guest who they think 'dunnit', it's normally the funniest time with everyone accusing each other, but unfortunately Angel had switched the CD on prematurely, then everyone knew 'who dunnit'.

The poor girl was devastated, she couldn't believe she had missed out on all the accusations. She had to be reminded it was only a game, all suspects had a fantastic time, eating, drinking and being merry, so what difference did a little mistake make? (None) Before the guests began to leave, there was a toast to the hostess with the mostest, Heidi, she thanked everyone for coming and said she had a fantastic time and hoped in the future her friends would have a night like this. A night of murder, mystery.

'You could never relive my pasta pie and handgun night but you could recreate your own night with all the passion and excitement.'

Heidi gestured to her friends:

'I bet you've learned a few tricks tonight. Oh, and by the way don't forget me when you send out the invitations, I'll be your best critic.'

This was followed by a big round of applause for Heidi. Someone shouted:

'You were the hostess with the mostest. I'll host the next night and we'll have a vote on who was the best host.'

Georgia knew without even looking over, it was Cameron's voice. She could hear him clear his throat. 'Ahem, Ahem' he said with his poised hand over his mouth. He had actually offered to host the next night. Georgia hoped Cameron was offering to host the night with her. Oh what a way to introduce her friends to the new couple, gosh, it could be fun. She was beginning to imagine their night of murder, mystery called the night of 'The ten priests in the convent of a thousand nuns' (whittled down to ten). She'd heard the song *'On this night of a thousand stars, let me take you to heaven's door, where the music of love's guitars plays for evermore'* sung by Madonna in Evita.

'Just before you leave the blood stained carpets of my home and forensics arrive, ladies and gentlemen, my wonderful guests, Georgia has a few little words to say.'

Georgia took her opportunity and announced she was moving in the morning into her new rented accommodation.

'I urge you all, in fact I beg you all, if you have an hour or so with nothing to do, (but get over your hangover) would you please come and help me move my belongings from Tanya's apartment to my new tiny abode and in exchange I promise you, the nicest, well prepared pint you've ever tasted in your life, from the pub next door, sure you'll be licking your lips for hours afterwards. I need some kind of van, even if it's battered, bruised or without an exhaust pipe, it doesn't matter, please help a damsel in distress.'

She wasn't expecting Cameron to offer and he didn't disappoint. She took out a little envelope from her bag, inside were little tags with her old and new address and her phone number. She passed around one to each of Heidi's guests, she even presented one to Cameron. He looked down at his and missed her glance as she drifted to the next friend and presented them with the same little piece of paper. In came the voice of Rocco Scarfazzi, who looked a little worse for the wear, a great sport who offered his van with a man, who surprise, surprise, was him and thank God, BeJasus offered to be beside the man with the van. Some of the girlfriends also volunteered, the deed was done.

'Oh and by the way' said Georgia 'after all the hard work is done don't forget there's a drink in the cosy snug, in the little pub beside my new abode.'

Georgia couldn't take Cameron to Tanya's place, after all she didn't know they were practically a couple, so instead they just sat in Georgia's car, outside his flat and chatted. It was nice to just talk and hold his hand. Next to somebody's eyes and smile, Georgia loved strong hands. She felt he could do anything with those hands, all he needed to do with his right now, was hold hers. He was tired from his long week on the building site, the long journey home and the very enjoyable murder mystery night. She was tired from the long night, the thought of moving to her new home tomorrow and, of course, being pregnant.

'If all goes well you can stay with me tomorrow night.'

Georgia went to bed hoping her friends would remember her request when they awoke in the morning, if they awoke in the morning. Sure if all else failed she had their phone numbers. She had reminded them to leave their phones on so at least if they didn't turn up she could ring and get them out of their drunken stupor.

CHAPTER 24

Moving on

Meeting time is 12.00 pm at Tanya's house to give everyone a chance to rest after all the alcohol and fun last night. She thanked God she'd attended the murder mystery night because had she not, all this moving would have been left up to her and she knew that would have been impossible. Her friends all rallied round to help move her bits and pieces into her new abode. She had done a bit of cleaning, etc. etc. There were so many volunteers, Georgia only had to carry her prized possessions, handbags and shoes and direct all her friends to put all her worldly possessions in the correct rooms. She wasn't able to lift or drag furniture in her pregnant state. Her friends worked hard, maybe it was because of the promise she had made to buy everyone who came along a drink of their choice in the nearby pub after the work was done.

Now the terrible task was completed, every single solitary one of them had congregated in the snug, the cosiest part of the pub and there she was ordering the round, she was never so glad to part with money, it was so worthwhile. As Georgia sipped lemonade with all the team she remembered a saying her mum in her wisdom often used, 'A little bit of help is better than a lot of pity' and they had certainly helped. It wasn't just with moving the bits and pieces, they had done much more than that but perhaps they didn't even know themselves how much they're support had helped her, for one, she didn't feel alone. Even though this had been a mammoth task both mentally and physically, they had made her feel part of a team, a family. She'd forgotten the hard times, the leaving Ross, changing her career, being pregnant and not knowing which way her path was going, all of these things seemed a blur to her now. Her friends' good deeds had helped her step into the unknown with confidence and courage. As they toasted to her future, she could feel their positive energy spurring her on.

They left one by one, she said thank you and goodbye to each and every one and she meant every word. When the snug went silent with not a friend in sight, Georgia happily sat beside the warm cosy fire. She inhaled and exhaled slowly, coming to grips with her new life. She didn't feel alone, she could still feel their energy, encouraging, embracing, letting her know she had nothing to fear, her future would be coming up roses. From this moment on, Georgia would make sure to only think positive thoughts, block out all the negative ones and navigate her way to her future. Engrossed in her thoughts she sat looking into the fire as the colours changed and moved on up through the chimney breast.

She sat there staring into space watching all those colours in the fire, fading into each other. She could sense people beginning to come into the snug, after all it was now lunchtime and the usual Sunday patrons couldn't wait to be seated and get the best lunch that they'd been dreaming of all week long with those crispy roast potatoes and that succulent roast beef with gravy, parsnips, etc. etc. followed by the most scrumptious dessert. Georgia had booked herself in for one of these dreamy meals but like all the other guests she was ordered by the chef, to sit in the snug until he came in with his little bell and escorted all his guests into his restaurant, or parlour.

Georgia could feel people lightly moving past her, one touched her shoulder and kissed her cheek, she looked up into Cameron's eyes. That kiss had come from Cameron's lips, she was taken out of her dream, he smiled, her heart melted.

'Georgia. Sorry I couldn't make it this morning. I had to visit the monastery to tie up a few loose ends' and the priests were short of help, so of course I volunteered. It was nice to meet up with some of my friends but it felt so strange being back there in the monastery. I realized if I had any doubts at all about leaving, I know now for sure I really don't belong there anymore but when I've returned to Dublin and things have settled down, I would have no problem helping out at special times of the year, like Easter or Christmas, times when I'm needed and I'm on holidays from teaching.' Cameron went quiet for a moment then he said 'Is there anything left for me to help you with?'

'No thank you Cameron, everything is already sorted, job completed.'

Just now for the first time in her life she felt as if she was standing alone. Ross would have never let this sort of thing happen to his Georgia. He would never have left her alone to cope with everything on her own, he was a good man. Was she completely bonkers leaving him for a man who did not seem to even realize she was doing all this for him? There is more to love than sex and out of body experiences. Georgia had to really make a huge effort not to stand up and scream, you are an unfeeling, unhelpful blundering idiot. She was also tempted to shout out loud, and by the way I'm also pregnant. Does that hit home with you, Cameron, or are you also brain dead?

She said nothing, instead she took a few minutes away from the table and had a little cry. (Not from sadness but from temper) She tried to remain calm, cool and collected. Maybe she was just overtired, or suffering from a hormonal imbalance, or missing Ross. When the time is right she will discuss all of these things with Cameron one by one. On the way back Georgia passed by the kitchen. There stood the chef.

'Excuse me, is it OK if I add one extra guest to my table? It's a table for two anyway and it's set for two for lunch.'

The answer was yes. Georgia sat down at the table.

'Cameron, it's OK for you to join me for lunch. The chef had no objection to me having one extra guest. Cameron, how lucky are you?'

This was the perfect end to a perfect morning, in one way Georgia felt she stood alone. She shuddered at the thoughts of what could have been, had no one arrived to help her move this morning and the only reason she moved out of her home with Ross in the first place, was to eventually set up home with Cameron. This move was a stop gap between leaving her marriage, moving out of Tanya's apartment and renting a place on her own. Now Georgia felt a little bit closer to the day when she and Cameron would move in together but that thought obviously had not occurred to the man himself Cameron. She had moved to her new abode, she herself had organised all her friends to help with the move, she'd even organised the drinks in the bar for all the helpers and the lunch the two of them were just about to feast on. The only thing she hadn't organised was the perfect end to the journey, the love of her life, Cameron. Her poor little heart skipped a beat as she looked up into those beautiful eyes, then Maisie Coyne's words came back to haunt her. 'Break that spell.' Would she ever want to be released from his magic spell?

The big burly chef arrived, all dressed in white, complete with a big white hat and big white apron. He even wore a handlebar moustache and had rosy, shiny cheeks. He was Georgia's idea of the perfect chef. He held in his hand a big shiny silver bell that rang sweetly as he shook it to and fro and side to side, as he moved through the starving patrons announcing:

'All my guests please follow me into the dining room where I will present you with your best lunch ever.'

He spoke as he walked along in his spotless white, dazzling apron.

'You will taste the sweetest vegetables, munch on the most succulent roast and end your meal with a mouth-watering, scrumptious, surprising dessert.'

They sat down, the babble all around was astounding. Georgia always loved that, that feeling of life surrounding her, the din of voices, everyone in their own little group having their own conversations. All their little stories, if only I was invisible I could listen in.

'Do you realise Cameron?' said Georgia. 'I'll never again have to cook meals, when the best chef in Dublin works in my favourite pub, right next door to my humble abode. No more slaving on a Sunday when friends arrive, I'll just treat them to lunch in Stanley's pub.'

Cameron was happy for Georgia. He didn't say much, he just sat there smiling and agreeing with her all the way through lunch.

'You've done a great job, Georgia.'

'I know,' said Georgia. 'I used to think I was leaving Ross for you, Cameron. I can tell you, he was one of the best men I've ever met, we were just too young when we married. Maybe in a different life, (her thoughts drifted for a moment ...) things could have been different, but just now I've realised I didn't leave Ross for you, I left Ross for me, just to try to find myself in this great big world, where God knows we're all only dots in the universe. Cameron, I'm happy you've taken the step to leave the monastery and I'm extra happy that you still have some time left in London living a life of freedom (even if you're saving every penny for our future).'

Cameron nodded his head and smiled that happy smile, he was a happy man.

Lunch over, all patrons moving, some to the snug, some to the lounge and some just heading home, Georgia and Cameron took this route. They walked the short distance to Georgia's new rented accommodation. Next time she moved home Georgia prayed it would be to the house Cameron was saving the deposit for, that thought put a smile on her face.

'This weekend was a busy one full of travel and murder mystery but Georgia, I'm so happy I came just to spend time with you.'

She showed him all around her little place and encouraged him to sit by the electric, pretend coal, fire. Those little rosy lights she bought in Dunnes Stores were placed around the mirror that was the centre focus of the room. The lights were only cheap, run by batteries, but they just lit up everywhere. In the darkness the colours reflected on the glass of the mirror and made the whole place so welcoming and homely. Yes, Georgia was home, she could feel it in her being, this was her home. Cameron loved this warm, friendly house. He was beginning to dream of what it would be like when they had their own house together. He was a great listener and as they sat there by the fire, he did what he did best, listen. It must be all the psychology he studied while in college that gave him this great gift of listening to others. He encouraged Georgia to explore her mind and bring up the things she had held in for so long. Tonight was about her. Cameron put his two arms around Georgia and drawing her close he kissed her lips. She closed her eyes, she felt warm, oh! how she wanted him, wouldn't it be perfect to fall into her comfy bed with the love of her life but she knew he had to go back to his old apartment to collect his belongings, have a little rest and be ready for his early flight in the morning.

When he left, Georgia sat there taking in the silence and remembering the day and the night that was now gone, altogether it had been a great success and now, looking back Georgia felt content as she counted her blessings. She had great friends that were always there for her like angels. Brand new warm jammies complete with a logo on the front, 'early to bed and early to rise make a gal healthy, wealthy and wise'. Into her gorgeous sleigh bed complete with brand new sheets and duvet, she climbed and mooched around trying to find that comfortable spot. She lay there, quiet and peaceful in her new rented house looking out at a beautiful moon that lit up the whole room. She thought 'How nice it will be when I have my little baby lying beside me on a night like this with the moon shining down on their cot. How lucky am I, with a bright future to look forward to, perfect.'

She came out of a dream when her phone rang.

'It's Anna, Dr. Darcy's assistant. Your scan is for 11am, best of luck Georgia. Dr. Darcy will see you afterwards, I should think 1.30 would be about right.'

Just like a robot she showered, put on her clothes and drove to the hospital. She was in such shock she really didn't think of the baby as a person, her mind was just blank and then she was there. The next thing she was aware of was the tears flowing from her eyes as she gazed at the screen in amazement, while the nurse pointed out all the teeny, tiny bits of that little baby inside her. It was such a surreal moment. Time just froze, all Georgia was aware of was that tiny little speck on the screen. The lady was so nice, so kind, she didn't say much, she just knew Georgia was in shock and alone… it was over. Georgia was outside walking towards her car, holding the print of the scan in her hand. It hadn't dawned on her to put it away in her bag. Then she was back in the car driving towards the doctor's surgery. She was brought straight in, no waiting. As she sat down the realisation hit her like a brick. Without saying a word the doctor filled a glass of water and she was ordered to sip it slowly.

'Well Georgia the good news is your baby is healthy and so are you. At this point I cannot tell you what you're having, it's too early but what I can tell you is you're three months pregnant. As pregnancy is natural there is nothing you need to take. Just enjoy every moment.'

'OK, thank you doctor.'

'Come back to me in a month from now. My assistant will make an appointment for you.'

As she sat in her kitchen drinking tea and eating a sandwich she'd bought in the local delicatessen, Georgia browsed through her phone for baby clothes and prams. Seeing the scan had brought her baby to life for her.

This is one of those times that I will never forget. It's that moment that will change me forever. I'll look back on the romance with Cameron and I'll think beautiful, I'll look back on the marriage with Ross and I'll think, why am I not just sharing this moment with him. When everything else fizzles out I can see so clearly… Now I'm sitting here alone with no one to share my fabulous news with and the funny thing is I don't want to share this with anyone right now.

CHAPTER 25

A complete 360 turn

Sometimes the future has plans of its own. The days rolled on and on, Georgia just kept her head down and worked her socks off. The reality had really hit her, now that her shape was beginning to change. She would have to do something, confide in someone, because soon it would be very clear she was pregnant. She continued to keep her secret to herself for now, only sharing it with one person, her favourite client. She still hadn't told Cameron and since Ross hadn't been in touch there was no need to worry herself over him. But time was running out and Georgia was becoming very stressed. Sometimes she could feel panic attacks coming on and the only way to deal with them was first get yourself outside and breathe in the fresh air slowly, very slowly, inhale, exhale.

She had just suffered one of these panic attacks moments earlier when her favourite client, the only one who knew her secret, presented her with a present. She urged Georgia not to open it until she was somewhere quiet. So while the lady was waiting for her nails to dry, Georgia slipped into the staff room, locked the door and sat on a little chair that up until now she wondered what it was there for, now she knew it was for moments like this. She proceeded to open the parcel and couldn't believe how beautiful its contents were. The most beautiful knitted white shawl with crochet around the edges that looked almost like lace and the prettiest little cardigan that when she held it up it looked like lots of seashells all attached together, knitted in an A line design. It was the first present she had received for her baby but it was the only one she would ever want or need because it was so beautiful. Tears streamed down her face, for the first time the reality she would soon be a mum hit her like a tornado. The lady's nails would be well dry but Georgia was in no fit state to leave the ladies room.

Luckily for her someone had left their makeup. It was right there under the mirror, so having cooled her eyes down with cold water on loo paper and dabbing them dry with yet more loo paper she began to painstakingly apply some make up. A little bit of makeup, a very big breath to try and relax her, so the tears stopped flowing, then some lipstick. She was breaking all the rules by using other peoples' makeup, something her mother had always told her not to do but right now she didn't care. She needed colour in her cheeks, to give her courage to go outside and mingle with the clients in the beauty salon. She re-wrapped the presents and since she couldn't re-stick the cello tape, she took a towel and covered them over and then she unlocked the door and walked out into the staff area where she put the parcel safely away in her bag.

Out into the salon she marched, retrieved her lady's coat from the hanger, the receptionist took the bill, Georgia said her good-byes and a big thank you for the beautiful present and prayed she wouldn't cry as her lady left the beauty salon. She did all these things, managing to place a kiss on the lady's cheek and smile when the lady told her to make sure to decorate the shawl with pink or blue baby ribbons when her baby boy or girl was born. She should have been in the Abbey Theatre. For the rest of the day as she looked after her clients there was only one thought in her mind, she was going to be a mum, and nobody knew but her.

The present of the shawl and the prettiest little cardigan ever was a real turning point for Georgia, she realised a little baby boy or girl would be sitting pretty beneath the comfort of the soft baby wool in both cardigan and shawl. She just didn't know how she felt, with so many different emotions messing up her head. If she was logical she'd realise all of this was part of a normal pregnancy with hormones jumping all over the place but on top of all that, there were lots of other things going on. Ross was gone, her rock who'd been there with her through thick and thin. She had discarded him. She wondered, was Cameron worth all this? He had ruined a perfectly good marriage and she'd allowed it to happen. Georgia began to resent Cameron but in her heart of hearts she could only really blame herself. As the proverb says, you can bring a horse to the water but you can't make it drink.

Right now she should be celebrating her pregnancy with her husband, being looked after, petted, pampered and all the other things that go with a mum to be but instead of all this Georgia felt alone and it was all her own doing. She had distanced herself from even her mum and her friends. Her mum would have pampered and petted her. Georgia just wasn't ready to share her news, so no one knew what she was going through because she was so stupid. She didn't confide in them, instead she had isolated herself away from everyone, now there would be no one there when she needed a chat, felt down or just needed help. It's funny how sometimes you think your life is out of your control, she needed to take back control of her life.

Everything changed that Saturday night when Georgia was all alone. It was a quiet night, her friends were tired asking her to have a night out with them. They all knew there was something going on in her head that she didn't want to share. Georgia had changed, she wasn't the same girl they had been bridesmaid to and she certainly wasn't the same girl they'd met that night in the Trocadero, full of the joys of spring and happy in her new marriage, showing photographs to friends while she happily smiled and enjoyed their company. So individually, they had decided, without discussing it together and came to the same conclusion, Georgia needed space, they also needed space from Georgia. That five letter word that says so much in these modern times. Space to come to your senses, space to cool down and decide you really do need friends, space to feel how lonely it is to be in an empty space alone. Yes that word, it says so much, yes she had plenty of space that day, in fact she was all alone with empty space all around her when it happened and it wasn't a nice feeling.

Terrible pains began to shoot through her tummy and her lower back ached. At first she thought she was imagining things but then it began to hit home, panic set in, so Georgia did what she was told, tried to keep calm, inhale, exhale slowly, this was real, and to think she'd spent months pretending to herself she wasn't really pregnant. Right now Georgia said a silent prayer that her baby would be safe. There was no option for her but to get to the hospital as fast as she could, at least that was one decision she took. There was no way she could take the car, so a taxi had to be ordered and having ordered the taxi she made that phone call to the maternity hospital telling them how she was feeling and asking them to expect her. The taxi arrived in what seemed like hours. Off it sped towards the maternity hospital. She felt every bump on the road, it was almost like jumping over mountains and yet they were only small ramps and potholes that definitely needed looking after by the Corporation.

A very pleasant nurse stood waiting for her when she arrived and she was taken straight away to be examined. Afterwards the doctor explained everything to Georgia and just as he was talking her through it all she heard a nurse saying:

'Put the patient into bed and let her rest.'

The nurse made her comfortable. All Georgia wanted to do was sleep. Her doctor, Doctor Deirdre Clancy explained:

'Georgia, you will have to remain here in hospital, in bed, you cannot return home.'

Georgia didn't hear the rest, she just heard blah, blah, blah as she tried her best to hold back her tears but they just kept on flowing.

'Now Georgia, I have to give you an injection. It will help you feel calmer and a little more relaxed. You don't have to worry about anything. We'll be looking after everything for you.'

Doctor Deirdre Clancy delivered the injection. It was so sore Georgia could feel her head spinning. She wanted to shout stop, leave me alone, but this wasn't just about her, this was about her unborn child, who needed to be given every chance to be strong and healthy. Georgia had to do everything in her power to allow this little baby to stay in her womb for as long as possible to achieve all these goals.

The doctors and nurses did their best to keep the pain under control but nothing really helped. Georgia was inconsolable, she hadn't realised how much she was looking forward to having this little tiny bundle of joy. The pain was getting stronger and Georgia was getting weaker and more frightened. Then she heard the nurse ask the question.

'Is there anyone you'd like us to call?'

'No, thank you. I'm fine with all of you around. You're the only people who can help me now. It's between you and God. You see, I haven't told anyone. I've gone this far, (She wondered why she had gone this far without telling her mum, she would be here now holding her hand.) I might as well see it through with your help.'

The next few hours of Georgia's life were pure hell.

CHAPTER 26

Nightmare behind her... Facing her future

It was over, the dreams she'd had and kept to herself all this time. She had loved when her baby was in her tummy and she had dreams of a great future for the two of them with no complications. The biggest complication of all had just happened, she had lost her baby and now she was numb. Tears flowed, she couldn't stop them and all control was gone. Now she couldn't care less about that word, control. There was nothing left to control herself for, she felt empty and she certainly had lots of space, but not in her head. When it was over the nurse gave her an injection to help her relax and sleep and that's what she did. She was exhausted and seemed to sleep for hours, only to be woken for cups of tea and a nice piece of warm toast and then it was back to sleep for another few hours. Eventually Georgia awoke to a vision of beauty in the shape of Doctor Deirdre Clancy, who sat down beside her bed and held her hand.

'How are you feeling Georgia?'

'To tell you the truth doctor, I feel completely numb. All I'm doing in my head is looking back on the last few months. Do you know doctor, I have three of the best friends anyone could wish for and I have a mother who would do anything for me. I also have an ex-husband and a lover. I don't know why I'm telling you all this except to say for the last few months I've kept my pregnancy to myself because to be honest I didn't know which one was the father, I decided to let the pregnancy take its course and now I look back on those few months and realise how absolutely stupid I've been. Right now I should have all of my friends around this bed and instead of you holding my hand it should be my mother but nobody has a clue of what I've gone through or what I'm going through.'

'Now Georgia, don't be worrying about anything except you. I can assure you, you will have no problem having a full-term baby in the future. This was just one of those things, there's no explanation. Your pregnancy had been perfect right up until a few hours ago, isn't that right Georgia? Please don't go blaming yourself. Lots of women do that, they think they are to blame for everything.'

Georgia nodded her head in agreement.

'You're right Deirdre. I know it's not my fault but I feel so empty inside. Nothing is going to make me happy, I have nothing to look forward to.'

'Again' said the doctor 'Georgia, you know that old saying, this too will pass, it will but you'll never forget and you wouldn't want to forget your pregnancy.'

Georgia cried, Dr Deirdre Clancy handed her some tissues, a cup of tea and sat with her explaining:

'You must have a check-up in six weeks' time, in the meantime take lots of rest and remember you now can look to the future full of as many babies as your heart desires.'

Because nothing like this had ever happened to Georgia before, there were lots of things she wasn't aware of. One in particular, she certainly didn't know you're not kept in hospital for very long, so before she could say toodle pips she was outside the hospital sitting in another taxi, still feeling all the bumps, still numb and the worst feeling of all, nothingness.

As fate would have it, on her arrival home she spotted not one, not two, but three of her friends. Heidi, Coco and Tanya emerging from a spanking new cream Volkswagen beetle. They had actually come to show Georgia the new car and maybe take her for a ride but once they looked at her grey face, they knew this wasn't going to happen, so instead of asking a lot of questions, they helped her inside, put on the fire and the little pretty lights around the mirror, then they tucked her up in a warm duvet and insisted she sipped on scalding hot tea. How lucky was she to have friends like this and how stupid was she to distance herself and not confide in these friends, who were the salt of the earth? She never had to explain anything to them, they never asked, that's friends. She would never tell Cameron or Ross and now that it was over, there was no need to say a word to her friends. She needed time to process everything in her head and deal with the grief she was feeling. Now Georgia would concentrate on herself and her wellbeing. The only thing she could turn to was her inner strength, that was the one thing Georgia could depend on. She had been through so much in the last few months but she would keep it all inside and do her best to move on with her life.

CHAPTER 27

The dream

After she'd lost the baby Georgia just couldn't sleep, she tried everything, reading short stories, hoping the happy ever after ending would send her into a relaxed sleep but she just wasn't reaching her goal. Maybe controlling her breathing would do the trick, but still no joy. One lonely night followed the other, and so the pattern continued, crying, not sleeping, instead lying awake tossing and turning from one side to the other and thinking. It was on one of these nights Georgia must have drifted into a light sleep and began to dream. In the dream she noticed something above her head, there was no need to feel afraid. The vision was of a baby descending towards her bed. She held up her hands and grabbed the baby's fingers. The baby smiled the kindest smile that understood all Georgia's pain and Georgia, for the first time, felt completely calm. In her dream, that to this day seems so real, the pair soared up towards the clouds, the baby leading the way with Georgia gazing up into the baby's beautiful, kind eyes, they moved effortlessly, higher and higher.

She didn't dare to look away, not even for a moment, just in case this beautiful vision would leave her forever, (although she knew it would). Below her was the raging sea – cold and frightening. Then the waves parted. This beautiful child began to release its grip on Georgia's hand. Their fingers slid very slowly apart. Georgia just felt the beautiful, soft, silky skin on the baby's fingers as she lost her grip but she could still feel the presence of that beautiful child, the one she missed so much. She knew in her dream, although the missing link in her life was gone, her child would always remain in her heart, in her head and in her dreams.

Now Georgia could feel herself spinning down towards the clouds, she was frightened. She could see the clouds below her. They were getting closer and closer by the moment but there was nothing she could do to stop herself falling. In her dream she noticed a small gap as the clouds parted. She wondered if there was enough room for her to get through. It's strange but even though she was dreaming she was petrified, then out of nowhere her little baby appeared once more as a cherub. She knew it was her baby, the eyes, they glittered like diamonds in the sky and then it happened. Her beautiful baby kissed her right on the cheek. She put her hand up, her face was warm. She would never forget that kiss, so loving, so tender. Once more that child led her just to the opening in the cloud and then Georgia could see the light shining through. She looked back and at that very moment her baby smiled, a magical smile, just for her (so captivating). Now, still in her dream, Georgia glided through the cloud with no fear. There was barely enough room for them to move through. This magical apparition guided her down to safety between those torrid waves. She could feel her hand slipping away. This magical apparition encouraged her to walk on, she didn't want to walk alone but she had no choice, so she obeyed.

As she walked back to shore the sea returned back to its former calm state. Georgia took one last look up at the skies and watched as her baby disappeared into the marshmallow clouds and for the first time in a long time she felt safe once more. She now understood why her beautiful child couldn't stay. Somehow she knew her little baby, she had even named her, Connie (the sweetest name) was looking after her from up above the clouds.

Someday they would meet again. Then almost like an electric shock, Georgia could feel her body jump then settle, she was back in her bed in real time. The dream or apparition with meaning would stay with her forever.

Isn't it strange how a dream can have such a huge impact on your life and in her case take away a lot of the hurt because the dream had explained something to her and rationalised everything. She understood a lot but not everything... maybe someday.

She felt inner peace and from that night on Georgia could sleep and look forward to the next chapter of her life, when she would hope to be stronger both mentally and physically, when she would have at least reached one of her goals, to stop isolating herself away from the real world and the friends that meant the world to her. After all, nobody isolates you, you do it to yourself. She now recognised that for the last few months she'd only lived life in a magical place, a magical world, her head, her mind, while the rest of the world spun around her and while it spun it kept on taking her friends a step at a time further away from her. This she did all by herself.

CHAPTER 28

Cameron's return

He was coming home today. It was the first ray of sunshine Georgia had seen for a long time, his smile, his amazing eyes and his kind ways. He was coming back to look after his Georgia. Little did he know how much his Georgia had gone through since the last time they set eyes on each other, how mentally and physically broken she was. Normally when she thought of Cameron, thoughts of racy nights flashed through her mind, now all she could think of was anything physical with him would make her sick. Somehow she hated her body, the body that had rejected the pregnancy, she just didn't feel it should be allowed any feeling of ecstasy. She had already discussed all of this with her doctor who assured her it was just a matter of time before she returned to her old loving, bouncy self, ready for a romp in the sack (her words, not the doctor's). Georgia couldn't let Cameron know she was feeling like this because he would know something was really wrong with her. All he knew was that Georgia couldn't wait to be with him alone, couldn't wait to see his naked body, she was a good actress and had every intention of using all her skills to put him off the scent of her panic.

'Georgia' he said as they sat sipping a cocktail. 'I can't wait to tell you how much I've saved, how much we have towards our deposit. I've already spoken to my bank manager and made an appointment to see him tomorrow. I'm hoping you'll come along. There's something else I've been doing, looking up the internet for houses. I spotted a gorgeous one, not a house, it's actually a bungalow. It's just gone on the market. We can go and view it together. I'm hoping you'll like it too. Just think of it, Georgia, we could be in our new home in the next six weeks. To be honest with you, it will be about as long as I could spend in my damp apartment. Are you excited?'

'Excited, Cameron I'm over the moon. I can't wait until we have a home of our own. Because I love you, I want to say to you, I'm with you 100% when we buy this new house together. Since the first day I met you all I wanted was you forever. I walked away from Ross and a really good marriage to be with you. I was behind you all the time you were in the monastery wondering would you or wouldn't you leave. I was completely behind you when you did leave and when you went to London for those two months to save for this very important chapter in our lives. I was there pushing you to go because, Cameron, I felt two months of hard work would do you good and bring you back to me a real man.'

Cameron looked amused. Georgia continued:

'Now you're here and there's only 24 hours before we'll know our fate.'

Cameron finally got a minute to say something.

'In answer to your statement Georgia, I'm so well aware of everything you've done to be with me. Sometimes I don't feel worthy of you, I also feel your husband Ross didn't deserve the treatment we gave him and although I've never met him I know from the things you say he is a good, honest man who loves you just as much as I do. If I could go back to the moment I first met you and I knew then what I know now, I would have tried a lot harder to be a lot stronger and not so selfish. I would have made me do the right thing, and left you in his arms. I shouldn't have encouraged you to come into mine. I was selfish but I couldn't help it, it was just my deep feelings for you that overwhelmed me and caused my brain to override everything else. I'm madly in love with you and just longing for the day when we have our new home, only then will I feel secure. You decided to leave Ross, you said it really wasn't because of me, you said at the end of the day you wanted to find yourself. That explanation was good enough to give me the push to pursue the life I wanted to have with you.'

Georgia thought, if only life was as simple as that, Cameron, if only you knew I still love Ross, I just can't help myself.

'Georgia, If we don't get the loan, so be it, we can get a smaller house, we can move to the country, I can get a job down there, whatever it takes. I should know a lot more than I do about loans and mortgages, all I do know is, if you want something bad enough, you have to work your ass off to make it happen and when that opportunity comes you have to take it, grab it, hold onto it tightly with both hands and continue working your ass off to maintain your goals. That's what I've done in London Georgia, worked my ass off, I worked morning, noon and night to come home with a leprechaun's pot of gold. Now before we go to meet the bank manager in the morning I want to explain a few little things to you, Georgia. I already told you my grandad left me some money but I never said how much. Well it was €200,000. As I said to you before, I already had a little bit of cash and since being in London I've a little bit more, altogether now I have €250,000.'

'Cameron, I don't think all of your money should go into the deposit, I think you should keep around fifty thousand aside for our future, renovating our new home and maybe keeping some aside for when we have a baby and I can't work but we'll still have those big repayments. What do you think Cameron?'

'Words of wisdom Georgia, that's exactly what we will try to do. You are so right, we could try to buy a house that's not too expensive and renovate it ourselves with some of the money we keep back. There are so many TV shows and books out now, we could learn from them, sure it could be the beginning of a new career. First things first: Let's just go and meet with the bank manager in the morning and see where it takes us.'

'Yes' said Georgia, 'I have everything I need for the bank manager. Proof I am working and paying rent, that should help.'

Cameron nodded his head.

'One day in the not too distant future, Georgia, we will have a roof over our heads, that will be one more bridge crossed, one more box ticked, sure we're a great little twosome, together we will move mountains. Georgia this must be the most serious conversation we have had since the day I first clapped eyes on you.'

'Sometimes,' said Georgia 'that's exactly what couples have to do, some straight talking, it just has to be done.'

CHAPTER 29

A fate that would be decided for them

11 am Tuesday morning, already seated in the bank manager's office, it turned out Cameron already knew Mark, the bank manager. He was a constant member of the church where, in his previous life, Cameron worked and helped to serve communion on Sunday mornings. Mark jotted down a few things.

'The deposit we have is from the two of us' said Cameron. 'We're a couple now and we want to move in together, not into rented accommodation but into our own house. Mark, it's so important to us to get this loan. I'm starting as a teacher in a nearby school in September. I've spent the summer working in London.

As you know all my business is with your bank, I feel we have an adequate amount of money to put down and secure our new home. We're first time buyers if there's any perks in that.' Everyone laughed.

For a moment Georgia's mind drifted back to the house she shared with Ross. It hadn't cost her a penny, it was already his when she met him. How easy that life was, now here she was sitting with a bank manager, at the bank's mercy. Could they secure this bank loan? Answer unknown.

'Well now' said Mark 'having done a little calculation and listened to the price of the bungalow you're going to look at today, I feel you will both get the loan to cover what you need. Does that sound good to you?'

'Yes' said Cameron 'that sounds bloody amazing.'

'Now I can't promise you you'll get the loan but I feel you will. You're both well-established people. I'll do my very best to put your case forward. I have all the information I need so it's time for us to say goodbye for now. It will take a few days but I will get back to you ASAP with the answer. Do go and look at that bungalow but offer a little less than they want and tell them you do have the loan.'

'We have an appointment to see the bungalow at 2pm.'

'Well the best of luck to both of you.'

Cameron and Georgia stood up, they shook Mark's hand and left the office, feeling a little more in control of the life that was just an inch away.

As they walked along the seafront in Sandymount on that bright sunny day, they reminisced on the bungalow they just viewed. It had everything they wanted, real fireplaces and real fires and lots of kitchen presses from the seventies. Some fabulous old beds they had every intention of asking the owners could they buy. Yes, Georgia was already seeing herself painting them.

Georgia gathered up seashells. She had a bucket of them at home from picking them up every time she went to the seafront and in her head she had all kinds of ideas for them. She was thinking of making a kind of mosaic from them or using them around frames for the numerous magical photographs she hadn't framed. Yes, Georgia had great ideas in her head and she looked forward to seeing them come to life. The phone rang, Georgia at first decided not to answer it but Cameron encouraged her to.

'It could be the bank manager' he said and it was Mark himself, making that call very personal.

'I decided to ring you Georgia as I thought Cameron might be with you and then I could kill two birds with one stone.'

'Well he is, as a matter of fact. We're walking along the sea shore in Sandymount, soaking up the sun.'

'Would you like to put me on speaker?' said Mark 'and I'll give you the news.'

'Yes, you're on speaker now' said Georgia.

'You have both got the loan. Congratulations to both of you. How did you get on viewing that bungalow the other day?' enquired Mark.

'The bungalow has everything we want. It's bright and airy, just the right size and within our budget. If all goes to plan we will put down the deposit and it will be our very own bungalow in just six weeks.'

'Sounds good to me' said Mark 'best wishes to the two of you. I'll put you in for an appointment next Monday morning at 11am if that suits.'

'Absolutely, we'll be there.'

What a day, the sun beamed down as they walked the last few steps to the front door of hopefully, fingers crossed, Cameron and Georgia's forever home for a second viewing. It was the most delicious little bungalow they had ever seen. There was really nothing that needed to be done in that bungalow. They could just move in straight away but if everything worked out they would put their own stamp on it and pretty it up a little by changing the paint work and having the doors of the presses taken off and spray painted. Georgia thought it might be a good idea to add some wallpaper to one or two of the walls. It had three bedrooms, one quite small and two lovely big ones. They would keep the small one as their wardrobe space, for all their clothes and just in case someone came to stay it had been decided to invest in a pull down bed. The good news was, as the owners wanted to sell the property fast, they were giving a considerable discount off the asking price. Cameron was thrilled to hear there would be extra cash over to have every inch of this fabulous space deep cleaned so the finished result would be pristine.

Six weeks had passed when the two spritely lovers dressed in their best collected the keys to their new bungalow and drove the short journey, with hearts beating like drums, to their new abode. Georgia turned the key, Cameron lifted his happy partner up into his arms and carried her over the threshold into their hallway. The first view she had from the angle she was at, was the ceiling. Immediately a song flashed into her head. The name of the song was, *Oh what a feeling, when you're dancing on the ceiling*. She began to sing the song out loud, her voice echoed all around the empty space. The words of that song resonated with her.

Outside in the boot of the car sat buckets of paint. The two of them carried them into the house looking very silly in their best clothes. Cameron carried the larger, massive ones and Georgia, in her high heels carried the smaller heavy buckets of paint, one in each hand into the hall and put them down on an old sheet. Earlier that very day Cameron had met the tiler to get a price for tiling the floor and see when he was free to put down the tiles, already bought and being delivered later. It only took a few weeks to turn everything around, that included having the garden landscaped, something Cameron had insisted on. As he said himself, he was a culchie through and through and just loved the great outdoor life. They were in their, home sweet home. Now all they talked about was the garden, he wanted to plant every kind of vegetable he could think of, in his vegetable patch.

Georgia became so intrigued with the whole idea she decided to try her hand at planting flowers. All she would need was a lot of time and patience to have her little patch of the garden looking just right. At last, thank God, the time had come to move into their fantastic, comfortable, freshly decorated bungalow that was all sparkling clean and ready to embrace its new owners. Georgia loved the old saying, home is where the heart is. That's exactly where Georgia and Cameron's hearts were, in their pretty little bungalow they now called home.

CHAPTER 30

Georgia's demons

Isn't it ironic, when it seemed Georgia had everything her heart desired, she still had her demons inside her head, the same ones - Ross and Connie, the beautiful baby she had lost and the faithful husband she had betrayed. How she wished and longed for that baby to be here now and for her to reside in her own little bedroom, all pretty and appealing but instead there was a void she just couldn't seem to rid herself of.

It had been a long day. Georgia turned the key in the door, normally she'd sit down, have something to eat but this evening she felt absolutely wiped out, exactly the way she felt when she was expecting Connie. All she needed was to confirm what she already knew. She needed to see the word positive, in black and white in front of her eyes. With that in mind, Georgia had already purchased the pregnancy test, now she was in the bathroom with only moments to wait to confirm what she knew in her heart to be true. Positive, that word stared back at her, the proof she needed to confirm she wasn't going mad. That one word explained lots of things to her. The tiredness, the mood swings, the teary eyes if someone said boo to her, was all because she was pregnant. She needed a little time to decipher all her thoughts in her own head first, before she could put them out on the wider stage and tell her adoring partner their great news. Georgia believed when the moment was right she would know and everything would fall into place.

Alone holding the pregnancy test results in her shaky hand, feeling both fear and excitement at becoming a mother for the second time, knowing she should be ecstatic, feeling the glow of a mother to be, dreaming of a future with her new partner Cameron and a new little life in her arms but she just couldn't come to terms with her pregnancy yet. She was almost afraid to say a word even to herself and she knew why. All of this was bringing back her last pregnancy when all her happiness had turned to sorrow, when all her dreams had been crushed. She had held on so tightly to those sad memories, they were rooted deep down inside, hidden away for such a long time. Now, just like an explosion inside her mind they were back alive and kicking, stirring and churning around in her head again. It made her feel uncontrolled and quite desperate. Soon she would have to say something to Cameron. First she had to decipher all the feelings, pain and sorrow that were returning to haunt her. She was a strong woman and she would find a way to cope.

Georgia sat down to dinner with not an ounce of energy to even talk. While Cameron on the other hand was full of chat, all about his new job and the fabulous pupils he had, the other teachers that were so welcoming and how he loved the short distance he had to walk to get to the school he now worked in. Georgia just sat there trying her best to listen to every word her lover uttered and join into the conversation whenever she needed to. Unfortunately, she felt detached with thoughts of soon becoming a mother overtaking everything else.

'Sorry Cameron, I'm no fun, I'm just so tired, I feel like a wave of exhaustion has taken me over. It's such a strange feeling, one I've never felt before.'

'Relax, once you have had a cup of tea and a chocolate biscuit, you'll feel a lot more upbeat.' And she did.

The bungalow was so lovely and quiet, not a sound. These were the times she loved, having a big space all to themselves where they could just be themselves. Cameron also loved this bungalow and never stopped doing things with it to make it look even better than it already did, which Georgia thought was impossible. With that thought in her mind, she made a really big effort to make him happy. One thing led to another, she undid his tie and then unbuttoned his shirt. He unzipped his fly himself, this time with no sound… she missed that sound that used to echo around his cell. Cameron turned on the record player and played his favourite song for Georgia, *Big Spender*, great to strip to but it had a light side. Her favourite strip tease act followed, not up to Dita Von Teese standards, no burlesque moves or large champagne glass to perform from but she did have a creative mind and a desire to give her partner lots of happy memories. Cameron filled the bathtub with lots of lovely hot water and lots of bubble bombs. She lay there allowing the lovely bubbles and the warmth of the steam to engulf her. Slowly she began to come back down to earth. She was living in the moment, exactly the way she wanted it to be. All the tiredness slowly drifted from her body.

First thing the next morning Georgia booked that appointment with her doctor for 2 o'clock. Now as she left the surgery, having heard the good news she was coming to terms with her second pregnancy and almost ready to share the excitement with her partner. After all she had lived with him, eaten with him, chatted with him and made love to him, it should be easy but up until now she couldn't bring herself to tell him, even knowing that he would be so excited and so thrilled at the thoughts of becoming a dad. In a way, Georgia felt kind of mean, she knew he would have wanted to share this moment from the very beginning with her but the time was not right, until now. Georgia always felt the stars had to be in line, now they were. She just had to tell him. While she did facials and make-up in the beauty salon, she threw around the thoughts in her head, how would she tell him, what was the appropriate way? If any of her friends were pregnant, she knew exactly what advice she would give them. She would say, well, if you feel up to it, organise a meal for both of you in some romantic restaurant. Take a card with you with the words 'Congratulations, you're going to be a dad' and watch as his face lights up.

She had a lot of organising to do. Let's face facts she was pregnant, she needed to tell Cameron. So off to the shops she went and bought the presentation box in pale lilac, the card, Lily O'Brien chocolates and the booties in cream. She would present them to him in the beautiful presentation box. Last but not least, she booked a table for two at his favourite restaurant where, when the time was right, she would present him with that little package, card, chocolates, booties and the pregnancy test with the words positive facing him. Then she would observe, wait for that appropriate moment and take a photograph of him as his facial expression changed and he began to realise he was going to be a dad. All of this would help them to make memories.

CHAPTER 31

Perfect timing

Some of these things she had already done, others would happen along the way there, as they ate. There she was sitting in his favourite restaurant, at his favourite table and on the floor beside her sat a bag containing a nicely wrapped gift box that held inside the card, the chocolates, the booties and the pregnancy test with the word *positive* clearly displayed. She was prepared for this big occasion and looking forward to his reaction. First, soup of the day, next course, steak, onions, French fries, followed by fabulous dessert, chocolate fondue and then of course, the fabulous pot of tea for her and a gorgeous skinny latte for him, but still no words coming out of her mouth to tell him the good news. She wondered if he suspected something was going on because he was looking at her strangely but the poor fecker, he hadn't got a clue. Not a word did Georgia utter, instead she presented him with the gift box. He sort of looked at it, began to undo the bow and then unwrap the box. There inside sat a smaller, round box full of his favourite sweets, chocolates from Lily O'Brien.

'What is the occasion?'

He bewilderingly asked Georgia as he put his hand into the box again and took out another little bag. For some reason he opened it very gently and there sat the prettiest cream booties with satin bows. His mouth opened wide but he still didn't seem to get it.

'What are you trying to tell me, Georgia? Who are these for?'

He said in a weird voice as he delved into the box and took

out the last item folded in tissue paper. Cameron held that very important little item in his hand. He slowly began to unwrap it. Georgia could hardly contain her feelings, she was becoming so emotional. A feeling she had not prepared herself for.

'Let me help you open this little package' said Georgia as Cameron seemed to be in a daze.

She opened it and held up the pregnancy test with the word *positive* facing him. He could see the word positive clearly. He looked at her, he looked at it and he looked at her again.

'Positive! Who's positive?'

He was speechless. Georgia took the very last thing from the box, the envelope holding the card and handed it to him. He opened it. The front of the card said Congratulations. Still speechless, he opened the card and read the words out loud:

'Cameron you're going to be a daddy'.

He sat back in the chair and for a moment didn't quite know what to do. He leant across the table, kissed Georgia and gave her the best hug ever while tears streamed down his face.

'I have never been so happy' he said 'this is the best night of my life. Georgia you have made me the happiest man alive.'

Georgia cried too, she couldn't tell him she wasn't really crying for this new little baby growing inside her tummy but crying for the loss of her first baby. He would never know she would never share this information with him.

'I'm having your baby Cameron. You might take it in better if I read the card to you, slowly and very carefully.'

She took the lovely card from Cameron's shaky hands. She felt a huge overwhelming surge of emotion taking over her body as she heard the words being read out loud from her very own lips, it was as if she was hearing them for the very first time. There was a pause and then she continued,

'Dearest Cameron, you know the old song, *I'm having your baby*, well I am having your baby and I'm so happy. I was waiting for the perfect time to give you the good news and right now seemed like the perfect time.'

Cameron ran around to Georgia's side of the table, lifted her up in the air and announced again he was the happiest man in the world.

'I'm going to be a daddy'.

Cameron romanced about this new chapter in his life, one he'd waited so long for.

'This is the way it was meant to be, first falling in love with you, Georgia and then leaving the Seminary behind.' With his hands waving up in the air he announced 'This is the best chapter of our lives so far. It's like a fairy tale.'

The happy couple returned home to their gorgeous bungalow. Cameron poured a glass of champagne for Georgia and himself. It's always a good idea to have a spare bottle of champagne stashed away. She loved the bubbles but a drop of the champagne didn't touch her lips, the bubbles did tip her nose but she decided to have pink lemonade instead. Later on that night as she lay there just about to fall asleep, feeling relaxed and in heaven, Georgia heard a voice in the darkness asking her to marry him. She must be dreaming, and then she heard the words repeated again.

'Georgia, will you marry me?'

Georgia sat up in bed and moved towards the light, she was about to switch it on, when she felt Cameron ever so gently, pulling her back.

'Leave the light off, Georgia, just for now. It's more romantic in the dark. I know you might need some time before you decide, I understand Georgia.'

'I'm so happy you took the opportunity on this night when I've just told you we are expecting our first baby together, to propose to me, Cameron. It's very easy to say yes to you. You had me at hello. Right now I am not a free woman until my divorce has been finalized. I would love to wear a promise ring, to show all our friends we have made a promise to each other, it can be one sparkling diamond.' She smiled. 'I will always be yours. Please will you just propose to me again when my divorce is finalised?' said Georgia.

'Absolutely, I'm a very happy man. What more could I ask for than your commitment to me and a new baby to look forward to, Georgia. That's more than enough for me right now. Once I know we now have an understanding and a real future together I'm happy to wait. It will give me time to save a few more bob for a bigger diamond ring.'

Cameron's animal instincts took over. Georgia didn't need to do anything, just enjoy it. Instead of feeling tired and listless, she now felt like a young lamb, full of the joys of Spring, at one with another human being, his name was Cameron, a beautiful chocolaty sounding name. Georgia sank into his strong arms, they were warm and comforting. She could smell his skin and his Creed men's perfume. She took everything in. They were both so content and relaxed in each other's arms, it was as if stardust had fallen on their comfy bed. It was easy for them to fall into a relaxing sleep and dream of what was to come, until it was morning.

A few hours later Georgia was awake again feeling restless, uneasy and wide awake. She looked across at Cameron lying beside her. He looked so content with his gorgeous hair tousled and the happiest smile on his face. She was happy too. This was different from the last time and all because Georgia had someone to share this gorgeous journey into motherhood with, for her second time.

It was a strange feeling, being pregnant again. She felt lots of different things, but there were two that really stood out. First, she didn't realise until now how much she had longed for another baby. She'd blocked all those thoughts out of her mind. The second thing she felt was guilt, afraid the start of a new life inside her might make her think less of the baby she lost. She would refuse to let that happen. In her heart she knew she would never forget Connie. After all, Georgia continuously had vivid memories of that dream she had after she lost Connie. She would always believe in her heart, Connie her baby had appeared to her and only her, so every day on this journey and for the rest of her life, she would include Connie in everything. As long as she lived, Georgia would never walk alone.

There were a few little things she wanted to discuss with Cameron.

'Cameron, I haven't had a chance to tell you how long into my pregnancy I am. First I just want to say to you, I honestly didn't think I was pregnant, I thought the exhaustion was from moving homes and making so many big decisions and of course, working. I let time pass and then, there I was in the doctor's surgery having already taken a pregnancy test myself at home. It was positive Cameron but I really wanted to hear what the doctor had to say before I built your hopes up and then crashed them to the ground. To my astonishment and my surprise, I was actually four months pregnant because I haven't put on a lot of weight, perhaps that's also to do with the moving, etc. etc. So sit down beside me Cameron, you thought it was great news last night when I told you, you were going to be a daddy. Now I want to tell you, if you haven't already done your sums, you really only have five months to wait for our baby to arrive, to be precise the beginning of December, please God, a Christmas baby.'

Cameron was stunned but ecstatic with happiness. Now he wasn't sitting, he was jumping around the table.

'We're having a Christmas baby.'

As the weeks turned into months, the nights got darker and Christmas got closer, the happy couple enjoyed the way this chapter of their lives was unfolding and taking them in a new direction. Georgia decided it was time to buy Christmas decorations because they hadn't got one Christmas decoration. The question was where would you get Christmas decorations in October? She decided on Brown Thomas where every year they have an early Christmas shop on the third floor. This day was the best day ever, no crowds pushing and shoving, early morning just Cameron and Georgia sifting their way through the fabulous decorations and ending with a lights-on Christmas tree. Georgia couldn't stand for too long so into the café on the third floor they headed with all their Christmas bags. Another thing on the to-do list ticked, done.

Every night Cameron drifted off to sleep with a happy smile on his face. On the other hand, Georgia's sleep pattern was all over the place. She would fall asleep quickly, then awake a few hours later as bright as a button. It was at this time every night Georgia did her thinking, she had to admit she was still holding a torch for Ross but she prayed that once Cameron's baby was here on planet Earth, that torchlight would be quenched, blown out forever. She didn't want to forget Ross just as she didn't want to forget Connie.

All the things that happened in Georgia's life were big milestones, each one she loved and didn't want to miss or forget one moment of the life she had led, after all this is and was her life, the life she was given. Why is it that somewhere deep in her soul she never really wanted that torch light to ever disappear? Surely life shouldn't be a struggle, why is it when one fantastic thing happens there's always that other little thing that niggles at your heart? Once you see there is a light at the end of a tunnel there's always hope! When you love two men in different ways in your heart, and you really haven't allowed yourself to decipher your feelings, there will possibly always be reasons to fight with yourself, while you deal with the Yins and the Yangs of your life now and your life in the future. Sometimes Georgia felt as if she was in a dark forest covered in big, big dark trees, trying to find her way out.

If only I could find my way out of that forest I could completely free myself, both mentally and physically from that feeling of being trapped and instead completely immerse myself in this amazing new chapter of my life, this amazing future that is mine to have, once I embrace it. That's what I must do, just focus, become like a horse with blinkers on and only see what is in front of me, not what's to the left or right or behind me, just in front of me, that would surely help me cope. I mustn't look back.'

CHAPTER 32

Amazing friends

With that thought in mind and Georgia concentrating and looking forward to her future she made a phone call to each of her friends individually and invited them to meet her in the Trocadero for a little reunion. It seemed as she spoke to them individually they all had stories to tell and were thrilled with this opportunity to share their news, good or bad, with Georgia and so they met. Four pals, a little older, a little wiser. They ordered some lovely food and sat there just enjoying the ambience of their special restaurant. Heidi may be getting married, Tanya still flirting with Frederick, Coco still with her French man. Oh how their lives had moved on, they were becoming women of the world now, all four. Georgia sat there enjoying the conversations until they turned to her and asked the question

'Well, Georgia, what's been happening to you?' Tanya butted in 'Georgia when we lived together for that short time I knew everything that was going on in your life and you knew everything that was happening in mine. Now when we meet I look forward to hearing your stories. Come on, Georgia spill the beans, we're all waiting.'

'Where do I start?' said Georgia.

'Please just bring us up to date because we know a lot has been happening,' said Coco.

Heidi said 'No matter what's happening I want you all to be happy on the day when you're my bridesmaids.'

'Well' said Georgia 'first things first, Ross and I are no longer together. Lately I've said to myself, I've got to face up to everything if I want to move on with my life. I have faced up and I am moving forward but you are my three best friends, I just want to bring you up to date with everything. Our divorce should be through soon, it's been a hard time. I asked you to come here tonight because this is where it all started, the end of my marriage and the beginning of my romance with Cameron.'

Tanya said 'Georgia this isn't coming as a surprise to any of us, we've known all the time there was something going on.'

'Yes.' said Heidi, 'The electricity in this room the moment I introduced you to Cameron, went wild. I knew you'd fallen in love with him without even speaking to him. I saw him looking at you across the table. I knew you had been with him, but hadn't seen him for a while, that's why I asked you to come along with me to his apartment. It wasn't just to keep me company, it was a great excuse and I knew you wanted to see Cameron. Remember that phone call I took when I vanished from the room? That phone call came from Coco. We had it all arranged so you would have time to talk to the love of your life.'

Coco said 'We've all grown up together, Georgia. We've been through the good, the bad and the ugly. We're your friends so we just left you alone to come to us when you knew the time was right.'

Heidi said 'Do you remember the night we drove to surprise you with the new car, Georgia. We thought you'd be so excited but the only ones that got a shock was us when we saw the state of you getting out of the taxi on your way home from the hospital.'

'Yes.' said Tanya 'We had gone around to your house that night telling you we wanted you to see the new car but we were really concerned about your health, the car was just an excuse for all three of us to arrive at your door at the same time.

We are your friends, I know we said it before and we'll say it again you have always been there for us. The three of us worked together, Coco ringing you one week, me ringing you another week, Tanya ringing you another week, just keeping you in the loop. I actually met Ross out some time ago. I have to say he was distraught but determined to start a new life without you. You were always such a lovely couple. When you came to stay with me I never asked you anything, friends don't do that, they wait until you are ready to talk.'

'My little part in all this was liaising with your mum. She has been so upset over you. Looking at you when you were very mixed up, when you were tired, when you didn't want to talk to anyone, she would go into your house, run up the stairs, giving that little Yoo Hoo, always letting you know she was there for you but not interfering. You see we all took part in secretly looking after our best friend.'

Here was Georgia sitting beside her three friends, tears streaming down from her eyes, feeling closer to them than ever. They were remarkable people. She couldn't believe they'd been working in the background all that time and now in her mind's eye she could see them popping in and out of her life in the last while, never pushy, just friendly. They sat quietly drinking tea and having dessert.

'Cameron and I are very happy in our new bungalow. When can you all come to visit us?'

Her friends were so happy with the invitation.

'I'm looking forward to having so many celebrations with all of you in the next few months and I promise I'll never leave you out of my life again.'

The girls shared a taxi to their homes, the taxi stopped and dropped them off one by one. Georgia was last to leave the taxi, as she stepped out onto the street outside her little bungalow, inside she felt the happiest she'd felt for a long, long time. It was working, not looking back, instead with imaginary blinkers on looking straight ahead.

CHAPTER 33

Friendships never die

Nellie arrived bang on 1 o'clock.

'Come on Mum before they all arrive let's sit down here and have a little chat. I've already put two spoons of coffee in your cup, I know you like it strong. You'll be so full of energy you'll be funny. Mum, I'm glad you came early because we have a few things to share with you before my friends arrive.'

'So what's the big news me darlin girl?' said her mum.

'Mum, Cameron and I have something to tell you. Cameron, go ahead, tell Mum our good news.'

'Nellie you've probably guessed by now.'

'Cameron and Georgia when I came here today I had no expectations, I just wanted to see your new home.'

Cameron just blurted out the words:

'Nellie, we are expecting our first baby and before you ask we don't know if it's a boy or girl and we're not sure if we want to know but we do know our bundle of joy is due at the beginning of December, just in time for Christmas.'

Georgia continued 'We really want the surprise. We don't mind whether it's a boy or a girl as long as it's a baby.'

There were hugs and kisses and more hugs and kisses.

'Well Georgia and Cameron, congratulations. Your baby whether it's a boy or girl is going to be so happy in your beautiful new bungalow. You know Georgia I just love the bungalow, I wish it was me that owned it. If I see one in the area for sale I might just buy it.'

Cameron joked 'Oh gosh Nellie that would be great for

babysitting, we would just have to wheel the baby to you.'

'On second thoughts, maybe I won't buy one so close.' Nellie laughed.

'Now, Mum, you cannot breathe a word of this until we tell our friends. That's why I've invited them and Maisie Coyne over, an hour later than you. They're just coming for lunch and they'll be gone home by 7. That is all except Tanya, she wants to stay over.'

Friends arrived at 2pm. Maisie arrived at 2.10pm. After introductions, they all loved Maisie and Maisie loved them. Beautiful lunch – Duck a l'orange and all the trimmings. Pavlova for dessert, lots of drinks and chat. Then there was silence. Georgia joined Cameron.

'We have a little announcement to make. Are you ready now? Drum roll please.'

Everybody banged the table.

'We're standing, we're ready.'

'Are you ready Maisie?'

'I'm ready to raise a glass to anyone' said Maisie.

Georgia stood up to her 5 foot 3 inches height and felt the tallest she had in a long time with Cameron by her side. Cameron gazed at Georgia with so much love in his eyes, then he turned to the anxious friends and announced.

'Nellie, Georgia's lovely mum and Coco, Heidi, Tanya and of course, our new guest Maisie, I'd like to introduce you to the new expectant parents.'

The girls, the mum and the new friend, clapped, kissed and hugged Georgia and Cameron. It was definitely a moment not to be missed. Georgia had her little piece to say:

'Let's raise a toast to Cameron, who is about to become a daddy. Now Mum I know you'll always be there to help and bestow as much love on our new baby as you did on all of us, and girls I know you'll all come up trumps as usual, you might even babysit the odd time and then there's Maisie Coyne, I love having you as a new friend. I know Cameron cherishes the friendship you've both had over the last six years. We're hoping that you also will be happy to take a little part in our baby's life.'

Maisie looked like the cat who got the cream.

'Cameron and Georgia if it's ok with you, I'll start knitting straight away' said Maisie 'I love knitting for babies, and don't worry Georgia I'll knit everything in cream and yellow, no pink and no blue.'

'Oh' said Georgia. 'I have a request Maisie, would you mind knitting a tiny Christmas cardigan for our new baby?'

Maisie was over the moon, speechless. Georgia could see she was already creating the design in her head, something to look forward to.

What a lovely afternoon, what a lovely meal, what a nice new friend, what lovely old friends, what an amazing mother. Georgia and Cameron had real back up now, friends who would be there to help them if ever they needed help. As the Beatles song said *Help, I need somebody, Help, Not just anybody…* What a lovely day. Now that the news was out Cameron threw all caution to the wind and behaved like a real excited civilian and soon to be father.

'Georgia, please sit down and rest' those were his words.

Then he kissed Maisie on the cheek, he just didn't know which way to behave but the most important thing was, at this moment in time he was the happiest man and Georgia the happiest mama to be, in the world.

CHAPTER 34

The happy bungalow

As the birth of Cameron and Georgia's baby drew closer, their bungalow seemed happier, brighter, warmer, cosier and even more beautiful than ever before. What a lovely, well-established part of Dublin to live in. The bungalows were built in a circle around a green space not too close and not too far away from the neighbours. Georgia was beginning to take in everything around her as she left for work in the mornings, getting to know and love the area a little more with every step she took. She began to imagine pushing her peaches and cream, perfectly pretty pram along past the other bungalows. Sometimes as she day-dreamed, she could in her mind's eye imagine the locals coming out to welcome the brand new baba boo into their leafy green area. As the day got closer and closer, Georgia and Cameron continued to prepare for the birth of their baby. They had one other big surprise to look forward to... was their baby a boy or a girl? By now the pram, the cot, wash basin and set of drawers had been delivered. They only bought one toy, a cuddly teddy bear and some new baby clothes. Oh! the size of them, teeny tiny. How could a baby fit into them?

Cameron looked after Georgia so well she began to wonder if he thought she was a precious artefact or the queen bee. His brown eyes never stopped glowing with anticipation and excitement as he gazed at her now non-existent figure. It didn't seem to bother him as much as it bothered her, the fact she no longer had a waist. That's true love! He must be wearing special rose tinted glasses that only saw perfection. As Cameron lay in bed that night fast asleep, with that look of contentment on his beautiful face, Georgia felt he finally had re-found his faith. Only yesterday Cameron in his own words said to Georgia,

'I truly believe the dreams I had for my future are beginning to fall into place. God has cleared my head of all the doubts. The, should I, shouldn't I, now I have a clearer head and a better mind-set.'

Georgia knew now his heart was open to embrace the changes.

'Being with you and sharing this journey with you is truly my vocation. Everything and anything is possible as long as you are by my side.'

She loved the way Cameron could see his life's path unfold. Georgia continued to lie in the stillness beside him, gazing out through the window at the night with a beautiful full moon sitting prettily up there, lighting up everywhere, especially their room. She felt Connie's presence. It was a surreal moment, her mind floating back to that dream when Connie had appeared to her. That dream was more an apparition than a dream. In it she had felt herself floating through the clouds with her beautiful baby girl. Now in her mind she was reliving that dream. Her spirit floated back towards it. When it ended, she felt content inside and ready to face her future knowing and feeling in her heart she now had a wonderful future with Cameron and their new baby to look forward to.

She blocked out any feelings of betraying Connie, because at this moment Georgia realised this new baby would make her feel closer to Connie. It was clear to her as she said a little prayer, Connie would be spiritually there by her new baby's side always. Connie's memory and that dream, for her, would always be paramount. Georgia felt content, happy, empowered and ready to face her scan tomorrow with Cameron. Calmness descended on her and she drifted off to sleep.

CHAPTER 35

A dream come true

When Georgia awoke she could still feel that lovely calmness engulfing her being and butterflies in her tummy. Today, Monday was usually Georgia's day off, one where she just lay around and maybe took a trip to town but this Monday was different, she had a date with Cameron. They were going somewhere very special. Cameron was taking Georgia to the hospital for another scan. She would have loved to have toast and tea, served by her favourite waiter, Cameron, but unfortunately for her those luxuries were not allowed. She felt like she drank Lough Erne dry with all the water she'd consumed from the night before, her tummy felt like a whirlpool. How could she cope with all this water retention, well it had to be done. She had tried to be sensible and book the earliest possible appointment but even at that it was pure torture to walk. She felt heavy, bloated and uncomfortable just when she wanted to feel all feminine and pretty. Cameron tried everything to keep her stress free but it was impossible, she felt her blood pressure soar and wondered how she could possibly put up with it for much longer, if she felt so bad right now. Still it had its compensations, she was being waited on hand and foot. Georgia decided to dwell on the positive and forget any negative thoughts as she sat into Cameron's car and tried her best to keep herself occupied on the journey.

The traffic wasn't so bad, at least that took some of the stress away. The CD played out one of Barry White's old songs, one of Cameron's favourites, *My first, my last, my everything*, the words rang out and Georgia hoped in some way this was meant for her, her second child (on the way) and her last child, the way she was feeling now that's exactly where it was at. The last few words really said it all, *her everything*. And then she was there lying on the bed and that white jelly being rubbed on her poor waterbed tummy. That's what she felt it was like, a waterbed, just squelchy, uncomfortable, unbelievable.

'Oh my God! Was that my baby's heart beating?' oooh, it was. Georgia's heartbeat seemed to be beating in time with her unborn baby's.

Cameron's hand tightened on hers. Tears welled up in her eyes, she had to rub them away and then her nose started to run. There was poor Georgia fumbling in her bag for tissues to blow her nose. No, It wasn't a pretty sight, this was supposed to be a very special time for Georgia. She should be glowing at this magical moment. Then like a wave of a magic wand Georgia forgot all her little problems, runny nose, waterbed uncomfortable tummy, none of it mattered now, this was the moment they would savour for a long time to come. No, there weren't two babies, there was just one baby but how she longed to hold this little infant in her arms. She didn't care how long it took, she vowed. The nurse handed them a photo of the scan, she looked at Cameron, his face was glowing and his beautiful eyes were beaming as he gazed at the first sighting of their baby.

She had spent about ten minutes in the ladies loo and the relief was so good when all those gallons of water had disappeared, she was back, would you believe, to feeling slim and attractive. For the happy couple there was, love, excitement and longing surrounding them knowing they would soon become a little family. Yes, she was ready to embrace all the changes her body would take on before that big day. To hell with it, she thought, it's just part of being a woman.

Georgia had turned off her mobile, so if Cathy, the reception-ist at work, Coco, Heidi or Tanya were trying to get in touch it wasn't going to happen. She was leaving the phone switched off as she embarked on a big lunch of grilled salmon and a gorgeous side salad. To wash it all down, she sipped a huge glass of freshly squeezed orange juice. Exactly what an expectant mum needs, lots of vitamin C and fresh fish, they say that's good for the brain. Cameron had taken the day off work, he wanted to be part of this special time in both their lives and she was determined he would share it with her. Just like any couple expecting their baby, they had something special just between the two of them. Something no one else could share, it was a wonderful feeling. Every now and then he'd smile that secret smile or grasp her hand and she just knew things were going from good to fantastic. They were on top of the world.

The beauty salon was going really well. Unfortunately Georgia was finding it very hard to work, all the standing was causing her legs to swell, yes, poor Georgia felt uncomfortable. Her aim was to work right up until the day, well almost until the baby arrived. She did her best to keep that goal in mind but with two weeks to go she just couldn't do it any longer. She was begin-ning to feel sorry for herself and shed bucket loads of tears at a moment's notice. Georgia knew she had come to the end of the road. She just couldn't stick one more early morning, one more late night, even the thought of the alarm going off at 6.45am was enough to bring goose pimples out on her arms. There was no time to waste, so donning her jacket that by now, only barely fitted her, she said goodbye and very happily swapped her day job with all its mayhem and at the same time wonderment, for being a homemaker who just enjoyed peace and quiet and a big slice of the good life.

After all, this was her first full term baby and no matter how much Cameron did for her, he did everything, including painting the baby's room in lovely colours to suit either a baby boy or girl, she came to the point where she didn't care, she felt so uncomfortable. At night she could only sleep for a short time with a pillow underneath her bump. It was at these times she would look back at her last pregnancy and thank the man above for getting her this far. Oh how she would love to have Connie now and just about to give birth to her second child, one pal for the other, but as they say God has his wise ways and after all she had to leave it all in his hands.

Thank God for morning time and the birds' chorus, to her it meant the dawn was breaking. She pushed herself to the limit, dragging that body of hers out of the bed. The hardest part was sitting up, so she found a new way around that, she would mooch herself to the edge of the bed then put one leg out onto the floor, then the other, gradually turn her body around, hold on to the frame of the bed and haul herself out onto the floor. Standing up straight was the only way to be. She couldn't sit for any length of time and although standing was uncomfortable, once she started to walk around her body loosened up. She prayed the last two weeks of her pregnancy would roll by, just like her, who like a rolly polly ploughed through the moments, the minutes, the hours, the days. In the meantime she made up her mind to enjoy every loving gesture and all the petting and pampering Cameron bestowed on her. Georgia wondered how she would put in her days, would she walk up and down the high street. Would she water some flowers, definitely not? Would she mope, well in fact she did none of these things because one ordinary night and when I say ordinary, I mean a sleepless, uncomfortable, unpleasant night, it came to a brief end. What she thought of as a normal pain in her back turned out in fact to be contractions. It had taken Georgia some time to cop-on to the fact that she was about to give birth.

In the meantime she walked up and down the floor, spent numerous moments in the loo but at last she just had to wake Cameron up and that took some time, it was like trying to wake Dracula in the middle of the day. When he finally came out of that stupor, Georgia made the big announcement, those words that send some men into a frenzy.

'It's time.'

Cameron answered, 'For what?'

Georgia felt like she was in a sci-fi movie and repeated the words, message to brain, message to brain. He slowly came around, the robot's words finally hit his brain cells, message understood. Up, dressed, keys for the car and bag for the hospital in hand. They were ready to roll, a terrible word but very suitable for the occasion. Just that one very important phone call to be made to the hospital, to let them know Cameron and mother to be, Georgia were on their way.

The car made its way to the hospital, there were lots and lots of potholes and bumps along the road and Georgia felt the car hadn't missed one bump, no not even one, she felt them like kicks to her back. On a normal day when you're not pregnant and you're in a Merc, you wouldn't even feel the slightest movement as the car glided along, but this day was different. Georgia felt like she was in an old banger with no suspension, going down a mountain, tipping every large stone on its way. It's funny that even though Georgia was in such agony her mind was focussed on one very important task she'd like to have completed before she came home with her new baby.

'Cameron' she said, 'remember I told you I want the Christmas Tree up and lit when I come home from the hospital. Oww, I really felt the car going over that stone, Cameron. I have laid out all the decorations, you can decorate it yourself or you can ask my friends to help you. I've already told them and they're all more than happy to oblige. Oww! Cameron you shouldn't have pulled the brake on so hard.'

It was a great relief to Cameron to finally entice Georgia to step out of that car with his help, meet that friendly porter, sit her into the waiting wheelchair and have someone take the pressure off him as he walked beside her straight to the delivery room. She insisted Cameron rub her back. Since all he wanted to do was please Georgia, he did everything that was asked of him until his hands were sore but still Georgia insisted he continue to massage. He wasn't a trained masseur, that was true but he certainly could hit the spot with the determination of a man obsessed.

CHAPTER 36

The time had come

Then it was time! With lots of encouragement and help from the doctor and midwife and many pushes and shoves their beautiful baby girl, Juliet, arrived on planet Earth. She emerged into this world with really no bother at all. She had beautiful slightly tanned, creamy skin just like Cameron's, dark hair, dark eyebrows and long lashes, beautiful little fingers that moved and even now had that artistic look about them, as for her tiny little toes they were just perfect. Cameron thought she smiled up at him as he held her in his arms for the first time. They looked just perfect together.

The two of them had become like all new parents as they sat together gazing in a trance at their little miracle. Juliet was the baby, you know, the one that everyone admires, with hair that looks as if it had been restyled for its entrance into this world, black and shiny with a full fringe that adorned her pretty little face. Georgia was exhausted but elated, she just couldn't wait to present her daughter to her mother and friends, but first there was one little thing Cameron was required to do by the mother of his new born baby girl. Georgia begged Cameron to purchase a pretty little pink baby grow, she had a white one and a yellow one but she didn't have a pink one and she wanted a pink blanket also, to let all their friends know Juliet, their little baby girl had arrived. She wanted nothing to be left to their imagination and although Cameron, at this point couldn't even remember his name or where the stores were, left and sometime later returned with a bouquet of pink and white roses, a pretty card, the pink blanket and that gorgeous baby grow.

Georgia had great fun watching as the nurse took orders from her and dressed the baby up in her new little outfit then placed her in the pink blanket and then into the little cot. The proud parents gazed down at their little gem. Cameron had informed all his and her friends by text message and had requested that they wait until tomorrow to come and visit. The thing Georgia liked most and had always known she wanted was a room all to herself, where she could get better in her own time with no one looking on, telling her how well she was doing. When you work with the public, you really understand how precious quiet time is and Georgia was enjoying her quiet time while their baby slept peacefully.

The proud parents were served tea and toast by the friendly staff. This was definitely magic toast, buttered to perfection and still warm. They nibbled the toast quietly and sipped the warm tea. It was a lovely little chunk of time for both of them. To be honest, they were both in shock. Cameron couldn't believe that he was now a father and responsible for a little tiny baby girl, he loved her name, the beautiful Juliet. He also couldn't believe he already felt that urge to protect her. It's funny how all these natural human feelings begin to show straight away when you become a parent. As for Georgia she could now only recall the pain of the last nine months both mental and physical. The mental pain was to do with Connie. She had carried that fear with her, the fear it might happen all over again and she just knew she could not have faced that. Luckily for Georgia she didn't have to face it, Juliet was as healthy as could be. This was the moment to thank Connie for staying by her side through the whole pregnancy and to confirm to her, in her heart she would always be her first child. She felt at ease with herself as she recalled the last nine months of her life that were now history and behind her once and for all. She wouldn't have missed any of it for the world even with all the pain. She was still very weak going in and out of hot and cold sweats. All she wanted was fresh air.

'Just let me breathe in fresh air, not this dry heat that always surrounds a hospital.'

With all the excitement Georgia thought the feeling she had of lightness in her head was normal. She was really unaware of what was happening to her body. The nurses seemed a little anxious so they decided to feed the baby themselves and put her down for the night. Nurse Aoife encouraged Cameron to go home as there wasn't anything else he could do.

'If you have a good night's sleep behind you, then tomorrow you could look after Juliet while your Georgia rests, now isn't that a good idea Cameron?'

A warm hug and a kiss was bestowed on Georgia, then she watched, her heart melting as she gazed at Cameron gently kissing his baby daughter on the forehead with tears of joy rolling down his face. He had to almost prise himself away from his little baby girl. As he walked out he looked back longingly and smiled, then off he went on his merry way, feeling like a schoolboy being told to stand in the corner, when all he wanted to do was stay in the room with Georgia and Juliet.

As soon as Cameron had left, Nurse Aoife came back into the room.

'Now Georgia' she said 'one of the doctors is coming up to see you, I just want to check to make sure everything is in order before I settle you down for the night.'

In walked Doctor Brian, a nice young man, who explained to Georgia he was checking her for a few different things as her temperature was a little bit erratic. By now Georgia was beginning to realise something was wrong, she felt freezing cold although her temperature was sky high. Doctor Brian took control and prescribed intravenous antibiotics. Straight away the nurses organised them and immediately Georgia began her treatment. Nurse Aoife advised Georgia to try and rest. There would be no need to worry about Juliet as the nursery nurse would look after her. Nurse Aoife assured Georgia she would be in and out to her. Doctor Brian would return periodically to keep her monitored through the night.

'Should I call Cameron?' enquired Georgia.

'No, not for now, we'll wait and see' said Nurse Aoife.

The night dragged on, who could imagine after nine months with no problems and a pretty straightforward birth that something like this could happen, but it did. Nurse Aoife was finishing her shift at 8am so she took the precaution of ringing Cameron at 6 o'clock to explain how the night had been for Georgia. It was explained to him on the phone, there was no need for him to rush in. The nursery nurse was taking care of the baby and the nurses and doctors had Georgia under observation. She was improving but she kept asking for Cameron and they felt it would be better for her recovery to have him by her side. When he arrived Georgia was talking gibberish from all the medication and upset. She was trying to ask Cameron to go and see Juliet but Cameron couldn't understand a word so Nurse Aoife translated.

'Georgia would like you to go and see your baby girl. If you stay here, I will push her cot into the room and you can both see her.'

'That's a good idea, nurse. That would make Georgia happier.'

So that's what happened, baby Juliet was pushed in, in her

cot, still looking beautiful and well fed. The nurse put the cot right beside Georgia's bed, Georgia put out her hand and placed it on the baby's tiny hand. Cameron could see the smile on Georgia's face and felt she was on the way back to full recovery. He sat beside the bed and watched Georgia as she fell into a very peaceful sleep. When the tea lady came around Cameron accepted and had some tea and toast, piping hot and delicious. Cameron didn't feel like celebrating because today was to be the day when all Georgia's friends were due to arrive. In Cameron's mind's eye he could see Coco, Tanya and Heidi gathered around the bed but unfortunately today the note on the door read 'No Visitors Allowed'.

When Georgia awoke, it was around ten in the morning, all the hot and cold sweats had gone and she felt more like her old self, if a lot weaker. She encouraged Cameron to go home and gather a few things for her because she thought she would only be in for two days and now she had just been told by Doctor Brian she would have to remain in hospital for another, at least, two to three days until her temperature had settled and all the dizzy spells had gone. She would remain on tablets until the prescription had finished and then come back for a check-up, she was still weak so she must take it easy for a few days. She felt very sore and uncomfortable but positive and looking forward to getting home. She knew the only thing to do was, do what she was told by the nurses and doctors. Georgia always found that very hard. The next day friends and family were allowed to visit through the day.

Cameron called everyone he needed to contact and gave them times that suited them. Nellie was the first to arrive. She couldn't get in the door fast enough in her high shoes. She couldn't get over how beautiful little Juliet was and once she held her in her arms she never wanted to let her go. That's the effect an infant has on everyone. Once her friends began to arrive Georgia felt a little bit like Rachel in Friends in the episode where the camera panned up on the friends' faces as they made cooing noises and sounds to her new-born infant but it was all in good taste. They came with beautiful gifts, she received so many and would have loved to open all of them but she was still very weak and decided to wait until everybody was gone and the room was quiet. Then she and Cameron could pass the time unwrapping the baby girl presents and savour each and every moment. Georgia also wanted to make sure she kept the cards with the presents so she would know exactly who, each and every present was from.

In the meantime, she chatted away until exhaustion hit her. Cameron escorted the last of the visitors from her room while Georgia began to fall into a peaceful sleep with a little smile on her face and memories of Tanya, Coco and Heidi kissing and hugging her and telling her how lucky she was to be a mum, but they didn't need to tell her that, she knew it already. It was the best feeling in the world to have this little pet depending on her, her very own baby doll. It was nice to be a family for the first time.

CHAPTER 37

Tomorrow
IF TOMORROW NEVER COMES

Tomorrow Cameron would arrive on the stroke of 10 to take Georgia and gorgeous baby Juliet home. The bungalow was already prepared. The little light in the baby's room that was left on and her little cot was the way Georgia left it, perfectly ready for her little angel. Now he was at the hospital. Inside he was feeling like a soldier outside Buckingham Palace on duty making sure to do everything right. In fact, little did Georgia know how hard Cameron had worked to make her final farewell to the hospital a pleasant one. He had the list, he checked it twice, yes everything was present and correct. He had the boxes of chocolates for each one of the nurses and tea ladies who looked after her, also the cards hand written by him when he was alone in the early hours of this morning. He also had a special present for her doctor that was given to Aoife to be delivered later. Now was the bigger task of dressing baby Juliet for her homecoming. Oh how Georgia would have loved to complete this task alone but she was too weak. Aoife listened to her instructions. She knew these special moments in a young woman's life can never be relieved or rehearsed. Cameron was over the moon with excitement when he looked down at their baby girl lying there.

'I've just realised she's very like me.'

'Yes Cameron, she really is like you, she has your sallow skin and gorgeous black hair, just like you.'

Nurse Aoife trying to keep things nice and steady butted in,

'Georgia, as time goes on you'll see a lot of things that resemble you, babies change so much.'

'Don't worry Aoife, I'm delighted she's like Cameron.'

This was all said while Aoife continued to get Georgia ready for going home. Poor Georgia was so weak she couldn't even pull her tights up. Cameron had tried to help her pull them up, now he was good at pulling them down when it suited him but pulling them up was definitely not his forte. Nurse Aoife took over, Georgia was ready to sit into the wheelchair and be wheeled to the hospital door, while Cameron carried the wicker basket with baby Juliet inside. In the car, as weak as she was, her mind had turned to home mode.

'Cameron, did you get the Christmas decorations up? Did you buy a pudding and a cake? Did you get all the groceries ordered?

'Holy Jesus' said Cameron in his most religious voice (not) 'You'll have to wait and see Georgia, it will be a surprise.'

In his head he was thinking Christ, I hope Nellie and her three friends have completed the task. I pray to God the lights are on and the decorations are all up the way she wants them, or my life won't be worth living.

Home safe, Cameron opened the door and there was Georgia's mum, Nellie, waiting inside. He carried baby Juliet over the threshold just like he did Georgia, a couple of months earlier and Nellie helped Georgia into the hall. Georgia limped her way to the sitting room, where she was dazzled by the lights of the Christmas tree and the sparkle of the decorations and the boxes of presents underneath the tree. She couldn't have been happier as on this winter day the reflection of the lights hit her face and gave it a little Christmas glow. First things first, a bottle for Juliet, of course a change of nappy and then back into her wicker basket. Then Nellie took over, she had the kettle already boiled and a fried breakfast cooked, including the ould fried bread. Everyone tucked in and enjoyed the best brekkie ever.

Cameron insisted Georgia go straight to bed. She didn't argue, she knew she needed sleep and rest. She would have loved to sit by the fire and cradle her baby. It was nice to be alone, no nurses, no doctors, no tea ladies, no friends, just Cameron, Georgia and Nellie. They were so excited but Georgia knew she would have to stay in bed and rest and Daddy Cameron would have to take things into his own hands, with the help of Nellie, and look after their baby daughter Juliet. Then it began, the routine, checking the clock to make sure the bottles were on time, listening for her cries if they left the room, with the help of the baby monitor.

Georgia did her best to remember she had to continue the antibiotics and for her to realise she still wasn't very well and needed a lot of rest, that's where her mum came in. Ever happy to oblige, Nellie moved into the spare room for two weeks. She felt she needed to put a time limit on it or maybe she'd get too comfortable and overstay her welcome. Two weeks was long enough for Georgia to get a lot better and into a routine. Nellie knew from experience that is one of the hardest things to do. Sometimes new mothers can be upset if they feel anyone is interfering or trying to be very bossy. Nellie knew how to stay out of the way and not invade the privacy of the new parents. She was just there to assist and make the transition to parenthood a little easier.

When the two weeks were over Georgia felt almost back to herself. Cameron was still making and taking notes to do with Georgia and Juliet. Nellie was preparing the house for Christmas Day. Georgia had been so focused on her game before the birth of her baby girl, she had all of her Christmas cards written, now her mum posted them. Hopefully they would arrive on time for the celebrations. It was at this time Nellie was meant to vacate the house but at Georgia's request she decided to stay over for Christmas. She was used to making Christmas dinners, cooking the turkey, making sure the roast potatoes were crispy. Nellie was a vital part of Cameron and Georgia's Christmas. She helped in a lot of ways but mostly she kept the two of them sane as they were still navigating their way.

Their bungalow was so beautiful and such a happy place to be in for Christmas. Tanya, Heidi and Coco were in and out all the time and Maisie Coyne arrived with her Christmas presents for Juliet. Beautiful cardigans in peach, white and she added two pink ones. For the pièce de resistance, two amazing Christmas cardigans, one red with tiny white snowmen and one white with reindeers, two Christmas hats to match and of course, bootees. Sure her poor fingers must have been worn away from all the knitting she was doing over the last few months. Maisie really deserved the name Auntie Maisie. On Christmas morning the whole entourage walked to the chapel nearby. Cameron pushed the pram and Georgia walked happily beside him holding onto the side. It took them ages to get to the church with neighbours stopping to admire the little red cardigan and the pretty Silver Cross pram. They enjoyed the Children's Mass, very sweet, lovely and holy and when they finally came home they enjoyed, courtesy of Nellie a great big brekkie. For Christmas dinner Nellie looked after everything with the help of Cameron. They had the most magical Christmas in this beautiful, enchanted bungalow. When all the presents were given out, all the meals eaten, all the friends gone home, including Auntie Maisie and all the lights turned off, just leaving the Christmas lights on Georgia, Cameron and baby Juliet sat in the room just lit by the Christmas Tree and thanked God, Nellie and all the friends for everything they'd done for them over this beautiful Christmas. It was time for Nellie to leave and go back home but when she did she left them a little better organised and a little wiser, to face a new year with new challenges and wonderful memories made.

CHAPTER 38

Daddy's girl

Cameron took Juliet's hand in his, It was so, so tiny. Georgia just had to capture the moment in a photograph. He looked so lovely holding his new baby daughter. In the hospital Cameron had been shy, self-conscious and almost afraid to hold her. To him she seemed like a china doll that could break into smithereens, so he left most of the holding and petting to Georgia but now he was in his own territory and so at ease, all his self-consciousness had gone. Cameron was really coming into his own, he was beaming, Georgia could see that new Daddy look on his face, she just had to capture it. Click... She looked at her screen, she had captured it, that precious moment. Such a nice sight, a new Dad beaming with pride, it was a moment to be savoured. Juliet was such a good little baby, she hardly cried at all except when she was really tired or really hungry and this made things so much easier for the new parents.

Georgia hadn't been outside the door for 2 weeks, certainly a record for her as she never stayed indoors for long but today was different, they were taking Juliet out in her new pram for the first time. Well, it wasn't a new pram exactly, in fact it was one of those old Silver Cross prams with great suspension, and after all the months of her wondering what type of pram they would purchase, would it be a bug-a-boo or would it be a silver cross, in the end she had both Silver Cross and Bug-a-Boo. The silver cross pram was a present from one of her three best friends, Coco. She had very gracefully accepted Georgia and Cameron's request to be Godmother. It had been a hard decision for Georgia because she had equally loved all three friends, so to be fair to all of them this was how the decision was made. Coco was the first one Georgia had met at kindergarten, decision made by pecking order worked to keep them all happy. Coco had been wracking her brain trying to come up with something unique, a very special present for her best friend. It wasn't exactly new, in fact it was an antique, it had been her pram when she was a baby.

Her mum had treated it so well, she packed it away with love. It was so well looked after you would honestly think it was brand new. It had been wrapped in almost cotton wool and put away for all those years. Coco was giving it to Georgia but only on loan.

'I have one request, please Georgia. I hope you don't mind me asking. Would it be ok if I took the baby for a jaunt in my old pram and her new pram? You can come too. You see I just want to experience what my mother must have felt like pushing me in that beautiful, Rolls Royce, Silver Cross pram.'

'I will grant you your wish Coco, I can't wait to be holding the side of the pram with my baby cuddled up inside as it glides up past the houses on my street.'

Georgia had purchased her bug-a-boo and that would be the one she would use once her baby's bones had got stronger. It would fit nicely into the boot of her car. For now she was as proud as punch of her Silver Cross pram, it was blue and white. Juliet was dressed in a pink dress, pink cardigan, little bootees and pretty pink hat. Both parents were very happy with their choice of clothes for Juliet. Cameron could not believe he was taking such a big part in choosing baby's outfits. First Georgia put two warm baby blankets over her pretty baba and then pink satin covers, soft and billowy. Georgia was taking no chances. Thank God she had the Silver Cross pram as the suspension was fantastic, it just glided over the many bumps on her road (which she honestly hadn't noticed until now). She didn't want to pull any of her baby's little muscles.

Now you would think taking a baby out for the first time was a pretty simple task but not for Georgia and Cameron, they had never pushed a pram before and were very self-conscious but excited. It was time, a great moment for the very proud parents. She pushed and he steered, while every neighbour, people Georgia had never spoken to before, stopped the couple to gaze into the perambulator and look at the little holy picture that hung down from the hood and admire Juliet who lay there sleeping. What is it about a new baby that makes people smile and go gaga? Whatever it was, was infectious, everyone was smiling, people coming towards them and people leaving them. This baby was doing wonders for the whole neighbourhood. Georgia was feeling hopeful they might make a few new friends along the way. Babies give you a new purpose in life, far away from waxing, massaging and all the other beauty treatments that helped her make lots of money, right now she wasn't making a penny but she was happier than she'd ever been before.

CHAPTER 39

Maisie Coyne

'Oh Georgia, I nearly forgot to tell you I had a phone call from Maisie today. She rang to ask how we were getting on with Juliet and Georgia, I did something I normally wouldn't do, I invited her over for tea, well actually for dinner, tomorrow, Sunday. She's so excited, sorry I didn't tell you earlier.'

'I can't wait to see her, Cameron.' said Georgia 'She has a special place in my heart and I'm sure in yours. Maisie was the only one who knew our story almost from the start. Remember Cameron when she caught me sneaking out of your room. She was the one who made tea for me, in the parlour when I couldn't stop the tears flowing and she always seemed to understand what we, as a couple were going through. I remember her saying to me, you should run from a man of the cloth. He will never be happy, if he stays in the monastery he will be sorry he stayed and if he goes with you he'll be sorry he left. But here we are today, with our new baby girl, both of us over the moon with happiness. I know Maisie will be happy she was wrong. I'm happy we had the courage to take this road, turns out we were right, both of us made the decision. It was a good one Cameron.'

The smile on Cameron's face faded.

'Gosh Georgia I never knew Maisie said that to you.'

'Well she did, Cameron, but in fairness she was just trying to protect me from being hurt.'

'She was a brave woman' said Cameron 'to say that to you.'

'She was a staunch woman, Cameron. We had better have a hearty meal for her tomorrow or God knows what her verdict will be on us as a couple. Yes, she might say we can't cook. It has to be a meal fit for a farmer. It has to be a good pot roast to keep her strength up. Don't worry we'll have a pot roast, it's a hearty meal fit for a farmer and his wife, easy to make and sure Maisie will love it. Did you give her a time, Cameron?'

'No, I never mentioned any time.'

'Then, just let her arrive when she arrives. My mum is also coming for dinner, the two ladies will have great fun together discussing life's ups and downs.'

On Sunday morning Cameron was up like a lark, peeling potatoes, cutting up turnips, slicing carrots and putting on the pot roast. Georgia's mum, Nellie arrived carrying a huge bouquet of mixed wild flowers, all Georgia's favourite colours, pinks, lilacs and blues. Her arrival was followed swiftly by Maisie Coyne. In her arms she carried a beautiful big pink presentation box. She handed it to Georgia. Over a glass of champagne the four of them celebrated, yet again, the new arrival. Nellie placed the flowers in one of Georgia's large vases. She moved them this way and that way until she was satisfied her display was perfect.

Georgia couldn't wait to open the present from Maisie Coyne. It was so easy to open, there were no bags or paper cluttering this present, just the big pink presentation box, gorgeous. This box would be their treasure chest where they would hold their treasure trove. It was big enough to hold lots of things. Georgia already had her mind made up as to what would go into this box. It would contain in future, all the small things belonging to Juliet, her first tooth, her little curl, magically contained in this beautiful box. But, first she would have to take the lid off and see what lay inside. Georgia and Cameron didn't know what to expect but to say they were surprised was putting it mild. Lying on top of a layer of pink silk was a statue of Our Blessed Lady.

An absolutely beautiful statue, not one of those ones that were dragged and the face long, this was pretty, it had a woman's figure. They loved it, it would be put in pride of place by the side of Juliet's bed and they hoped in the future Juliet would always keep that statue in her life.

'Take that piece of silk off the top, there's more underneath.'

There lay the prettiest pink dress with smocking all across the top. The prettiest cardigan ever, white with pink flowers, little white tights and in the corner of the box lay a smaller box, it looked like an old fashioned jewellery box.

Cameron had the honour of opening this. He was jumping up and down with excitement, all these things contained in one big box, out came the last and smallest one, like a burst of beauty. He opened it, there were two things inside, a beautiful little rose gold bracelet and the tiniest little necklace. Juliet was far too young for necklaces, Maisie already knew that but she also knew Georgia and guessed she would let Juliet wear it one time, for her Christening. After that it could be kept as a memory and what a memory Maisie was making for Juliet to enjoy at her eighteenth birthday.

The pot roast turned out to be absolutely delicious, falling to pieces on their plates, the vegetables were magnifique and the dessert courtesy of Nellie, Georgia's favourite, chocolate bombs, delicious. Over dinner Cameron and Georgia had one question for Maisie which they had both discussed last night.

'Maisie, would you like to be Juliet's adopted auntie? We really need you to be and want you to be, because you know her mother and father more than most people know them. You have been the kindest person to us when we really needed kindness. You were there for us every step of the way as we navigated our future. Really, only for you Juliet might never have appeared on this earth. We can't think of a better name for you, you're officially the baby's auntie' agreed the happy pair.

Maisie was silenced with emotion, tears streamed down her face.

There were hugs and kisses all round. Nellie was delighted to have another auntie in the family, one that really looked like an auntie, really huggable and lovable. Just the extra ingredient Juliet would need as she grows up. What a lovely Sunday this had turned out to be.

Just before Maisie left, there was one more drink on the menu, pink champagne. They'd had one at the beginning of the meal, now they were having one at the end of the meal, to celebrate the new auntie. Cameron handed Maisie a box. This was their turn to do something nice for a woman from a different world to their world. This time Maisie was flabbergasted as she undid a turquoise ribbon that decorated the white box. Very slowly she opened it as if it was very precious. Inside was a gorgeous, pretty rose gold watch attached to the prettiest rose gold bracelet, it had that olde worlde charm, perfect for Maisie. Cameron put it on her wrist and clicked it closed. Maisie gazed at the watch, speechless, for what seemed like ages. Cameron, Georgia and Nellie didn't know whether she liked it or didn't like it. Not a word was coming from her lips. Nellie saved the moment.

'You love it don't you, Maisie?'

'Honestly' said Maisie 'I have never had a present like this in my whole life and nobody has ever made me feel as welcome as you three today.'

Nellie was delighted she was included in the special three, the three musketeers.

'We're happy you're happy,' said Nellie.

The day had turned out to be a perfect one and now with

Nellie and Maisie gone home, Cameron sitting, feeding Juliet with her lovely bottle, Georgia kicked off her shoes, sat back and flicked through the Hello magazine. What a lovely end to a lovely day.

CHAPTER 40

The final straw

Happy go lucky Georgia was still on maternity leave, alone in the house, perfect. Juliet fed and fast asleep, all her baby clothes purring away in the washing machine on a gentle wash. Georgia asked herself a question, should we get a dog? That would complete our little family. Followed by the doubts, you're gone mad, Georgia Brown, you don't need a dog, concentrate on your flower patch, it can't bark back.

She almost missed that call, so engrossed was she in her thoughts and the peace she was experiencing all around her bungalow and in her heart.

'Jesus, it's my phone.'

Georgia rushed and grabbed it out of her bag. All she was thinking of was keeping the silence in the house and praying the ring of the phone wouldn't wake Juliet.

'Hello' she said in the quietest voice ever.

'Hello Georgia, it's Ross.'

Yes! That was Ross, quick and to the point. No clearing of his throat before he spoke.

'I wonder if you could meet up with me, Georgia? Could you make it a priority?'

She could tell by the tone of his voice, it was certainly an urgent request.

Straight away she could hear the words of a song, sung by Reo Speedwagon coming into her head, *Keep On Lovin You.* The line that brought this song to her mind was: *You Should Have Known By the Tone of My Voice.*

She knew by the tone of his voice this was really urgent. She also knew this was the something she had avoided broaching, like a lot of things in Georgia's life she put them on the back boiler and hoped they would go away. In haste Georgia fixed the meeting time for 8pm knowing Cameron would be home from work to look after Juliet.

'I'll book a table for two, in the little bistro on South William Street, if that's ok for you Georgia.'

Gosh, he's well organised, thought Georgia.

She parked her car in the car park, stepped across the road and straight into the friendly bistro where Ross sat fiddling with a napkin, looking slightly uneasy. Georgia slid around the little table and sat opposite him, in this packed little bistro. Georgia needn't have worried if anyone recognised her. She had bluntly told Cameron she was meeting Ross tonight, he wanted to talk things over with her.

'I'm glad you're finally meeting, Ross. I've been wanting to talk to you about it for ages but I just couldn't seem to broach the subject. Please do your best to have your divorce sorted out. Now that we have Juliet, it's time we moved on with our relationship. As long as you're married to Ross, I can't marry you. So believe it or not I'm very happy that you're meeting him tonight' said Cameron.

Who could have imagined Cameron would be pleased Georgia was meeting Ross.

Food hadn't really passed her lips that day so by now she was really hungry (wall falling). She ordered Carbonara, Ross ordered Spaghetti Bolognese. In moments, the order was there before them, piping hot and delicious. Georgia was so hungry she just attacked the Carbonara and detached it from the plate and into her tummy in what seemed like a flash in the pan, when she finally looked up from her food to take a breath, and sip on some ice cold still water, she realised Ross's food was not having the same effect on him. There were times when he endeavoured to lift the spaghetti from the plate, twist it around on his fork but for some unknown reason the spaghetti still managed to remain on the plate. He was so upset he just couldn't eat. Eventually he put the fork down, looked directly at Georgia and announced:

'The first thing I want to say to you is congratulations on your new baby Georgia, I wish it was mine, ours.' He said quietly almost to himself. 'Our lives took a different path.'

This was followed by a deadly silence. Georgia almost blurted out and with every moment that passed it got harder not to say the words, Ross I lost a baby a while ago. Her name was Connie. It could have been yours. The enormity of that thought and the words from Ross brought her back in time. Because of Juliet's birth and the happiness she felt with Cameron, all because of Juliet, she never gave Ross a second thought. Ross's feelings had until this very moment evaded her. She'd been living in cuckoo land. As usual reality hit home, Georgia was a mess, she felt her world was falling down around her. She looked at him, she had left him a broken man, but now she knew he was making a life for himself.

'Juliet's a lovely baby Ross, she takes up all of my time, but she makes me feel as a woman, whole.'

'It must be lovely for you both.' said Ross, staring back at her.

She knew in some ways at this very moment he hated her. He had come here tonight to say his piece. He would not leave without completing his promise to himself.

'I have loved being married to you for most of the time, even though it was a brief encounter, it has taken me a long time to realise we were obviously not meant to be together. It's time to do something about it.' (He smiled the saddest smile and continued) 'Now that you're with someone else and have a new baby, it's time we made a decision. I'm sure you'll be quite pleased to know I've already been to a solicitor.' Ross continued 'If you give me the name of your solicitor, I'll have the divorce papers sent over. All you have to do is to make an appointment with your solicitor, sign the necessary papers and soon we'll be out of each other's hair forever.'

Georgia's look of astonishment must have been very obvious, even though she knew this conversation had to be on their agenda tonight. The bloody idiot was almost struck dumb. (How could she be feeling like this? She brought this all on herself. He was right, she did have a new life and it didn't include him. It was no wonder he wanted closure.)

'Well, Ross I still have the same solicitor as I always had. You have her address so please just send all the information to her and I will sign on the dotted line.'

Georgia began to cry. She didn't know where all these tears were coming from but they came from her eyes like a waterfall. She just nodded her head, unable to speak another word. He was doing what he had to do, keeping his pride and making the final move to change his life.

'If you need any help in the future, I'll always be there for you, but just right now I have to make the proper decision for both of us and I feel this is it.'

There was nothing he could add to that sentence. He had said everything in such a short space of time. Ross produced the papers from his briefcase. Georgia continued crying. Where did she go wrong, acting the idiot and falling in love with a deacon, Cameron, who at the time, was unobtainable?

'Ross, I wish I'd listened to the wise words of Maisie Coyne. I know you don't know who she is but she was a very wise woman and recently she has been a very important part of my life. Her wise words were, girl, just stop dreaming of a different future, hold the future you now have in both hands and continue on your journey. If I'd heeded Maisie's words, Ross, I would still be with you, loving you a little more every day, we would still be happy. At this moment I feel empty.'

'So do I' said Ross 'and what a horrible feeling. Why didn't you listen to that lady? She made perfect sense.'

She could see anger in his eyes. Ross steadied himself, regained control, focussed on what he had come here to say. Every move he made and every word he uttered was rehearsed, automatic, Georgia shook her head.

'I'm sorry Ross, I started this horrible episode in both our lives, I never wanted my life to go like this.'

Georgia wanted so much for Ross to say something, anything. Instead the silence was deafening. Ross lifted his hand to hold hers but he stopped, he didn't want Georgia to feel he was needy and wanted her back, he wanted her to know this was strong Ross starting to stand up for himself. It was that strength that Georgia always loved. She knew no matter how bad things were he would always stand in her corner, all she would have to do was ask. Back in their lovely bungalow Georgia had Cameron and Juliet waiting for her return, why was she so upset? The reason... the way she saw her life was in little groups, her friends, her mum, even Maisie Coyne was part of those groups, then there was Cameron, Juliet, her pretty bungalow, her new life, then there was Ross who had been a very big part of her life, the one she'd really given her heart to and taken vows at the wedding altar with. She loved the life she now had but at times like this she missed the life she used to have. The harsh reality was she now felt she was in a dark corner, with no one there but her, stupid Georgia. Just now, Georgia wanted to forget she ever knew Cameron and wished Juliet was her and Ross's baby. Oh, what a price they had both paid all because of Georgia's mistake. She'd lost a wonderful, strong, loving individual, who she still loved deeply.

It was her who had started this whole miserable journey with Cameron that day when by chance their paths crossed. How could she have known back then, that meeting would mark the beginning of the end for a marriage she was so happy in and lead to this moment? There was a little voice in her head saying just tell him you love him, shout it out, she couldn't do that.

'Georgia, Are you OK? You're looking very pale.'

'I'm OK Ross.' She blurted out. 'May I excuse myself for a moment? I need to go to the ladies to powder my nose.'

She grabbed her bag and her phone from the table and scurried along into the ladies room. As she closed the door behind her and stood leaning against it the tears continued to flow. She sobbed and sobbed. One of the young girls fixing her make up at the mirror seemed very concerned as she asked in a broken English accent:

'Can I do anything to help you? Please sit down on this chair for just a few minutes and I'll get you some cold water. Take some deep breaths. Have you anyone you'd like me to call?'

'No thank you.' sobbed Georgia 'I will be alright. It's just a sad time in my life, I'm breaking up with my husband. He's sitting out there and I don't want him to know I'm crying like this.'

'If you like, I'll help you to freshen your makeup. First you'll need some water on your face and I'll put some cold water on one of those hand wipes and I'll put it on the back of your neck. It'll help you cool down. Now, don't you feel better? Where's your make up? Let me help you.'

And so this angel in a Prada suit, with a nice crispy white shirt, applied fresh make up onto Georgia's warm, tearful skin. She even fixed her lipstick and rubbed a bit of the lipstick on her cheeks to give her a blush. Then she stood with her for a few minutes until Georgia had composed herself and was ready to return to her table and finish this meeting. In that moment Georgia's memory drifted back to the evening walking towards the Trocadero, as happy as a little lark with her wedding photographs tucked safely away in her bag, all ready for their big showing. Perhaps it was fate, the night that changed her happy life.

She said 'Thank you for helping me. You're a real earth angel.' and walked out to where Ross was seated.

All she could feel were tears and sadness inside. A little voice in her head gave her the advice she really needed to hear right now, pull yourself together Georgia, give yourself time because as they say time heals everything. A final decision had to be made sometime. You could never have made that decision yourself. Thank God Ross has taken control for both of us. She continued to take deep breaths, slow, very slow, inhale, exhale, inhale, exhale, keep going Georgia, she said to herself. Eventually calmness began to return.

She wondered what had made Ross take this final decision. If he loved me so much why hadn't he fought to keep me? Perhaps Ross has a girl tucked away somewhere just waiting to be unveiled, something must be making him see things this straight, maybe it was the need for change or final stability in his topsy-turvy world. For whatever reason Georgia would give him his moment. Ross sent a text, paid the bill, stood up, donned his heavy coat, it was cold outside. He kissed her gently on the cheek and he was gone. She felt that spark that was always between her and Ross, like someone had ignited a fire the day they met and it refused to be completely extinguished.

He walked to the restaurant door. The doorman opened the door, Georgia felt the cold wind sweeping through the restaurant. The door of the restaurant was still closing ever so slowly with the help of the doorman. She was happy when the door finally closed. Ross was no longer there, he had left her, numb. Little did she know he had to leave quickly before his tears began to spill. If the truth was known he was broken-hearted and even though he had something to look forward to, the only thing he ever really wanted to look forward to was a happy married life with Georgia. It was almost over, he almost had closure.

Her heart pounded in her chest, she looked around at the waiters, wondering could they hear it too. Of course, she knew she was just being silly, these things were happening inside, she alone was suffering and she had brought all of the suffering on herself. Georgia remained seated in total disbelief, wondering how Ross could have walked away and left her, the trouble with Georgia was she always thought Ross and her were a complete unit. He could never live without her and she could never live without him. It was in this moment she realised how much she had depended on him. She didn't need his money, all she needed was his strength and knowing that he understood the way her mind worked. Her needs, her welfare was all he ever worried about until now, until this minute, now he was almost free. Was he feeling as the words of the song says, *A dusty road going down the highway?*

She had burned all her bridges, ruined all her chances of ever returning to Ross but why would she want to when she had a lovely life with Cameron now? It all came down to one thing, in some weird way Georgia still thought she had control over Ross, this evening he had proved her wrong. The world she had with Ross was now completely gone, disintegrated right before her eyes. She was always the one who called the shots and in her mind had total control of most situations. She'd spent many months analysing it all, thinking the ultimate decision was up to her but No, for once Ross had taken control and taken things completely out of her hands, in the end, he had made the decision for both of them. I suppose someone had to be decisive, this was his show and good for him to take back control, he was allowed to call it any which way he liked and he had.

Little did Georgia know this poor man was shattered completely. He just wanted to run back and beg her to go right back to when they got married and just continue the loving relationship he cherished, but that was all gone now that he knew Georgia had a baby with another man. How could there be any chance for the two of them? Even so, maybe he thought she would have run out after him and begged him for forgiveness but neither one did anything. No shouting I love you from the rafters.

Outside in a car parked around the corner from the restaurant sat someone who saw his text and had just arrived to pick him up. Someone he'd grown quite close to in the last few months, someone who was a friend for now but if he could manage to lift all his barriers she could be something more. He hadn't told her why he was meeting Georgia tonight, she hadn't asked, he just asked her to pick him up afterwards. He wanted to keep all of this to himself for the next while until he could get his head around it. In a way he was biding time. They were both somehow still connected and although they didn't know it, their bond would be the hardest bond to break. (If it was ever possible to even break it!)

Georgia was in no fit state to leave the restaurant so she ordered a Cappuccino. It seemed the waiter was tuned in to the problem in his section, so no sooner had the order been placed than the Cappuccino was there sitting in front of her. The waiter smiled sheepishly, almost pityingly, then he backed away into obscurity. Georgia sat sipping the Cappuccino alone, until all that was left was the white froth that once decorated the brim of the cup oh so prettily. Ross had paid the bill, all she had to do was pay for the Cappuccino, leave a tip for the understanding waiter who had looked after her so well during the meal and now declined charging for the cappuccino. Georgia was still feeling Ross's kiss on her cheek but she heard no words of goodnight, goodbye or see you sometime in the future, nothing.

She pressed the fob, click, opened the door and stepped into her car, turned the key in the ignition and began the short journey back home. In the calmness of the night and the quietness of the car, her mind began wandering. Thinking back to her past and knowing in her heart that anyone who would hear her story would say, just like she would say, what kind of woman is she? How could she have the right to be sad because her husband is divorcing her, when she was the one who had the affair and caused the whole mess in the first place? How could she be so remorseful now when it was too late? Question: who would feel sorry for her? Answer: No one, unless they had this challenge in their own lives. Sometimes we all fall from grace, people in glass houses shouldn't throw stones and in some ways we're all in glass houses. How judgemental are we human beings, including me? Georgia thought, no one has the right.

CHAPTER 41

Return to the happy bungalow

She made her way home. Georgia couldn't lift her spirits, she had thought that once she walked through the door of her gorgeous bungalow all the feelings she had would disappear, how wrong she was. Cameron took one look at her, he didn't say a word, he just handed poor Georgia a cup of hot chocolate, a biscuit and sat with her very quietly. They stared at the flames disappearing up the chimney.

'Cameron there is nothing to say I just feel so sad. I'm very happy with my life now but I don't know if it will ever feel completely right. Now there is no going back. As an old friend of mine used to say, it's onwards and upwards. I can't believe I'm saying all these things to you. I would never want to change the life we share now, you have to believe I'm so totally committed to everything we have together and I want you to know, I fall in love with you a little bit more with every day we spend together. I'm totally in love with you but Ross was such a huge part of my life. I would never want to change the life we share, I just felt so sad when he said how he wished we had achieved more in the time we had been together.'

Georgia couldn't say the words Ross had said to her, she never told Cameron the words he actually said, how he wished Juliet was their baby. Those words would be too harsh, she just couldn't say them because in that moment she had entertained that thought. Cameron left Georgia to herself that night, he had questions to ask like, had Ross asked for a divorce? Had he told her in spite of everything he still loved her? No, all his questions were for another day. Would she have answers for his questions? He hoped so. Georgia lay in bed, her body felt numb but did she sleep? Yes.

A new day, a new chapter. She convinced herself Ross had done the right thing, cutting all ties with her. He really had to do it knowing Georgia as he did, knowing decisions weren't her strong point, so he had taken matters into his own hands and sorted the problem out for them. There was no time to look back. In that moment she remembered that gentle kiss on the cheek from Ross and she also had a very clear vision of Ross as he left the restaurant (not looking back). Last night she felt sure Ross had made the right decision but now she could feel her lips quiver as the reality hit home, how final things were between her and her husband (Had she any right to call him her husband?). When would she get the letter from the solicitor to come in and sign the papers and get everything done and dusted? Her heart was beating like a drum. She began to hyper-ventilate, Panic surrounded her being, to think a marriage that had started so well could end so bad.

She felt frightened and alone, up until now Georgia had always felt in control of the situation. She must have been delusional to have convinced herself that somehow Ross would always come back to her with just a click of her fingers. She had left him in mid-air, with him not knowing what would happen next, but now it was her who knew what would happen next and she didn't like it. The loneliness she felt was unbearable and all self-inflicted. She should have been stronger and walked away on that night when she met Cameron and went home to the warm arms of her gorgeous young husband but the kamikaze, adventurous side of her needed the challenge and just look where that challenge had taken her. Now she felt as if Cameron was an intruder, a nothing in her life. Cameron could see she was in a reflective mood, he sensed that little bit of tension.

In his innocence he thought it was just Georgia working things out in her mind after her meeting with Ross. Since it was the weekend and he was free he did the changing of the nappies, feeding Juliet and all the other little things that needed to be done. Georgia continued to wallow in self-pity, she'd never been like this before in all her life. As the time passed she began to realise this swing of moods wasn't brought on by post natal depression, this was in fact, Georgia dealing with something equivalent to a bereavement. Ross's words, *I wish Juliet was ours,* had left her completely shattered. If she said those words in her head once she said them a thousand times. She just couldn't move forward, she needed someone to talk to but who could she talk to? She remembered something one of her friends, Heidi, had said, 'when you can't cope and you want to talk something through, I always feel you've got three choices:

1. Talk to your mother or your best friend, (someone who can keep a secret) but most of all someone who under-stands you.

2. Write everything down as if you're writing a letter to yourself, read it through, understand it, come to your own conclusion then burn it.

3. Find a time when there is no one else around, sit down in front of the mirror and talk it through with just you, in person and your mirror image staring back at you.

When can you get more honest answers than when you are looking straight at the culprit, victim, the fool, you, yourself. Sometimes talking things through with just yourself, getting no reaction from anyone, only your own reaction and after all it's only you who knows how you feel. It is the best way to understand your problems. (In the end you're left to solve your own problems yourself anyway) Which choice did she take?

First she worked it out, If I confide in my mum or Heidi they'd be worried for me and it'd be written all over their faces, I'd get continuous phone calls checking on my mood swings.

X... No to that.

Georgia felt with a baby to look after she really had no time for writing letters to herself that also was a big:

X... No, not for me.

√... 3 is perfect and right now. I'm going to confront my demons and myself through that mirror.

Cameron was in work, Juliet was fed, washed, dressed, asleep.

There she sat looking at her reflection in the mirror. She looked absolutely awful, indeed a sorry sight, her eyes were dead in her head. She had to admit to herself, this one time she had to be truly honest if she wanted to move forward because in her head she feared if she couldn't come to terms with this problem she would end up in hospital. That was how bad she felt. Now it was stalemate. She'd had a rough ride in the last few years. This was the first time she had the determination to try and sort herself out. She had first to face herself in the mirror and look face to face at the one who had inflicted everything that had happened to her in the last few years.

Today was Monday, the start of Cameron's school week. When he closed the door and left for work their bungalow felt insulated, warm, cosy and a very happy place to live in. Quiet enough for Georgia to do what she was doing right now, sitting in front of the mirror trying her best to come to terms with the good, the bad and the ugly results of her actions, that had brought her to this place. While Juliet slept peacefully Georgia had time to do what she needed to do and had to do, because she wasn't a happy bunny. She'd known that once she began to blame Cameron completely for this and not taking responsibility for herself she was on a downward spiral.

Falling in love with him (not his fault)

Leaving Ross for him, again not his fault - (her decision)

Living with him, buying a house with him was (their decision).

Having a baby with him was their decision. (Just happened)

Now everything was crystal clear, as an adult Georgia had to take responsibility for her actions - actions have reactions, she was painfully aware that was true. It seemed to Georgia, in this moment, that she was just a selfish bitch. Always only thinking of her needs, all of this had to change if she was to get back to her happy place in life. She had written these three truths on her mirror in red lipstick. Now the truth was her image was now looking back at her, straight in the eye. She couldn't look away. She continued to write just two words, actions/reactions and that's exactly what had happened, she had acted and had to suffer all the reactions as a consequence of her decisions. She used to feel the secret life she was leading with Cameron, while she was still with Ross, was her secret, her view at the time was if no one knew, then no one would get hurt. How wrong was she, Ross got hurt.

She was grateful for the space and time she now had to talk this through with her, the only one who knew the complete story. Once she had, at least some of the answers she could talk everything through with Cameron, when her brain wasn't topsy-turvy and she was heading back home on the yellow brick road. She needed to become more like the lion in the Wizard of Oz and somehow muster the strength from somewhere to get back on the straight and narrow.

She began to sing the words from the Wizard of Oz.

Follow the Yellow Brick Road
Follow the Yellow Brick Road
Follow, Follow, Follow, Follow
Follow the Yellow Brick Road

Am I going mad?

Georgia didn't know how but facing one problem at a time and working through it, she began to understand a lot about herself. For the first time she was honest, with this young lady looking back at her. She admitted to herself where she went wrong. Eventually, slowly, very slowly Georgia began to admit her faults. There were a lot of tears, soul searching, recognising her flaws and taking the decision to move on learn from her mistakes, stop hating herself, blaming herself, the truth was, this was all past tense now, well and truly behind her.

Conclusion: There is a reason for everything.

My future starts now.

Decision: When I begin to doubt myself in the future, I will draw an imaginary line between me and my insecurities.

CHAPTER 42

Questions answered at The Shamrock Hotel

As they say another day another dollar and the only way to earn that extra dollar was to pull her thoughts together and head to work. She was taking things slowly, doing short days for the moment working them around Cameron's hours, massage, eyebrow tint, leg and bikini wax, just busy, busy, busy. In between appointments Georgia had 15 minutes to relax, grab a quick mug of hot chocolate and catch up on any gossip the other beauticians would like to share with her. Then she was back home opening the front door of her gorgeous bungalow, straight into the kitchen. Juliet lay fast asleep in her pram, Cameron looked all flustered and secretive as he hurriedly put his phone away. She would have loved to ask him who the phone call was from but thank God she didn't. He explained everything to her over a cup of coffee while Juliet remained fast asleep.

'Remember Georgia, I told you all about my friend Mikie's hotel, The Shamrock?'

'Yes' said Georgia 'You said it was all beautiful and gorgeous. It's on my bucket list. I can't wait to stay there.'

'Well your wish is my command, Georgia. I've booked us in for a night. Now don't get all nervous, your mum is minding Juliet, here in our own home. We're leaving early on Saturday morning and returning late on Sunday night. The journey will take about an hour from Dublin. We'll have lots of time to relax, just the two of us. If there are any problems with Juliet it will only take us one hour to get back. Nellie, your mum has promised to keep us informed by text message all the way through.'

Georgia was so excited and at the same time anxious for her new baby who she didn't want to leave. She didn't feel like going anywhere, her spirit was still very low. Should she go or should she not go? When she thought about it logically she came to the conclusion she might as well be sad in a beautiful hotel being looked after like a princess, than stay at home wallowing in self-pity. Maybe, once she got out of Dublin she might be able to continue working out her problems in her head in the luxury of the gorgeous Shamrock Hotel.

'It will be the first chance for you to dress up after having Juliet, so bring one of your beautiful dresses. I have a very special meal organised for us while we are away.'

Georgia's imagination ran wild. This Hotel must be a really very special place, where privacy was top of their list. It must have been built with Georgia and Cameron in mind, the high class guests. As usual Georgia always had the words of a song in her mind to fit every occasion. She knew exactly the song she would sing to suit this occasion and most definitely up to the standard necessary to appeal to the high society VIP. (Song - *High Society* from the film with Louis Armstrong)

If they were lucky enough they just might have a brush with some well-known film stars as they glide through the fancy bar. Lord knows she would need a lot of energy for her weekend trip. Just before Juliet was born Georgia had bought a lovely pale green vintage dress, size 10 to wear as soon as she lost all her baby weight. She had also purchased some underwear in Victoria Secrets and a pair of sexy silver vintage shoes with gems and a little baby doll nightie. She was indeed all set and ready to go. Wednesday, long discussions with friends on the phone, Thursday, no time to talk at all, Friday, rest time, Saturday, deep breath. 9.30 am Nellie had to almost prise their fingers from the door, ding dong, they were gone. Special dress tucked away in the boot of the car along with all the other sundries Georgia had packed ever so neatly. You would think she was going for a year, instead she was only going for a night. As the car sped along Georgia wondered if she had packed her lovely Chanel perfume. After all, no dress, no matter how beautiful, would be complete without Chanel.

The journey was swift, soon they arrived at the hotel and went straight to Reception. Cameron was as usual Mr Calm, Mr Cool, as he registered quietly and took time to make a very short phone call. Then with the porter holding all their luggage Cameron marched almost like the Captain of a luxury liner to their suite with his Georgia in hot pursuit. Why all the rushing she thought. Little did she know, just like the captain of a luxury liner, he also was on a mission to check if the suite was fit for his queen and if it lived up to his expectations.

Hurriedly he unlocked the door. For a few moments she was transported back in time to the monastery and those heady days when the love, lust and anticipation drove them wild. She ran ahead and began to excitedly open each door one by one in her quest to discover every nook and cranny. The lights hadn't come on yet, the place seemed a little dark, then it all happened. Cameron just tipped on the switch that he had located with the help of the light on his mobile phone. Light flooded the rooms and there to his and her delight stood a bed dressed to perfection and sprinkled with rose petals, beside the bed stood a round table. On it lay one single rose, the most gorgeous bottle of pink champagne sitting in the cooler and the prettiest chocolates in a golden box. What a view! What a surprise! What a vision! Every day should start like this, Georgia truly believed. If most women with romantic minds and romantic thoughts started their day with a golden box of chocolates and a bottle of pink champagne, their world would be a far better place. And as for the bathroom, Georgia was mesmerised by the freestanding tub, surrounded by scented golden candles in the perfectly golden lit bathroom. Georgia looked in amazement at the beautiful bathtub with steaming hot bubbly water. Beside it stood yet another bottle of champagne with two of the most beautiful old fashioned champagne glasses holding strawberries waiting to be drenched in champagne. In case the pallet required some extra strawberries they were already waiting on a silver tray.

Georgia dipped her hand into the beautiful sudsy water, Wow! The temperature was just perfect, not too hot to make her pretty skin red and wrinkly and not too cool to make her come out in goose pimples. The bathroom was all cream and gold, warm and inviting. It looked amazing, Georgia wasted no time in stripping off leaving a trail of her clothes behind her. As usual two feet first she plunged in (not so dignified). She could feel the light-as-air bubbles, as the water swayed like a wave, engulfing her and her hair. No! That wasn't part of the plan but sure, in for a penny, in for a pound. She was a happy girl and even happier when Cameron joined her. She decided she was meant to be a water baby. So, just as long as the company remained interesting, the champagne flowed and the deliciously sweet tasting strawberries lasted, she would endeavour to drink in moderation, No… still it would be wrong to get tipsy (No) and spoil what was proving to be a weekend like no other.

'Cameron, how did you organise all of this? Yes I was surprised by the champagne and the strawberries but my question to you is, how could you have the hotel organise the vintage champagne glasses, hot water in the tub and have it at just the perfect temperature when we arrived?'

Cameron smiled, cleared his throat and announced the obvious.

'It was the phone call I made in the lobby, Georgia. That was to the housekeeper who promised she would have everything tip top on our arrival.'

'And she did.' said Georgia as she raised her vintage champagne glass and tipped it off Cameron's.

It sounded like a high note in a choir, oh so romantic. It's always good to start on a high note.

Every now and then they would top up the hot water just like they topped up their vintage champagne glasses. Until the last drain of champagne had vanished. Then it was time to leave one of the wonders of the world, step into the hotel's comfy slippers and that gorgeous bathrobe and wander back into the lounge. There was so much to admire in this room, an elaborate comfy settee, with the biggest comfy cushions, beautiful paintings on the wall, everything you'd ever want in a hotel room, not forgetting that huge big TV.

'I could live like this forever' Georgia heard herself say out loud.

Cameron smiled. 'Wouldn't it just be amazing?'

'Ah no Cameron, not as amazing as our beautiful bungalow.'

They felt at home without being at home but they'd best not get too comfy. Cameron reminded Georgia, the restaurant in the hotel was booked for 8.30pm. Their energy was low after sitting in the tub, drinking champagne, eating strawberries and doing all the other little things that make sudsy water interesting. They could stay relaxed and chilled like this for the evening, but they just needed to get their glad rags on, get that energy from somewhere and then drag themselves from their suite to the restaurant.

Cameron dressed in his best in the sitting room while Georgia retreated to the bedroom to perform miracles on her makeup and hair and of course, step into her gorgeous 50's dress and those 50's shoes. Cameron mustn't have a glimpse of his beautiful partner until they meet in the restaurant at 8.25. Cameron got all dressed up in the sitting room, he was the first to leave for the restaurant. Georgia hadn't seen his completed look and couldn't wait to meet him downstairs. She left her room at 28 minutes past 8, (after all it's a woman's privilege to be late). As she skipped down the stairs, the light hearted words of a song came into her mind. She danced down the stairs and sang to herself the first lines of the song from Alice in Wonderland.

I'm late, I'm late
for a very important date.
No time to say hello, goodbye,
I'm late, I'm late, I'm late.

Georgia arrived at the last few steps of the stairs. She looked up straight into his eyes, she nearly fell off the stairs with the surge of excitement that came from inside her. He looked more than handsome in her eyes, dressed in a dark navy suit, white shirt and pink tie. Now she knew the answer to everything, there was no point in her tormenting herself, hour after hour, day after day, month after month, repeating the words in her head over and over again.

Why did I leave Ross for Cameron?

Why did I give up the life I had with Ross for Cameron?

How did I come to the stage where Ross is divorcing me? And:

Why did I let everyone down, my mum Nellie, Ross's lovely parents, my friends?

My biggest question to me is, why did I feel so mad inside,

that I wrote three things on my mirror and had no answers until this moment?

This moment, as I gaze at Cameron, reconfirms for me that everything I did, I did for love. Yes I broke Ross's heart, yes I've been messed up ever since in my head but now in this moment, everything is crystal clear. Thank you God.

The truth was, I just loved Cameron too much to let him go. It was completely out of my control. My heart led the way and my feet followed. I am removing the imaginary line from my life. From this moment on I refuse to feel the guilt I carried with me for far too long, after all you don't find love, love finds you and at the end of the day, love conquers all. With those words she had just said ringing in her ears, Georgia could feel all the weight from such a long time and especially the last week falling from her shoulders. Things have a way of working themselves out.

All Georgia could see was Cameron, the father of their baby girl Juliet. They just stared into each other's eyes as if for the first time. The variety of food at the Shamrock Hotel was second to none. It was a perfect night in a very special hotel where the world was your oyster. The service was brilliant, the staff were friendly, all of them knew to distance themselves and give this couple the little space they needed. Time to revisit the feelings they had when they first met and realise, now they had baby Juliet, that perfect ingredient for a little happy family, they were on cloud number nine, together in heart, mind and spirit. Here they had the uninterrupted time to exchange thoughts and ideas. They left the table with a deeper love and understanding than they'd ever thought possible. This was the place to come for a perfect night together. As they sat by the fire, Georgia announced:

'I'm so happy you took me away for the night Cameron. I

needed a little time with you to explain what happened when Ross and I met. The meal was really nice, he was very quiet and didn't say a lot except to say how much I'd hurt him and how he wished things had been different. He's started a new life without me and he's come to terms with the fact we weren't meant to continue our journey together. He's also very, very happy we have a new baby Juliet.'

There was a silence after that sentence. Georgia almost blurted out, he said he just wished Juliet was his and mine. She said nothing. She continued:

'He said he has come to terms with everything. He said he needed closure and without closure he felt he was in no man's land. Now was his time to look to his future. He said, once everything is finalised, then and only then will this nightmare be over for both of us.'

'Were you devastated, Georgia?'

'To be honest with you Cameron, I was completely shattered. I just kept on telling myself, it was all my fault, my weaknesses had caused this fiasco. Then when I came down the stairs tonight and saw you there, I realised your love had just found me, I just couldn't say no to it. I'm feeling a lot better now and coming to terms with everything. To be honest, it's as if a weight has been lifted from my shoulders. I'm so happy with you and our gorgeous baby, this is the way my life was meant to be.'

'Do you know Georgia?' said Cameron 'When you left that night to meet up with Ross, I was terrified you might not return home to our happy bungalow or our little Juliet. I feared you might go back to him. Honestly I wouldn't have blamed you, I know your feelings for him run very, very deep but now I'm happy that we're happy and with the divorce looming we will be able to proceed with our lives without that dark cloud hanging over both our heads. We have something that you and Ross didn't have, we have Juliet.'

Georgia hadn't been expecting him to say those words, she was dumbfounded. To cover up her feelings she blurted out:

'And we have our happy bungalow.'

The flames in the fire glistened and threw up so many different colours, while the flames in their hearts burned brightly. They were in unison with a bond that couldn't be broken. This was a new beginning for both of them.

CHAPTER 43

Lazy day

I wonder if Cameron imagined this night would be as mad, crazy, full of lust? Georgia thought. She had gone there with an open mind. Her memories of the Shamrock Hotel would be the fabulous suite, the gorgeous bath tub with all its bubbles, the lovely meal in the restaurant but most of all the one memory that would stay with her was that first look at Cameron when she came down the stairs of the hotel. All of that was romantic enough for her. They slept like logs. 6am in the cold light of day, Georgia lay in bed beside the sleeping Cameron, thinking back to the words Ross said to her, that of course she'd left out when she had described her time with Ross.

'I have told myself and I've warned myself to listen to me, tomorrow morning when I wake up, my past with you will be well and truly past tense. I will only see the bright side of everything. I want you to know, Georgia I still love you and I'll always be there if you need me but for you and me as a married couple, I never want to remember the pain. I will have truly moved on and away from everything we had, when I awake tomorrow morning I will be a new man, baptised and born again.'

Tears of sadness streamed down her face as in her mind she said the words, I'll always love you Ross. I pray you've already woken up and the words you said to me about being born again and a new beginning for you are the first words that come into your mind and I pray your new life has already started. I'm sad I'm in your past but I'm very happy for you, that you are finally ready to move forward without me. I have to be strong enough to let you go too. I will always love you and if I ever need you I won't hesitate to ring, but for now and for all of our wellbeing this new chapter begins now.

Georgia wanted to do something to mark this moment, she crept out of bed, showered, popped on a little bit of makeup, pulled on an easy dress, grabbed her jacket and took a last look at Cameron who still slept soundly. She opened and closed the door very quietly, then she was in the lobby. It was now 7am.

'Excuse me' she said to the receptionist, 'Are there any churches near here?'

'You just have to go out the door, turn right, back off the road, there's one just there.'

'Thank you,' she said.

Out she went into the lovely fresh air, the little flowers swayed with the breeze as she walked up the little walkway to the front door of the church. She was surprised to see quite a congregation for that hour of the morning. Maybe people in the country loved their religion a little more than us city slickers.

The priest was saying Mass, she could hear everything, the bell rang for Communion. She walked up to the altar and received Holy Communion. When she came back down, she stopped at the first statue she saw, candles were already burning on the stand. She put the money into the slot, it made quite a bang as it reached the bottom. She lit four candles, the first one for Ross, the second one for her, the third one for Juliet and the fourth one for Cameron. She said a little prayer, she asked Mary to help Ross on his way and to keep her little family strong as they continued their journey through life. She just waited for the blessing and as the priest left the altar she left the church, walked back into the hotel, smiled at the receptionist and answered her question,

'Yes I found the church.'

She rang Cameron and asked him to meet her in the dining room.

'I left you sleeping' she said 'You looked so peaceful. I just went for a little walk, I'm going to start my breakfast, come down when you're ready. See you then Cameron.'

It was only one night but as the old song says, One night in Bangkok makes the hard man humble and if it only takes one night to make a hard man humble in Bangkok it had taken Georgia too long but that one night in The Shamrock Hotel where the world is your oyster, had made her understand a lot of things her mind had blocked out for too long. That night away would be marked on her calendar as the night when something different happened.

Georgia was so happy to be back home getting a warm hug from her happy mum, Nellie. As usual Nellie had her little stories to tell, she announced:

'Juliet had tried to speak a few words, they were all googoo, gaga but they were lovely. She drank all her bottles and she slept like a princess. Oh! and Georgia I had a phone call while you were away from a friend of mine who has booked a weekend in London for both of us and he just would not take no for an answer, we'll have so much fun, gorgeous meals and we're going to see the show *Chicago*. I'm so excited and I don't have long to wait, if you need to have a night out and you'd like me to babysit please organise it for any other weekend except the bank holiday coming up. I'm going to London, Georgia.'

Georgia had to admit her mum would brighten up even the grumpiest person, she should have been called sunshine instead of Nellie.

There was no avoiding the two men who had shaped her life

up until now, her lost love, her new love and father to their baby Juliet. Yes, it was time to take the phone call when it came, to deal with the letter when it arrived, in other words it was time for Georgia to kick her life back into gear. This Georgia decided as she lifted up a pile of letters the post man had delivered. She sat on the floor in the hall sifting through them, lots of bills, luckily all paid by direct debit, various leaflets from all the pizza places, Chinese take away even the chip shop announcing they do deliveries. Now, Georgia would definitely stick them behind the door of the cupboard with blue tack, who knows when her friends arrived unannounced and felt a little bit peckish, she would just open the cupboard door, pick the telephone number of the take away to suit the occasion, call, order, sit with her friends, waste no time on cooking food.

Right underneath the pile of post was that one big envelope she lived in dread of receiving. She left it until last to open, she knew well what it was and even though she knew what it was she kept praying that it wasn't what she thought it was. The quality of the paper in the envelope was so superior to all the others and the white label with her name printed so perfectly gave the game away, it had to be it. Georgia didn't want to open it. She felt there was too much pain in her life that she was only beginning to cope with, how could she cope with more but she did know one thing, in order to move forward with her future with Cameron, she needed to face her past even if it was going to be painful. Georgia stood up from the floor and walked into the kitchen, opened the cutlery drawer, took out a scissors, cut open the envelope across the top so very slowly and so very carefully. She knew this letter, document, would need to be preserved. She didn't want to preserve it, she wanted to set fire to it.

Oh My God, I can feel my legs turning to jelly and my knees

knocking. I don't want my future to be muddled by holding on to my past. I want a future that is a really happy one. OK, it's time to quit the crap, Georgia, take control, you already sorted your mind out on that night away in The Shamrock Hotel, now just read it. You're going to meet an awful lot more obstacles as you go through life. Once you read it you can deal with it, read it. That voice in her head repeated, read it, you have to.

The paper was high quality, not something you'd buy in the local store, definitely from a solicitor's office. As she expected, the words were strong and to the point. Boiling everything down, the documents simply confirmed that the divorce would proceed once Georgia visited the solicitor's office and signed the divorce papers. The realisation hit Georgia, soon she and Ross would no longer be married. The consequences for him didn't quite have the impact it would have on her, she would return to her single name and do her best to respond when someone called her, while Ross would carry on regardless. Georgia had to take deep breaths and try to calm the panic attack she could feel engulfing her body. From now on she would take everything in her stride, everything in stages. Someone had once said to her when everything seems on top of you, imagine, in your head, filing each problem in a different box, taking one at a time and dealing with it. That was the only way she could properly move forward, she would have to take everything in her stride, take everything in stages.

(1) She had caused the divorce,

(2) He had filed for the divorce,

(3) She had drifted along until this letter. Now she would simply have to continue on this journey knowing full well where it would lead her (the divorce courts).

I'll be free, but that's all a farce. How can something that was so real be reduced to something that evaporates, right in front of your eyes. She was happy to know Ross kept his dignity by being the one who took a stand. She knew, the law is the law, it was inevitable divorce would happen. As a song said *Saying Goodbye Doesn't Mean Forever* and somewhere deep in her soul, Georgia hoped herself and Ross could still be friends.

CHAPTER 44

All things bright and beautiful

Georgia thought, memo to brain, I need something to brighten me up after all this serious stuff in my life. I know, a House Warmer. Our Bungalow is a great place for entertaining my three best friends and catching up on all the old gossip. I'll send them a little invitation and for a bit of fun, I'll give them my home phone number and ask them to call that instead of my mobile. Then when I answer their calls I'll say, in my best impression of Hyacinth:

Hello, this is Hyacinth Bucket, the lady of the house speaking. I have all my Royal Doulton with the periwinkles on display. She just knew her friends would burst into laughter because like her they had also watched the carry-on of Hyacinth Bucket on TV for years and loved every episode. What a nice way to start their visit to her bright, airy bungalow, with fun and laughter. And so one by one the phone calls came, with each phone call Georgia tried her best to hold it together and somehow in between the laughing, she recited her party piece,

'Hyacinth Bucket the lady of the house speaking.'

No! there was no Royal Doulton with periwinkles on view but there was Georgia's very best china cups and saucers and no, there was no need for any friend to become nervous in case any of the china would fall from their tiny hands, like Hyacinth's neighbour afraid she'd break a cup. Most of it was Georgia's mum's presents or bric a brac bought at Christmas fairs or collected from her travels. All three came together that evening, Coco, Heidi, Tanya, all they wanted to do was stare at

Juliet lying in her cosy cot, fast asleep.

Dinner arrived courtesy of one of the restaurants whose leaflet was conveniently blue tacked to her cupboard door. The food was hot and steamy just like the stories from her three friends. Yes, there was a wedding coming up, Heidi's, with her ever-loving Sugar Daddy. The four friends jumped around the place quietly, in case they'd waken Juliet, anyway they celebrated and there was a lot to celebrate. They would be the bridesmaids at the forthcoming nuptials. The three pals had already accepted the challenge at the Trocadero. There were stories upon stories, they all had to tell. Coco had someone she really wanted to introduce her friends to but not just now. She was expecting wedding bells too, just like Heidi and of course the ever-loving Tanya always had a story. She was still flirting with Frederick, the steward from the airlines. She'd made love in granny's place over in London and the sordid details were so funny it made everyone smile and laugh. Cameron sat in for the meal, Georgia was reminded of the first time she met him, when Heidi had practically dragged him over to their table. It was love at first sight for both of them and now they were here, the end of one journey, the beginning of another. The lovely thing was it was still all friends from kindergarten together again celebrating yet another milestone in their lives.

CHAPTER 45

Guess who's coming to tea

Guests came and went all the time to visit them in their gorgeous new bungalow. Cameron's family and friends from the country and from the monastery made their appearances, so also did Georgia's family and friends. Most times they arrived unannounced. Cameron and Georgia didn't mind, they loved every visit from everyone. First priority looking after Juliet, working and having friends and family up to their new beautiful bungalow and making time for themselves, for love. Mixing everything all together in the mixing bowl of life had a very tiring effect on Georgia, maybe she was run down, maybe she was overworked, maybe she was all the above. Georgia decided once they had Maisie Coyne up to dinner she would take a break, have some quiet time and enjoy their beautiful bungalow. One phone call

'Absolutely Georgia, I would love to come and see Juliet, yourself and Cameron. This time I won't have to keep watch in case one of the priests wants to go to Cameron's cell while you're there.'

'Christ Almighty, Maisie, I didn't know you did that for us.'

'Indeed I did,' said Maisie. 'I diverted many priests in the opposite direction. I'd say things like, I think Cameron is outside in the gardens praying Father, or actually Father I asked Cameron to get me an apple tart in Apple Pie while he was out. He should be back soon. Oh! Georgia if the truth was known I lied through my teeth all to save you and the love of your life.'

'Well Maisie, I think to celebrate that, I will buy an apple tart for you in Apple Pie and have it piping hot when you arrive.'

'I'll bring the cream.'

'Great idea Maisie. I'll see you then.'

So Maisie arrived, 5.15 on a Wednesday evening. She just loved the bungalow from the first moment she had put her foot inside the gate and walked up that little pathway. Georgia opened the door.

'Why hello Maisie, you are very welcome to our beautiful bungalow. I have just taken the apple pie out of the oven, it's warm and on the table just waiting for you.'

Maisie was dressed to kill, this time she wore a dusty pink hat, deep grey coat, pink gloves, pink bag, pink shoes. A lovely sight to behold. Georgia needn't have worried was it going to be awkward sitting there with Maisie, not really knowing her that well but no, it was really nice. It was as if she was a close relation, everything just went with the flow. As they sat down and enjoyed a slice of apple pie Maisie asked:

'Georgia would you do me a little favour, would you go onto the internet for me and see if you can find my Fergus or maybe a trail that might lead back to him. I'm just looking for another friend in my life. I'm not going to do his washing or anything. He could be lonely like me. I'd just like to see him again and have a chat and having spoken to you before about him I did start to wonder, what better place to get the ball rolling than here today.'

'Maisie, let's not wait, you have had a slice of warm apple pie. The dinner is on but Cameron's not home yet so why don't you sit over here with me at the computer and we'll mosey through the names. Now, what did you say his full name was?'

'Fergus Breen.'

In went the name to the computer. So many Fergus Breen's existed. They sifted through but there was nothing to be found that seemed to resemble the man Maisie loved. Then Georgia suggested putting in Father Fergus Breen? They did and just like an angel appearing from heaven he was there on the screen.

'My God, it's easy to find people these days' said Maisie.

His parish was in London and he was the parish priest. Now Maisie had a decision to make, would she call the parish or would she just let it lie?

Georgia insisted:

'Maisie I don't think you should make any decisions now. It's too soon.'

'No Georgia, it's not too soon. I have wanted to talk to him for years. He might be ancient but so what, I'm no spring chicken either. Would you call the number for me?'

The two of them became like giddy schoolgirls as they laughed, joked and messed around... Georgia dialled the number. There was no Hyacinth the Lady of the House Speaking, instead a nice English accent:

'Good evening, how can I help you?'

'I'm looking to speak to the parish priest, Father Fergus Breen.'

'Who will I say is calling?' Enquired the quiet voice on the other end of the phone in London.

'Please just say it's a friend from long ago.'

'Hold on, I'm connecting you now' said the English lady.

Then Georgia heard:

'Hello, Father Fergus Breen speaking.'

Georgia composed herself... 'My name is Georgia, I've been looking you up for a friend of yours from the past. She's here with me now. Just hold on a moment and I'll put you on to her.'

Maisie took the phone from Georgia. Georgia walked out of the room and as she was closing the door she heard Maisie say, 'Hello Fergus. This is Maisie Coyne from the monastery. I used to be the housekeeper, I used to be a friend of yours. How are you keeping?'

Georgia closed the door and heard no more. She set an extra place at the dinner table for Maisie. Poor old Maisie needed a friend right now and some real food. Luckily there was enough in the pot for everyone.

Georgia heard the door in the sitting room open, Maisie walked in, tears streaming down her face, she ran over to Georgia and gave her the biggest hug ever.

'Only for you this would never have happened, Georgia. You made me strong enough to let you make some enquiries for me. Thank you from the bottom of my heart.'

'Compose yourself Maisie.' Georgia looked into her eyes, 'You're happy to join us for dinner?'

Maisie nodded her head in agreement.

'Yes Georgia and I'm even happier to have heard Fergus's voice on the phone. It brought back many memories. I just wish he had looked for me but sure something is better than nothing.'

'Now sit down there at the table, Maisie. Dinner is being served now on my periwinkle plates.'

That little comment broke the mood and made Maisie smile again. By now Cameron was home and had changed his clothes into something more casual. Georgia served the dinner, they ate like men and women returning from the war, they were all so famished. For dessert they enjoyed more apple tart with lashings of cream. Cameron thanked Maisie for all she had done for him in the time he had been in the seminary. How she had taken him under her wing and treated him like a son and even made food for him at times when he was feeling down and out, wondering which way to go.

'Yes' said Maisie 'you had great times and hard times there.

Sure I saw them with my own two eyes, Cameron. Sometimes I used to feel sorry for you, you looked so lost… but on a brighter note, look at you now. You're as shiny as a new button, as happy as a lark and into the bargain you have found the girl of your dreams. That was God's plan for you Cameron. You had to leave the country life, take that journey to the monastery and the religious life to find yourself where you are now with a new life. Now you have a new partner, Georgia, you're enjoying working in your new teaching post and of course, your beautiful Juliet… you have the complete hat trick.'

Just before Maisie left, she whispered in Georgia's ear, 'sorry I couldn't talk about that phone call. Just hearing his voice brought me right back, Georgia. I'm not in work tomorrow at all, would you like to meet me in that little coffee shop and I'll take you up to date with my story.'

'Actually, that would fit in very well with my plans tomorrow, Maisie. Would 12.45 be ok for you, I'll be needing a cup of tea then.'

Maisie left for home happy as a lark, maybe now she had found her new family and a blast from the past.

CHAPTER 46

Stories and declarations

Georgia pushed the pram in through the doorway of the café, she didn't notice Maisie arriving. The two women practically bumped into each other going through the door of the little blue café. Just as well Georgia arrived in slightly before Maisie or their two bottoms would have been wedged forever in the door. Georgia positioned the pram as neatly as possible in the corner away from the other diners. Maisie looked longingly at Juliet. She didn't say a word but the big smile on her face said it all. They sat down. It was close to lunchtime so it was soup and a roll all round, gorgeous creamy vegetable soup and crispy rolls. There was no talk until the last morsel had vanished and the fresh cream slices were sitting on the table, ready to be devoured.

'I can't wait to tell you the news, Georgia. Fergus was very surprised I took the time to call him again and to be honest with you he had me in panics of laughter when he reminded me of all the things we used to get up to in that monastery. He could hardly believe I was still working there and informed me that he had his own housekeeper who looks after him very well... a cool silence. On a good note, he has invited me to London for a very special night for him, a big celebration of twenty years as a priest. Family, friends, loved ones and foe will all be there. He said I couldn't have called at a better time because he'd previously block booked rooms in the hotel and they rang him, this very morning, to ask if he needed all of those rooms as they could take some of them back and release them for other guests. He was just about to ring the hotel when you called his number.

It was fate Georgia, fate. And guess what Georgia, I will have one twin room, all to myself paid for by Father Fergus Breen. Maybe you'd like to come with me? I can think of no one better to share Fr. Fergus Breen's celebrations with. If it wasn't for you encouraging me to call him this invitation would never have happened. Is it too short notice for you to organise Juliet because the celebrations are this coming weekend? We would both have to work very swiftly if we would like to take the journey.'

'Give me a minute, I'll call Cameron and see what he thinks.'

Georgia had thought this lunchtime conversation would be all about Juliet and all the little stories that Maisie would have to tell her, but instead of all the small stories there was just that one big story, the invitation.

'Hello Cameron, love of my life' said Georgia 'I'm just wondering are you doing anything special this coming weekend?'

'Yes, Georgia, I'm spending the weekend with two beautiful people, my beautiful little daughter and my gorgeous Georgia.'

'Well Cameron, instead of spending it with your gorgeous Georgia and your beautiful daughter, would you just spend it with your beautiful daughter, because you see Cameron, your beautiful Georgia has had a better offer, an invitation to a big celebration in England. I would be the guest of Maisie Coyne, who has been invited to Fr. Fergus Breen's celebration of his twenty years as a priest. Years ago he was in the monastery where you were, that's where he met Maisie Coyne.'

'You're not serious' said Cameron 'so Maisie got in touch with him, did she?'

'She did' said Georgia (and I encouraged it)

'Absolutely Georgia, you should go, you really should. I'm great with Juliet now. It'll be my treat, I'll pay for your flights and also for Maisie's. I was trying to think of something special to buy her for all she has done for me through the years. My mind was blank, now I am delighted with myself. I will pay for the flights and accommodation.'

'No Cameron, there's no need for you to do all that. We would be delighted if you just paid for the flights. The rooms are already paid for by Fr. Breen. Maisie has asked if I would go with her today to a boutique down the road so she can choose an outfit for the big celebration. I'll be slightly late home. Is that OK Cameron?'

'No Problem. See you later Georgia.'

CHAPTER 47

London baby

Out of the taxi, into the airport, purchases in the duty free completed, (perfume, to be collected on arrival). Plane up into the blue skies, coffee, tea and croissants vanished from the plate, landed, perfume collected, outside in arrivals and on the train bound for London. A song came to mind, *Trains* (√), *and Boats ? and Planes* (√). They made their way to the Strand Palace Hotel where the celebrations would begin later on that very evening.

'I really don't want to see Fergus until I'm all dressed up' announced Maisie 'so we'll just go into the hotel very quietly, incognito, get to our room as fast as we can, order some sandwiches and tea and get ourselves ready, because all the celebrations begin at 7 o'clock on the dot.'

Georgia started with Maisie's makeup and left her just shampooed hair caught up in a towel to take all the heavy wet out, while she concentrated on her eye makeup and eyelashes, so Maisie could do lots of flirting (with Fr Fergus Breen) with her long eyelashes. Then Georgia blow dried her new great friend's hair into a nice bouncy curl, caught one side up and placed a little flower for decoration on the side and left the other side down, to show Fergus just how lovely Maisie's hair was. Then while Maisie began to dress for the evening in her brand new dress from the little boutique close to the blue cafe, Georgia prepared herself for a celebration that she never thought she would ever attend. This was Maisie's night, a night when she would shine as bright as the stars. Georgia was dressing nicely, she wanted all of the attention to go to Maisie, not her. She was merely a companion.

When Maisie appeared in her brand new beautiful dress, with her makeup applied perfectly and her hair looking gorgeous, she was barely recognisable from Maisie Coyne the housekeeper, who worked in the monastery. She didn't look at all matronly, in fact she looked simply divine. Her dress had a sweetheart neckline, the skirt was skater shape and the colour was powder blue with a pink belt to match the flower in her hair. To finish her ensemble Maisie wore pink shoes with kitten heels. Georgia's dress was a luscious red to match her lipstick, kind of a 50's figure hugging dress, with white 5 inch high heels. Georgia realised she did look a bit showy but they were a pretty pair as they entered the dining room, that was designed for the night with a lot of thought. There was a dance floor in the centre and a live band sitting perched back from the dance floor. The band was made up of young teenagers, every instrument was on display, guitars, piano, violin, cello, saxophone, tin whistle, drums and one young man carried an accordion.

Georgia couldn't wait to hear the music that would come from those fabulous instruments. On closer inspection, Georgia realised this must be a school orchestra who'd possibly given their time free to celebrate this big occasion for Fr. Fergus Breen. Already sitting on chairs around the bandstand were teenagers, who she guessed were singers and backing singers, all presented so beautifully. On the left hand side of the room stood a table laid out and decorated with champagne and all kinds of beverages and in the centre a big cake. On the right hand side of the room were the tables all set out with tiny vases of flowers on each table. The room was nice, bright and airy, decorated with balloons and streamers. The two glamorous ladies made their entrance to the little desk set up in the dining room and stole the show. They held evening bags, Georgia's one was a small white and gold bag, while Maisie held the pink evening bag she'd borrowed from Georgia. Everyone else there had that lived-in look, not a lot of glamour around at all, that was except for Maisie and her friend Georgia who shone like the brightest stars.

This evening had the promise of amazing things to come. So far there was no sign of Fergus or at least the Fergus that Maisie remembered, all young full of the joys of spring and the wondering, but there was one gentleman there that seemed to be getting a lot of attention. He was dressed in a black evening suit, pristine white shirt with gold cufflinks, a black sparkly bow tie and black shiny patent shoes. His hair was dark with just a sprinkling of grey throughout. His eyes darted around the room at his guests as if he was looking for someone in particular, then they stopped and stared, as into his vision came the two beautiful ladies, Maisie and Georgia. He rushed past the other guests, straight over.

'Maisie, it's you, it has to be you. You look utterly fantastic. I was just going to dress ordinary, Maisie, but something told me you would go all out for tonight, so I decided I might as well be hung for a sheep as a lamb. Oh! my patent leather shoes are my only new purchase. I took all of this clothing from the archives and they still fit me. Here I am in all my grandeur, presenting myself to you, your long lost friend, Fr. Fergus Breen.'

Maisie was speechless. It was a very emotional moment for all three.

'Can you introduce me to your companion?' he asked.

'This is Georgia, a friend I met at the monastery.'

'Pleased to meet you' said Georgia.

The band struck up and the night of celebrations began. The

first song must have been one of Fergus's favourites or maybe it reminded him of Maisie, *On the Street Where You Lived.*

'May I have this dance please Maisie?' said Fergus (Fr.).

Maisie excused herself but before she shimmied towards the centre of the floor she whispered into Georgia's ear 'I feel honoured to be the first person Fergus invited to dance with him.' Then with her prince in tow for the first dance of the night, Fr. Fergus Breen and Maisie glided onto the dance floor. Her dress just looked gorgeous on her, the prettiest dress in the ballroom. Georgia stood there in awe and watched as they waltzed in perfect timing to the perfect song with the Maisie's new watch, her prize possession from her friend Cameron, shining on her wrist. All of the other guests clapped for the priest who had served them so well through the years. Georgia guessed some of them were wondering who his perfect partner was. For this special night, all of the songs played were selected personally by Fr. Fergus Breen, obviously songs that brought back beautiful memories.

The meal began, every course was supreme and delicious. There were lots of speeches given, some by parishioners who had known him for lots of years, some friends who told silly stories. Maisie had nothing prepared, all her memories and all her thoughts were personal. She hoped to discuss them with Fr. Fergus Breen when the time was right. Then it was time for Fergus to give his little chat. He thanked everyone who came from near and far to celebrate with him tonight. It was a short speech well thought out and ended with a request from Fergus for everyone's attention for just a moment.

'To a lot of you, this will come as a surprise tonight but after a lot of thought I decided that since this would be a big celebration and the people who have meant the world to me throughout my life, would all be here.' With those words he gazed over at Maisie Coyne. 'I decided to wait until now, the perfect moment, to say that within the next three months I will be retiring from my post as Parish Priest.'

There were gasps of dismay.

'I have really enjoyed my time here in London. All of you have made my life as a priest so very special and well worth living.' He looked down at all his happy guests and continued 'Now I'm going to take some time for myself. My heart has told me it's time to return to my roots in Ireland.'

Maisie felt her heart jumping up in the air.

Fergus continued 'Until my successor takes over from me, I will continue to work within the parish. I will make home calls if needed and we will have time for our little chats. I have given my all to all of you for the last twenty years and I feel I have nothing left in me to give, my job here is done. You all have my phone number and you're welcome to call me anytime for a shoulder to cry on, or someone to laugh with. I will be just on the end of the phone line. Most of all tonight I'd like to thank the singers and the fantastic orchestra who will continue to play for you and me for the next hour or so. You'll recognise a few of the songs they sing, because I picked each and every one with all of you in mind. Maybe they will have some connection to you and me and the times we've shared.

As a lot of you know, the orchestra is from Saint Mary's School, they're a wonderful bunch of people. I know you will enjoy listening to a live orchestra playing and all the young singers singing just for you and me. So when I finish talking in a moment or two, would you all be happy if we did a little whip around to pay for their bus journey here tonight, carrying all their equipment and their stay over in the hotel. There's just one other thing I'd like to say and this is directed towards the orchestra. For the majority of you who live in London, this is your first night here alone without your parents. I ask you to be very careful and only have good memories of your time here. I also want to say because a lot of you are finishing school soon, please enjoy your summer, before you settle down to study for your music degree in autumn. I wish you a lovely warm summer.

In the meantime your music teacher has arranged to have different directors of music and musicians to come and meet with you when you have lunch here tomorrow at noon. (I'm coming too) I would like you to look your best at 12 o'clock tomorrow when you arrive for your meeting. Thank you one and all for all the joy and happiness you have given me through the years. For now I'd just like to say, let's dance.'

All the guests stood up and gave the most fantastic round of applause in appreciation for all Fr. Breen had done through the years and a second round of applause for the fantastic musicians who played and the wonderful singers who sang. The full orchestra and singers again took their places on the stage and began to perform. The night's entertainment really began when the words,

Let's dance

Put on your red shoes and dance the blues,

Let's dance to the song they're playin' on the radio etc. etc. etc. echoed around the room. The song belongs to the multi-talented David Bowie.

That one dance Maisie had with Fr. Fergus Breen was the first dance and the last dance she had with him for the night. He was so busy dancing with all his guests but she would always have the memory of being the one he chose, from every other Lady in the room, for his very first dance. Georgia also danced the night away and met so many new people. She had so much fun and two very sore feet. It was good to be away from home, she loved little short escapes. The musicians played an amazing variety of songs and such lovely music, something to suit every guest. It had been Georgia's first time to have an orchestra play while she danced. Oh! How special was that? There was even a young comedian who did great impressions of famous film stars in such funny situations. She had everyone rolling around with laughter.

When the final curtain call came and the last few guests danced back to their rooms, Georgia sat with Maisie and Fr. Breen as they went over old times but you have to know when to leave, there's always that moment. When it came Georgia excused herself from the table and went to her room, kicked off her tight shoes and smiled with happiness as she felt all the pain disappearing from her poor aching feet. She folded her dress, packed it away in her suitcase, donned her luxurious dressing gown and sat watching TV. As she sat there, not concentrating at all on the television, she began to wonder what Maisie and Fergus were talking about, were there any sorrys, or we should have, or will we in the future? She would leave the storytelling to Maisie. Unless Maisie told her she'd never ask. It was too late to ring Cameron, she might wake Juliet so instead she sent him a text.

The night has been a great success. Maisie wore the watch you gave her as a present. The rose gold gleamed. She looked gorgeous. I'll see you tomorrow night, the love of my life. From your gorgeous Georgia.

Exhausted but very happy, next morning the two ladies sat down at a pristine table. White immaculately clean tablecloth and beautifully set for late breakfast the next morning.

'Well Georgia, I'm sure you're dying to know what happened between me and the great Father last night. I'd love to tell you there was romance in the air and he had fallen in love with me all over again but I'm afraid not Georgia, it was all very cordial. He said he often thought of me and the great times he had in Dublin as a young priest and now he was looking forward to returning to his homeland. He hoped that we could meet up for maybe the theatre, or a film and maybe I could help him with some book work, as his one wish was to write his biography. If you're lucky Maisie, he said you might even get a mention. Then he kissed me on the side of the cheek and headed off to bed.'

'Oh I'm sorry to hear that Maisie. I had great hopes for the two of you. I could see you joining dancing classes and having bridge nights.'

'Don't worry' said Maisie 'To tell you the truth, Georgia, I'm very happy with the outcome. If he'd been falling over me and asking me for things that I wouldn't feel ready to give him, I know I couldn't have coped. This way we have a chance of letting things get better and the worst thing that could happen, we would just remain friends and I wouldn't say no to that either. I've had a lovely time in London and thank you, Georgia, for coming with me. It wouldn't have been the same if I was alone. I'm thinking my time at the monastery has come to an end. I want pastures green just like Fergus so when I go back I'm going to be a very busy lady getting all my things in order. Only then can I move on to a new chapter in my life.'

All they had were glasses of fresh orange juice so they tipped them together and made a toast to a sweet and sugary future.

CHAPTER 48

Time waits for no one

That's what they say, time waits for no one, it's such a true saying, just now she'd had that short stay away with Maisie Coyne. Her life was like a whirlwind between moving out of her house with Ross, moving in with Tanya, then going it alone in her small rented house, followed by two's not a crowd when she shacked up with Cameron in their gorgeous bungalow. Then she became pregnant, had a proposal of marriage from Cameron and, of course that was followed by the magical birth of Juliet. Getting used to nappies, bottles, baby washes, smiles and goo goo, gaga. Just for a bit of fun she might as well add the enjoyment she had from the Silver Cross pram that had pride of place in her gorgeous bungalow, it had turned out to be the icing on the cake, a real gem. Georgia didn't know how she was going to let it go back into Coco's arms but that was the deal, the time was coming very close. While the old Silver Cross pram was magical the new Bug-a-Boo would be so simple to move in and out of her car and she would need to be out and about a lot pretty soon when she would be back working away in the beauty salon. They often invited guests over for meals to their humble abode, in other words they were living their lives.

Cameron, herself and Juliet couldn't just say goodbye to the pram without having a celebration which of course, would include Heidi, Coco, Tanya, her mum Nellie and her new friend Maisie. Celebrations were easy to organise, there always had to be a victoria sponge cake and a chocolate sponge cake from Cadburys. Nice fresh biscuits courtesy of Marks and Spencer's, baguettes packed to capacity with all her friends favourite fillings and cut into three by the lovely assistant in the local delicatessen. There had to be two bottles of pink champagne, just barely enough to give each guest a well filled glass. Some pink lemonade, lots of tea and a few bits and pieces from Mr Kipling. Not hard to organise and lovely to eat. Everyone who was invited arrived. Cameron poured the champagne into each glass. The bubbles did bounce and if you were lucky some might tip your nose. As usual the first to vanish from the plate were the sandwiches, in fact everything from the table was gone in a flash.

When it came to the silver Cross pram leaving Georgia's, the whole event turned into a ceremony. The friends stood in two lines and made a less than impressive archway as Juliet, who was already sitting inside the pram smiled happily. Georgia, followed by Cameron, escorted the pram through the archway where Coco waited. She took over from Mammy and Daddy and continued to walk out through the front door pushing the Pram, with baby Juliet still on board. Georgia and Cameron stared sorrowfully.

Tanya announced, 'A thing of beauty is a joy forever' as she proceeded to remove baba boo from the pram that had been her very cosy place to sleep during the day, for a long time.

'May whoever sits in this pram in the future be as happy as this baby Juliet.'

Everyone clapped as the perambulator vanished into the back of Coco's car and the boot closed. There was a sigh from everyone. Tanya sighed because she was so happy cuddling Juliet, Heidi sighed a sigh of hope that one day she would be the proud mother of a baby boy or girl with the happy disposition of baby Juliet, Coco's sigh was a sigh of relief at getting back her pram and Georgia, Cameron and Juliet sighed a sigh of disbelief as the

Silver Cross pram vanished from sight into the boot of Coco's car. Nellie and Maisie Coyne sighed because they just couldn't understand what all the fuss was about. The Silver Cross Pram had vanished from their sight for the foreseeable future. Nellie and Maisie were gone home in Nellie's car, Coco and Heidi said goodbye, leaving Tanya who was having an overnight stay in the spare room with Georgia (so as not to waken the baby with their loud laughter).

CHAPTER 49

A glimpse of freedom

Time was passing by so fast and except for the odd push towards the local shops or the little trip in the car to the big supermarkets, Cameron and Georgia hadn't had one night out. Then a phone call from Coco confirmed they were having a meal out that very night. It would only give them hours to organise themselves but the one thing they didn't need was a babysitter because they had three. Yes the three friends were paying for the night out and coming up to babysit as well, now how good can things get? Normally Georgia would have showered, dressed, hair blow dried, makeup on, in under an hour but this was different, there was no longer just her, there was a baby to be fed and changed and sang to at bedtime. So her routine was completely messed up but eventually everything came together, Juliet lay sleeping, the happy pair were all dolled up and ready. Georgia was a little apprehensive but she knew from all the stories clients had told her through the years, this moment had to be overcome, there was life after babies, she was about to find out what that life would be like.

Her friends waved them on their way. Georgia looked around for one last time as the car slowly drove from the area, the front door was closed. Everything looked just as it used to look before Juliet arrived but Georgia and Cameron's hearts were still inside that door as they tried to make it alone without their little daughter. It seemed to take ages but eventually they were there. Cameron parked the car in the Drury Street car park, which was so convenient, as the restaurant they were having their meal in was in the Clarendon Pub opposite the School of Music. It had been renovated with lots of glass windows, which made it bright and modern. The food was brilliant, you could get anything from fish and chips to whatever else your heart desired. They chose the healthy diet, steamed salmon, jacket potatoes, a mixture of sides and two large glasses of champagne to celebrate after the meal.

They talked about everything, all their hopes and especially the dreams they had for their little girl. Georgia was feeling so healthy and happy, no baby blues, just a great feeling of relief at the pregnancy being very far behind her, pure happiness at being a mother to Juliet and really elated with their achievement. Cameron had a surprise for Georgia. He hadn't decided on exactly when to give the present to her, now was the perfect time. For Georgia this night out was more than she could have dreamt of.

She felt extra excitement as she opened the little string on the tiny box from Sheeran's Jewellery Store in the Westbury Mall, to discover a diamond eternity ring that glistened and gleamed and fitted her tiny hand. The diamonds weren't too small or too big, just perfect. Georgia was astonished, she felt this was just too much but Cameron assured her she was worth every penny he had spent and he wanted her to always remember this moment. How could she forget with every sparkle of her diamond ring reminding her this ring was presented by a very happy Cameron, to his gorgeous Georgia, for presenting him with beautiful baby Juliet. Georgia loved nothing more than pure bling!

When every scrap of food had vanished from their plates and they'd covered every subject they needed to cover and exhaustion set in, it was time to return to their bundle of joy, and the friends who'd minded her. It was lovely to be home and see Juliet's little face. She had been fed, bathed and was lying sleeping peacefully, in her comfy cot. Georgia's three friends announced 'this whole evening was a team effort' and now they were happy to leave Juliet back in her mum and dad's care. They joked of how exhausted they were and announced they were only fit for bed as they left the couple to get on with looking after Juliet.

Georgia and Cameron collapsed into their bed, fell asleep on connection with the mattress and there they lay until a little cry from their beautiful Juliet woke Cameron up, while Georgia still remained in the land of nod. In the coming weeks Georgia would face new challenges, having Juliet cared for while she started working part-time back in the salon. Still all those things could wait, right now there was a certain peace and contentment all over the house and all because of one tiny little human being who had transformed this house into a home. Sometimes, in a peaceful moment when Juliet was fast asleep in her cot, Cameron was at work and the sun shone into the room as Georgia sat sipping a cup of tea, she would take a look at that gorgeous ring on her finger and be blinded by the dazzle of the magnificent present Cameron had presented her with to celebrate the birth of their daughter, her eternity ring. Work and all that earthly stuff would just have to wait.

When Georgia awoke she wondered, was last night just a dream but as she held her hand up and the sun hit the diamonds, she knew it was for real. She rubbed her eternity ring as if it was magic. She made a wish. If only she could lie on in bed for a few minutes longer beside cuddly Cameron, unfortunately beside her in her little cot Juliet was wide awake, looking for attention. A cuddle with Cameron wasn't possible. Georgia was very organised with a bottle warmer on the table beside her and another one in the kitchen beside the kettle. Well, friends had said be organised Georgia and you'll enjoy the whole motherhood thing so much better. Never bothering to put on a pair of slippers, Georgia ran to the kitchen, popped on the kettle, made herself a cup of tea and filled a hot water bottle, retrieved a bottle from the fridge for Juliet and popped it into the second bottle warmer.

She returned back to the bedroom, put the hot water bottle into the bed at a safe distance from Juliet. She then got back into bed with her little bundle of joy in her arms and soon baby Juliet was being fed all the nourishment she needed. As Juliet snuggled in and sucked on her tepid bottle, Georgia used the time to contemplate her next tasks and there were lots of them. Gone was the time when she awoke to all the frivolous things in life, such as what dress to wear and where to go for morning coffee. Now it was the first bottle, wind, bath, cuddles, what to dress Juliet in and where to take her for a stroll. This was mind-boggling, enjoyable but Georgia definitely was not the stay at home type and unease was now setting in.

She needed a new challenge, so today when all the chores were done she'd advertise for someone to come to the house to cook, clean and mind Juliet while she returned to work to perform more miracles on her waiting public. She was aware, with the cost of nannies these days, there wouldn't be much money left over but that wasn't the big issue. Georgia was a free spirit, she needed her time and after all everything comes at a cost, as they say, there are no free lunches.

CHAPTER 50

Returning to what she knew best

The advertisement for a nanny had been in the local newspaper for a few days. They were both very surprised at the amount of nannies who applied for the position. They vetted each one very carefully and eventually decided on a pretty Parisian, highly qualified nanny called Maria. She had a lovely bright and happy personality and lots of energy needed to look after a young soon to be toddler. The best thing was, she was very happy to take on the post, even if it did include some light housework. Juliet took to her like a duck to water, she just relaxed in her arms. Cameron and Georgia were very happy with their decision. Maria seemed to know everything there is to know about babies. In fact, she put Georgia to shame but Georgia didn't mind, after all everyone to their own. Maria was so qualified for the job and could start the next day. The first two weeks would be spent working alongside Georgia until Georgia and Cameron felt the time was right to leave young Juliet in her capable hands. That day did dawn and although a little apprehensive Georgia felt comfortable with their choice of minder and confident to leave her toddler with Maria, happy in the knowledge, Juliet was in safe hands.

Georgia felt at ease and ready to return to work in the beauty salon to perform miracles on her clientele with her fabulous makeovers and enthusiasm. Some of the clients came in feeling dull and down from all the work they had to do but once inside the beauty salon they began to relax, then when they were all beautified and pampered they left feeling bright, cheerful and gorgeous. Georgia loved getting all dolled up for work, it was a great feeling to be part of the beauty industry. When she was there she had great fun hearing all the stories from the other girls and the clients. She had learned to listen but keep her opinions to herself and at all times remain professional. Georgia needed to work to earn that extra money but much more than that, she needed time away from home to give her a taste of a different life. Yes, time when she could be just her, Georgia Brown. Once her work day was over she was happy to return to where her heart lay, at home in their gorgeous bungalow with Cameron and Juliet, the loves of her life. That was the only place Georgia always felt free and at ease with herself. Yes, still only looking forward, with those blinkers on.

Little Juliet was fascinating and coming on in leaps and bounds in Maria's hands. Georgia was relaxed, rested and her life was taking on a new meaning with someone to help at home. Life was great and as she only worked Wednesdays, Fridays and Saturdays, there was plenty of time to spend with her million-dollar baby. When Maria arrived in the mornings to look after Juliet, it was time for Georgia to leave for her work.

The day she enjoyed most was Saturday because that was the day the house was cleaned from top to bottom by Maria. Saturday was also the day Cameron looked after Juliet and at 5pm sharp arrived at the salon to collect his beautiful Georgia, with baby in tow, dressed in one of her prettiest little dresses that Georgia had left out, ironed and ready for baby Juliet. She had so many gifts from clients but Georgia's favourite one was a little satin number, with pale pink flowers scattered beautifully and the tiniest deep pink cardigan to put a glow on her little baby's cheeks. Georgia looked on every Saturday evening as an adventure when Cameron and Juliet came to the salon and picked her up. Once she stepped her foot into the car, she was with her little family and she loved that feeling. Georgia left it to Cameron to pick the restaurant. Nothing too posh, just somewhere close to home with great food, flowers on the table and of course, it had to be bright, cheerful, quick and easy, where the waiters flurried around serving gorgeous hot food. It was nice to be in the middle of all this bustle but there's always a story.

On this one particular Saturday night the happy, footloose and fancy free couple plus baby arrived at the little restaurant. Cameron was tired from his daddy duties but nevertheless very, very happy and eager to please the two girls in his life. Georgia loved Saturday night, when the week's work was behind her and relaxing Sunday was looming. Now sitting in this little restaurant or indeed any little restaurant Georgia's heart was singing. She was content to just wait on her meal to arrive and as she did her eyes gazed over at one of the waiters. She watched as he bent down to put a plug in the wall and then there was one loud bang. The plug blew and lots of black dust surrounded him. Complete darkness in the restaurant except for the candles on the tables which gave a very romantic glow. Maybe this is the way the restaurant should really look, very, very cosy and romantic with glistening candle lights. It took a few minutes for the manager to find the trip switch, soon everything returned to normal and serving food continued. Georgia had watched the whole incident, poor man, he was in shock but insisted he was fine and just wanted to continue to work, a real trooper.

The time had come for home, after all Juliet had to be in her cot, washed, fed and changed for 8pm. Maybe then Mammy and Daddy could take time to watch a movie by candlelight. For a few months the seas were calm, the new parents gave each other a clap on the back for taking to their new task like ducks to water (maybe lambs to the slaughter) and then the tables turned. Poor baby Juliet began all her teething problems, the hardest time for mums and dads, with no rest for the wicked. Georgia was beginning to feel the strain. Juliet dribbled and whinged quietly to herself in her bad moments but in her good moments she was beginning to make wonderful sounds. She had discovered how to cough, and seemed to enjoy the sound of her own voice. It was comical to look at her big red rosy cheeks as she opened her mouth to make all these sounds, woo and ahh ahh ahh and then look around to see where the sounds were coming from with a look of great surprise in her eyes and her ears on full alert as she heard the sound of her own voice.

This was fascinating stuff for Georgia and Cameron, everything was a new experience, every sound, every smile, every cough and every tear. They looked on mesmerised at this little creature they had produced, their very own little mini me. She brought out so many new emotions in her bewitched parents. They just loved when friends remarked on the resemblance between Juliet and both of them. A true love child, Georgia felt fulfilled. To date this was the best experience of her life. Once Georgia was in the room, Juliet followed her with her eyes and once she was in sight that little baby was completely happy. All in all Juliet was a very good baby, happy, smiling, gurgling and enjoying all the attention bestowed on her by her doting parents.

CHAPTER 51

An unexpected invitation

One Sunday, no Maria, kitchen in turmoil, pots and pans everywhere, bottles, nappies, all strewn around. This was one of those days when Georgia just couldn't come to grips with the normal day to day chores. What had gone wrong? Well, for whatever reason, today she just couldn't get her head around anything. In the distance she heard the phone ring and really wasn't pushed to move herself to answer its call. It stopped for just a brief moment and then it started to ring again. This time she couldn't ignore it.

'Hi Georgia', came the friendly voice down the phone line. It was none other than Tanya. She was indeed a happy little camper but Georgia knew Tanya had some little question to ask her.

'Think about this one, my dear friend' Tanya chirped. 'Would you like to do something really exciting?'

'Yes' came the feeble reply down the line. 'Anything but stay in this kitchen, wiping babies bottoms and ironing babies clothes.'

'Then how about a trip, just a short few days to help your old pal at London Fashion Week?'

Georgia gasped.

Tanya continued 'I've been invited by one of Ireland's top designers to help dress the models for her shows. She has two big shows throughout the week. Personally,' said Tanya 'I'm so excited so why don't you come and share in the excitement. I think you'd be the very person to accompany me. You're always telling me you love the buzz of work and this would be the buzz to eclipse all others.'

'I'm on a high already.' Said Georgia in a high-pitched voice that matched how she felt. 'It's a great idea, but surely it's impossible for me to do that Tanya, gone are the days when I was free and single and could do anything at the drop of a hat, I have responsibilities now.'

'Well just sleep on it.' Said Tanya 'Have a think I won't ask anyone else until you come back to me.'

Georgia listened to her friend's chatter and felt so drawn to the idea.

'All expenses paid, including meals. Just imagine a chauffeur driven car to and from the airport and a few great days at London fashion week, where the days are busy and the nights are mayhem. There is one catch however, you'll have to work.'

There was a silence, Georgia hadn't thought about work but there's always a catch, there's nothing for nothing, no free meals that was something Georgia had learned a long time ago.

'Just think of it, Georgia, all expenses paid.'

'That sounds good' said Georgia. 'All meals included, that sounds even better. Being chauffeur driven in London, that's the icing on the cake but work!!!'

Tanya butted in, 'You're the one who always says if you're doing something you enjoy, you're not working.'

'But what about my baby Juliet? I can't very well hide her away in a little corner where no one would notice her sleeping quietly.'

(Definitely not, Georgia's little dream was certainly not an option.)

'Tanya I will do my best, thank you for asking and thank you for brightening me up on this day of muddles.'

'Keep your sunny side up, Georgia, hide the side that gets blue. I'll wait to hear from you, but I'll have to know by early tomorrow morning.'

There was a silence. Tanya was gone, Georgia tried her best to settle down to her motherly chores but now thoughts of London were swirling around in her head. She was going to try to make it happen. In fairness Juliet was a very good little baby, it was only if she was in pain, teething, that she cried, otherwise she just smiled, cooed and gave no trouble at all but with all her heart Georgia would love to take this job. So what could she do? Then like a bolt of lightning, the answer was written in the stars, yes right up there in that blue, blue sky… Parisian Nanny. Those words glistened and gleamed up above in the blue skyline. This could be her answer. Maria was hungry for money, so surely with the promise of extra salary that would allow her an extra bit of financial freedom to help her stay in Ireland for a little longer, she just might oblige. After all, she knew Juliet so well by now and Juliet loved her. Miracles do happen!

Cameron was no sooner in the door than dinner was on the table, dessert delicious, glass of wine, the scene was set. It was a lovely meal, the time was right. Georgia kissed him on the cheek and out came the question:

'I've been invited by Tanya to London Fashion Week. Tanya and I would be working on the show with an Irish designer. All our expenses will be paid, we'd also have a chauffeur driven car, if you don't mind, to and from the airport and a bit of free time to buy some new clothes. I'd just love to go Cameron. Do you think it would be at all possible for you to rearrange your schedule and take a few days off work? I really feel it would brighten me up and give me a little bit of a spurt, after all I've gone through bringing your beautiful daughter into this world.'

Cameron sat there quietly, not saying a word. Georgia had to work extra hard.

'Please Cameron, see what you can do. London Fashion Week

starts in seven days so I have to let Tanya know in the morning. Oh! I almost forgot, if you're happy with me going, I was going to ask Maria would she stay here for the few days and help you look after Juliet.'

She tried to explain to him how good it would be to start earning some extra cash. Georgia put on her begging face. It would be worth all the trying if she was released from mammy duty for three whole days. That now seemed attainable. She'd given it her best shot, as the farmers say, the answer lies in the soil.

Not even an argument, just 'why not. I'll really try to move things around' he said, as he opened up his laptop and began organising, hopefully Georgia's freedom. She could see he was trying to do the best he could to give his darling wife just what she needed, a few days away, after a nine month pregnancy, non-stop bottle feeding and nappy changing.

Although Georgia was really keen to travel to London and have all that freedom, deep in her heart she really only wanted to be with her little girl. She loved every bone in her little body and like all new mothers felt no one could look after Juliet quite like her. But sure, maybe a few days away would clear her head and bring her back to bouncing that new buggy up and down the neighbourhood. She'd have something other than bottles to talk about. Instead of telling Cameron how many times she had to change Juliet she would be talking about the bright lights of London. That could be good for her and Cameron and as the old song says everybody needs a little time away. Georgia lay in bed that night imagining three days of freedom from all her chores. She decided not to push the issue, she would give Cameron space to try to reschedule his work.

Breakfast was the usual Shredded Wheat, slice of toast and glass of orange juice. Of course, that was after baby Juliet was fed, bathed, changed and she lay sleeping in her cot. Cameron picked his moment and cleared his throat. She knew he had a statement to make.

'I've got it sorted Georgia, I've just checked my laptop, the last piece of the jigsaw is in place, I'm covered. One of the guys I did a favour for is returning it. So off you go, make your phone call to Tanya and just relax. If Maria can come and stay, fantastic, if Maria can't come and stay I'm well capable of looking after our little girl. It will give us a chance to bond. It will be nice to have her to myself for a few days. First, you will just have to go through a few things with me and I'll take notes.'

'What do you need to know, Cameron?'

'Like how to prepare her bottles, how to change her nappy without all her baby grows getting drowned?'

'Now is that all you need to know? Are there any other questions?'

'Loads' said Cameron, 'I'll think of them, write them down and ask before you leave. One springs to mind, how do you take the brake off that pram and what do I pack for her when we're going out? How?'

Cameron was nervous at the prospect of being alone with Juliet. He was just about to ask another question.

'Cameron, relax, you have a million and one questions, we'll sit down and I promise I'll answer all of your worries before I leave for three days that somehow, I imagine, you think is for three years.'

The pair hugged, both very happy that the problems were sorted. In a way Cameron would have three days free from his work too and maybe when Georgia returned, Cameron would have a new respect for mothers all over the world who stay at home to nurture their children. Cameron went off to work and

Georgia wasted no time in calling her friend Tanya. She was overcome with excitement and couldn't wait to get the words out.

'Tanya, I'm going with you to London Fashion Week. I cannot wait, I'm so excited. I feel I've got energy that I never knew I had. I can't wait to use it all up in London.'

Poor Tanya couldn't get a word in.

'Will you call over to me later and we can go through everything over a cup of tea or maybe a glass of wine. There're bottles of all sorts of drinks here, presents since I had Juliet. We haven't touched a sup, so if you play your cards right you could go home tipsy Miss Whitley.'

At last Tanya got a chance to say something.

'I'm thrilled you're coming with me. If it's ok with you I'll call over around 3pm but I can only stay for an hour.'

She did come over at 3 and they did chat about the two shows they would take part in, there was a lot more to discuss but that could happen later. Georgia had been to many places, many shows, mostly hair and beauty. They did include fashion but hair would have been the main theme, whereas this time it was all fashion. With no time to go through the itinerary it would have to be tackled on board the Aer Lingus plane. Georgia liked that idea, it would take her mind off the altitude the plane would fly at. If she kept busy panic would hopefully not set in. Her legs wouldn't turn into jelly, her lips wouldn't tremble with fear as they usually did from the moment she boarded an airplane until the moment she disembarked. True to form it worked. By the time they touched down at Heathrow she knew where she'd be every moment. It was going to be fast and furious.

CHAPTER 52

London fashion week (three days)

Georgia could feel the adrenalin rush as her little feet did their best to keep in time with Tanya's brisk strides. The journey to the arrivals seemed endless, thank God for the escalator that left them close to the Hertz desk, where sure enough a man stood with a plaque held high. Tanya's name was there for all the world to see. She smiled at the gentleman, he insisted on carrying their cases. They began to walk through the automatic doors and out to the black limousine that awaited their arrival. In moments they were speeding towards the centre of London to a little hotel in Soho. Although it was small it was beautiful, everything about it was pure chic, every girl's dream and right in the centre of everything.

No sooner had they laid their cases down than the phone rang, they must go straight to *Claridges Hotel* for the big and beautiful fashion show. Out came the big Irish badges, with the Irish flag in the centre and pleated satin surrounding it. Straight onto their black tops the badges went. They'd been asked to wear these as people from all over the world were exhibiting here and everybody loved the Irish.

Georgia had never met the designer before. She was so lovely with the softest Irish brogue imaginable. While other designers rushed around like mad hares, Deirdre did everything calmly and methodically. It worked out perfectly well. This was the first time Georgia had ever visited London Fashion Week and what an experience it was turning out to be. Everything Tanya asked her to do, she did to the best of her ability, loving every moment.

It was funny how this show was bringing out Georgia's patriotic side, believe it or not she wanted the Irish models to look the best they could be on the catwalk and they did. She couldn't help but notice the models' amazing height, shapes and bone structure. No big boobs, in fact sometimes quite flat chested but all oozing charisma. Soon it was lights, camera, action and from a little spot backstage Georgia and Tanya gazed out as the lights hit the diamonds and sequins that adorned next season's creations.

The models just focussed on one spot and strutted their stuff. It was a sight to be seen with photographers perched like a choir, flashing bulbs everywhere catching the sparkle from the chic hats decorated with sequins and following on through to the dresses, each one different, each one magnificent. Georgia especially liked the sequined collar, cut almost like a sailor collar at the back, hanging loosely and moving with every sway of the model's shoulders, finishing at the bra strap and leaving the rest of the back bare.

The paparazzi were already in the room in little groups for such a long time before the show began. Georgia only now realised there was an art to this. In her naivety Georgia thought all photographers just pushed their way to the front, but no, these guys and girls cooperated with each other. Some were down on one knee, others crouched, some standing on platforms, giving everyone space, a clear view, it worked. Hopefully every photographer would get that one shot they desired that night. The cameras flashed on celebrities and their companions sitting in the audience, familiar faces they recognised in the ballroom, no doubt with today's technology those photographs would reach their destination in minutes to adorn the morning's papers. Every designer needed celebrity faces to draw notice to their exquisite designs and in fairness the celebrities seemed to enjoy being photographed.

In all, the fashion show was amazing, from the spectacular hairstyles, to the funky makeup and the glittering clothes and shoes. Every move was so well timed, right down to the very last moment. Georgia was mesmerised. Where did she go wrong? How she would have loved to have this life but if there was any chance before, there was certainly no chance now, her life was sorted. She was a young mother and even though she loved her role she felt a little bit envious of these single, young girls only starting out on their long road to fame and fortune. Once the show was over all the backstage crew, including Tanya and Georgia, got to work frantically undressing the models and passing on the clothes to be hung up, numbered and making sure all the exquisite dresses were back in their rightful places. This was a very busy time for anyone in the fashion industry. It was so vital to have their designs noticed.

The young models changed speedily back into their own clothes and rushed towards the door for their next fashion show in some other part of London. Some were picked up by cars and others left, wearing crash helmets and jumping on the back of big, strong motorbikes as pillion passengers. Motorbike taxi was the quickest way to get in and out through London traffic as everything came to almost a standstill while London Fashion Week was on. It's just as well the models are so young and able for this very busy time that is known as London Fashion Week.

Once the show was over and the clothes gathered, Georgia and Tanya took to the flight of stairs to take their place at a little table with big comfortable armchairs where they ordered tea and cakes and gazed down towards the black and white marble flooring, all the time scanning the area for celebrities. This hotel was surely the most perfect place to host such a fabulous event. As the two girls sat there chatting, they wondered if it was possible to get their hands on some little souvenir to remind them of the time they spent at the fabulous show in London town.

Then Georgia noticed two little girls, whom she'd seen earlier amusing themselves running up and down. Guess what they wore apart from their pretty dresses? Yes, your first thought was right. On their little heads, perched ever so perfectly, lay pretty berets covered in large sequins displaying a designer's name, one that had exhibited at the show. A copy of the very berets the models had worn earlier. On closer inspection Georgia realised there was a big box of berets sitting on a chair. These young ladies weren't alone, they were accompanied by two models who in turn handed the berets to them to be presented to whoever they chose. That day the luck of the Irish was with Tanya and Georgia, the two little girls presented a precious beret to each one and requested Tanya and Georgia to sit down so they could place the berets correctly on their heads. Tanya and Georgia loved the attention they got as the berets glistened and gleamed against the bright lights in the room.

'We must have a photograph taken with you, we look like sisters' they said in their best English accents.

As one of the professional photographers passed by he insisted on taking a photograph with the four beauties sparkling and made sure to get all their information, names, etc.

'Maybe we'll be in the paper tomorrow' said Tanya. 'If only.'

Once they got home these berets would take pride of place in both girls' bedrooms.

One Irish designer's show over, one to go.

CHAPTER 53

The end of an inspirational week

The two beauties had two hours to spare next morning, so they made a beeline for the shops dressed in jeans, runners and their diamante berets. In and out of every shop they shimmied. Zara, H & M, Mango, Office and let's not forget Top Shop, their very favourite, where you were guaranteed to never leave empty handed. If you couldn't find a beautiful dress on the main floors of Top Shop on Oxford Street you could head downstairs and maybe find something beautiful and different in the concession area or maybe skip on towards vintage where, without a shadow of a doubt, Georgia and Tanya would find something completely different, a real once off especially at this time of the year when London fashion week is in full swing. Fashion stores really put on their best displays allowing young designers to exhibit in the concession areas where they can feel part of London Fashion Week and display their fabulous designs.

Georgia and Tanya's minds were completely blown away with on-trend clothes and futuristic designs. It was great to meet some of the new young designers who were filled with enthusiasm. Their enthusiasm brushed off on Georgia and Tanya as they flew around the shop and spent far too much money. How could they help spending money, with the buzz surrounding the store all they could do was pick out little pieces of heaven. For Georgia a pretty turquoise dress with a princess neckline and for Tanya an exquisite orange halter neck dress. Of course they had to have one of those trendy belts, each one hoping it would change one of their old plain dresses into a fashion statement. What an environment to be in? What an amazing atmosphere? This was why Tanya and Georgia had left the show for just a little while, to feel the London buzz.

In true girly fashion the two emerged laden down with trash, but classy, trashy clothes to be worn and torn and eventually used as dusters but for now pure fashion. They had a deadline to meet, this time they were even more prepared and like all troopers they were there right on the button, on time. It would take the next few hours to get everything moving but the two girls were comfortable with each other and always worked well together. Then of course, the models were professionals. The clothes yet again, surpassed themselves, they were simply magnificent, the colours delicate and the lines perfect. The models carried them off to perfection as they enjoyed the paparazzi flashing their cameras. They took it all in their stride, more celebrities, more photographs, presentation of designer, followed by encores. Then for Tanya and Georgia it was over, the last night of London Fashion Week.

Tonight was party night at a swanky hotel, organised in honour of all stage hands, dressers, hair stylists, make-up artists and anyone and everyone who took part in this year's fashion week extravaganza. The vibe was red hot. This was a huge occasion, so of course, Tanya and Georgia were dressed to kill in their new ensembles. Tanya in her perfect purchase, the pretty orange halter neck dress, that hugged her curvy shape while Georgia on the other hand wore her amazing newly purchased pretty turquoise dress with a princess neckline. It seemed as if everyone who worked on fashion week was there and much to Georgia's surprise, Tanya knew almost everyone, but seemed very drawn to one very attractive, well dressed, well-built male. Georgia could swear it was Creed aftershave he was wearing. She just loved that men's fragrance. Tanya smiled and laughed, she was happily keeping busy as she circled in and out of the crowd, always glancing back in the hunk's direction and returning to the gorgeous male every time she got the chance. Georgia began to think, I wonder what his name is? I think it's great to see Tanya looking as happy as a lark and getting so much attention from her gorgeous admirer but all I can think about is my baby girl and my other half Cameron, who is hopefully waiting longingly at home for my return. But for now, I'll live in the moment and enjoy the atmosphere. A great night was had by all with lots of dancing, lots of wine and lots of heady laughter. It was a great time to let your hair down after such a gruelling few days.

They could get used to this way of life but like all good things they come to an end. As they slipped off their strappy sandals and limped their way to their comfy bed, the two girls looked and felt the worse for wear. Tomorrow morning they needed to be up, packed and gone from their room by 10am in order to make a 2pm flight. This weekend had turned out to be one of the most amazing weekends they'd had together, full of organised chaos, happy smiles and wonderful moments. There was one thing for sure! Georgia would never forget working on London Fashion Week and Tanya made good contacts, had rekindled some of her old contacts (male wearing Creed aftershave) and had some promises of work and dinner dates to come in the near future. They had some goody bags to take home with a variety of perfumes, T shirts and jewellery inside. No one went home empty handed and the most fantastic thing was the moment they bumped into the two little girls who presented them with a newspaper with their picture on the front page. The caption read *Every generation loves London fashion week*. Underneath were the little girls' names and the big girls' names. That photograph was the icing on the cake for all four.

'Thank you for presenting us with our lovely berets.' Georgia and Tanya said to the little girls, 'If you hadn't we wouldn't have this gorgeous photograph to show off when we go home.' There were kisses and hugs all round.

CHAPTER 54

Home is where the heart lies

Cameron stood at the arrivals door in Dublin Airport with little Juliet in his arms, awaiting the arrival of the love of his life and her friend, smiling from ear to ear. They dropped Tanya off at her place and as their car drove towards their home Georgia thanked her lucky stars she had her little family. Glamour and glitz is one thing but home is where the heart lies.

Once Juliet was packed off to bed, surrounded by her little teddies, the two love birds settled down to fill in the gaps on the last 3 days they had spent apart. They both had stories to tell. Georgia had the one that included the beret. To Cameron's delight she made sure to dress up in the beret and not a lot else. She strutted up and down the kitchen doing her best impression of the models strutting on the catwalk to show the full impact, explaining that the whole show glittered just like the sequins on her hat, it indeed was a sight to behold. As for the shops, they came up to their usual standard, retail therapy was certainly the best way forward. To finish Georgia presented firstly the paper with the photograph of the four happy girls at London Fashion Week.

Cameron was so thrilled to see the love of his life's big beaming smile looking back at him from the newspaper and even more delighted to open the present she had spent so long choosing for her favourite man. A fabulous jacket, which, thank God, fitted him perfectly. Those broad shoulders looked even better entwined in the fabulous, cosy wool, herringbone cloth and the colour, wow, deep navy. She was falling in love with him all over again.

Cameron went on to describe his last few days alone without the love of his life. Well, he really wasn't alone, as it seemed Maria had taken up Georgia's offer and stayed over for one night only to cook some of her special French cuisine. (Really trying to impress him. huh!) Georgia could feel a surge of jealousy, this wasn't usually her style but she definitely recognised it. Her body temperature soared so she took a few deep breaths and did her best to look nonchalant as she continued to convince herself there was nothing to worry about. Cameron hadn't noticed that hot flush at all, he just continued describing the French wine, it was just a bottle she'd brought with her, to take away his blues. (And it seemed to have worked!) He described how Juliet remained sleeping soundly all night long. (Hmm he must have been awake all night with Maria, happy Juliet was sleeping!)

Cameron continued. 'The time passed relatively fast, Georgia, I was so busy with Juliet.'

(I bet you were busy with Maria. You probably wished the weekend would never end, jealousy, jealousy, jealousy) From that moment on Georgia felt uncomfortable with Maria. She vowed she would never again stay in Georgia's home. Maybe it's just women's intuition, or Georgia's imagination working over-time but why put a spanner in the works. She began to notice just how pretty Maria really was, how her beautiful hair moved and shone as she dusted and cleaned like a tornado around the house. She began to feel Maria was a threat and so it started. On the days Georgia worked she rushed home like a mad woman to make sure there was no hanky panky going on. This whole situation was taking its toll on her, she felt so tired. She just had to cop on, calm down and realise how stupid she was carrying on. She did what she did best, sat down at the mirror in her bedroom, stared at her own reflection in the mirror and did some straight talking to herself.

In her heart she knew Cameron loved only her and Juliet. There was absolutely no room in his heart for anyone else. The jealous feeling she had was beginning to subside, soon she was putting everything down to her insecurities. She began meeting up with her friends again and getting back to her old self, but the seeds were sown, her doubts were locked in her mind, she felt as if she was going mad. It was time to take a stand and do something.

So she did what she had to do, make an appointment with a therapist and right now she was on her way for her very first meeting. First things first, there would be no car involved in this, it was staying at home. She had confided in Cameron and told him about her insecurities. She did not tell him she thought he was up to something with Maria. (That was the cause of her insecurities)

'I need to talk to someone about all the different feelings I am going through.'

Without hesitation Cameron took the day off work and was very happy to mind Juliet. He was so understanding, it must have come from all his background in the priesthood, theology and psychology, or just maybe, he was doing his best to keep her happy so she wouldn't realise he had strayed?

She jumped off the LUAS, then crossed the road at full speed and jumped into the first taxi cab available. In moments the taxi was speeding towards Merrion Road. She had to almost pinch herself to remember the reason she was going there in the first place, maybe she'd have been better off spending her money on sexy underwear instead of delving deep into her inner thoughts to find out where she was going wrong. Was it not crystal clear?

She just didn't ring his bells anymore. Her dull and dismal ways were obviously rubbing off on him. Maybe all she needed was those sexy undies and an evening at home to convince Cameron that she was the woman for him.

CHAPTER 55

Therapist

It's not good manners to stand up a therapist, God knows what evil spell they might bestow. No, she'd face her demons, face all her flaws for once and see where the journey led. She was there, paying the fare and a tip. The therapist was ready for her, she must go into the lion's den. In fairness the lady was extremely nice and understanding, she allowed Georgia to get all her problems off her chest. The therapist did very little except listen, nod her head a little from time to time, take a few notes, give the odd smile, the odd frown. I suppose letting Georgia know she was still interested and deeply concentrating on her every word. You'd really wonder what goes through these therapists' heads as they listen to their patients' woes and sorrows. Do they think we're all nuts, or maybe they just drift off and think about their own problems? No good pondering on those thoughts, Georgia would never know the answers. This lady was good at her job, that was all that mattered. It was time to leave the consulting room. You always know when the time has come even though no bells ring, no alarms go off, no clocks buzz. There comes a moment when you start to repeat yourself, there's nothing left to say, the therapist begins to fold up her papers and pile them neatly in front of her. Her desk looked immaculate and in her own silent way she was letting Georgia know the moment of dismissal was nigh.

Georgia stood up and thanked the therapist for helping to clear the fog from her head and returned to the waiting room. Glancing at the clock she realised she had been chatting for 45 minutes, hardly without taking a breath. Her throat felt dry, she needed some cool water fast, although bleary eyed and exhausted her head felt a lot clearer, all she had to do now was act on the information she had. It's amazing how all of this information came from herself, all the answers came from her. For now, she'd spent enough time talking, thinking and knowing she would have to wait until later on to put her plan into action. She would draw a curtain on everything and head back in a taxi. After the stillness of the counselling room, Georgia was delighted to be out in the air with lights flashing, car horns beeping, people shouting, real life, ahhhhhh. Only 45 minutes spent sitting with a therapist and she felt bowled over, imagine what she would feel like if she had to spend 2 weeks in a psychiatric unit. Georgia guessed, after that length of time she'd be completely institutionalised and need more therapy to bring her back to the land of the living.

Yet another taxi but it was all in the name of pampering and she knew she needed it. Georgia couldn't say she'd come to terms with Cameron's infidelity, if in fact there was any infidelity on Cameron's part. Now as she went over everything she discussed with her therapist, Georgia began to understand that maybe it was indeed her insecurities that had all these pent up feelings going through her head. She could only put it down to her baby brain and realised she might need another session or two with the therapist to bring her up to scratch. She'd come to realise it wasn't all her fault, after all to err is human and let's pour all the blame on him for the moment, unlike years earlier when she would have blamed every problem on her making. This was a whole new phase for Georgia, therapists are a wonderful thing. She would recommend hers to a friend, in fact any friend who needed to talk through their problems. It was easy to think like that when her spirits were rising again and she wasn't feeling like the victim. She needed to take Cameron by the hand and get him outside that door and into a beautiful restaurant, just the two of them, no baby on board and for a plan like this she needed her mother. Would Nellie mind her little granddaughter now that Juliet is getting a little older and there's more to be done for her? To hell with the negatives, the positive thing is I do have a mother, she's always helped when I was stuck, ever since Juliet was born, the time has come, I'm calling her right now. Georgia was a girl who always acted on impulse.

'Hello Mum. It's me, your ever loving daughter, Georgia. I've quite a big favour to ask of you. Remember you're my minder in waiting? Well the waiting is over, I really need you to mind Juliet for a night. You see, I want to take Cameron out for a meal, just to celebrate the fact that we've got this far with baby Juliet and it has been reasonably smooth sailing. Mum I don't mean to sound smug, I'm just saying we could do with one night out together, just the two of us.' … Silence.

'I can't believe it' said Georgia's mum, 'No problem, Georgia I've been here ready and waiting. When the house phone rang I grabbed it so fast, it nearly fell, I just knew it was you requesting my services. Will I put my hat and coat on now and run for the house?'

'Whoa, Mum, hold your horses. First, I have to tell Cameron and then I'm wondering would next Saturday night suit you. We could have an early meal and sit by a nice fire somewhere reminiscing with a glass of bubbly in our hands.'

'Saturday night would suit me grand, if Cameron Oks it. Sure why wouldn't he when I'm offering my services free? Is it OK if I bring a friend with me, just to keep me company when I'm there?'

'Now Mum, you're going a step too far here, I think it's best if you come alone.'

'That's grand' said her mum 'I was only chancing my arm.'

The die was cast and the babysitter organised, Georgia felt she had soared from the muddy streets in her head right up into the clouds. Let's hope this mood will last. Well today is Thursday, only two days to go, when myself and my lover will be painting the town red, if Cameron accepts my invitation. He did. I love when you don't have to wait too long for a glass of bubbly and a night on the town.

CHAPTER 56

Romancing the stone

Mum was here, taxi waiting outside, holding hands, romantic journey into town. Dillon's, always the place to be when you're all glammed up. Steaks medium rare, sauté onions, mushrooms and of course, some French fries. The pair were so tired and hungry they just ate and hardly a word was spoken as they enjoyed every morsel. For dessert, Georgia ordered the chocolate bomb. What she liked best about this was when the hot chocolate is poured so creamily on top, then it all melts onto the plate in one big creaminess… delicious. Still not a lot of talking as Cameron enjoyed his apple pie and cream. What a meal! A hot chocolate for Georgia and a Bailey's Coffee for Cameron. It was only then they began to relax, sit back and talk. Cameron admitted how sorry he was that he hadn't made the first move and taken Georgia out for this meal. He'd left everything to her and poor thing, she was so busy with all her chores but she still found time to find time for them.

'I can finally say I am completely and utterly happy with my life. When I was in the monastery I continuously questioned myself, asking should I stay or should I go? To tell you the truth Georgia I spent far too much time delving into my inner thoughts but that's what I had to do in order to make the right choice that I am completely and utterly happy with. I'm in a great place. Thank God I made the right decision. I'm not trying to just talk all about me but I knew you would also have suffered if I made the wrong decision and I didn't want that for you.'

'I know Cameron,' said Georgia. 'I remember when we moved

in together first, I was so worried because you didn't seem to be settling in to sharing full time the bedroom, the kitchen, the whole thing.'

'I know' said Cameron. 'it was a complete U turn for me. I'd only had that tiny room, the cell, but it was my tiny room. My clothes sat tidy in my tiny wardrobe then all of a sudden, it was your clothes that seemed to take over. I had no say in the kitchen and quite honestly, I didn't know if I liked sharing or not. After all, I was six years in the seminary, it's a long time. I became very singular, then all of a sudden, I was a partner... it was very hard. Now I know I just needed to adjust my thought pattern. I had to change the way my mind worked and include you in everything I did but, Georgia, it was all so well worth it, every day I'm with you I love you more and more. I love the quiet times, the baby changing times, the us times, the sharing.'

'Cameron, I know it's been hard for you, I watched as you tried your best to re-adjust but I'm a patient broad (she laughed).'

He nodded his head in agreement. Georgia continued. 'I do my best to get from life what I need and want and Cameron all I ever wanted since the day I met you, was you. You have just blown my mind from the first moment we met and I know as the years roll on, I will just love you more with every day that passes.'

There was nothing left for either of them to say. The night was a pure success. They had an understanding... Georgia need never worry about Maria or indeed, any other woman taking her man. She was determined to keep the love alive forever and a day and he vowed to always put her first no matter how many other children they had, no matter how many other friends they had, she would be his priority. Always was, from first glance to eternity. The love birds sat side by side in the taxi cab, silent, both of them going over and over their conversation, their commitments to each other, to feel so secure in a relationship was everything to both of them. They felt so content there was nothing left to say.

Nellie, Georgia's mum had Juliet tucked up and fast asleep in her perfectly padded pink cot. Things were already changing slowly... perfect. Hopefully Nellie would continue her position as head babysitter to baby Juliet, what a nice way to build up a relationship with her granddaughter. From now on, Nellie pledged to give them time out to eat, drink and be merry at least once a month, when she'd stay over, get up early and feed Juliet her first meal of the day. Great expectations in the bedroom, lots of good vibrations, some man for one man... Ooh la la!

CHAPTER 57

Fr. Fergus Breen returns to Ireland

Georgia was really in a very happy place she said out loud to herself, I'm so lucky to have Cameron and all my friends around me, my mum on hand to baby sit and when I'm feeling down she's always there to give me that little bit of moral support to help boost my morale. I also have my work colleagues, all in all I'm surrounded by love. On the other hand Cameron's friends from school and more importantly, his mum and dad all live in the country and I don't know any of his work colleagues but on the bright side Cameron is so lucky to have one dear friend since he was 18 years old, in his last two teenage years and on and on since then, Maisie. She's been like a mother to him, she alone shielded him sometimes when he didn't even know he was being shielded. She always tried to give him the best advice, then when I came along she helped me through the turbulent times. When I didn't know what to do she advised me. In fairness, I listened to her advice but very seldom took it but that's me, headstrong. It's nice to know Maisie is still in both our lives, adopted auntie to our little girl Juliet, new fond friend of my mum, Nellie, and guiding star to both Cameron and myself. I'll call her right now, invite her over, it's time we caught up on our chats. Message to brain, don't let Maisie's love, kindness and dedication fade into oblivion. Keep it always here present.

'Hello Maisie, just a quick call, would you like to join myself, Cameron, Juliet and Nellie for Sunday lunch? … That's great Maisie, if you could be here for 2.30, we'll start with drinks and see where we'll go from there.'

'I can't wait,' said Maisie. 'I know it sounds cheeky of me but could I take along a friend?'

Georgia wanted to say no, I can't cook for four and Juliet but she knew better than to say anything, after all Maisie was an auntie now, part of the inner sanctum of the family. Right there in the heart of it and any friend of Maisie had to be a friend of Cameron, Georgia, Juliet, Nellie and the three friends. In order to not show that slight hesitation, Georgia rushed through with:

'Of course, you're more than welcome to take a friend along.'

Phone back on the receiver, Georgia wondered who is this friend? Maisie hadn't said if they were male or female but Georgia assumed it would be male and so the days drizzled on towards Sunday. With lots of encouragement Juliet began to eat from the spoon, she loved the desserts much like her mum and dad, all that sweetness, but getting her to eat anything that tasted like dinner took a lot of effort. Juliet shook her head and stuck her tongue out. The food looked dreadful all the way around her mouth and down onto her bib but Georgia persevered. She was beginning to see a light at the end of the tunnel. Another one of Juliet's tricks when she was beginning to walk was to hold onto the chairs, let go and fall down in a pile on the ground but as the song says, *I get knocked down but I get up again, nobody's going to keep me down, I get knocked down but I get up again.*

She'd come to the next phase of her growth, the high chair had already been purchased, it now had pride of place at the table. Every day, at meal time, Juliet was placed into her high chair, sometimes when she didn't want to get in she straightened her whole body and screamed, Georgia or Cameron, whoever happened to be holding her at that moment, would take her back up, comfort her and start the whole process over again. Juliet was beginning to understand it was safe to sit alone. She was a very active child, she didn't like sitting for too long, she'd start bending her leg up through the chair and try to lift herself up and out of it. Sure maybe when she's older she'll be a gymnast, jumping up on bars and twirling around.

And so the days passed quickly, then it was Sunday, 2pm sharp. Nellie had her little apron on helping Georgia dress the table and light the scented vanilla candles. Dinner in the oven, ham, chicken, carrots, turnips, Brussels sprouts, brown gravy, it was all there to be followed by chocolate cake with whipped cream. Georgia heard the doorbell ringing, she ran to the door holding Juliet in her arms and opened the door wide. There stood Maisie dressed in a lemon dress and dark golden shoes with a matching handbag and there beside her, lo and behold stood Father Fergus Breen. Holy Jesus, were the only words that came into Georgia's head (at least they were holy words, fit for a priest). Cameron didn't know how to react when he was introduced to Father Fergus Breen. He had never met him but he had heard lots of stories about him, all good stories, he was a happy priest, dedicated to his work and loved his parishioners, they still spoke of him to this day. Now he was inside the lovely bungalow sitting at the table.

At the head of the table sat Cameron, at the other end of the table sat Nellie, at one side of the table Georgia and Juliet sat and on the other side, Maisie Coyne and Father Fergus Breen. The atmosphere was a little tense and awkward. Maisie seemed to be really on her guard, watching her P's and Q's, so the flow of conversation was extremely slow. Nellie sussed out the situation, she hated when things went like this, so she did what she had to do, broke the silence and said:

'Everyone here at the table, I just want to tell you all about my weekend away.'

The small party at the table were pleased someone said something to break the awkwardness. Everyone sat up and listened attentively, even Juliet sat up straight. She loved the excitement, so she gurgled, laughed and was fantastic.

'Just to fill everyone in' said Nellie 'I spent last weekend away in London. I stayed in the Hilton Hotel. It was just amazing, you should all take a break in London and stay in the Hilton Hotel.' She continued to speak directly to her little audience. 'Breakfast is just lovely there, you'd really enjoy it, lunch was intoxicating, a few drinks always lightens the mood' as she said these words she looked around the room. 'We always had sandwiches followed by champagne. Our evenings started with the early bird meal followed by a West End show. My favourite one was *The Phantom of the Opera*. Although I saw it lots of times, it's always a show worth revisiting and then of course, we wanted to see a new show so we went to see *Waitress*. You'd all love that, especially the ladies.'

Everyone nodded their heads in agreement and Nellie continued to entertain her captive audience.

'What I love about London is when the show is over there's a variety of restaurants that open late where you can sit, eat, drink and recap with your friends on the show you've just seen.'

Father Breen contributed to the conversation.

'Yes' said Father Fergus Breen. 'I love the shows in London too, we always made a point of going once a month for the pre-theatre dinner and then on to a show. Because we belonged to a musical society we could buy the theatre tickets at discount prices, so we could go very regularly to visit the West End. I always feel alive when I'm in the heart of London going to a show.'

'Maybe you should have been on the stage.' said Nellie.

In fairness the timing was perfect, the meal was over, the dessert had been enjoyed and now everyone had tea, coffee or a glass of something in front of them. Yes, perfect timing for Cameron to stand up straight, place one foot on the chair, cradle his guitar and strum the perfect notes to the perfect song. *Georgia on My Mind.* Georgia was blown away by how absolutely handsome and sexy her partner was. Cameron had broken the ice for everyone and for his efforts he received a standing ovation.

'They said I had a good voice.' said Fr. Fergus Breen. 'It's a bit rusty now.' He added 'I'm looking to join a musical society here. I'm told the R & R is the place to be. Would any of you like me to sing a song for you?'

He stood up proudly, opened his mouth and began to sing a song from the musical Mikado.

A Wandering Minstrel I,

A thing of shreds and patches.

Of ballads, songs and snatches. etc.etc.

What a theatrical afternoon this was turning out to be.

'Maisie' said Father Fergus, am I right in thinking you were once part of a musical society?'

'You're right Fergus, I am actually still a member of a musical society, The R & R in Rathmines. The One you are thinking of joining. They're looking for new vocalists. I'll put a word in for you.' Maisie said jokingly. 'We're working on something at the moment, it's a Gilbert and Sullivan light opera, *The Pirates of Penzance.* I'm singing one of the songs, well I'm singing more than one. Since you have sung a song, I think I should sing one too. Would you mind Cameron, Georgia, Nellie and Juliet if I give you a little rendering?'

Everyone nodded in agreement, (What else could they do) even Juliet said 'ba ba ba' With so much confidence and absolutely no inhibitions, Maisie began to sing the song:

Three little maids from school
Pert as a school-girl well can be
Filled to the brim with girlish glee
Three little maids from school are we.

Georgia, Cameron, Nellie and even baby Juliet were left with their mouths open when they heard Maisie singing. She had such a fabulous voice. Maisie Coyne had lost her calling, she should have been an opera singer. Georgia thought, the bloody idiot had spent too long scrubbing floors and licking up to Fergus Breen, when she could have done so many other things with her life. Georgia wanted to scream out loud, something Maisie had warned Georgia of, Maisie you have wasted too much time chasing a dream, but it was too late for that statement, instead she said nothing. To everyone's astonishment and not to be hard done by, Nellie also sang her song and took her bow. Nellie's song was not quite as highbrow as Fergus and Maisie's. She sang one of her favourite songs of all time, Leo Sayer's *When I need You*. Cameron accompanied her on guitar. This song for her was filled with memories of someone she once loved. Everyone at the table clapped and felt a surge of emotion as Nellie gave it her all. She took her bow to loud applause.

This Sunday afternoon was the way Sunday afternoons should be, with close friends, relaxing and lovely. Georgia would remember it as, warming up and getting to know Father Fergus Breen. But most of all, she would remember it for one very exciting reason, watching Cameron, standing straight, placing one foot on a chair and cradling the guitar as he strummed the perfect notes to suit the song her mother Nellie sang. Now Georgia was falling in love with him all over again for the millionth time. Everyone was so relaxed, conversation began to flow, most of it came from Fergus, he explained how he'd been back home in Ireland for almost a month. He'd spent three weeks in Kerry winding down in the town where he was born. For the last week he stayed in the monastery where Cameron had been.

'I'm retiring completely from my job within the next month. I'm just going to do all the things I have wanted to do for a long time. Take walks, climb mountains, maybe buy a small house, I'm not sure whether it will be here in Dublin or in Kerry. That's really it' he said, 'that's all I have for you.'

The afternoon rolled on with more singing and chatting. Then it was 6 o'clock, almost Juliet's bed time and time for all the guests to go home. When they closed the door, having said goodbye to Fergus and Maisie there was a calmness and peace around their gorgeous bungalow, also a promise from Maisie to meet up in the little pink café, (Apple Pie) in a week or so. Nellie stayed on for a little longer helping to fill the dishes into the dishwasher, clean all the crumbs from the table and play with Juliet before she lay in her cot and fell off into a beautiful slumber. As Georgia lay in bed that night cosying up to Cameron, she looked back on the lovely Sunday they had all had. It was so good to have a few extra grown up friends. Yes she was exhausted and no wiser as to what was to become of Maisie and Fergus. Were they an item now or would they be an item in the future? Only time would tell.

CHAPTER 58

Night at the flicks (pictures)

Heidi, Coco, and Tanya decided it was high time to do something good for a friend who needed a night out with her pals, Coco, Tanya and Heidi. A night out at the flicks (pictures), first a few drinks, a light meal, a car ride and then on to Liffey Valley, Cinema 2, to see *The Aviator*, based on Howard Hughes' life. The girls were in great form having overcome all the obstacles to make this night happen.

Obstacle One: Cameron had meetings impossible for him to change.

Obstacle Two: Maria, the babysitter, had family from France visiting her and she needed time to show them the sights of Dublin's Fair City.

Obstacle Three: Who would mind Juliet?

Obstacle Four: Getting the four friends together on the same night had been an almost impossible task.

When obstacle one, two, three and four seemed impossible to overcome a solution was needed, it came in the shape of Heidi. Her generosity to forfeit her night out with her pals had saved the day. Yes, the friend since kindergarten had offered her services to baby-sit for the beautiful Juliet. She said:

'This is my chance to bond with your gorgeous daughter, Georgia. How lucky am I, no Cameron, no Georgia and no Maria. I'm going to have such a fun time, as you know I love babies, all I want to do is cuddle them. But I'll be a good friend,

Georgia, as soon as she's fed, changed and winded, Juliet will be placed back in the comfort of her little cot, this I promise.'

Georgia knew she could trust Heidi. She felt so lucky to have such fabulous friends.

Heidi was the first to arrive. She needed to be briefed as there was no point in her not knowing where everything was. Then she encouraged Georgia to leave with her friends who'd just arrived to pick her up. The three amigos headed for the bright lights of Dublin's Fair City. For Georgia it was a very well earned night of not being mammy, just being Georgia. So everything was great, popcorn in one hand, a huge carton of orange and a large packet of Minstrels, the scene was set. The girls joined the queue as it inched its way towards Cinema 2. The atmosphere was electrifying, everyone happy.

Georgia looked up from the little chat she was having with her friends. Her eyes fixed on the back of a head and shoulders she recognised, Ross's head and shoulders. She may not have seen them for a long time but they were definitely his. Please don't turn around, she thought. She had thought of this someone every day since they parted and had hoped that one day they would meet, but this was not the one day she imagined they would meet. It was definitely Ross, totally oblivious to her being there. Georgia froze to the spot. Jesus, he'd better not look back and see me, she thought. I'm not feeling great, I don't look my best, I've extra pounds I don't want, I'll have to avoid him at all costs.

She was so busy looking ahead that she tripped and almost fell to the ground. A speedy reaction from her friends saved her but guess what she was still holding onto the popcorn and drink, who said little miracles don't happen anymore? All around her people were laughing and joking, including her friends, she began to think that maybe they were laughing at her and then she realised how stupid and silly she was. Since she'd had Juliet she just felt so uncertain of everything, new mother syndrome. She'd best just kick herself out of this mood and enjoy the night out.

Ross vanished into the cinema and to be honest she felt a little bit of relief. Now she wouldn't have to worry about being out of shape, not in control and a bit ditzy. The company was great and the popcorn, minstrels and orange fizzy drinks that they passed between each other, made lots of noise and had the people in front looking back in anger. All their goodies tasted better than they tasted out in the real world. The seats were fabulous with nothing to obstruct the view and then the film started, first, of course, all the advertisements. Usually Georgia enjoyed this part, it was always so colourful but tonight nothing, she just stared in front of her, passing around the popcorn from friend to friend and trying to make out, in the dark cinema, was that shape and hair sitting about five rows in front of her Ross's, or was she just delusional? She hoped she was right and it was Ross, she'd longed for this moment and wondered how she'd feel if she looked into his eyes. Would she find out what she felt? Again after having Juliet she didn't really know what she felt. Between looking after the bungalow and working she was all over the place. Who was he with? She wondered as she gazed through the blackness trying to make out the figure sitting beside him. Lucky for her she was sitting down when she realised the figure was none other than Therese, a next door neighbour from days gone by when she lived with Ross.

She decided not to say anything to her friends, she just couldn't bear to hear any of their comments. Georgia hadn't got a clue of what the film was about, she had wanted to see it for so long but now there were even more important things she wanted to see in the cinema. It was over (the film). Lights on! Brightness all around, she could see Ross in the distance, how she would have loved him to turn around so she could see his face but he couldn't see her. She had to think quickly.

'Girls, I can't move just now.' Georgia wailed. 'My leg has gone dead.'

With that she did a brilliant impression of some old actress in bygone times, in the silent movies. She began to rub the back of her leg, pretending to get her circulation back to normal. Her friends sat on each side, rubbing her shoulders, trying to comfort her. It worked, everyone was gone, the cinema was empty. The usherette began to check the seats making sure there were no valuables left behind and when she reached their seat, Georgia took all the courage she had inside and began to hobble towards the exit doors, praying Ross was long gone. He was. Georgia smiled and laughed and continued the girly night. She would analyse her feelings in bed later. She deserved an Oscar. (Why are all awards called after men? Why not call them a Julie or a Sadie, or maybe a Nancy?) Coco did the driving that night, first she had to drop Tanya home and then it was Georgia's turn. The two girls chatted in the car for a few minutes but Georgia's mind kept drifting back to that glimpse of Ross in the cinema earlier and not on Coco's conversation.

Just as Georgia began to turn the key in her hall door, it opened from the inside and there stood the ever beautiful, smiling and unruffled Heidi with the gorgeous Juliet fast asleep in her arms. Heidi had the kettle boiled and two Galaxy chocolate muffins, still in their plastic wrapping, sitting on a pretty plate waiting to be devoured. Heidi explained how she'd bought them specially for her old pal, knowing she was a chocoholic and with that she gently handed Juliet to her loving mum. While Georgia gazed lovingly at her beautiful daughter, Heidi made two piping hot, mugs of tea and stirred them gently with two nice heaped spoonfuls of sugar. Then she placed Georgia's right in front of her on the little pretty table. Heidi switched off the television and the two pals chatted for a long, long time about everything including the film which really Georgia hadn't any knowledge of, so as they say, she winged it every time the subject came up.

'Was the film good?'

Georgia avoided the answer, the truth was she didn't have a clue.

'I'll tell you what, Heidi, I'll take you to see that film next week. I enjoyed it so much I really need to watch it one more time.'

She almost believed herself. Having removed the plastic wrapping the two girls set upon the Galaxy chocolate with great gusto. They were just delicious, not a crumb left, there's nothing like chocolate to make you feel good, let your guard down and that's what Georgia did when she opened her mouth and said:

'I saw Ross tonight at the pictures and guess what Heidi, he was with our next door neighbour and can I tell you I felt sick. He's absolutely gorgeous. By the way I only saw the back of his head.'

'So how could you say he's still gorgeous?'

'Ah well his hair is gorgeous. I also saw his broad shoulders and that was enough for me to draw my own conclusion.'

The two girls spoke quietly so as not to awaken Juliet.

'I suppose it takes all kinds to make the world' said Heidi.

'I was so blinded by my sexual desires for Cameron I didn't realise what I was giving up. God! I wish I could roll back the clock. I wish I never got myself into this situation. It's all too painful, and I've hurt too many people along the way, even though I am madly in love with Cameron. Perhaps it's possible to fall in love with two people but we're just not supposed to' continued Georgia, trying to make all the wrongs in her life sound right.

Heidi was never judgemental.

'It's not the falling in love with them that's the problem, Georgia. It's the choices you have to make because you've fallen in love with them. When you see someone you've loved after years, it's only natural you have feelings for them.'

Georgia began to cry.

'These feelings you are feeling will pass Georgia. You're probably very tired and have so much on your plate at the moment.'

'Maybe you're right, Heidi.'

'Don't worry Georgia, in a few weeks you will settle down and Ross will just be a distant memory.'

Georgia said 'Heidi, he was never a distant memory, he's ever present in my mind and in my heart, always.'

She'd never said this out loud to anyone before and here she was pouring her heart out to Heidi. Sometimes it's nice to talk about things to relieve the tension and who better to talk to than Heidi, she was so calm and peaceful and always just understood Georgia. She pulled herself together and almost whispered,

'I do hope you're right Heidi, maybe tomorrow he'll just be someone I loved and think of every day but not someone I have regrets for leaving.'

It was a blessing in disguise having Heidi there that night not only to mind gorgeous Juliet but to be there for Georgia. She was a little gift from God, and she didn't even know it. Georgia hoped someday she would get the chance to return the favour.

Heidi was gone, porch light was off, Georgia was still holding her little bundle of joy, she must be very careful with little Juliet who she was holding in her arms. She gently laid her down in her cot. Georgia knew by the contented look on Juliet's face, she would sleep soundly for the night. Teeth cleaned, make up off, baby doll on, Georgia gently rolled herself into the nice cool bed, occupied by only her as poor Cameron was out working his fingers to the bone. She slept so soundly and so happily, she didn't even hear Cameron coming into the room or into bed and sure that was grand, she needed the sleep.

The night out on the town had been the best medicine Georgia ever had. It gave her a new spark of life, a feeling that maybe after all, there was light at the end of the tunnel. The feeling of isolation was slowly disintegrating. Georgia knew why it had been such a tough time, all because of the deep sadness she still could never speak about, that feeling she was betraying Connie by having another baby and especially as Juliet was a girl. She felt if she had had a boy things would have been a little different. There was something else that really worried Georgia all the way through her pregnancy – the thought of Connie's memories and her beauty leaving Georgia's mind forever as her thoughts would inevitably turn to her new daughter. The fact that she had felt when a new baby would arrive, Connie would only be a distant memory but instead of being a distant memory, Georgia felt pain in her heart every day for what she missed out on Connie. She had no one to compare Connie with. She couldn't say for the first few weeks she watched her mum, smiled (maybe that was only wind) but whatever, she never saw Connie doing any of those things and that left a huge void in her heart. One thing she was very happy about was she would never and could never forget Connie. She would always look at Juliet and say to herself, wouldn't it have been lovely if Juliet's big sister Connie was here today but God had other plans for Juliet, maybe someday she would have a younger sister or brother. Connie's star would always shine in Georgia's heart and she was very grateful for that.

That night as she lay in bed a calmness fell on her. She acknowledged the truth, she had two daughters, one who would live inside her heart forever and help her through life's ups and downs and ultimately they will meet again when this life is over and her other daughter Juliet, she prayed she would watch as she grows into a young lady. In the calmness of the still night Georgia recognised, Juliet still has her big sister Connie, helping her not from planet Earth but from far above the white clouds.

CHAPTER 59

Freedom

This morning to make up for his sins, Cameron had taken the day off and now freedom was a dusty road heading down the highway for Georgia. No way was she hanging around the house for the day, she just had to escape from these four walls to keep her sanity. No need to let that guilty feeling take over after all Juliet needed to bond with her daddy (but what a great excuse to take a day off). Cameron was probably secretly longing to spend time on his own with Juliet. There must be lots of little things he would like to say to his little girl when Mammy wasn't around. Baby could coo and gurgle and start the process of wrapping Daddy around her little finger like all little girls do (that doesn't take long) and, Daddy would just lap it all up and enjoy the smiles, gurgles and bubbles she would blow while he sang songs and maybe played his guitar to his little pride and joy, away from the listening ears of Georgia. (Sure Georgia would fall around laughing if she heard him singing) Daddy and baby will have time together to make memories, that's what life is made of. In all everyone would get exactly what they needed from the next few hours.

1st - Juliet not irritated by crowds in the city (if Georgia took her with her)

2nd - Georgia Freedom,

3rd - Cameron Bonding.

Georgia wouldn't stay away too long, just a little while and early is the best time to get yourself into those busy streets. She'd start with breakfast in the Dome in Stephen's Green shopping centre. That was the place to be early in the morning and even better when she had Cameron's Visa card to pay for a really nice, sumptuous breakfast. She just sat there, it was always nice and bright, even on the dullest days the light shone through the glass dome and brightened up the whole area. It was a good place to start the day, with the surround sound of soft music playing throughout the centre. Georgia sipped on a glass of orange juice. She almost forgot the time, she almost forgot where she was as her mind floated away on a beautiful, soft, frothy cloud. The frothy cloud evaporated fast when a passer-by suddenly bumped against her chair and as the sound of the chair scraping the floor irritated her ears, back down to earth she came with a jolt.

She glanced at her watch and realised time was moving on. Breakfast over, she swiped Cameron's Visa card. Let's start small, my spending can only get better, I feel so empowered using Cameron's Platinum Visa Card. I'll have to get one of those for myself one of these days, she thought. Georgia strolled out of the shopping centre, across the road and continued down by the pretty shops at the top of Stephen's Green.

She couldn't believe her eyes when she saw the notice that read: SALE STARTING AT 10AM... EVERYTHING REDUCED BY UP TO 70%. Even though the doors had been opened only a few minutes, customers were packing in and running in the direction of the dress their heart desired. Judging by the looks on some of their faces, maybe they felt they needed that bargain more than life itself. After all, everyone loves a bargain. The thought of being able to get so many dresses, for a few euros, that actually fitted her now that she was beginning to get her figure back, made Georgia feel ecstatic. Her heart skipped a beat.

Would she be her beautiful size 10 again? Reality would soon set in!! Georgia almost danced into the shop. Now that she was there, she felt as if she was in the middle of a candy store with the variety of dresses, suits, shoes and underwear, in all colours, WOW. Jesus! what happens to your heart when you see a shop full of amazing clothes. It's dawning on me I haven't bought myself anything new in such a long time, desperation must be setting in, Jesus! I think I'm deranged. Georgia flipped through the clothes on the rails with her hands (as if possessed), she just couldn't get enough of them. She had to calm herself down, this was ridiculous, she just wanted everything that was on offer. In her arms she held a white linen suit in size 10 and 12, a turquoise dress in size 10 and 12, a beautiful pale lemon dress, size 10 and 12 and just on the way to the fitting room her eyes glanced in the direction of an amazing pair of 5" high heels, she'd try them on the way out.

The assistant must have seen her desperation, trying to hold all the clothes in her arms and enthusiasm at the mere thought of trying on and maybe buying these beautiful designs, or maybe the assistant had a baby herself and recognised Georgia's deranged state, or maybe she was just a brilliant assistant. Whatever was the true answer Georgia felt relieved when the girl lifted the weight of the clothes from her weakening arms and hung them up in the large fitting room.

'If you need me just give me a little call' and with that the assistant with the beaming smile and cheerful voice pulled across the curtains and left Georgia to delve into all these clothes, try them on and discover was she truly a size 10 or had she still got some way to go to return to her pre-mam curves? Size 10 in most things fitted perfectly, but the odd dress like the figure hugging turquoise one had to be a 12, it's a pity they don't make a size 11!! The lemon dress in a size 10, to her relief, slid on to her slender body, wow, the look was perfect and the White suit was perfect. As Georgia pulled back the curtain the amazing shop assistant was there, like the fairy godmother, ready to yet again make things easy for Georgia by carrying dresses, etc. that would soon be hers (as soon as Cameron paid for them on his Visa card). As she continued on up to the cash desk, Georgia took a moment to sit down and try on the pretty shoes and, of course, decided to buy them too. She convinced herself no outfit would be perfect without pretty shoes.

Thank God this shop had everything a woman could desire, especially that little sexy bra and pants. She forgot for a moment, she was buying these clothes to look good for the man in her life. Yes, she'd forgotten about him as well, isn't retail therapy just fantastic? With Visa card in hand (not just any Visa card – Cameron's Visa card), she would soon be getting that huge discount once she got to the top of the queue. She was there faster than she expected. Georgia frantically watched as the bill got larger and larger. Calm down, calm down, she jested to herself. Remember, it is Cameron's wish that I spend this money on me and I must abide by his wishes. A smile of devilment and contentment lit up Georgia's face. And how lucky is he, after all I've got so much discount. Thank God for sales and discount days.

When Georgia arrived the store was really busy but now it was getting busier with every moment that passed. She was very pleased with herself, because she'd been the early bird and caught the worm. The happy assistant with the beaming smile and a lovely musical voice packed all of Georgia's new collection into the prettiest bags.

'I hope you get great wear out of all these beautiful dresses, you purchased today. Myself and some of the girls have bought nearly all the same things as you have, they're all such good value and mine look great on me and I know they'll look even better on you.'

Feeling very happy inside Georgia moved towards the exit, trying to stay focussed until her eyes glanced towards a little section of the store where a bar had been set up. It looked amazing, with all kinds of light colourful non-alcoholic cocktails. Georgia was lucky to be presented with a pink one. She didn't know what was in it but it looked good and boy it tasted even better. The bar staff were quite impressive, all dressed in black with white dickey bows. They shook whatever they mixed for the cocktails and placed them in beautiful little cocktail glasses. Georgia had a cocktail from both waiters who smiled at her and made her feel free, if only for a few moments. She felt fabulous and had to agree it just wasn't a myth that retail therapy could make your spirits soar. Retail therapy without doubt makes your spirits soar, right up to the sky and she was living proof as she floated out through the doors and back onto a sunny Grafton Street.

CHAPTER 60

Second impressions

A quick glance at her phone, no messages, no phone calls. Cameron must be coping very well. A quick look at the time, 1 o'clock on the dot, it's no wonder she was a little peckish, yes! she had a bright idea and yes! She was going to see it through. Down Grafton Street, cross over just past Dunnes Stores, a left turn, down a bit, cross over, down the lane and out. The Westbury Hotel, what a lovely vision standing there spotlessly clean, sparkling like the sun. In through the revolving door she glided to be greeted by Carlton the Doorman (a name she always gave to doormen).

'Welcome, your bags look heavy. Can I take you to the lift?'

There she was inside sitting on a very nice comfy velvet bench, imagining herself as Julie Roberts in Pretty Woman. The lift ascended to the first floor. She got out, he got out and walked her all the way down, holding all her bags with Georgia in hot pursuit. She could feel all eyes on her as she took a seat beside one of the big windows looking out onto Harry Street, just off Grafton Street. He bid farewell and off went Carlton to his next conquest.

'Yes, I'll have a toasted ham and cheese sandwich please' she said to the waitress, who'd arrived on cue like a magic fairy to her table, 'and a nice pot of tea. Could I have a fine big glass of water with ice, thank you?'

Ahh, so peaceful, I've got to judge my time, I can't go back too late. Poor Cameron no matter how good he is, he must be getting a bit overwrought trying to keep his concentration while he continues to look after our Juliet. I'm so lucky to have my gorgeous Cameron and my bouncing baby girl. Her mischievous side set in, there's a little while left, I've a lot to do. Then it was there, delicious food, piping hot tea, so beautifully presented. They say presentation is everything. Well I hope Cameron likes the way I'm presented with my new clothes on my homecoming. The last morsel of the sandwich vanished from the plate, the last drop of tea consumed, the large glass of water gone, tap on the machine, the money was gone. It's so easy these days, just tap, so effortless. You feel as if you're not spending money at all, (this is possibly how most people go broke! Little amounts of money too often) before you know it, it's all gone.

Georgia looked around the room packed to capacity with people having business meetings, and families enjoying time together. She could see the business men and women conversing with each other, explaining this and that, (it's amazing what you notice when you're all alone). There must have been a lot of money on the line. Here, somehow in the calmness of the Hotel, it would be hard to hear the beating of the hearts, or feel the fear they must be feeling, those poor business men and women as they tried to get a business deal across the line. To think that in most hotels, on a calm day like this in Dublin, with all the tea, coffee, scones and drinks being passed around, most people fail to see that underneath it all there are life changing deals being made and everything depends on that one meeting.

Georgia was happy to say she wasn't part of any of this, instead she was here to rest her weary feet and decide which outfit she was going to go home to Cameron in. Up from the seat she stood and with all her strength took the bags into her hands and walked as elegantly as was possible to the lady's room, a beautifully decorated, quiet area. By now she had decided which one she was wearing. She'd wear the figure hugging dress that was meant for evening, in the middle of the day (God was she mad). Ah well, it's all about living in the moment, proving she looked just as good now as she did before she was ever pregnant and silly as that sounds to some people, it made great sense to Georgia. First she took off all her makeup and re-did it. Put her hands through her hair and made it bouncy and soft and when all that was sorted and in the privacy of the lady's loo, Georgia changed first into her gorgeous new lingerie and then into her figure hugging turquoise dress. Outside she came, put all her new purchases on the chairs and re-organised the bags. Then she sat down and changed her shoes, stood up and looked into the long mirror, and if she said so herself, she looked great. Oh! just one more thing before my audience with the doorman, another coating of that fabulous glossy lipstick. Back into the lift, sitting with all her purchases beside her on the sexy bench covered in luscious velvet while she admired herself in the mirror in front of her, again she re-lived another scene from the film Pretty Woman. Doors opened, Georgia floated out, to be greeted by an astonished Carlton, as she called him (not his real name)

'May I say you look fabulous and your dress is amazing.'

Again her thoughts returned to the film Pretty Woman. This time in the scene when Julie Roberts walked past the concierge, he gazed at her as she sashayed (walk in an ostentatious yet casual manner, typically with exaggerated movements of the hips and shoulders – [Google Dictionary]) her way through the foyer in possession of fabulous clothes from a fabulous store. OK, I know I'm dreaming or I'm delusional, I haven't been to expensive stores and furthermore nobody has spent any money on me (Cameron gave me his Visa Card but come on, that wouldn't hold a candle to the lavish amount of money Richard Gere had on his card in the film.) Well, this is my poor woman's version of Pretty Woman, even if it is the half price version. These few hours away have rejuvenated me, I'm ready for anything.

'Carlton, It's all the gorgeous clothes I bought. There's a great sale over there in that shop but don't tell anyone except your wife. Give her your Visa Card and let her go and buy something nice.' The two of them burst into laughter.

'I'll hail a taxi for you if you like.'

'No, I'll walk around the corner and pick one up. Time is starting to drift away on me and I need to get home. You know, I have a baby, her name is Juliet.'

'Well congratulations and can I say you're an inspiration.'

CHAPTER 61

Expect the unexpected

Outside, standing with her back to the Westbury hotel, Georgia took a right turn and walked to the end of the road very slowly as the paths weren't the best and after all her shoes were brand new. As she turned the corner a stranger rushing, probably to the Westbury to close a deal, bumped straight into her and with all the bags she was holding she couldn't keep her balance, down to the ground she fell like a pack of cards (now she didn't feel like Julie Roberts in Pretty Woman, that illusion was completely shattered). Why is it that every time she gets too big for her boots, God gives her a kick in the behind and she falls to the ground with a bang. Usually Georgia could laugh when things like this happen but not now when she was just beginning to feel fabulous again. In this moment, she felt more like Dawn French in one of the episodes of The Vicar of Dibley. You know the one, when Dawn French jumps into what she thinks is a small puddle of water that turns out to be a big deep pool of water. She goes right down and comes up looking mucky, deflated and terrible and that was exactly how Georgia felt. There was no water involved, instead a man's shoulder, then a rough wall and of course, inevitably the ground.

She couldn't believe it was happening to her but rise from the ashes she must just like the Phoenix. How can I do that when my beautiful dress is ripped from rubbing off the wall? she thought. Her arm was sore and her beautiful new shoes lay in two separate places on the ground. Pretty Woman was long since gone, for the moment the Vicar of Dibley had left the building and in

313

her place stood Joanna Lumley in Absolutely Fabulous. In true Joanna style Georgia pulled herself together and tried to focus on the goal of getting up from the cold, dirty, uneven ground. What kind of fool am I? I should have just let Carlton, the doorman, hail me a taxi. I won't be home any earlier and I'm in bits, I feel awful, how can I go home to Cameron looking like this? Her mind was miles away, then out of the blue she heard a voice. She knew that voice. Was she in Heaven? Had she indeed been struck by a rock? Was that St. Peter's voice? Had she arrived at the Pearly Gates?

'Jesus Georgia. Am I seeing things or is it you? 2.30 in the day and you look as if you've just finished a photo shoot.'

Georgia looked up and straight into Ross's eyes.

'Christ' she said 'Well I felt like I was coming from a photo shoot until you nearly killed me. Now I feel sore but most of all deflated. Of all the places in all the world, you had to be in my place.'

Ross got down to the ground, put her shoes back on her now dirty feet (was she Cinderella with two shoes?) took her two hands in his and hauled her back up on her feet. She looked down at her beautiful shoes, lucky for him they weren't scraped. She looked down at her dress, torn and frayed but apart from that Georgia knew, she'd live to see another day.

'Do you know Ross, you've been on my mind a lot lately and I've had every intention of ringing you when the time was right.'

'Funny enough I had the same idea about you. When is the time ever right?'

'Hardly now' she said.

'Maybe now' he said 'Come on, we're so close to that little pub, opposite the school of music. Please, I'll help you all the way.'

'Fuck, do you want to make me feel like a real old woman?'

'No,' said Ross 'more like a damsel in distress.'

'I can live with that. OK come on and help me as I limp my way there. Now you know Ross, Cameron has been minding Juliet all day so I only have a little while to spend with you. This is not the way I had planned our meeting in my head but it's the way the cards were dealt so we might as well go with the flow.'

Into the pub she limped, like a wounded soldier, with the help, of course, of the gladiator. She had to have tea with sugar and milk, to give her energy and to her delight the pub also had chocolate biscuits, that were on the plate one minute and gone the next. Ross sat there quietly smiling happily to himself. She could see that smile even in his eyes. He seemed really pleased to have bumped into his ex-wife and she couldn't hide the little burst of excitement she felt. It seemed they both wanted this for so long and it happened in the most uncanny way. Maybe it's true when they say what's for you won't pass you by. He knew she must leave, she knew she must leave but it was hard to drag themselves apart. Time is a great healer and they'd had plenty of time. They both agreed the timing was perfect for their re-introduction. Ross insisted on paying.

'After all if it wasn't for me' he said sheepishly 'You would have been home by now with your dress and your pride intact.'

'I can't wait to sit down with you for a nice long chat, because it's something I've wanted to do for the longest time, but when we do sit down and chat I want to have the time to give you, and right now I'm already running very late. Please Ross don't take this as an insult I honestly really can't wait to sit down with you. Just tell me where and when and I'll be there.'

'Have you changed your mobile number, Georgia?'

'No, my mobile number is still the same and will always remain the same. Please, please Ross, ring me tomorrow.'

'Abso, bloody, lutely' Said Ross.

Those words brought back memories to Georgia of the series *Sex in the City* and Carrie's boyfriend Big.

Now, out on the street Georgia had just noticed a taxi coming into view. Her hand went up, the taxi stopped. Ross opened the door for her, she sat in and spread her purchases across the seats. Ross paid the taxi man for Georgia's journey then closed the taxi door. Georgia pressed the window down. She held his hand for a second and told him again how great it was to see him. He leant in through the taxi window and kissed her forehead. She could smell his aftershave, it was the one he always wore. Such a true blue was Ross. He always knew what he wanted, and once he got it he did his best to never let it go. Unfortunately for him, he had no choice, Georgia had let him go. As her hand slipped away from his, something changed inside her head. The taxi edged its way out into the traffic. He smiled, she waved, something happened just there, she thought as she looked back and saw him vanishing into the crowds.

She turned back around and faced her future and the huge mood swing she was now having to deal with. The taxi came to a stop right outside her house, Georgia hobbled to the front door. Cameron opened the door and stood looking confused when he saw the state of his poor Georgia, who had left him only hours earlier looking radiant. Now she looked more like Nicole Kidman as she walked into the water, in a scene from the film *The Hours*.

Nevertheless, as usual Cameron was intrigued by Georgia and looked forward to her telling the story of how this unfortunate incident had occurred and hoped it would end up better than when Nicole Kidman began her walk into that water. He loved her new dress (if a bit raggy) and he loved her new shoes (if a bit dusty), he loved her hair (if a bit scraggy). Let's face it he just loved her.

'So tell me all and spare me nothing' said Cameron. This was the bit where Georgia said she would tell Cameron that she met Ross so why wouldn't the words come out of her mouth?

'I fell on that bockety pavement just up from Westbury Hotel and I felt such a fool, Cameron. I was just on my way home but I had to sit down so I went into the nearest pub and had tea with sugar and milk and chocolate biscuits and it was only then I could come home to you. My mistake was wearing the shoes straight from the shop. I should have waited and worn them in the house for a little while, to wear them in, but you know me, always pig headed, when I buy something I want to wear it straight away. I really wanted to dress up for you, that's why I wore the dress, I put on fresh makeup and I really looked the part, Cameron. Now I'm home and you look amused, you seem to never get fed up with all the silly stories I have for you.'

'That's because I never get fed up with you and your silly little stories always amuse me.'

Georgia thought to herself, if he knew the real story would he be so amused? She felt a cold shiver going down her back. Was she right back where she was when she met Cameron, beginning to set the seeds of deceit? She should have just told him as it was. She'd bumped into Ross or he bumped into her and that's all that really happened, it wasn't intentional, it was meant to be and the truth is the best story to tell. By avoiding it Georgia could be making real trouble for herself but there was something holding her back from telling the longer, honest story of what really happened and after all you have to go with your gut feeling.

Cameron had visions of his Visa card maxed out, and yes it did make his heart beat faster, after all he wasn't loaded and they did have a Mortgage to pay and a little daughter to feed and look after. But, Georgia had been through the mill giving birth to their beautiful little girl and he had promised her that when she felt back to herself, he would give her his Platinum Visa card to go out and buy the dresses she wanted to wear instead of him buying dresses for her that she didn't want to wear, because eventually he would have to return each and every one back to the stores. When that day dawned Cameron kept his promise. Even now when Georgia looked a bit dishevelled he could tell she had enjoyed her day and for a little while she had returned to carefree Georgia. He was happy she had the freedom to spend some extra cash on herself because to him Georgia was very special and as they say in the L'Oreal advertisement... *Because I'm worth it.*

'You've got a great glow about you, Georgia' he said. 'Those few hours have done you the world of good, you look as if the weight of the world has been taken off your shoulders and you've got me to thank for the whole thing.'

'How was my little angel?' Georgia whispered as she gave Cameron a warm embrace.

'She was so good, I loved the time I spent with her all on my own. I feel I've got to know Juliet better and my confidence with her is right up there in the moon. I know I can go anywhere with her now and take her anywhere with me from now on and not be afraid. You know it used to worry me that someday I'd have to mind her on my own and not be able to do it but I've done it.'

With that he stretched his hands out in front of him and exclaimed:

'I've jumped the hurdle and we both survived. So now I'm

going to take her with me once a week. How does that sound to you, my gorgeous Georgia?'

'That sounds like music to my ears, Cameron.'

They kissed and hugged and ate some nice food already prepared by Cameron. Juliet woke up, feeding time at the zoo began. Bath time came and went. Lights went on in her little room, nice and dim but still there. (It was a special light, a fairy light that stuck onto the wall, flat, you pulled a little string and a light came on inside, just delightful) Georgia could never leave Juliet in a dark room, never ever, that must make babies very frightened. Somehow that little light had such a warm glow Georgia always felt content to leave her baby in her glowing fairy room.

Georgia and Cameron were too tired to get up to anything that night, one was tired from minding baby all day, the other tired from her day's escapades. Every ensemble she'd fallen in love with she bought (they were all cheap and cheerful and in the sale), Cameron's Visa card had suffered a little for this but Georgia made sure it hadn't suffered a lot. After all (she convinced herself) we now have a little daughter, it's definitely something to celebrate. Sometimes in life you've just got to spoil yourself. She lay in bed, motionless, trying her best to fall asleep but how could she when her thoughts were in such turmoil. Bumping into Ross on her way home from the Westbury hotel had brought back memories of how she nearly collided with Cameron at the South William Street crossing. She wondered had God got a plan that she had to bump into someone, fall on the pavement or almost push someone over to meet a man? Yes, her mind was all mixed up, as they say she didn't know her ass from her elbow, she was a complete mess and all because she turned to the right instead of the left when she left the Westbury hotel and then went around the wrong corner. The pledge she made to herself before she fell into the land of nod was:

1. I will tell Cameron I met Ross.
2. I will tell Cameron I'm going to meet Ross, just for a little chat.
1. I will tell Cameron and everything will be above board.
2. I will tell Cameron and all my dealings with Ross will be honest and true, after all, I only love Cameron.

Did Georgia believe what she was telling herself ? NO.

CHAPTER 62

Deja vu

Deja vu, that's what it felt like, that afternoon when Georgia sat in a little restaurant in Wicklow Street with Ross. They had decided to keep it low key, not visit one of those fancy restaurants instead they would just sit chatting about old times and listen to some melodious French Music, La Vie en Rose, etc. while they indulged in French pastries and a bottle of French wine. Then Georgia would kiss Ross on the cheek and say goodbye. But did she, of course not. Instead they sat there drinking hot chocolate, eating pastries and sipping wine with so much enthusiasm, trying to fill in all the twists and turns their lives had taken since they parted.

Yes, Ross had lived with Bernadine and everything had been great for a while but as he said, he realised things had moved too fast and he wasn't really ready for another relationship, so it fizzled out, she moved out and now he was all on his lonesome. Now, when he needed company he would go to the pictures with Theresa, his next door neighbour, it was always a happy occasion because there were no strings attached. Yes, he was feeling better, he could cope with his life now and actually admitted he quite enjoyed being a singleton. He could come and go as he pleased and just for now he was steering away from relationships (he made this point very, very clear). For her part Georgia felt this was as good a time as any to confess to Ross that she hadn't told Cameron about their collision (bumping into each other).

'Ross, I should have confessed to Cameron and said, the reason I look so bad, Cameron is, when I left the Westbury

Hotel, took a right turn and walked to the end of that road, I turned the corner and guess what happened next, I bumped into Ross. I just lost my balance and fell to the ground with a thud. It wasn't until Ross bent down and pulled me up onto my feet that I realised it was him, and at that point my dress was torn and my shoes were all dusty. Ross, since I wasn't upright and straight with the father of my child, if he ever finds out it will seem like I did something sneaky behind his back.'

Ross gave Georgia a look that spoke volumes. She continued: 'If I had been honest with Cameron, he would have understood and known everything I told him was true, all above board. So why did I leave the whole story out? After all we are just friends now, who happened to bump into each other (literally). And yes, we did have a stroll down memory lane, but that's what friends do. You don't want a relationship and I'm in one, there was no need for me to leave that big chunk of information out, Cameron is a man of the world, he would have understood.'

Georgia wondered if these little meetings were to continue would they in time fizzle out? Would they remain friends meeting from time to time? Or would they, because of the history they had, turn into something else? After such a long time they had a lot to catch up on, things that interested her and Ross, especially their mutual friends, Tanya, Coco and Heidi, the three girls who had stood by Georgia through thick and thin and had also become great friends with Ross. They were still always there on the horizon ready to tell stories, waiting to listen, always eager for the night out and loved to chat. Georgia felt the need to talk to Ross about her friends because right now it really was the one thing that they still had in common. She told him all the stories about her friends, which he loved as he knew them all so well and all about her work. Of course, Georgia spoke about her beloved daughter Juliet. In fairness Ross listened with interest. She found herself telling him all the little stories about the recent photo shoot she'd had. It was one of her cousins, Bertha whom he knew. She had just finished an extra artistic course on photography and now specialised in toddlers and baby photography,

'You know, Ross,' Georgia said 'she now knows how to artistically position the baby's hands and cross their little feet in the photograph to make them look gorgeous and almost edible.'

Ross smiled, but Georgia noticed sadness there in his eyes when she spoke of Juliet. Suddenly she realised her nerves had made her babble on about Juliet without giving a thought to his feelings. She knew he was thinking Juliet should be our baby.

It was getting late, they just had to leave. In the time they spent there they really hadn't noticed anyone else, people had come in and gone out, waitresses had changed shifts, the pastry chef had baked dozens of pastries and the waiter had taken away trays and bottles. Now outside, they were back to reality on Wicklow Street. It was fair to say the conversation had been a bit too intense but the warmth of the feelings they still had for each other could have kindled a fire in the coldest hearts, but there was no talk of romance and that was good and healthy for both of them. There wasn't a feeling of an elephant in the room, meaning Cameron.

Georgia spoke about him naturally and honestly. So everything between Georgia and Ross was above board. It was a pity she couldn't say the same for herself and Cameron. Georgia felt Ross was doing exactly the same as her, convincing himself that this whole shenanigans was ok but in their heart of hearts both of them knew it was anything but ok. In all the time they'd been apart, unbeknownst to Georgia, Ross had never stopped loving her and in his heart of hearts had dreamt he would get her back one day. That thought had kept him going and to be fair to him he hadn't lost sight of his goal.

His long term aim still was to have Georgia and himself living together, back in the house they once shared. In fairness to Georgia she had always imagined that maybe in some different universe they would return to the lovely life they had before she absolutely fucked things up, but she certainly wouldn't like to return to the house they shared, she'd rather wipe the slate clean, a new house, maybe even a new country, but right now it was just a platonic friendship. Would it blossom into something else? Only time would tell. Their next meeting was chiselled in their hearts for next Monday lunchtime. This would be a very special meeting, one where Georgia would take along Juliet, of course with Ross's permission. It would be a good time to do this as Juliet was too young to tell Cameron about the man she'd met with Mammy. Georgia could cover it up with a nice warm hello in a restaurant and that look, as if I haven't seen you for years.

CHAPTER 63

The day that changed Georgia's life

Monday morning, 9am, Juliet washed, dressed, fed and now playing happily in her highchair while her mummy, Georgia, plastered on some make up to her pale cheeks and added a little bit of blusher, then, of course, the mascara and that dark pencil to give the eye brows definition, all that was left to do was slide into one of the beautiful dresses she'd purchased in that big sale. She was beginning to get into character, you know, like an actress dressing up for her role and today was certainly going to be one of her finest roles. Just imagine, introducing your daughter to your ex-husband, that has to be one for the books. It's right to say that Georgia was scared, in fact she was petrified, not so much about the introduction but more about his reaction, would he ever talk to her again, would he just get up and walk away or if luck was really on her side would he think the baby was beautiful, ask to hold her and just go on as if nothing big had just happened? Georgia would soon know the answer to her questions, after all she was meeting him at 12noon, it was now 11am, just an hour to organise her little girl. As my mother used to say, it's best not to make arrangements when you have a child, every day is different, you just don't know what tomorrow will bring. Georgia had decided not to take a pram, to just carry Juliet wrapped in her blanket. The hotel would provide them with a baby chair. Georgia would perch little Juliet in the chair, give her something to play with, while herself and Ross had a chat.

The taxi came, the twosome sat there and it was no time

until Juliet was sitting in the high chair beside her mammy in the hotel. Georgia ordered a cup of tea and put a lot of sugar into it. She'd also ordered two fruit scones, they were delicious, the way scones should be made with all the right ingredients, she always said and continued to say the same, you get what you pay for. No dried up scones, you know the ones that if you rubbed them they would just flake like flour, these scones had substance, you could tell they were made with butter and all the right ingredients and tasted delicious. Georgia knew she was eating like somebody in The Famine who had just been given a feast to eat but it was just her nerves. The second scone had almost vanished when she felt his presence and looking up she confirmed it was indeed her ex, Ross. For once, he looked a bit uneasy and she knew why. She jumped up, nearly knocking the high chair over and almost shouted,

'Ross this is Juliet.'

It must have been her head telling her to get this bit over as it was so delicate and then it was as if time stood still, there was pure silence and in slow motion Ross went to the high chair and lifted Juliet up into his arms. They both sat down, the silence continued, it was a surreal moment only broken by the words from Ross:

'Your little girl is beautiful, Georgia. I can't believe it but for some reason I've become very emotional.'

She looked at him as tears streamed down his handsome face. Now this was a situation she just was not prepared for and in that moment she realised she had been very uncaring and unsympathetic. I mean if the shoe was on the other foot, how would she feel if Ross introduced his daughter to her? She couldn't speak. In her head she went through all kinds of scenarios but nothing came out, maybe that was the way it was meant to be, both of them had different things to deal with right now. For him this was one of the saddest moments of his life, for her it was one of the most awkward moments of her life. Then her brain started to work and all she seemed to repeat in her head was how could I have been so stupid as to do this? It's totally out of character for me to want to hurt another human being and especially Ross, one of the kindest people I've ever met and someone I love deeply.

Georgia began to cry, the situation was carnage, it was quiet carnage though, but the poor waiter who came over to ask was there anything they needed must have got the shock of his life, as his training had taught him if something is happening right before your eyes between two people just back away until the moment is right and that is what he did. Hands behind his back he actually backed away from the trio, it was as if he was leaving the Queen, you know you never turn your back on the Queen, you have to back away and this is exactly what he was doing. He put his two hands behind his back, took steps, very large ones at that, steps back into oblivion (the corner of the room behind the reception desk where he couldn't be seen). Lucky for the two of them there was a big jug of water and two glasses on the table. Ross poured two full glasses of water and before you could say Bucks Fizz they were gone. Lucky for them it wasn't a heavy drink like Gin or the two of them could be in a drunken state by now.

'I'm sorry I didn't buy you a present when you had your baby. I prefer to give you a few bob to buy something you really need' said Ross, gathering himself together.

'I'll tell you what I need right now, Ross. A stiff drink and I'll tell you what I need to do right now, Ross, is to apologise profusely for putting you in this position and upsetting you the way I have. It wasn't my intention, I was just trying to share little things with you and it's completely backfired.'

'I'm OK, Georgia I've pulled myself together, I know you didn't mean to hurt me, it's just that I would have loved all of us to be a little family but in life things don't always work out the way we'd like them to. I think it's as if I've been trying to block that part of my life out, you know when you left I couldn't understand why and I blocked it out and got on with everything and I was doing fine, but now I feel like a blundering idiot. I'm sorry Georgia, another time, another place. I'll have to leave now.'

And with that he kissed little Juliet and gave her back to her mum. He then kissed Georgia, slap bang on her lips. Now that was something she really hadn't thought would happen and it was something he didn't think would happen either. She might have expected a peck on the cheek, a hug, a kiss on the forehead, even a shake hands but never a fast passionate kiss at a time like this, but it had happened and to prove to herself it had happened she could still feel the tingling of his lips on hers and the heat of her body, as he vanished with some speed down the stairs of the Westbury. Once more she saw the back of his head and his broad shoulders as he disappeared out of her sight. She was left sitting there with Juliet whom she loved more than life itself but she had this awful feeling that she did something uncaring and out of character. Yes, that's how she felt, hopeless. She had nothing but regrets as she poured herself a cup of tea and pondered on her life.

Somehow she got herself home that day. Ross had left some money for the bill. How he even thought straight enough to leave money was still beyond her but he did - in true style, always the gentleman. Carlton, the doorman, insisted on getting her a taxi this time.

'After all Miss, you can't take the baby around that corner, you might just fall with her in your arms.'

Little did he know that indeed she had fallen the last time and that moment had changed her life in so many ways and today she was living proof of that. In fact, it was that fall just a few weeks ago that had led to this moment and she certainly didn't want a repeat performance, especially with Juliet in her arms. God knows, with her luck, who she'd bump into this time? Carlton knew there was something different about her, she seemed a little tense, not like her usual bubbly self, especially the bubbly self he'd met a few weeks ago, arriving into the hotel with bag loads of bargains and leaving the hotel dressed to kill and so full of life, but this was another day and people change all the time. His training had taught him to take people with all their various mood swings, just embrace the guest and never make any judgements. He had the taxi sweeping her away from the scene and then they were home, where the moments turned into minutes, the minutes turned into hours, the hours turned into days, the days turned into weeks, the weeks turned into months and she still had not heard one word from Ross and she still felt powerless to pick that phone up and ring him. What could she say? What could she have to offer him? He had to ring her, it just had to be that way. She'd messed him up twice, really badly. If he chose not to get in touch with her, then that was his prerogative. If he chose to call her, then it would be on his terms and that was what it needed to be, this time he had to be in control, not her, only time would tell.

CHAPTER 64

Busy bee

Her decision was to keep herself busy, invite her friends for combination evenings of dinner and vodka, the old saying (vodka makes you wanna) or maybe champagne or gin, because you know what they say about gin, (gin makes you sin) and she even threw in whiskey, cause they say (whiskey makes you frisky).

All four girls would bring their ingredients and have a pick and mix to create a meal together. As the friends continued to drink and get fluthered the evenings just got better. The drinks relaxed everyone and cooking the meals showed off the culinary skills, or lack of, they had achieved with time and, of course behind every meal was Georgia trying to keep herself busy and surround herself with happiness and love. These evenings were only workable if Cameron was free to do the bathing of Juliet, the feeding of Juliet and the telling of a little story before bed to Juliet. Even though she was only a toddler, they always did this to awaken her senses to the wonderful world of imagination and to be fair to Cameron he never let her down, not even once.

He would chat to the friends and even join them in a glass of whatever was on offer for the night, then he would quietly leave them to it and head to the bedroom with Juliet in tow. Georgia knew Juliet would be asleep in no time at all with such a loving daddy and once she was quiet and resting he could read, something he loved doing. He might even watch a little television or just go to bed and wait on Georgia to join him around ten thirty, once friends were gone.

Georgia had to say, although this idea was born out of

desperation, it turned out to be a great idea. A great way for friends to relax, laugh and joke between themselves. It's true what they say too, when you're cutting up potatoes or making a salad or even baking a little cake it makes you happy and you feel at one with friends around you. Sure, they would fall around the place laughing at the things they used to do. They'd reminisce about the first time they baked a cake or made dinner, their triumphs and their failures and would you believe, now that they were adults they were getting to know each other all over again in a different way. The evenings were great fun and it was true to say they all looked forward to that evening once a week. If they felt they needed to change things up a bit and have a night out on the town instead, once in a while, Cameron would babysit for his little baby girl, but if he had to work one of Georgia's friends would step in and let Georgia have a night out with two of them and enjoy harmless fun.

Georgia needed her friends, she needed to be wrapped around with love from people who really cared. Being in a happy place in life was always her goal, someone once said, you have to choose to be happy and in the early days after her collision with reality when she failed to imagine what another human being would feel by putting in front of him a future he had dreamt of but a future that wasn't his, she had to re-assess where she was going with her own life and how she should be treating people including her friends. Georgia just couldn't believe how uncaring she'd been. She realised that in her own little way she had used her friends to flit into her life when it was hard and then leave them out when she was on top, floating along, oblivious to everyone in her world, in the end she knew it was her who caused all this pain. She knew she'd done all this damage to someone she loved. She had to live with it, he had to live with his broken heart, but the void in her life was so bad she was finding it harder and harder to get through the days until she began to make changes.

She dismissed dwelling on her feelings and worked on continuing to reach outside herself, things were getting a little easier. She started to meet up with Coco, Tanya and Heidi more often because she'd come to realise friends are very special people, like flowers in a garden you have to nurture them to keep the friendship alive. Not just expect them to be there for you when you need them and boy had she needed them the last few months but also to be there for them when they needed her. It would have been impossible to get this far without them, even though she couldn't discuss her meeting with Ross with them, having them there gave her solace.

She daren't talk about this problem to the closest person in her life, Cameron. If she did he would also be hurt, just imagine her bringing his daughter to meet her ex-husband without even asking him. She often went to say something to him and then realised, I can't tell Cameron that. This conversation could never be up for discussion. It was her fault she had to bear the brunt. It took a long time, then one evening as Georgia sat with Cameron and Juliet watching a colourful baby story on TV she began to feel the weight of the last few months slowly starting to lift from her body, very slowly she was beginning to like herself again.

Georgia thanked God she was starting to recover, along the way she had added another few things to her to-do list, to try to make things right. She'd set herself tasks like bringing flowers to someone who wasn't feeling too well or chatting to an old lady on the street, giving some of her old clothes and any clothes that didn't fit Juliet, to Vincent De Paul and the latest thing she added was lighting candles for people who had no one to pray for them. Believe it or not somehow all of these little good deeds had a healing effect and slowly, very slowly Georgia began to love herself again and not keep bashing herself down, telling herself she was mean, spiteful and basically didn't consider others at all. Now she was starting to admit to herself, yes, she had done wrong, she had hurt someone who didn't deserve to be hurt again, all because she was feeling good about herself and was in a really happy place. She'd lost all traces of reality thinking that everybody was in the same happy bubble as she was after the birth of her baby. Georgia had to admit she had not considered Ross's feelings for one moment when she introduced him to Juliet. It was all too soon, just like a whirlwind. One evening seeing him at the movies, second literally bumping into him as she turned the corner and thirdly, introducing him to another man's baby when he still loved her and his feelings were still raw. The question was: How could she have done it? She had blamed everything but the truth was her lack of consideration for her fellow man. Now that she was owning up to herself, all her sins, she was beginning to find herself in a different place. It was all working out slowly but surely. The cracks were beginning to close and her heart was beginning to open, life was good. She could now see a light at the end of the very dark tunnel.

She needed something to celebrate, that's what she needed, something to lift her heart, lift her spirits, that something to celebrate was Juliet's first birthday. There it was, written in the stars, crystal clear, something to work towards, in fact she had already started to work on it with one month to go before it would even happen. Cameron had his little list and she had her little list. They even checked it twice and agreed, sure if the weather was good enough they could have a garden party. Altogether, between the two of them there was a list of about twenty friends to invite, most of them would no doubt bring a wife, husband or partner and children.

CHAPTER 65

A night to remember

Just when the time was right, the dinner parties began to fizzle out. The girls had other commitments and Georgia was very, very busy organising baby's birthday and dealing with Juliet's teething problems. The poor little thing, her gums were so sore, she had to have teething rings waiting in the fridge, cold as ice, to numb them. Georgia thanked God for those teething rings, she had at least a dozen of them. They had to be almost ice cold and had to be replaced every twenty minutes once they thawed out, to keep poor little Juliet's gums numb. This wasn't the right environment for friends coming around because all of Georgia's time was taken up looking after Juliet. Of course, as God says when one door closes another one opens and that door came in the shape of Juliet's first birthday. At this stage she had begun to walk holding onto every chair, people's legs, the curtains and the piano stool and anything else she could grab on her way around the sitting room. Georgia kept saying to her little first prize daughter

'You're going to be one year old in a little while and all your aunties are coming to see you and you'll get presents and you'll have a party frock and we'll have balloons.'

The poor little girl didn't understand a word but she had her own language. She gurgled and smiled, gurgled and fell, gurgled and ate, gurgled, talked nonsense and cried with the pain of getting her first milk teeth Ahhhhh. This was the hardest time for Georgia and Cameron as they tried to navigate their way through sleepless nights, endless exhaustion and trying hard to control their bad tempers caused by the lack of sleep and endless exhaustion. Thank God they had their little girl's first birthday party coming around to distract them (after all in order to organise the party they had to stay focussed and awake). There were no invitations, just phone calls and messages put up on Instagram and sent to the chosen few. The pink fluffy birthday cake and the pink and white meringues were all ordered from Butler's Pantry and of course, the bubbly, marshmallows and birthday candles were collected from the supermarket. There had to be a pink drink in there somewhere, it came in the form of a non-alcoholic fizzy pink lemonade specially bought for their little girl's first birthday party.

'I need to check if I've set the scene properly for the coming of the friends to the birthday party.'

First to arrive was the well trained Father Fergus Breen and Maisie Coyne, holding the most beautiful pretty little box, all white with pink hearts and inside a pretty Harrods Teddy. Coco, the gorgeous one, loved parties, even children's parties. She loved dressing up for them and for Juliet's party she made a really special effort. She wore the prettiest short skater dress in baby pink with a big white flower brooch and white high shoes and her shiny hair caught neatly back in a diamante slide. She certainly was a sight to behold but then that was Coco and that was what you expected from her, perfection at all times. Perfection in her clothes, perfection in her overall look and of course, perfection with her gorgeous Italian stallion who looked like he could live up to his name. Tall, broad, well built, a guy with dark curly hair and sallow skin, who would stand out in a crowd.

Of course, Sugar Daddy was there holding his brand new video camera. He immediately took it out from its case and began to video the birthday party. He started the video with his gorgeous wife Heidi, who looked so sophisticated, dressed in a white beautiful Koopla suit and a pair of red Louboutin shoes holding a small red clasp bag. Her presentation was pristine. Tanya arrived in her fun dress, white with red cherries and a big red bow on her hair and of course, bearing gifts. She also brought along her little niece to make the birthday feel special and of course, her niece also had a big bow on her hair and a red dress. Two or three of the children next door, on either side were also invited. They arrived with little presents all wrapped by them and presented them to Juliet, the little girl they came to visit whenever they had the chance.

There she sat at the head of the table in her high chair, all dressed in a pink and white, frothy, pretty dress. She had the loveliest little pink flower pinned onto her blonde curly hair which made her look like a present to be handed around. The sore gums, by now were beginning to be a thing of the past and now in their place were her smiles and gibberish talk, something all the guests really enjoyed. She was, as her daddy would say, the prettiest bundle of joy he had ever had the honour of holding. Then there was the cake and candles. How many times had that one candle been blown out and another one lit, in order for everyone to get that one special photo? This was the moment Cameron chose to present Juliet with his very special present. This was also the moment he chose to give a little speech. Georgia thought he wanted this speech to be at her eighteenth birthday party. So for this moment he was prepared.

'This is my little present to my gorgeous daughter Juliet.'

In the pretty wrapping everyone could tell it was a storybook, after all if it looks like a book, is the shape of a book, it must be a book. Cameron and Juliet tore the paper away. She had great fun and there it sat, The Velveteen Rabbit, a hardback book, unusual in itself for a 1 year old child.

'I know' he said 'this is the hardback version of The Velveteen Rabbit but I do have the other version for now.'

He held that up and showed his audience.

'The hardback one I will present to Juliet on her eighteenth birthday. For now I'll only read from the soft covered one. This particular book means an awful lot to me. I myself was given this book, the hardback one, as a child and now it's Juliet's. That book meant so much to me as I grew up. It helped me find myself as a little boy and made me understand you're only real when you've worked hard and deserve it, in fact, I think I only deserve to be called real now. I have a real life, my real Georgia and my pretty and gorgeous daughter Juliet. She will realise when she looks at this version. My book was presented to me by my parents and I hope she gets from it what I have got from it for years. Enough about me, I will start reading it to you tomorrow night, Juliet, once you get over the tiredness from your party.'

Cameron was applauded by the birthday party guests and Sugar Daddy made sure to get every single word and every single frame in.

Of course, in true spirit all the guests were there, beautifully styled. They remained very patient while all the photographs were being taken and the video camera continued to roll. After all, the first birthday is a momentous occasion. Georgia imagined she would have all these same guests at Juliet's eighteenth birthday. When these very photographs they were taking right now would, on Juliet's eighteenth birthday be displayed on a screen above the birthday table. With all of this in mind at least a hundred photographs were taken that day. The first very special one with Juliet's grandparents, then Georgia holding Juliet, Georgia and Cameron blowing out the candles with their beautiful daughter, Georgia and Cameron with all their friends, including the new ones, Maisie Coyne and Father Fergus Breen and of course, the special one, each of them, with the birthday girl, individually and collectively, a group photograph was taken with Mammy and Daddy and all the children and friends who had arrived for the party and that was the nicest one of all. When you looked at the photograph it looked as if Juliet knew what was going on, she did a lot of gurgling and had a go at blowing out the candles. Poor little pet really trying to talk and express herself but she had already discovered the art of blowing kisses in the direction of her Mam and Dad.

Lots of bottles of bubbles were bought and now were being used to their full capacity as they swirled around Juliet and Mam and Dad, this photograph would have to be a truly memorable one. Georgia was tired and could really think of nothing more to say or do to make this evening the success she had hoped it would be and indeed it had been, she just needed sleep, hours and hours of uninterrupted sleep. Everyone else there seemed tired but happy as they left for home or a night on the town. Unfortunately poor Tanya was three sheets to the wind, having consumed too many aperitifs and a lot of her favourite drink, Champagne. The little girl she had taken with her had already gone home with her daddy as she had school the next day.

'Will you please stay tonight?' begged Georgia 'you can't take your car, it would be far too dangerous.'

'Not to worry' said Cameron 'I'll drop you home.'

On went his coat and a kiss on the cheek for Georgia.

'I'll wake you when I get back.' He said and off out the door the two friends trotted.

Georgia crawled into bed and fell immediately, into the deepest sleep she'd ever fallen into. The hours ticked by, Georgia lay in her bed motionless, just looking beautiful but exhausted, half way through the night she awoke. The house was so quiet, baby Juliet was still asleep probably from all the crawling and playing she had done during the day. Georgia crawled out of bed, grabbed her dressing gown, put it around her cold shoulders and she went to join Cameron for a cup of tea and chat all about how the evening had gone and what a success it had been. The room was in complete darkness. Georgia switched on the light and looked at the time on the clock on the wall. It read twelve, fifty five. He must have a lot to talk about, she said to herself out loud. Wouldn't you think he'd just get her home and put her into bed, cover her up and tip toe his way out of her house. After all, the only thing that would be any good for Tanya would be a good night's sleep after the big drinking session she'd had at the party.

Georgia sat down at the table, drank a glass of water and wondered was he ever going to come home and what the hell was he doing with Tanya at this hour of the night. She didn't want to go back to bed and miss his home coming as he always had stories to tell, she loved that and she loved when he told her she looked lovely and she especially loved when he said, you are the girl of my dreams. She just loved that line. She'd have to wait 'til tomorrow as right now she needed sleep and if Juliet woke she wouldn't get any at all. She'd have to leave Cameron to his chatting. Overtired, overworked and over sleep, yes she was exhausted but sleep just wouldn't come and then she heard that sound, the key turning in the door, that hollow sound, her body began to relax, only Cameron had a key so it couldn't be an intruder. Then she heard footsteps, it was definitely him. He pushed the door open, the light poured in behind him from the bulb on the landing. She just caught that smile, the one she loved, then he cleared his voice as usual and that chocolaty sound, the one she just adored, flowed.

'I'm so sorry I'm late, Georgia. Tanya was so out of it I just couldn't leave her but I have to say I learned things about you tonight that I never knew before. In her drunken state she just kept talking about all her three friends. The funny thing was, she told the stories you told me but from a completely different angle. I almost felt I was in the classroom with all of you in kindergarten. In my mind's eye I could see the four of you feeling so lost and unsure, looking for someone to play with. Then you found each other. That proves to me even as children we are all drawn like a moth to the flame, to the people best suited to us. It also proves to me we should really listen to children. When I was a youngster adults would say to me, children should be seen but not heard. That was so wrong. Children should be encouraged to join into most conversations. I imagine when the four of you met for the first time symbols clashed together in heaven and a spark fell, split into four little pieces and tipped your hearts and you became friends forever. Now I really know the friendship all of you have is as strong today as it was all those years ago.'

CHAPTER 66

The worst time of her life.

'Cheerio Georgia. We're off for our walk, you know bonding time, me and my baby girl, Juliet. I love her name, it just rolls off my tongue.'

'Aw Cameron, you know I don't like competition.' Georgia said laughing out loud.

'You know, Georgia there'll never be competition with my girls, how could I not love you more every day for presenting me with our amazing little dream girl.'

'Yes Cameron, since Juliet arrived we haven't stopped smiling, she's just the icing on the most sumptuous birthday cake. But you know Cameron, today I feel quite tired, it'll be nice just to sit down with a biscuit and a nice cup of coffee.'

'That's exactly what to do when we're gone walkies, just slip off your shoes, grab yourself a coffee and do what you like best, listen to music on the radio. You really do need a bit of you time.'

'You're not going anywhere until I grab my phone' said Georgia. 'I just have to take that photograph and video of the two of you all dressed up, snugly-bugly. It's going to be a great one for Juliet's eighteenth birthday, when she's watching mortified and we're just enjoying the memories on the big screen.'

'We'll be back in about an hour' said Cameron.

Georgia enjoyed the big kisses and the warmest, loveliest hugs, from Cameron. Then it was Georgia's turn to cover their little girl in kisses too. Then up again with her camera and she was delighted she captured that beautiful smile from Cameron on video, an enthusiastic wave and Juliet was gone out for that long walk and bonding time with her daddy. Georgia could still feel those big teddy bear hugs and her lips still tingled from the long lovely kisses and the gorgeous smell of Juliet. All that lovely powdery, creamy baby smell lingered with her, that smile on Juliet's face and the little gurgles just haunted her in the nicest way.

She turned on her music, made herself a big cup of coffee and did what Cameron had advised, slipped off her shoes, sat on the big comfy sofa with her feet to the side. She sipped the coffee and nibbled on a nice chocolate biscuit and time just passed. It's lovely to just sit down and forget about everything but already she had decided she wouldn't like a life like this. The room was too quiet, even with her favourite songs playing on the radio. As stupid as it sounds, Georgia was already missing her loved ones, her routine, checking on her gorgeous daughter, her little family. She had something very beautiful and let's face it, in her past life she had plenty of time to sit, drink coffee and ponder on life's questions. Where am I going?

Georgia continued to listen to the songs on the radio and as she crunched on the biscuits and sipped her coffee she realised all she wanted from life right now, she already had. She felt at one with herself, the pondering and wondering about life was over, she was just happy. Her life was back on track, she still thought of her little heavenly baby but she always knew she was somewhere up above. She took comfort knowing in her heart from somewhere up above Connie was looking after Georgia's little family. The coffee and the biscuits had vanished but the music still played softly in the background. Georgia was really missing her two oul pals. Maybe she should have gone along with them; sometimes a walk outdoors can make everyone relax and talk freely. She put the kettle on again, and began to prepare the dinner. Cameron was always so kind in every way, so she needed to be kind to him in return too. It was quick, just chicken pieces thrown on the pan with a little butter and some new potatoes boiling away in the pot. She'd added some broccoli and a few carrots just to give a little colour to the meal. Everything was simmering, everything was peaceful, life was good. She heard the doorbell ring.

Cameron has a key for the door, why is the doorbell ringing? She never bothered to put her shoes back on. Once Georgia had her shoes off she always walked on her tippy toes. She gracefully walked to the door and opened it, hair in a ponytail, no makeup, just casual. But it wasn't Cameron and Juliet at her door, it was two police officers, one male, one female, they looked serious. She just knew something was wrong, she could hear herself screaming inside, what's happened, where's Cameron, where's my Juliet? But outwardly Georgia looked calm and didn't say a word.

'Can we come in Georgia?' Said the Garda.

Georgia nodded her head and walked backwards into the kitchen still looking straight at the pair of them, as they moved along trying to get into the kitchen. Georgia automatically turned off the radio, and sat down at the little deep blue, old, newly sprayed table. The place was quiet and still. They said my name. How could they know my name? Her brain was alert, her senses were on high, she could smell the fear she was feeling. Something was wrong, she just knew it. In her head she was repeating over and over, they couldn't know my name, I never saw these people before in my life. They are police officers. She was thinking all these things but she hadn't uttered a word.

The male Garda, put the kettle on and made her tea. She could see him from the corner of her eye and heard the spoon as he stirred it in the cup, every sound was crystal clear, as clear as a bell. It was like there was a silence all around and in the silence every sound was magnified, everything happening around her was exaggerated, sounding sharp in her head. Georgia wanted to cover her ears so she could not hear a word being spoken. This was too hard, she didn't want to hear what they had to say. Every fibre of her being was on red alert. The Bean Garda introduced herself to Georgia:

'My name is Louise' and then she stopped... cold silence.

The male Garda arrived back holding a big mug of, scalding, boiling hot tea and placed it on the table beside Georgia. Louise handed the mug to Georgia and made sure she was holding it correctly before she let it go. It would be terrible if it spilled all over Georgia and burnt her hands and legs. At times like these the Irish Gardai are trained to take control and be of great assistance to everyone who needs them. Louise encouraged Georgia to take a sip. The sugary taste hit her tongue. The male Garda pulled a chair over and sat down, beside the two women.

'My name is Tom. We are here for you Georgia,'

'What's happened?'

Georgia heard herself say almost wailing like a banshee. She had only heard herself cry like that once before when she miscarried her baby and she never thought she'd hear herself cry like that again. She just wailed, not knowing if every grain of happiness she possessed had been taken from her again.

'Now, there has been an accident' said Louise 'your baby is absolutely fine.'

'Oh Thank God.' Georgia cried. 'Where is she? I want to see her, I want to see her now.'

'She's just being checked over at the hospital. We are going to bring you there just as soon as we chat. You have nothing to worry about as far as your baby is concerned.'

Georgia could feel a rush of happiness, at least God wasn't taking her little girl away from her. All the pain she felt from losing her last baby came back on top of her swiftly like a tornado. Then she felt panic engulfing her being again. She thought she might collapse as a cold sweat teemed down from the back of her neck, she heard herself crying out:

'Where's Cameron? Is he all right?'

Louise did all the talking and handled the situation so sensitively and with so much care and consideration.

'Cameron has some injuries. To what extent we really don't know yet but we will take you to the hospital now and let the doctors explain everything to you.'

Georgia grabbed her shoes and ran to get her bits and pieces to take with her. Louise followed close behind her into the bedroom and helped her pick out a few warm things to wear because by now Georgia was shivering, she felt so cold as if she was walking in snowy, cold, frozen weather, scantily clad but instead she was dressed in a warm coat, with a big jumper underneath. Louise, the policewoman, encouraged Georgia to pack a few extra things into the baby bag for Juliet and some nightwear for Cameron. Like a child she walked out with the policeman and woman and did something she never thought she would do, sit in a police car. She glanced back at her front door as the car drove away and in her heart she just knew for her, things would never be the same again. Her brain had conveyed the message, when she would return to her beautiful bungalow her life as she knew it would have changed forever. Her home, his home and baby's home would have changed forever. What could she do? Nothing, just be taken along on a cloud of despair. Louise had been in touch with the hospital all through the journey and when they arrived, there was a team waiting for them.

As Georgia slowly got out of the car, the first sight she saw was her baby girl in the arms of her friend Heidi and beside them stood Coco and Tanya. Georgia couldn't wait to hold

Juliet as tight as she could in her arms. Then, on that cloud of despair, with the slightest hope and holding her baby girl, she was escorted into a private room where she was greeted by a lovely doctor and a very nice young nurse. She realised the nurse was there to help her and the doctor was there to give her the bad news. Louise and Tom the Garda excused themselves and left the room and Georgia, in an environment she'd never been in before. But then, who's ever ready for bad news or grief? She knew she'd have to get the strength from somewhere.

The doctor explained what he heard had happened. As Cameron and baby Juliet were crossing at a pedestrian crossing, a car had gone through without stopping. Cameron had pushed Juliet's pram to the side and took the full brunt himself. He was in a serious, critical condition but if he pulled through the next twenty four hours and his condition stabilised there was every hope he would pull through completely but first they would have a waiting game.

Like an apparition Georgia's mother was there by her side. Nellie put her arm around Georgia's waist, they walked together into the unknown, right over to the bed where Cameron lay with tubes coming from everywhere. He was indeed a pitiful sight and it was hard for Georgia to compare the two, Cameron earlier as he left the house with Juliet, his happy way and the words he said to her were all coming back. She needed the comfort of those words and his sincerity right now. She prayed that God would save his life and she promised God that if He did, she would always be true to Cameron and never again look for something that really wasn't there, outside of her happy home. Beside Cameron's bed stood his mum and dad and sister. One of her friends must have got in touch with them. Thank God somebody did because Georgia couldn't think straight. His poor parents and sister were distraught but thank God they were there.

CHAPTER 67

Night vigil

Georgia, her mum and Cameron's family sat quietly beside his bed. All that could be heard were the sorrowful sobs and all that was there to be seen were white faces and red eyes. Outside the room, friends were still rallying round, her childhood friends, the old reliables, Tanya and Heidi. Georgia never tired of thanking God for them. They made sure that at all times one of Cameron's family or Georgia were by his side.

By now Juliet was back home being well looked after by Coco, who had put her life on hold, because she loved Georgia and Cameron. After all, she knew if the chips were down Georgia would do exactly the same for her in a heartbeat.

Nurses and doctors floated in and out of the room checking Cameron, but in the end it would be the specialists who'd make the final decision on what path to take. For now all they could do was keep him stable. When someone is sick it's always the night time that's the longest, sitting beside the bed feeling useless and wondering what the daylight might bring.

Georgia's mind drifted back to Connie and she prayed to her to just keep her sane and alert. What in God's name would she do without her belief that Connie would always help her through the worst crisis in her life? What would she do without Cameron if the worst came to the worst? It was at this moment Cameron became very uneasy and began to move erratically in the bed. Georgia pressed the alarm bell. Just before the nurse entered the room, Georgia looked over at Cameron, his eyes were wide open, oh those beautiful, haunting eyes. She was so happy her mum and his family were right beside her to witness this moment. Did he recognise her? Maybe he was trying to tell her something. She thought she saw him smile.

Then the nurses were there and the doctor was there. It's wonderful how they take control of a situation that is completely alien to you, at a time when you feel completely useless and unable to help in any way. All she could do was be there, hold his hand, wipe his brow and sit silently. The doctor had been swift in his actions, he gave Cameron an injection to calm him down and thank God for that. Once he was settled, the nurses could see how upset everyone was and urged Cameron's mum and dad to go home and come back in the morning. They would feel better after a few hours of sleep. Nellie took control of the situation and insisted that all of Cameron's family should stay at Georgia's bungalow. There were plenty of beds, plenty of food, for now it would be their home because it was important that they were close to the hospital. Georgia refused to leave, she wasn't going anywhere, all she wanted to do was be by his side, sit with him and just be there, in the stillness of the night, beside his bed holding his hand.

Her thoughts drifted back to their journey together, how long he'd been in her life, how she'd met him, how the romance had developed, how she'd left Ross for him, how she'd become a mother to make him feel complete, not realising how complete it would also make her feel. Now at this moment she couldn't bear to think of facing a life on her own while everyday trying to keep Cameron's memory alive for Juliet. She had never imagined that responsibility, she'd have to make sure she had photographs of him all round the house so Juliet could say daddy and know what her daddy looked like. She would always tell her how much her daddy loved her and all the good things her daddy had done for her, like taking her for walks and chatting and singing to her and creating a great bond between the two of them in her short little life. Georgia's body shuddered, she didn't want that to be the outcome of this awful accident.

As time dragged on, her insecurities kept popping up their ugly heads and every now and then she'd panic, she'd feel her pulse racing and her head spinning when she'd realise this wasn't a dream, this was her reality, a living nightmare and she was living it minute by minute, hour by hour.

She looked at the monitor, had she heard it beeping or just imagined it? Then doctors and nurses seemed to flood the room. She had to stand up, let his hand slip away from hers, (Oh my God she could still feel his hand in hers). Her brain was telling her Georgia, stand back and let the team do whatever they need to do. She just stood there, motionless staring at Cameron, lying there trying to breathe with the help of the life support machine. She tried to breathe, it was too hard. She felt as if she was up in the air looking down and this was all happening minus her but instead she was being ushered outside the room by the nurse. She could still feel Cameron's hand as it slipped away from hers. Now outside the door Georgia was trying to hide from the pain of seeing Cameron so distressed but she couldn't. She ran back into the room where Cameron lay.

All she could see was the nurses and doctor standing back from his bed. It was then she realised it was over, he was gone. They could do nothing else for him. She was helpless and beyond consoling, in her worst nightmare she had never imagined this moment. It's funny at times like this all the little things don't matter anymore, Maria... all in her imagination, Ross... in her past. Why had she continued to try to bring him back into her life? He had made a new life, she had made a new life, so why had she pushed to meet him again after that chance meeting? Now all of that seemed silly and stupid. Why hadn't she just enjoyed what she had, this charismatic man who knew her inside out, who never questioned her, who did everything in his power to help her have the life she craved. At that moment, Georgia realised that since the day she met him they never had a disagreement, were always on the same page and lived together harmoniously. He'd taken time off from work to give Georgia time for herself and give him his time to bond with his little baby girl. At all times he had looked after herself and Juliet and made this new life they shared together a fantastic life. Now, just like turning off a light switch there was darkness. No light in her heart, it had disappeared in one flash, all gone.

She could feel someone's hand on her shoulder. Georgia took a little look back and there she stood, his mum, even in her grief she was trying to be kind to Georgia by showing solidarity to the partner of her precious son. Cameron's dad and sister, stood silent and so alone. Georgia felt sick in her heart realising in her grief, she almost forgot that Cameron was the most loved person in his mum's, dad's and sister's lives. Georgia put her hand on Cameron's mum's shoulder, re-enacting what she had done for Georgia just moments earlier.

'I insist all of you have time with Cameron alone. Stay here with your son. We will be outside if you need us. We will be in the little private room.'

The look on Cameron's mum's face was so humbling, it said it all. Cameron's parents just nodded in agreement, together the little group walked closer to Cameron's bed. Georgia and her mum left the room. It was just a few steps to that private room but they seemed endless. Isn't it funny, how all the hard knocks you've had in your life somehow give you inner strength to cope with the worst times of your life'. Cameron's mum and dad had been so proud of their son when he joined the religious life and equally proud of him since he became a father to Juliet and a partner to Georgia. In their quiet way they were always supportive and now they were frightened to their core knowing what they had to witness and what they had to accept. Their Cameron was gone forever.

It was a while before Georgia came back into the room but she was right on time to witness the two women sitting down. Cameron's father just stood at the opposite side of the bed quietly gazing down at his beautiful son, his skin white and tears flowing. Cameron's mum and sister sat quietly crying, with tears of disbelief streaming down from their eyes. Georgia knew there was no point in hugging her in any way, this was her time with her son and she needed to grieve, so Georgia stood back, this was an out of body experience. Eventually they all sat down on the chairs as close as they could get to the bed. For Georgia this was an honour to sit beside his mother, such a charismatic, wonderful lady who even in grief was so dignified. Cameron's father remained standing beside the bed for a few minutes, then he re-joined his family and sat down.

Georgia's mum and Cameron's family quietly left the room, Georgia could hear the door gently close. Now it was her turn to grieve. She could hear herself sobbing, it sounded like nothing she'd ever heard before. When she'd lost Connie there was a different sort of sound, it was a mother's loss, right from the pit of her stomach, and now it was a grown up loss, the loss of a partner, lover, comforter, father to her daughter, all gone. His life swept away in a moment. For her a life changing experience, everything that had been hers was gone, she felt empty, alone. What would she do, without him? Georgia began to panic. Who would she tell her stories to if it wasn't him? Who would laugh at her jokes, if he wasn't around? Who would she get dressed up for? All she wanted to do was look beautiful for him. All questions, no answers, just a horrible void, an empty pit, that's what she felt she was in. How could anyone understand that feeling except people who were going through it themselves?

As she sat on the chair alone, she could feel the stillness and absolute utter silence. She held his hand that was still warm. She began to do silly little things, first she fumbled in her bag and took out a brush and began to brush Cameron's beautiful hair. Her hand moved to the back of his neck, she could feel his warm perspiration. She took up a face towel, damped it down and patted his face. Then she just gazed at him and said all the things she wanted to say to him and needed to say to him. What a difference he had made to her life, how much she loved him, in fact how much everybody loved him and what a good daddy he was even that day to his very last moment. How proud she was that he'd bonded so well with Juliet. Georgia would always tell Juliet all about her daddy, show his photographs to her, in fact Georgia would always make sure he was forever alive in her eyes.

Then Georgia looked at Cameron and thought how absolutely beautiful he was and even though he had passed on she could still feel him beside her in the room, yes his spirit was still there all around her. She stood up for a minute, walked to the window and because she could hardly breathe she opened it just a little to let in some fresh air, there must have been a breeze outside because the very light curtains on the window swayed. She felt a surge of energy and a sense of peace from her toes right up through her head. She believed she could feel his spirit leave the room out through that window and up into the blue sky, even though his beautiful body was still lying there. It was an unbelievable feeling, she just knew he was happy.

Cameron had always been a religious man. He at all times had felt at peace with himself. He had lived a good life and now it was over. His time on Earth had abruptly come to an end but she knew he truly believed death can come like a thief in the night, so even though he was only a young man he was always prepared, always ready and felt death wasn't the end, it was the beginning, there were better things to come.

Georgia found some peace in knowing Cameron didn't die in vain, he died saving Juliet's life. Calmness descended on Georgia, maybe that's the feeling you have when shock sets in, when you feel nothing. By now her favourite nurse had arrived, Elaine, she was beyond nice, beyond caring, beyond understanding, beyond compassion, just a wonderful human being (an earth angel). She pulled over a chair and sat beside Georgia, that's just what Georgia needed, Elaine giving her the strength to get through these moments. This nurse could work wonders. Georgia felt the anguish and panic attack she was just about to have, leaving her mind and body. It's funny the little things you observe at times like this, thought Georgia. First, how fresh Elaine's clothes smelled, how her shoes were so perfectly laced, at this moment in Georgia's mind Elaine looked like a perfect Florence Nightingale.

Elaine knew when it was time for her to get up and leave Georgia alone with Cameron. When she did go Georgia didn't even notice. Time was moving on, the evening was settling in, darkness was falling. Someone put the lights on. Her eyes remained fixed on Cameron, she just couldn't let go of his hand. Elaine returned at just the right moment to save Georgia from herself. Georgia just didn't want to leave him, she kept holding onto his hand. Elaine gradually and gently slipped Georgia's fingers away from Cameron's hand. She then put her right arm around Georgia's waist to give her support, while her left hand held Georgia's hand to give her some comfort. She guided her outside. There stood two of her friends, Cameron's family and her mum, of course Coco had stayed behind to look after Juliet. The nurses returned, they needed to get things organised in Cameron's room, all the things Georgia didn't need to know about.

'Now Georgia, come on outside' said Elaine 'I'll take you to that nice quiet room and organise some tea, coffee and a few biscuits, to give you some energy, while I take your friends in for a moment to see Cameron.'

Elaine left, Tanya remained beside her friend Georgia. Tea and biscuits arrived, they sipped the tea and nibbled on a few crunchy biscuits, somehow the hot tea and biscuits worked wonders but still all Georgia felt was cold, shaky and empty, she thanked God for all of Cameron's family, her mum and her friends who were there all together, lending support to each other. Heidi returned to the room and Tanya left to join the other mourners in Cameron's room. Elaine came in and presented Georgia with a few personal items belonging to Cameron, tucked in his canvas backpack. Georgia held Cameron's backpack with his personal belongings inside. She was immediately engulfed in a wave of sadness. Just in the nick of time friends and family began to return.

Together the little group walked out into the open air where a warm breeze seemed to dance on their faces. Two cabs had already been ordered and were sitting there waiting. Home to Cameron and Georgia's bungalow the taxis sped, where Coco had a big fry prepared, enough for everyone. Easy things like rashers, sausages, tomatoes, all kinds of greasy food that they needed. Georgia didn't eat that much but what she ate she really enjoyed and what she enjoyed even more than food was her little girl Juliet who just hadn't got a clue about anything that had just happened. There she was smiling, gurgling and just being herself, a happy little girl. In that instant Georgia knew she would have the strength to go forward, Cameron would have wanted that... yes! Cameron would have wanted his little girl to grow up smiling. They all just ate, drank tea or coffee and spoke about little things, just nonchalant. The friends knew there was a lot Georgia would have to go through in the coming days but for now it was all about keeping her sane and coping.

With Juliet being looked after by the three friends Georgia had time alone. She sat on the side of her bed, in her hands she held the canvas backpack. Inside in a plastic bag lay the little parcel Elaine had given her with all of Cameron's worldly goods. She opened the parcel that was so neatly folded and his watch was the first thing she saw. The watch she had given him, she loved that watch on his wrist and she knew he loved it too. Beside his watch, wrapped in a piece of tissue paper lay his gorgeous chain and cross. The other things were just the things he'd worn that day, his jumper, jacket, shirt, trousers, underwear, stockings and shoes. Everything he had been wearing that fatal day was now sitting on Georgia's lap, it made her realise that the possessions you own are really worthless. All you really have at the end of the day is you. She just stared down at his trousers that were dusty and torn, his shoes that were scratched, the soles that were loose, she felt nothing. She looked back on her phone to find the photos she had taken as they left the house on the one day in her life she would never forget and there they were, pictures of Juliet in the pram being pushed by her very happy dadda.

Something fell to the ground and Georgia bent down to

pick it up. There were two letters addressed to her. Her hands trembled, tears flowed, she sobbed uncontrollably, she knew she could not open those letters now, they would have to wait until another time, when she was calmer, an awful lot calmer. All his clothes she packed and placed back into his drawer, his shoes were put back into the box in his wardrobe and the two letters she put them in the safest place to be read at a later date. Tanya walked in at the perfect moment.

'Georgia' she said 'have you thought of the clothes you'd like Cameron to wear?'

'What clothes?' said Georgia.

'The clothes you loved on him. Maybe his newest suit, shirt and tie?'

'Oh yes' said Georgia 'I completely overlooked the whole thing. All I can think of is the day he left our bungalow with Juliet and the two of them as happy as larks as they bestowed on me kisses and hugs, and smiled for my camera. Then they were gone. Now, he is gone forever.'

Coco and Heidi arrived and gave Georgia the biggest hug ever. She continued to sob.

'I'm trying my best to block out in my head Cameron lying in that bed with tubes everywhere in his body and the pain he must have been going through. It's all just too sad, too soon and too horrible to allow myself to remember.'

'Come on' said Heidi 'for a few minutes let's all just remember the good times we had with Cameron. He was great fun to be with, he was so understanding and the best thing of all was, he loved you and Juliet to the moon and back.'

'So let's pick his clothes' said Coco 'and imagine he's going to the best party ever, he's got to be dressed in his best.'

'It's his best suit,' said Georgia 'that's what he'll wear.'

She took it down from the wardrobe, conveniently everything was on the hanger, suit, shirt, tie, the lot.

For a moment or two she didn't feel sad, instead she felt happy as memories drifted back to her of their date night in the Shamrock Hotel. They had both decided to get dressed separately and only meet downstairs in the restaurant when they'd both be glammed up to the nines. In his own words Cameron had said 'I want it to feel like a date night, Georgia, so I'll be down there all dressed up in my new suit waiting for you, my date, to arrive.' When she got her first glimpse of him that night, she fell in love with him all over again and just knew, in her heart of hearts, she had made the hardest decision of her life but the right decision, when she left Ross for Cameron.

'Who'll dress him?' said Georgia 'Should I?'

'No' said the three best friends together. 'We'll go, we'll sort everything out for you.'

'Would you do one favour for me please Coco?' said Georgia. 'When he's all dressed up and looking his best would one of you put on his watch and his chain and cross for me?'

The three friends vowed to do everything just the way Georgia wanted.

'He will look his best, Georgia. You will be proud.'

It was the day before the funeral and funnily enough Georgia had slept most of the night with her little girl by her side, keeping her warm. This was the day she was dreading, the day before the funeral. She just followed orders and found herself being driven to the undertakers to see Cameron and believe it or not she was starting to feel happy just to see him again. They were inside and being ushered down the hall and into a room with soft music playing and there Cameron lay, in his newest beautiful suit with his treasured watch on his wrist for everyone to see and around his neck his gold cross and chain glistened. Her mum and all her friends were saints! After all, sure it's only a saint who could have everything so perfect for Cameron. She could hardly believe he had passed away, he just looked as if he was asleep.

The time had come, the moment she was dreading was now here, Georgia stood to the side and allowed everyone to pay their last respects to Cameron the man they all knew in different ways. Then out of respect for the family, everyone but family stood back, some of the mourners left the room. Eventually her time had come, her turn to walk right up to Cameron, bend her head and kiss him for the last time. Now his body was cold. She felt his spirit had already soared up into the blue sky, leaving just a shell that looked like him but definitely was not him.

Without anyone noticing she slipped his watch from his wrist and without a lot of fuss she removed his chain and cross from around his neck. Georgia stood back and although the lid of the coffin had been placed and it was very clear to her she would never see his face again, she still had a little smile on her face, just knowing he would always be there for her and Juliet. She was doing the right thing. You could hear the sobs of everyone that stood there but Georgia was just aware of his mum and dad and family. They would have nothing to go home to while she had Juliet.

The rest of the night was a blur. Georgia allowed friends and family to take her and Juliet under their wing. Her mum stayed with her overnight. She felt she was on a dark cloud drifting towards tomorrow, the morning of the funeral.

CHAPTER 68

Morning of the funeral

Georgia sat surrounded by her mum Nellie, her friends Heidi, Coco and Tanya, Miss Maisie Coyne and Fr. Fergus Breen all there to lend their support. Some of the neighbours whom she hardly knew had gotten together and bought the food for the funeral breakfast. They cooked it, served it up, and when there wasn't a crumb left they cleared the table, cleaned everything up and left the bungalow spotless.

What a nice humane thing to do and all in such a quiet caring way. As she sat there surrounded by love, she began to remember the dream she'd had last night. Maybe she was only imagining things or maybe it was an hallucination, whatever it was, it was only coming back to her now. She could see Cameron, she felt he must have been trying to tell her something. She was trying to make out what it was, trying to get the vision clear in her mind. She concentrated, what was he trying to tell me in my dream, what was it? Let me remember. Then very slowly it came to her, it was something to do with his watch I just know he wants his mum to have his watch, and what was it about the gold chain and cross? I feel he would want me to keep it for now and give it to Juliet when she is older, maybe on her Communion Day? Perfect she thought.

Thank you Cameron for making me do things the right way. In that instant she just knew he was there all around her. Georgia knew in her heart she would never feel alone again. He would guide her frail body and mind through the stormy seas of her life. Until she was able to take back control all she would have to do was close her eyes, concentrate on him and he would be there. Just like the song sung by Leo Sayer, *When I Need You, I Just Close My Eyes And I See You*. Her body began to relax, she felt really happy that somehow his wish was now her command and not only was it his wish but it was her wish too and the right thing to do.

CHAPTER 69

Final goodbyes

The time to leave for the funeral had arrived. Georgia hadn't a clue who organised it, but she was so glad that Cameron's mum, dad and close family were all there to support each other. His family were all so nice, Georgia felt sad they hadn't been included enough in their lives so far and vowed, at Cameron's funeral, she would include them even more in Juliet's upbringing and make them a bigger part of her life from that moment on.

Of course, as usual her mum and friends had everything top drawer for Cameron's day. It was a small funeral, just his and her families, close friends, teenagers from the school where he taught, colleagues from the beauty salon and Ross. Yes Ross! Unknown to Georgia, Ross had been part of the little organising group for the funeral. They had gone as far as going back to the religious order Cameron had belonged to and obtained a lot of his details from them.

The order insisted on hosting the funeral in their church surrounded by all the priests and the church choir. They said Cameron would have liked that and all Georgia's friends agreed that she too would be happy with their decision. Georgia was very, very happy with how things turned out that day. From the first moment her mourning car turned into the driveway she could see in the distance pupils from Cameron's school lining each side of the road. That one gesture of camaraderie made Georgia so happy, to know he had made an amazing impression in such a short time on his pupils.

The morning went like a dream from an organising point of

view and like a nightmare from Georgia's point of view. Lots of priests attended the ceremony. It was held in the beautiful church in the monastery where Cameron used to pray, where he had made mad passionate love with her, a beautiful memory (Forbidden Fruit). The pews were situated face to face with a big walkway through the centre. It was such a warm inviting church and the words the priest said about Cameron were out of this world, there wasn't a dry eye in the Church. The choir was made up of priests, locals and teenagers from Cameron's school who joined in with the choir and sang. They started with *Nearer My God to Thee*. Then the priest took a moment to thank the choir for their beautiful singing and announced:

'I just want to say a few words, a big thank you to the school choir who have joined us today, they are absolutely amazing. Their voices have added extra depth and warmth to the hymns. You've already heard the beautiful hymn *Nearer My God to Thee*, in a little while they will sing *Ave Maria* and later on *Panis Angelicus*. For our final song, Audian, our soloist has asked to sing a song that was very close to Cameron's heart. I won't disclose the name of the song, it will be revealed in a little while.' Father Joe added, 'As Audian was one of Cameron's best friends he's been nominated by the rest of the priests to say a few words.'

Audian came down the stairs from the choir, walked up through the church and stood in the centre of the altar. He spoke to the congregation.

'I would like to speak on behalf of the deacons, sub-deacons and priests who were here during Cameron's time. I've been elected by them' he smiled 'to say a few words. Cameron was one of the calmest, most charismatic people I have ever known. He often spent time with priests individually, to listen to their worries and concerns. All of the congregation of priests here would like to stand up and applaud Cameron, to thank him for all he achieved during his time here at the monastery. The real reason I'm standing here today is to sing Cameron's favourite song, from him to you Georgia. It's a song that Cameron sang on the corridors and in his cell, so loudly that not a priest could miss it and from that day forward it was the song that reminded all of us of him.'

With that Audian stood straight, put one foot on a chair, cradled his guitar and began to strum the chords, the organist and the choir joined in and accompanied Audian. He sang in the most beautiful voice, the fabulous words of the song *Georgia on My Mind*. Georgia could feel the hairs on the back of her neck stand up with the absolute thrill that song gave her, she could visualise Cameron singing that song and standing exactly like Audian, just like he stood in their pretty bungalow on the lovely Sunday with Fr. Fergus Breen and Maisie Coyne. You could hear a pin drop in the church. Some mourners smiled, some mourners clapped and some of them remained silent. Georgia's mum was one of the mourners who stayed silent, her job was to hold on to Georgia and give her the strength to carry on and to let her know she was there for her through thick and thin, no matter what. Cameron's sister, mum and dad turned to Georgia and just hugged her. Georgia said:

'Oh! That song means so much to me. It was our song.'

There were no more words needed, she could feel the love. Again she vowed to keep them in her and Juliet's lives forever.

As Georgia began to walk to the church door, the singing continued. She stopped at the end of the stairs that led up to the choir and waited until one by one the choir members began to descend from the stairway, still singing. She thanked each and every one of them for making such an effort and invited them to the little gathering after the funeral, for a light snack.

Unfortunately the school girls had to return back to school once they had formed a guard of honour for the cortege, as it drove past on its short journey to the graveyard.

Georgia couldn't help but look up at the little windows on the building as her car slowly made its way to Cameron's final resting place. She remembered looking out from one of them at the luscious green grass and the pretty flowers. Back then she was looking out, out at a life she dreamt would be hers with Cameron and for a little while that life she had dreamt of, was hers but now God was not willing to share Cameron with her any longer. Georgia had his love for a very short time but God was always going to win. As the tears flowed down her face she said her private goodbyes to Cameron, the most charismatic man she had ever met and vowed to love him forever until they meet again.

The burial itself Georgia had very little recollection of but there were a few things that stood out in her mind. The sadness in Cameron's mum and dad's eyes even though their family surrounded them and tried their best to give them strength and comfort, they were just broken.

There was something else she became aware of something that she didn't really dwell on at the time but turned out to be so important to her. Just like her having little dreams in her head for her little girl, Juliet, they must have had those dreams for Cameron when he was a young boy, then when he joined the priesthood, and when he met Georgia. Yes, when Juliet arrived on the scene they must have felt that all the boxes had been ticked and all the wishes they had for their son had come true, like happiness, self-fulfilment and having someone to listen to his stories and love him. They had had so many reasons to visit Dublin more frequently, especially at times like Easter, Christmas, St. Patrick's Day and of course, this year the very special first birthday for Juliet and sharing that time with Cameron. Hindsight is a wonderful thing. That birthday had been so special, Cameron had been his charismatic self, listening to everyone's stories, giving his mum, dad and sister plenty of time to talk, even Georgia's mother (Nellie) and friends were entertained by him.

As for Georgia herself, she would have the memories of all those lovely smiles, kisses and haunting gazes in her heart and soul forever. The best part of it all was, all of that was captured on video. What a wonderful thing to have for Juliet as she grows. Georgia decided at that moment, once everything settled down, she would invite Cameron's family to her home, to see Juliet and view the video of the birthday party. She would put 100% into making them happy by bonding with Juliet, yes Georgia would make sure Juliet grew up knowing her country grandma and grandad and the aunties now that Cameron was gone. Her skin burned from the tears and her heart just broke but all the time she felt grateful for having met and shared a small but very precious part of her life with Cameron.

As her car was just about to pull out from the graveside there was a little tap on the window, outside stood a young man, around the same age as Cameron. At first Georgia didn't know him from Adam, then she realised he was the soloist from the choir. She lowered the window and bewildered, she looked out at him.

'Excuse me Georgia' he said 'could I have a word with you? Firstly I hope you liked the song I sang *Georgia on my mind.*'

Quietly Georgia answered 'I loved it.'

'I'd better introduce myself to you.'

Georgia knew Audian didn't need to introduce himself to her. He'd already been introduced to the congregation, by the priest in the church. Georgia just let him do the honours.

'My name is Audian. I studied with Cameron. He loved that song. As I already said, he sang it all the time, but there was one other thing he used to do, he constantly wrote letters to you.'

'I found two letters with his clothes that the nurse in the hospital gave me. The dates on the envelopes coincided with the dates I went to see him in London, but I never received any letters in the post from Cameron.'

'He never sent them. He said he hadn't got the courage. He left them in his drawer together with a lot of my things. He left the monastery before me. When I was packing I found an envelope addressed to you. I called Cameron and promised to look after the letters and return them to him when I saw him the next time. Every time we moved digs, Cameron's letters came with us. He told me to look after them and keep them safe. There never seemed to be the right time for passing them back to him so they just remained with me. Now I know why. Each one is in their own envelope and each envelope is sealed. So here they are Georgia. I'm presenting them to you. I truly believe this is the way it was supposed to be. Cameron was never meant to post them or have them returned to him. I just know these letters were meant for you, on this very day at this very moment. You were meant to be presented with them now. Georgia, I'm so happy to give you all these letters from Cameron. He wrote them especially for you, to you.'

Georgia took the letters, all piled together in a big brown envelope. She noticed Audian's full name and telephone number on the front of the envelope along with her name. At this point she got out of the car and stood with the young man, her hands were shaking.

'How can I thank you?' she said and began to sob. 'I really mean thank you from the bottom of my heart. I won't read any of them until the time is right.'

She gently hugged Audian, he returned the hug and whispered in her ear:

'I'm so happy that at last Cameron's letters to you are in your hands. I feel a huge responsibility has been lifted from my shoulders. I just wanted you to know that even when Cameron left you for a little while and returned to the seminary, he never forgot you. He told me you were the love of his life. I hope my words will give you some comfort.' Audian continued 'Oh! How I would love to meet someone who I would call the love of my life.'

'You will Audian. She is at this moment looking for you. Your paths will cross. Just like my letters eventually found me. When the stars align, just wait, she, love will come to you.'

Audian looked at Georgia, she noticed that lost look in his eyes. She remembered seeing that lost look before, in Cameron's eyes. Georgia made a mental note to keep his number safe. She also knew one day soon she would call him. She knew Audian needed someone to talk to. Georgia got back into the car and watched as Audian walked slowly away. Most of the mourners adjourned to the friendly pub for a little gathering after the funeral and a light snack. Georgia made sure to sit close to Cameron's mum, after all she was on a mission. She found the perfect moment. She turned to Cameron's broken hearted mum and declared:

'I have a little personal presentation I would like to make to you today.'

She rummaged in her bag and out it came the watch she had presented Cameron with. Now it wasn't loose, it was back in its own box.

'This is for you, I hope it brings you some comfort.'

Cameron's mum began to open the box and looked in amazement as her eyes caught sight of the beautiful watch.

'This watch was meant for you. I feel you need something to hold onto and Cameron would have wanted you to have his watch so you will never lose track of time because every second of your life counts. You probably wonder why I'm presenting you with Cameron's watch when I bought it for him but you see I had a dream, an hallucination or a vision, I'm not sure which but in it Cameron came to me, he was trying to tell me the little things he wanted me to do for him. It took some time but eventually I worked it out, you were to have his watch.'

She told Cameron's mum all about her dream or vision and in her heart she knew Cameron's mum loved that story, it made the watch even more special to her. Sometimes you just know when it's right, it's right. The day was over, the worst day of her life, all friends gone, all except her mum, her best friend. Yes Nellie was there as usual quietly organising Juliet, knowing when to dip in and out of conversations, making sure Juliet was fed and Georgia never missed a meal. Nellie constantly encouraged her to eat a little bit more 'just a little bit.' She was only short of spoon feeding Georgia as well as Juliet.

Georgia had gone to bed early that night, she sat on the side of her bed and as she sat there she remembered the two letters she'd put away in her safe place - her locker at the side of her bed. The drawer sounded loud as she opened it. She opened the woolly bow on the letters Audian had given her and before putting the two letters with them, she numbered them 4 and 5 the way they were turned towards her when she picked them up off the floor. She packed them all back into the box and put them into her noisy drawer where they would stay until she knew the time was right to read them.

CHAPTER 70

The sun beginning to shine

Even weeks after the funeral Georgia could recall her last look at Cameron's beautiful face, she would never forget it, his sallow skin, his curly hair that she had continuously combed and combed on that fatal day, just everything about him. She knew why she was drawn to him and she didn't quite know how she would live without him. (She felt as if every piece of their life's puzzle had fitted together perfectly, they were meant to be.) Now she would have to depend on all her friends and of course, her mum and her own inner strength to get her through this awful heart-breaking time. The only problem was she didn't know if she had any inner strength left inside her body. Georgia agonised inside thinking about the months passing by and friends not coming to see her so often, how would she cope then? She had to rely on the things her mother taught her.

'Georgia, remember to only take one day at a time. There's no point in looking months ahead and visualising friends having reneged you and leaving you lost and alone. Live in the moment, take one step at a time Georgia, it's the only way. No friend of yours will ever leave you alone and you know in your worst moments I'm only on the other end of the phone (or with you in your house). Just stay reassured, when you feel alone, you're not, we will at all times be thinking a step ahead of you and be there to catch you when you fall. Take lots of deep breaths and go for walks out in the air with Juliet, don't stay inside on your own and become a recluse. Organise yourself so you will have something special to do every day that will keep you focussed.

There are going to be times when agonising as it will be, you will want to think of Cameron, after all he was the biggest part of your and Juliet's lives and you certainly don't want his memory to ever die. So Georgia, when these times present themselves to you, just go with the flow, don't panic, think of someone that you loved but has now passed on to a different life and ask them to help you.' Her mum also promised Georgia, she would pray to Georgia's angel for her. 'Sure, between all of us up above and down here on planet Earth we'll lighten the load, ease the burden and help you cope.'

Georgia felt reassured by these meaningful words her mum had said. Georgia's friends also reassured her,

'We promise we will look after you until you get back on your feet and you can look after yourself.'

It was weeks later when Georgia sat down one cosy evening by the fire – Juliet was fast asleep – the time was right. She ran to her room and removed the tidy bundle of letters from her noisy drawer, took them with her to her comfy chair by the fire, removed the bundle of letters from the brown envelope and just stared at them. How neatly they were packed, with a string of wool tied in a bow holding them together. With trembling hands Georgia first opened the string. The letters fell onto her lap , they were marked 1, 2 and 3 plus the two from the hospital 4 and 5, the date and then a long arrow pointing to her name, Georgia. She opened the first one, his writing was so clever and easy to read. She began to cry, tears streamed down her face. It took a lot of effort to even begin to read the first one. It began with:

FIRST LETTER:

Dear Georgia,

I'm back here in the seminary. I'm listening to Georgia on my mind, a song that reminds me of you, playing on my record player. It was a record my mum and dad had for years in the house and when I was leaving to join the seminary they presented me with a record player and a bundle of records. One evening just after I met you, I decided to rummage through some of my records. My mum loved vinyl records and she loved the song Georgia on my mind, so I just thought with a bit of luck she might have given me that song hoping it would remind me of her. As sure as day turns to night it was there. I put it on and played it quietly in order not to upset the other young men trying to sleep. That was when I decided to write you this letter. As the song says Georgia on my mind, that's exactly where you are with me, on my mind every minute of every day. When I should be praying my mind is off thinking of you. There's not a prayer said by me. I hope I'm on your mind even for a few moments. For me it was love at first sight. Is it too much to ask you to come with me?

xxxx

Cameron

Silently Georgia said to herself *I would have gone to the ends of the Earth to be with you Cameron and I did.*

CHAPTER 71

Trying to move forward

Juliet needed even more attention as she was starting to grow up. Now she was walking and trying to say words that only a mother could understand. Yes, she was interesting, still cuddly and warm and loved attention (she didn't get that from a stone). Georgia's mind drifted back to when she feared Maria, her babysitter, her fear was that Cameron would fall in love with her. Now she was thanking God for Maria, it's amazing how the tables can turn. Georgia knew she needed her help more than ever now, if she wanted to get back to work and make a life for herself outside the home.

Together they had conjured up a nice plan, Georgia would work two days a week, Maria would cover for her and from twelve in the day until eight in the evening on the late night. Georgia felt a little more in control, inside she was pining away for Cameron but outwardly she was doing a great job of acting her way through her mornings, her evenings and her nights. It was on one of these evenings as she sat looking at the television her mobile phone rang. She didn't even look to see who was calling, it just had to be one of her friends, it always was. So she pressed the button, said 'Hello' and almost jumped off the chair with fright when she heard Ross's voice.

'Hello Georgia' and a pause 'I hope you don't mind me ringing. I've been keeping in touch with Tanya and the rest of your friends so I'm up to date on how you are, but I wonder would you mind if I called around just to say hello and have a little chat? Sometimes we all need a little chat, you know.'

'Yes, Ross, that would be nice. I'm only working two days a week but one is a late night so could you make it about eight on Thursday evening when Juliet is in her cot fast asleep?'

'That would be fine' said Ross. 'I'll be just on my way home from work and if you like I'll take some fish and chips up to save cooking.'

'Sounds like a good idea, Ross.'

Georgia had a spurt of enthusiasm and felt sort of strong and happy after talking to Ross. It was time to read letter number 2.

When she opened the first letter, she had made the decision to buy one of those little letter openers to make sure there were no jagged edges on the envelopes, they had to be preserved for Juliet. One deep breath, inhale, exhale.

SECOND LETTER:

Hello Georgia.

I'm wondering where we are in our lives when you read this letter. Are you just flashing past the words on the pages or are you reading them looking for some meaning.

This is a very important night for me here in the monastery. It has been a day like no other. Today I saw my mentor. He has always been wonderful, inspiring and demanding, always wanting each deacon and sub-deacon to reach as high as they possibly could in all aspects of learning. To his delight we achieved every goal he set for us. In the meantime we have all lived wonderful, happy lives in here. We were taught how to sing properly, you know Georgia, how to harmonise. Then we were taught how to take a group of people who want to sing and turn the group into a choir. It was another string to our bow and I have every intention of using that skill as soon as possible. We have also learned to read music, and play musical instruments, now we could become music teachers in the future! One of the priests was a qualified mechanic before he joined the priesthood so he taught me all I need to know to fix my car, if I ever have one. Some of the young men I have studied with are moving on to fulfil the training and become priests of God and some of us are moving to new careers outside the monastery. One of my friends, Audian is beginning a career as a policeman, one is taking up a career in Social Work, one is becoming a Psychologist, one is a tenor and is singing all over the world and I'm praying I will marry the absolute love of my life… you. I hope you're happy with the decision I've made to leave. I'm not leaving because of you, I'm leaving because I know my place is not here anymore, but I do pray we will get married and as man and wife have children and build a dream life that without me knowing was always on my horizon. If all of this ended in the morning I'd still be grateful for everything we've had. I love you so much, Georgia.

Cameron.

She found the sign in the last lines of his letter *If all of this ended in the morning I'd still be grateful for everything we've had. I love you Georgia.* (She might be pulling at straws but Georgia needed something to cling on to.)

CHAPTER 72

Bravery and long conversations

Georgia's life was beginning to have a routine again and in some ways it was like old times when herself and her friends had long conversations about nothing but loved every minute. She was older and wiser and so were they and they had such a fondness for each other. She told them Ross was coming over and they were all delighted for her.

'Nice to have someone outside the circle to chat to' they said. Their lives had all moved on.

Tanya was still dating the hunk of junk she met at London Fashion Week. They did every second week, he would come to her and then she would go over to him. It seemed to work out very well.

Heidi was very happy with Sugar Daddy, their lives seemed to be full of love. She didn't say too much about her love life but it was obvious she was such a happy-go-lucky girl and even so Georgia always felt there was something on her mind and it wasn't until one day when the little group met, all pals together, out for that little meal and that little chat every one of them looked forward to, that everything became clear.

'So here we are girls' said Tanya. 'All sitting at our favourite table in the Trocadero, unfortunately one of the saddest experiences we have all been part of and need to talk about is still very sad for all of us because it affects our hearts, our minds and our best friend. Please Georgia don't cry. I feel if Georgia is able for it we should talk about Cameron now. Sorry Georgia, we don't want to make you cry and feel sad. We know how you feel. We feel it too – all for one and one for all, that's our motto. We have to talk about the sad times and the happy times.'

'Just a moment' said Heidi 'I just want to put something in here and it's happy news.'

'Yes but first let's just talk to you Georgia, then we can't wait to hear your news Heidi' said Tanya. 'How are you Georgia, remember you're with friends you can tell us how you really feel, the truth, the whole truth and nothing but the truth and we'll listen.'

The friends sat there sipping their favourite drink, as they waited for their meal to be presented in the most beautiful fashion at the fabulous Trocadero.

'OK' said Georgia 'I know the light is on me, I'll share my feelings with you. I'm very lonely but I'm very busy. Juliet is just so lovely she makes every day of my life worthwhile. When I look into her eyes I see Cameron looking back at me. She is just the image of him, the curly hair, the little sweet smile and the happy ways, all the proper ingredients for a right little darling.

I try to look forward with my life and honestly can only take one moment at a time, because that's what my mum told me to do, so I'm trying to be, as they say these days, mindful, aware of everything around me that's positive and blocking out the negative. That doesn't mean that I don't think of Cameron all the time, both when I'm awake and asleep but the worst time for me is when I get into bed each night. That was the time when we used to have a laugh and a chat over the goings on of the day. I think we both looked forward to that time of the evening all day and I didn't realise it until he was gone. You know, the sharing, the little secrets and the fun things people did at work. All the little things that add up to a night time story.

Yes the nights are the hardest, I wake up looking like a zombie from all the tossing and turning, panic and the realisation he'll never come back. Sometimes I feel I can't go on because most of all I miss the heat of his body and listening to him quietly breathing and the way he looked when he was asleep, so beautiful.'

Georgia came out of her little daze, lifted her head up and looked around at her friends, tears were streaming down their faces. They needed tissues even more than she did and since she brought a box with her knowing she was going to be crying, she put the box in the middle of the table and let them all help themselves and they did.

'Cameron's up there, he knows I have to stay focussed and strong for my own peace of mind and for Juliet. People say time is a great healer but I don't find it like that. Sometimes I wake up with fear, hyperventilating because I think I'm forgetting his face, sometimes I just can't focus on his face. I keep saying to myself, I'll never forget you, Cameron, I'll never forget you.'

Tissues were vanishing by the minute as all four girls wiped their faces and with that pulling their black mascara across their eyes, what a funny sight.

'There's one last thing girls' said Georgia, 'before I finish the sad bit of the night. To tell you the truth, I didn't know if I could face coming to the Trocadero this evening. As you all remember I met Cameron here and when I was introduced to him I just knew my life would change forever. He was so charismatic; he just got me at hello (as they say in the movies). Do you know Tanya and the rest of you? I'm sitting in the very same seat and he would have been right over there in my eye view. When I look at that spot I can still see him there.

I have one thing that is keeping me going, you know his friend Audian who spoke to me at the car on the day of the funeral and sang the solo of *Georgia On My Mind* and also sang in the choir.

He presented me with the most gorgeous letters, hand written by Cameron, tied up in a woolly bow, all in separate envelopes and sealed by Cameron. Believe it or not girls, I read two of them, in one way I cannot wait to read all of them but there's another little bit of me that doesn't want to finish the last one because I feel then all my connections with him will be gone forever. I know my biggest connection with him is Juliet but the letters just helped me to cope. I felt that within his words in his letters lay answers to the problems I was trying to cope with in his absence. I read one before I left home tonight. I felt the time was right, because I knew I was coming to meet you tonight and you all gave me the strength. I still have more left to read, it will bring me right up to the day almost, when Cameron left the monastery. So now let's move on' said Georgia 'I think you've heard enough sad stories for one night.'

It felt like Georgia had released a lot of her pent up feelings and said as much as she could about what was on her mind, without taking a breath.

'Girls, you have my permission to start the happy stories now, starting with Heidi's. Please girls, promise me you'll never let me delve so deep into my feelings again.'

The three girls put their hands on their hearts and with their thumbs they made the sign of the cross on their chests.

'We promise, this was a once off Georgia, collectively we just knew you needed to talk. If you can't share the pain you're going through with us, who can you share it with?' said Tanya.

'We've been friends since kindergarten, Georgia, you needed to talk today but on another day one of us might need to share our joys and sorrows with our little group' said Coco.

'Now for some happy news' said Tanya as she pointed towards Heidi.

'Well my news is happy news' said Heidi. There was a round of applause from everyone including Georgia.

'All get ready to congratulate me because (Da Dum) Sugar Daddy and I are expecting our first baby together and we are so excited. This is top secret news and you're the very first to know girls, so feel very honoured.'

By now in the Trocadero the main course had been served to the table, everything steaming hot and beautifully presented. Georgia looked up at the waiter, he looked mesmerised because earlier when he took away the starters nobody had even noticed him, there had been so much sobbing and eye wiping and funny mascara all over the four girls' faces. Now, in contrast to that, as he looked around he could see happy faces with mouths wide open enjoying the happy story.

'I'm only twelve weeks pregnant, I'm having my second scan next week and we will know a lot more then. I'll fill you in on the news girls, as I get it. You know, every one of you have just got to be there when our little sweetheart arrives and I give you full permission to organise the party afterwards and the baby shower beforehand. Sugar Daddy is paying so your money is staying in the bank. Just give him the bill and he will pay for everything. He is over the moon with excitement. This is his first baby and at his age he feels as if the heavens have opened and the real god or goddess is about to appear (our baby) and come down to earth.

Everything I say goes, I never play on him because he is generous beyond words. He has never been anything but giving. I feel this is a fantastic time in our lives. He has me on the highest pedestal you can imagine, he wants to be there for every moment, the morning sickness and now that I'm beginning to get cravings, or I might be imaging I'm getting cravings, whatever, he would go down to the shops in the middle of the night if I want anything. He is the real hunter gatherer now and I feel like the damsel in the eighteenth century with a strong warrior by her side.'

Her friends stood up at the table and clapped for their friend. There was lots of hugging and kissing going on, smiles and more tears and then they all sat down and returned to the task of eating their meal. So with that great news now a group secret, Heidi passed the baton on to Tanya.

'What's happening to you Tanya?'

'My news is not all that exciting but I'm praying to God that in the next few weeks I might have something more to tell you so watch this space. For now I'll just say I'm still with Jean Luc from abroad. We're exhausted from travelling. Me Tanya, over to England and back or him over to Ireland and back to England. All I think about before I see him is amazing sex and I know he's thinking exactly the same as me, but after all the travelling, when we meet each other, the one of us who didn't have to travel is always up for a very passionate night but the one who has travelled is exhausted, having done the flight, gone out for a meal, then going to someone else's bed, they just crawl into bed and instead of amazing passion, one has a well-earned great night's sleep, while the other one has a night of frustration.'

The girls laughed so much their desserts were landing everywhere except where they were supposed to land, inside their mouths .

'Honestly girls with him coming here one week, me going there the next week, to tell you the truth it's wearing me out and if he was honest it's possibly wearing him out as well. Something's got to give or we'll end up breaking up, we're too exhausted for love. The pressure is on, we've got to salvage the train wreck, so he's thinking maybe he'll come to live here, with me, in Dublin or maybe and don't get frightened girls, I might go to live with him in fantastic London, you'll have to watch this space twice. Now' Tanya said with the final round of tea and coffee landing on their table with the guiding hand of the fabulous waiter, 'it's your turn Coco.'

'I suppose I have no choice' Coco said. 'I was just enjoying my apple crumble with cream. Firstly girls I need to say Raphael and I are no longer an item. That chapter in my life is well and truly over, in other words that ship has sailed.'

Heidi, Tanya and Georgia had imagined that Coco and Raphael's wedding in a vineyard in France would be only a matter of time, but now that was never going to happen. The girl's shoulders drooped, there were plenty of ahh sounds and shouts of tell us more. We want to know every little detail.

'There's nothing left to tell you on that subject, girls, I'm having a great time, life is good.'

At this point the tea, coffee and hot chocolate were going cold. A fresh round was needed, hot and comforting. What a night this had been. If the four girls were honest with each other, they would have said they were dreading the night because Georgia was so sad having lost Cameron, but instead of it being an uphill struggle it had turned into a mix of sadness and grief, happiness and new beginnings.

Tanya said 'Before we move forward I want to say as usual, the Trocadero has excelled itself. My friends are right on track, everybody looking forward and not looking back.'

'For me' Georgia said 'I'm beginning to see the wood from the trees.' (a little round of applause) As you all know Ross has been coming to see me every week or two. There's nothing permanent, nothing settled or nothing happening he's just being a friend to me, taking fish and chips up on a night when I haven't eaten all day, or bringing up a stew he'd prepared the night before all packed up and ready to go into the microwave just when I need nourishment.

He encourages me to take Juliet for a walk in the evening time all wrapped and snuggled up. He takes me for that walk at times when I feel I haven't got the will to go on. But do you know girls, it's at times like that, when we're just walking together we start to talk. We have begun to build bridges between us. So maybe one day something could happen between Ross and I, things could change, but right now it's too early, I just wouldn't be in the right headspace and I'd feel like I was letting Cameron down. I feel there is light at the end of the tunnel, but it is a very long tunnel and the light is quite dim. I wake up every morning and tell myself to be positive, to look the day in the eye, and make myself believe there's always light after dark. So one step at a time.'

That called for another little round of applause from the friends. They always liked to do that. The sound of the clapping sort of gave the friend that was down, energy and spurred them on. The night was over and the friendships were stronger. The love was everlasting.

CHAPTER 73

Third letter from Cameron

The house was quiet. Georgia's mum had babysat and stayed overnight. Georgia could imagine her two favourite people, Nellie and Juliet sleeping in the same bed with Nellie's arms wrapped around her baby girl protecting her and keeping her all cuddly, just the way Nellie used to wrap her arms around Georgia in bed, when she was a little girl. She would have loved to creep into the bedroom to witness them all snuggled up but Georgia didn't dare to, instead she was going to sit down with a glass cup full of hot chocolate, accompanied by a dark chocolate biscuit to dunk. This was her heaven and she wallowed in this quiet time. Hot chocolate disappeared from the glass cup and every crumb of the dark chocolate biscuits devoured, she just knew the time was right.

Mustering up all her courage, she trotted over to her little mahogany writing desk in the corner where she had re-housed the letters from Cameron. She had in the last few weeks read two. They contained all his beautiful words of love and all his hopes and dreams for their future. The one thing he had really wanted was to have at least one child and in his letter he had asked Georgia would she possibly consider having a baby real soon. Georgia was so happy Cameron had met his beautiful daughter and his wish had been granted. His last few lines read:

I know we're on the same page Georgia, I pray you'll get to read my letter. Little did he know that yes, eventually she would read all of the letters he had written to her, but sadly Cameron wouldn't be there to answer any questions Georgia might have relating to those letters.

She opened the third letter, as she read and read, she began to understand so much more about Cameron, the one thing that, to her, was crystal clear was in this letter.

THIRD LETTER:

Dear Georgia,

All of my life I felt I was living in a maze, going along with what everyone expected of me and what I expected of me. They're expectations and my expectations were too much to bear.

Then YOU were there. Georgia, only then I felt there was an escape from that maze, into your arms to start the life I was working towards all the time. A life that would not be lived in a seminary but in a home, my home, your home and hopefully our family's home in the future. I realised there were all sorts of vocations, I thought mine was to be a priest of God but my vocation is not in a seminary. It is not written in the stars that I should become a priest. My vocation is to be with you, marry you, live a good life with you, give good example – all the things I would have done in the priesthood, I will continue to do in the wider world. I have decided to become a teacher and I have been accepted into a really nice school. By the way I will be teaching Religion and English and in the evenings when I go home I will be returning to our home, not to the seminary life. Please Georgia, tell me, are we on the same page? I truly hope we are.

All my love

Cameron

Georgia answered Cameron and said out loud

'I absolutely loved every minute that I was there with you, Cameron. I'm looking up at the stars and hoping you are looking down on me and I'm telling you Cameron, I was on the same page as you from the first moment our eyes met. As they say in the films you had me at hello.'

She continued to tell herself, Cameron expressed himself completely in that letter. He said exactly what he wanted to say. I'm so happy inside that most of his wishes were granted. Handwritten letters should never go out of fashion.

Georgia was overcome with sadness when she realised that if she had a question about the letters or wanted a reaction, Cameron wouldn't there to react. She couldn't look at the smile on his face when she said, of course I wanted to have that baby with you or the worry when he said he was living in a maze.

CHAPTER 74

The meeting of the girls

As Georgia tried to navigate her way through her life, her friends did their best to give her something to look forward to, something exciting to take her mind in a different direction and nothing was ever as exciting to Georgia as meeting up with her friends who knew and loved her and boy did she love them right back, indeed she knew them right down to their core. Sure where would she be without them now, friends she could speak honestly to, have those conversations she could only have with friends of this calibre and whom she shared a history with.

They had all done the sad stories with Georgia, in their heart of hearts they were all so sad for her and agreed that when she was out with them, they would give her space to talk through her fears and challenges but then it would be time to clear the decks and give each friend their chance to tell their story. It would take hours to catch up, little by little all the stories would unfold and there had to be lots of them but there was one, in particular, that story that all the girls were looking forward to the next chapter of, it was the follow up of Coco's romance. Tonight she would take centre stage, after all last time everyone got to tell their story now it was Coco's turn. That's the one thing about friends, everyone must be heard, not just the chosen one.

The pals had arrived, Heidi, Georgia and Tanya. They pulled their chairs closer together. There was only one missing, yes, it was Coco and she was late. The girls put in an order for drinks for themselves and made sure to include one of Coco's favourite drinks, ice cold and waiting patiently for Coco to sip. They didn't have long to wait, she arrived moments later, just when the drink was getting used to sitting on the table and being part of the conversation. She slowly picked it up and began to sip, then while still standing, she nervously began to blurt out her story while her friends listened attentively.

'I'm so sorry I'm late but just look at my poor hands, they're still shaking.'

The girls moved even closer, afraid to miss a word. Something had just happened to poor Coco and her shaky hands were a real sign she wasn't coping very well with it.

'I was on my way to meet my gang (all of you) when just as I pulled out in my little 206 sports car, another car cut straight across and bumped into the side of my previous state of the art love machine. The driver got out of his car and began to shout abuse in my direction. My thoughts scattered so much I didn't really know if I was in the right or the wrong. Anyway luck was on my side in the shape of a plain clothes policeman who confirmed I was in the right. He left his number and was gone before the squad car arrived with a Bean Garda complete with spick and span uniform, who took details. Then the Bean Garda reversed my car just a bit further along to allow other drivers to pass. I stood beside them still in a daze.

Then I felt little hot burning sensations on my arms and when I looked up all I could see was smoke billowing towards us. A derelict building was on fire right behind my car and the hot sensations were pieces of ash falling. It seemed to take ages before the Garda would listen to me and look around. Now I was more worried my car might catch fire or be destroyed by the falling ash, anyway my senses soon returned. I insisted on retrieving my keys as the Garda rang the Fire Brigade Station for help. Then, just as soon as the Garda allowed me to leave, I drove over to be here to be with my friends on this special night' she explained as she sipped the last drop of her drink.

Poor Coco, she was still nervous from her experience. She churned out the story as if pouring milk into a big pitcher, so luckily her friends had another drink ordered, to curb the dryness in her throat. The bar man exchanged glasses and Coco continued to sip away to her heart's content forgetting her worries and her woes and letting her story unfold.

'Don't despair friends, you know me, I don't wait around for men, you have to let life just happen and with that in mind my story tonight stars a man who works in the American Embassy. He's tall, well built, with broad shoulders.'

The girls were so amused with the hands flying around the place as Coco described this man.

'Is that all you have to say Coco?'

'Oh no, one other thing, well two, he's blonde.'

'Come on Coco, tell us more, what's the second thing?'

'Oh yes!' her two hands are in the air. 'Wait for it girls, his hair is curly and when he smiles girls' Coco exclaimed 'I can almost hear the ping as a shining star appears on his pristine white teeth and that smile would melt the heart of a snow girl.'

The girls were really getting this picture, it was crystal clear, everyone wanted a piece of this hunk of junk and just couldn't wait to meet him. Coco's description had been so perfect, let's hope the man lives up to the image.

'Girls, he's everything I've ever dreamed of. Since I was a little girl I always loved American men. Maybe it was because my mum watched so many American army films and the men seemed to have just the right ingredients to make a woman feel secure and loved, but in all fairness once I grew up that little dream I had was well forgotten and pushed back into the archives of my mind until the night I met Bill' (moment to dream), she continued 'in a club on Leeson Street. That night I was knocked for six when he asked me to dance. I felt like I'd known him forever.

All the memories of the dreams I dreamt as a child, flooded back. He was just like that man, the love of my life, everything just fitted. In my heart I was praying that the man I dreamt of as a little girl and the man I had just met, would both combine and become the perfect man for now and forever. At first I thought I had met him previously at another venue or another time but then as we danced and chatted, the picture reappeared from the archives of my mind of the American hero I watched on screen with my mum as a child. He was standing right in front of me dancing his socks off and boy could he move (the girls moved closer, they were all spellbound). From the first moment everything fell into place, I felt the jigsaw of my life had just been completed and to tell you the truth we've been seeing each other nonstop.

Anytime he has a few minutes or I have a few minutes free, we'd meet up for a cup of coffee or a walk in the park and the walk in the park works well as the American Embassy is so close to Herbert Park. There's a lovely café right in the centre of the park and we can have as much coffee, tea and cookies (his words, not mine) as we desire.'

The girls leaned in on the table, mouths open wide, ears pricked up, listening intensely to every word Coco uttered. A phone rang, Coco's phone, no one wanted her to answer it but answer it she did.

'Hi' (her face was beaming, no one needed to be told who was on the other end of that line, it had to be Bill) 'Yes that's fine… OK… love you.' The phone call was over.

'What did he say? When can we meet him? Jesus, it could be another wedding, we need something to brighten us up.'

The door of the pub opened, a few people arrived and almost pushed their way past the friends trying to get to the end of the bar. One stopped right behind Coco. The girls weren't really watching, they were still enjoying the story and waiting for the next sentence to come from Coco's mouth but instead she jumped to her feet, turned around, lifted her arms high in the air and wrapped them around a tall, blonde, well built, broad shouldered, hot American man. He smiled, they all heard the ping, his smile was like an advertisement. for toothpaste. Then they noticed his blonde curly hair, it had to be him, it didn't take brains to come to that conclusion as Coco's description was accurate. She kissed him and it seemed like it would never end (All consumed with jealousy). The girls sat there mouths wide open, mesmerised, not a drop of alcohol being consumed. The pub was losing out big time. Then Coco prised herself away from the American hunk and uttered the words:

'This is Bill. I decided the best thing to do was not tell you too much about him but let you meet him so he could tell you all about himself. I'd like to do the introductions. Bill these three girls are my best friends, there's Georgia (Georgia moves in to embrace the new man in the girls' lives) and Heidi, that's her looking in shock with her mouth open and the one with the big broad smile that's Tanya. You've got to pass the friends' test before you can move into the inner circle, Bill.'

'Then I should assume there's no pressure, girls. I'm very nervous. I haven't had to pass a test like this in my whole life, usually it's one gal and me but today it's all the friends and one poor love struck American guy. Well girls, let me just tell it as it is. First can I say, in the words of Joey from Friends, *How you doin?* I'm single, I'm working and I'm in love with your pal and can I say girls this doesn't happen to me very often' (he hadn't even sat down and all of this was spilling out so naturally).

Eventually Bill sat down beside Coco, put his arm around her and kissed her on the cheek, ordered a beer and one for everyone in the audience and announced:

'My mamma and papa (what an American drawl) were Irish, so am I girls, I was born here too. Girls when you look at me and hear my accent you see an American, but I've spent so many years back in the USA telling everybody and anybody that would listen, I was born in Ireland, Westport, Co. Mayo. You know every time I say it I feel so proud. I really want to take my parents with me for at least a month and travel the roads of the country I've spoken of all my life. I'm a country bumpkin, my mamma always said, in Ireland I would be called a culchie, but during the short time I've been here I've been told on more than one occasion that word culchie is not acceptable for the 21st century.

I was born in Westport in Co. Mayo. My mamma and pappa emigrated to New York along with lots of their neighbours, during the hard times in Ireland. My mamma used to say, someday we want you to go back to Ireland, to see where you came from and with a bit of luck marry an Irish girl. Someone who speaks fluent Irish, because they did and so do I and preferably one with roaring red or jet black hair.'

Coco comes in with 'That hair colour can be arranged, Bill. Which would you prefer, red or black? Tell me later.'

'Is maith liom rua agus dubh ach tá do gruaige go hálainn.'

'As for the Irish language I can speak quite a lot but obviously I'm not as fluent as you. You'll put me to shame' said Coco.

The girls shrunk back into their chairs knowing the little

Irish they only had and feeling ashamed of themselves for not knowing more.

'I have never felt so at home in any country as I do here in the Emerald Isle and I'm praying to God my Irish colleen will be my happy ever after. I'm also hoping to extend my time here in Ireland for another year or two. There's something I've always wanted to do since I joined the army, I really want and need to bring my mamma and papa over here to Ireland and to see their faces smiling and lit up like the sun. Girls, you know way back my first memories were of my parents reminiscing about the land of their birth and now that I've been here a little over three months I just feel so at home and ready to visit the place where my parents and I were born.'

The evening drifted on, the friends sat there thinking how lucky Coco was to have met this hunk of junk. As Coco and Bill shared a few words, Heidi whispered to her friends:

'Maybe this time our beautiful Coco has met the love of her life.'

'Maybe answered Tanya.'

Georgia smiled and stayed silent. She felt she had begun to understand love and had already come to the conclusion, love is like a melting pot incorporating so many ingredients, love, understanding, caring, sensitive to your sexual needs and mostly being on the same page in life. That last one ingredient is the most important one because it keeps the seas of life calm and easy to navigate, so to stay in love it is imperative that most of the ingredients your whole body and mind require must be in that melting pot. Maybe, just maybe, Bill might be just the man to give her everything she needs to feel complete, all the compliments, all the love, all the excitement, that she's craved for all her *God damned* life, all wrapped into one. The girls couldn't get a word in edgeways with Bill crooning on, just like Bing Crosbie (An American singer).

'Girls, a moment's silence please.' Coco tapped the side of her glass. 'I'd like to say Bill and I are heading off to Westport, Co. Mayo this weekend. We're going to do a bit of sightseeing in Athlone and then we're heading to Westport to a farm that's just on the edge of the sea. It belongs to a friend of mine, a nurse who married a farmer and now lives in the most beautiful part of Ireland. They have invited both of us to stay in the farmhouse, along with the other farm animals. They have a small amount of sheep, dogs and donkeys but they're still building their farm and trying to decide which way to take it and believe it or not in this day and age, there're quite a few options. Now, don't get jealous girls, I know you'd love to come and walk on the silvery sands and see the little church right down at the end of the road. I can imagine all of you lighting candles there.'

They were imagining the scene too and then they heard the words they wanted to hear.

'So why don't you just do it? Join with myself and Bill on our Westport hurricane. We're moving fast in the direction of the chapel and we would love to have our friends there for the ride.'

Tanya sings 'We're going to the chapel and we're going to get ma..ah..arried, going to the chapel of love.' All the friends joined in.

'Chunais girls.' Coco stands up and again uses her hands to quieten the girls. 'The good news is we're hiring a Land Rover Defender, it's fabulous, all orange and black.'

At this stage Coco was giddy with laughter.

'Now I'll ask the big question again girls, would you like to join Bill and me to be blown along the roads of Westport on our hurricane weekend?'

A unanimous 'yes' from the pals followed by questions:

'What day are we going?' Heidi asked.

'What time are we going?' Georgia asked.

'How long are we going for?' Tanya asked.

Bill: 'The pick-up time in Dublin is Sunday morning at 06.00 hours.' Gasp from the friends.

Tanya 'Oh my God Bill you sound like a real soldier.'

Bill blushed and said 'Early to bed, early to rise makes a man healthy, wealthy and wise.' He continued 'We're all meeting at Coco's place, then we're travelling straight to Athlone for breakfast in one of those pretty cafes by the river that I've heard so much about. We'll have great fun looking at the big boats and imagining how life could be if we only owned one of them. Then we can do some sightseeing and a lot of walking and browsing in the shops.'

'There is one place I'd love to go to' said Tanya, trying to get a word in. 'I've heard so much about it and never been in it. The Hodson Bay Hotel, I believe it looks onto the River Shannon. I'd love to sit there and watch the Shannon River flowing by and just dream.'

'In honour of you Tanya,' said Bill. 'I've just had a great idea. We will have lunch in the Hodson Bay Hotel?'

Coco said 'I really want to walk through the winding streets of Athlone. I'm so excited at the thoughts of all those little shops, God knows what we'll find there. Girls, we'll have plenty of time to spend in Athlone as my farmer friends are not expecting us until around tea time.'

'I did my homework,' said Bill 'and it's clear to me when we leave Athlone, we should allow a good 2 hours to get to Westport.'

'Just to let you know girls, Bill and I have covered every

eventuality. If everything works out for all three of you, my friend has already invited you all to sleep in the little annex by the house.'

Bill began to laugh out loud. 'Gals, I think it's the pig sty you'll be sleeping in. Don't mind that posh word annex.'

Coco laughed 'Ah go on with you Bill. She swore to me she has an annex.'

Georgia added, 'Oh My God to think when we all met here it was looking like a dull weekend ahead.'

'Now we're promised a hurricane of a time' said Tanya.

Heidi: 'I can't wait to get into that jeep and start our journey.'

There were kisses, girly giggles and American bear wolf hugs all round as the group said their farewells and headed off home, leaving Coco and Bill living their dream.

Georgia lay in bed feeling peaceful, excited, exuberant, exhausted but really happy as she lay there looking out at the stars. She decided there must be a special angel that was just hers, right up there in that sky, looking down between the stars on this beautiful night, answering her prayers and saying, Georgia from here your journey will be wonderful, all downhill. In the meantime enjoy the hurricane, courtesy of Coco.

As she lay there she thought, I just have to sort out one very important obstacle… Juliet. Last night as I listened to that fantastic invitation being given out to all of us, that one thing was on my mind and I wanted to scream out loud, but what about Juliet? Would it be OK if I took her with me? It's too long to leave my mum minding her and I'd miss her too much. So why didn't I say something, I just sat there like an absolute moron. Unless she can come I can't go, it's too early to be apart from her. I would miss her too much and I know Cameron would want me to be with her. What am I going to do? She fell asleep with that question on her lips and awoke to the sound of her phone ringing and the answer to her question from Coco's pretty lips, only moments away.

'Georgia, I forgot to mention Juliet is welcome and if you really want to you can take your mum along too, she can mind Juliet when she needs to sleep.'

'TG' said Georgia 'It would have been awful to spend the day wondering, Coco. Thank you for putting my mind at ease. I couldn't have gone without Juliet, you see she's too young, it's too soon and I would be very sad to sit in the jeep knowing we were driving further and further away from her. Thank you so very, very much from the bottom of my heart for allowing us to go with you.' Georgia began to cry soft tears of happiness.

Heidi arrived home to an untidy bed, she'd only pulled it together before she left early that morning, forgetting it was the cleaning lady's day off. Message to brain, get a new cleaning lady to cover Phoebe's holidays and days off. I'll say a little prayer just before I go to sleep. This is to whoever is listening, I need a miracle in Westport, a seaweed bath, a full body massage, a facial, eyebrow trim and everything and anything else on the menu.

Tanya arrived home, made herself a cup of tea and began to talk out loud to herself, the only one listening. I know what I need, I need to drive that Defender right out on the wild roads with the windows down and the hurricane sweeping around my hair. I'd feel like Kate Bush singing *Wuthering Heights* I could scream the words out through the window, *Heathcliff, it's me, I'm Cathy, I've come home.* My friends would think I'd just gone mad and would allow me to work my way through the madness and Wild Bill Hickock, the American teddy bear, would possibly decide I was a banshee coming back to haunt the dark hills of Ireland.

That night Coco lay in bed in the arms of Wild Billy Hilly from the hill of Killy, thinking to herself, *Oh! What A Night* (song) All my friends and the man of my dreams together in a comfy bar, it just seemed fitting, sure my pals have shared everything in my past, my present and hopefully in my future, so why shouldn't they share my new hurricane journey. Her prayer was that they would all stay together in their hearts no matter how far apart they were in miles.'

CHAPTER 75

Bill and the girls on the hurricane express

And so it came to pass, the trip. There was Bill sitting in the black and orange Land Rover Defender looking every bit the soldier, sleeves rolled up, exposing those muscly arms and the shirt opened that one or two buttons, just enough to let everybody around view that perfectly tanned male form. The Hurricane's lover, Coco, sat next to him in her rightful place, glowing with love and devotion. Heidi and Tanya fell over each other, full of the joys of spring as they piled into the car. What a time it was going to be, all friends together, feeling the love and ready to begin their adventure to Westport.

Just like a hurricane Bill had arrived into their lives so there was an air of expectation, was it any wonder this trip was branded the Hurricane Express. The American had such a personality, he was quite comfortable with women both young and old. He just knew how to work a crowd, he joked and jibed with Georgia's mum, Nellie, as he helped her to sit up into the high seat in the Defender. Georgia took her time with Juliet making sure she was secure in her baby seat, then sitting beside her and feeding her a bottle as they began their journey and drove along out of Dublin onto the M50. Bill just hit the road running, smoothly driving the jeep. The Land Rover Defender was a smooth vehicle. (One smoothie with another smoothie) This jeep had no problem with the bumps and humps in the road, it just glided over each and every one, what a machine!

The girls chatted in the back while Coco made sure at all times to either rub Bill's back, stroke his face, tenderly touch his arm and on the odd occasion gently run her fingers through his blonde, curly hair. Bill didn't object. This man had more areas on his body to caress than most and Coco made full use of every one, living up to her usual style, always keeping things decent. This was the side to Coco that everyone embraced, the loving side. She could be so soft and gentle, it was a part of her that was so endearing. If he was a bit hot under the collar he wasn't showing it, what a brave soldier. He was a smooth dude, she was a smitten kitten and the girls were all along for the ride. They wanted to be part of this romance and watch it as it evolved into something more. With a bit of luck the wedding could be in the USA, all pals would be invited and it would broaden their horizons seeing how the Americans lived.

The Land Rover was so slick, not one bump, one jerk, one bounce occurred. The Defender glided down the roads as smooth as a glass of hot chocolate. Guess what! Coco had packed sandwiches and small bottles of orange juice. The sandwiches were beautiful, individually wrapped in pretty paper. As soon as the Defender drove onto the M50, Coco handed drinks around and sandwiches were there to be taken. All agreed no one had felt hungry until the first bite into those delicious sambos and as for that cool orange juice, it just hit the spot.

It was no time until they arrived in Athlone, the centre of Ireland. The fun really began when Bill parked the jeep down by the River Shannon. All out, stretching their legs, out came the buggy, in went Juliet seated like a queen on her throne on the well-padded seat. Now that she was covered up and snug as a bug in a rug, Nellie took the reins, so to speak, and began to push the little princess on their walk down by the river towards the centre, taking in all the little cafes on the way. Would they have something to eat right here and now or go into the centre?

'Here and now! Let's live in the moment!' said Bill as he marched the girls almost army-like; maybe he thought it was his platoon in the war zone. In fairness to him he picked a lovely café, pretty in pink on the outside with baskets of flowers in lilac and pink hanging up over the windows and very pretty tables and chairs outside. That's where they sat in the morning sun with a big pot of tea and cups you could get a grip of, followed by a nice big Irish breakfast fit for a king, the king of Ireland, Brian Boru. The girls were delighted with Bill, he was up for anything. He enjoyed the trip down, he loved his new Land Rover, he devoured this breakfast as if he hadn't seen food for years and he was a good bit of fun into the bargain. Tanya took her opportunity:

'Bill, I know you had all these dreams of going back to your roots, well I've had a dream for a long time too and my dream is driving a Land Rover Defender, especially when it's orange and black. Please, could you let me drive the next leg of the journey and you could sit there and enjoy the scenery. It would be good for both of us.'

Bill made Tanya's dream come true. So back down the road they went, climbed back up into the orange and black jeep, turned on the satnav, set the destination for Lough Ree, a beauty spot, one of the three lakes on the River Shannon, not to be missed and so close to the Hodson Bay Hotel. In fact the Hodson Bay Hotel is on the banks of Lough Ree. The drive along the River Shannon was just beautiful. Bill was so content, he had pictured this trip all his life way back in America, but he had to admit he was absolutely blown away with the scenery. So far so good Ireland was living up to his expectations. He said all these things and then there was silence. The little group took in the beauty and for this there were no words. When Bill began to talk again you could hear the emotion in his voice.

'I know I'm a big guy,' said Bill 'well certainly here in Ireland. In America they'd just call me average and no one expects big guys to have big hearts but I have and girls all of you have helped to make the dreams I had as a boy become a reality, especially you Tanya for taking over the driving seat and allowing me to sit here and take in the spectacular scenery. I wish my parents were here and I pray to God they'll be able for this trip because I gotta take them on it. Sure maybe we could hire a camper van and all of us could relive the beauty of today.'

Georgia sat there in the orange and black Defender and thought how lucky she was to have a friend who would include all her friends in this lovely romance of hers, not only that but she included Juliet and Nellie. What a kind hearted girl Coco was. Most girls would probably want to keep him all to themselves but Coco wasn't that girl, she had such confidence in their love even though it was only a new love. She didn't feel she had to protect him from her friends, in case he'd fall for one of them or one of them would fall for him. She knew their love would prevail and the only thing her friends would do was add to this love and this hurricane weekend. She was all loving, all giving and it really showed to Georgia how much the friends meant to Coco, to include them in her most private and personal moments.

Heidi's thoughts were similar. She thought the scenery was fabulous, the new man on the scene was fabulous and she couldn't wait to visit Coco's friend in Westport because she knew that would be just fabulous.

As for Tanya, all she could think of was driving the Defender, how fantastic the feeling was, it made her feel almost high and then maybe, this gorgeous hunk of junk and his fabulous lover might invite all of them to his hometown, what a thought! The jeep sped back along the River Shannon towards the Hodson Bay Hotel with Tanya still in control of the wheel. Tanya indicated, pulled in, turned off the engine, took out the key and handed it back to the ever loving Bill. She gave him a peck on the cheek and said:

'You've just made one of my dreams come true, Bill, so thank you. Gur raibh maith agut.'

Bill answered 'Na h'abair e.'

Check time, 1.30pm just on the edge of lunch time, the meal was already booked, so in they went. Firstly wash hands, freshen makeup, fingers through hair, ummm everything ship shape. Out they came from the wash room and into the restaurant where they sat in great style gazing out at the Shannon River. What a tranquil sight with Juliet quietly eating some food from a spoon in between sucking on her tepid bottle.

'A great selection of food, girls' said Bill with such excitement in his voice. 'Let's all order different things and share.'

Bill couldn't get over the fabulous helpings of food put before him and he devoured them like a lion in the wild. Nothing meek about Bill when it came to food, but in fairness he had driven most of the way down, he must have been famished. Such a lovely hotel, the group decided it would be well worth having a weekend there with spa treatments and anything else on the menu.

Tanya announced:

'I must have my moment of glory, would everyone mind if we took our tea and cake into the lounge area. This is my time to buy everyone a glass of champagne, my opportunity to make my own dream come true as I gaze out at the Shannon River flowing past. A little like in the film, Shirley Valentine asking the waiter to take her table and chair down to the edge of the sea, because she could always imagine in her heart that vision of her sitting by the sea alone raising a toast to life.'

She came back down to Earth with a bang as the waiter popped the cork on the champagne and poured six glasses. Tanya was host to this toast.

'So let us all raise our glasses and have a toast to the Shannon River and the fabulous Hodson Bay Hotel.'

The meal was over and then for the serious stuff. This was the last leg of the trip. Satnav as usual at the ready, onwards and upwards the jeep glided along the roads under Bill's control. They came to a lovely spot, Bill pulled the Defender over and parked at a visitors' viewing area. Everyone got out, including Nellie who had a tight hold of Juliet as they walked towards the edge. Cameras at the ready, click, click, click, pictures, pictures, pictures. These are the things everyone needs to do, take photos, make memories.

As Georgia lined everyone up to take her photographs, for an instant she was taken back to her wedding and the photographs of all her friends she had taken out that night in the Trocadero. What would happen when they go there next time with all these photographs? When they lay them out on the table in the Trocadero, to see the stories unfold, after all it's only when you look back you can see the story from start to finish. She felt sad but nobody noticed. Georgia wanted to make her own fairy tales, to have her own dreams become reality. It is lovely to share all your friend's adventures but we all need our own adventures, our own story, (happy ever after) and happy ever after was evading Georgia. Georgia began to think back on the last few years of her life. I started something a long, long time ago with Ross, I loved him, I married him, I left him, I became pregnant and miscarried, at the same time I did all the falling for someone else, (Cameron), that adventure I lived for a while in my head until I transferred it to reality and moved in with Cameron, then I had Juliet and lived a different life.

Georgia hadn't really dealt with anything she'd gone through, she hadn't shared any of her feelings with her friends. Yes, she told them her version of things at the time but she hadn't searched her soul and shouted out loud, I need help, I need closure, so here she was living someone else's dream and doing exactly what she does best, ignoring her own dreams and refusing to move forward with her life. How could she think of all of this while she's taking photographs? Why did every click of the camera bring her back? block, block, block. This is what I need to do now, go back to happy Georgia, live in the moment and when this weekend is over go back to my thoughts of today, of this very moment and make it happen.

Georgia came back from her thoughts with the sound of her friends shouting in her direction –

'Georgia, please stop going into those little daydreams, you're supposed to be taking our photographs but instead we're standing here like eejits while you're staring into space.'

'Come on' said Coco, 'get with the programme, time is marching, that Defender is calling us and I know there's a big Irish stew on the stove down in Westport. I can almost smell the stew from here.'

'My mom used to make Irish stews back in the USA but she always said, to get the real taste of an Irish stew, you need to be in Ireland. It's the air, the smell of the bog, the whole aroma of Ireland. The taste is only real when you're eating it back in the Emerald Isle.'

Nellie came to Georgia's rescue, 'Georgia, would you take over from me with Juliet and I'll take the photographs?'

What a relief Georgia felt. She knew that sometimes in her grief she would stare into space and lose concentration. Thank God her mum had come on this trip and she was here to rescue me this time. This was Georgia's opportunity to be quiet with Juliet, spend a little time under the sun freshening her up and slowly returning to normal herself. Into the Defender they all jumped.

'The Defender really grips the road' said Bill.

'It's such a lovely car for comfort on a long journey' said Tanya.

Bill was driving like a racehorse with blinkers on and eyes focussed knowing soon they could rest, be fed and watered, in the annex or cowshed of Coco's friends.

'It's typical of Irish wanderers, they must get to their destination before darkness falls.' said Nellie.

The passengers fell silent, Juliet slept and then they were there.

CHAPTER 76

Destination, Westport, County Mayo.

Bill and Coco were the only two people in the car awake, everyone else had weird expressions on their faces, which Coco captured on camera when they were in a deep state of forty winks. They were too comatose to notice. When they arrived a little shout from Bill almost had the girls saluting him, that was the kind of effect he had on women. Georgia thought of Little House on the Prairie as Coco's friend Roisin ran towards them on her gravel path, closely followed by her black and white sheepdog, Oisin.

Before you could say Cock Robin, the embraces began. There were the happiest big hugs, kisses and welcomes all round as they were led into the spotlessly clean kitchen, tiled floor, table dressed with a beautiful green check tablecloth, white place mats and a beautiful big bunch of yellow daffodils in the centre of the table. Soup bowls were standing to attention waiting to be filled with this gorgeous Irish stew. Candles flickered. Just as they imagined, the air smelled of a beautiful Irish stew. The aroma of the carrots and onions, turnips, lamb, herbs and potatoes was mind blowing.

Not a word was uttered as the happy group devoured everything in front of them and then went back for second helpings. There was so much catching up to do but this wasn't the night to do it. Coco wanted time with her friend, both to catch up and to listen to her if she wanted to tell a story. Roisin always said when she spoke to Coco on the phone or wrote her a card or letter, sometimes I just miss my friends and since I'm a city slicker I miss city life so much.

Roisin explained to everyone:

'I don't have many girlfriends here and sometimes I just want to go back to the big smoke, Dublin, and go wild for a weekend. I'd have something to think about other than the cows, the sheep and the vegetables we continuously have to look after, just to make ends meet. Yes, some weekend I'll do it, I'll go up to you Coco and we'll have that fun. This isn't a statement, it's a promise, please make me do it and take me back to the big smoke for therapy.'

Bill told jokes and stories, all about his mother and father and their memories of Ireland. The one that made his eyes shine and his smile broaden was his best story ever, it was the time when his mother and father brought him to Dublin for the St. Patrick's Day Parade. They were lucky enough to be in the line-up as the television cameras rolled past and their little son, Bill, was interviewed for a couple of seconds, all dressed up in his Paddy's Hat, Shamrocks on his face and of course, the Irish flag swinging back and forth.

He wanted and needed to go back to RTE to look back through the archives of film, maybe they could find him in the archives of one of the old programmes dedicated to St. Patrick's Day. He knew the year and of course everybody knows St. Patrick's Day falls on the 17th March, sure with a bit of luck Bill would have a roll of film to take back to his mum and dad. He knew they'd shed tears and smile and laugh when they'd look at their little boy all dressed up like a Leprechaun. That was one thing he must do, get to the bottom of that Paddy's Day, back in the day.

The craic was mighty, Bill gave as good as he got. Oh, what a night!

Roisin and Tomás have certainly done themselves proud. It seems all too good to be true Georgia thought, as they were ushered towards their sleeping quarters.

'Take a breath, we really could be outside with the hens and chickens' Georgia said out loud.

'You should always look at the advantages' laughed Bill. 'At least if we were in with the chickens we'd be sure of nice fresh eggs in the morning. You know girls you can turn every negative into a positive.'

Yes it was a shed on the outside but inside it was beautiful. Tomás had excelled himself, firstly by doing all of the work himself and secondly in the way he divided the rooms. He had two bathrooms along a corridor, one on each end and then small bedrooms almost like dormitories, two with double beds and four with single beds, all with different coloured bedclothes. One had the most beautiful patchwork quilt with blue and red, yellow and white, orange and gold squares all sewn together to make it the bed everyone wanted to sleep in.

Bill had to decline that bed, he needed a room with a double bed for himself and Coco. The other girls, of course, all wanted that bed so they had to toss a coin to see who the lucky sucker was. Of course, it was Tanya who was the lucky one. She almost ran into the prettiest bedroom ever, with wood divides and a wooden floor. She was elated, her friends stood around and watched as Tanya flew from one end of the place to the other, to clean teeth, etc. and before you could say twinkle, twinkle she reappeared.

'Please don't leave yet, don't go to your rooms, I want to try out that bed and see if it's like the three bears bed, so cosy you don't want to leave.' It was and she didn't want to leave. 'Just turn out the light as you leave the room, friends and close the door. Thanks a million I hope your beds are even half as cosy as this one.'

With that she fell into the dreamiest sleep ever, while her friends insisted Georgia, Nellie and baby Juliet would share the biggest bedroom that also had its own ensuite bathroom. Heidi was happy with her bedroom, although it was small, it had the best view across the sea. Everyone fell asleep with happy memories of a very happy day.

And then there was Bill and Coco. Bill closed the door and sat down full weight on the bed. Coco could see the mattress dip with Bill's weight. He didn't look heavy but he was a big strong guy and Coco wondered could the bed hold such a hunk of junk from America. Coco wondered if she would tell him to go lightly in case her friend's bed collapsed onto the ground but she needn't have worried, Bill pulled her close and gently, very gently gave her the nicest hug.

'Now, my little Coco, it's time for us, we spent the day with your friends and while I know you love them and they are a big part of your life, that door is closed, there's no one here only you and me and this bed is big, so let's make music.'

That was it, Coco forgot all about her friends and only had a warm glow thinking about the wonderful day they'd had, the fabulous drink and sambos, the views of the Shannon, the picturesque towns they'd driven through, the amazing scenery, the great food in the Hodson Bay Hotel, the anticipation of getting here, to their destination, to meet up with her dear friend and family again. The Irish stew, one she'd never forget, for it was so tasty. The here and now, lying with Bill, the someone she was destined to meet, the lover she had waited all her life for. Somehow in the very depth of her soul she'd always had this longing to meet her one true love and as they lay together she prayed to God this figure of the All American Hunk would turn out to be the soul mate she had longed for. Coco fell asleep feeling full of great expectations of the day to come.

CHAPTER 77

Great expectations.

All that weekend the sun had shone, in fact there were only a few clouds in the blue sky and the girls all felt really happy to be in this neck of the woods. It would never have happened if Coco's friend didn't live there. Georgia wondered would she like the country life. As much as she liked this neck of the woods, how would she feel if she were to wave her friends off and live here? Nowadays there's a lot to do in the heart of the country but the mere thoughts of living far away from Dublin gave Georgia panic attacks. A visit is one thing but actually living there, how would she be able to handle the country life? She thought, no a Dublin Jackeen like me, needs the beautiful noise of the big city. That song always came to mind *It's a beautiful noise* (Niall Diamond).

She wondered how Coco's friend had survived for this length of time having sampled the goings on in Dublin. Just imagine Temple Bar at night buzzing with excitement, the bars stuffed with students and holiday makers laughing and enjoying the black stuff. With that thought in her head Georgia joined all her friends and American hunk for breakfast. Coco's friend Roisin must have arisen at cock crow to prepare such a sumptuous brekkie, all laid out on the big brown wooden table. Black pudding, white pudding, fried eggs, fried bread, tomatoes, rashers and gorgeous Irish succulent, big juicy, sausages.

Everyone was ravenous including Nellie and Juliet, as they dug into the country food in a country kitchen, what more could they ask for, they ate every last morsel. Bill's favourite was the fried bread, every slice Roisin took from the pan was turned fried side down and then another perfectly fried slice placed right on top. It was like a whole sliced pan piled up, roasting hot, still almost sizzling from the fat and tasting delicious. It was only in Ireland you could get such gorgeous fried bread cooked in Irish lard. To see the big scoop of it on the pan slowly melting and digging its way into each slice and possibly into every one's arteries, but this wasn't a time for thinking of health, this was all about taste and their taste buds were certainly treated to the best breakfast Ireland could offer. Everyone licked their lips, wishing there was even more of the greasy stuff to eat. Georgia reckoned they would have sat all day in Roisin's kitchen eating that fry and getting even more of an Irish brogue as they really got into the ceol agus craic in their country, Ireland. They were beginning to sound more like culcies than Dublin jackeens, it must be the country air.

As they left the table and went out with Roisin, Tomás and the sheepdog Oisin, onto their farm, they encouraged Juliet to help pick up beautiful fresh eggs from the hen house and then they strolled across to see the little donkey, Neddy and his girl pal Una the donkey. Georgia encouraged Juliet to pat Una the donkey. They continued to stroll through the fields of grass, Juliet loved lifting her tiny legs high over the long grass, over towards the sheep, who just stood there and gazed at everyone nonchalantly.

Bill was so overwhelmed with the whole thing, he exclaimed:

'God girls, this is the way I imagined Westport. It's just as if the constant dream I had in my childhood has come alive and is dancing with the leprechauns. I feel completely at ease in this neck of the woods. Oh God Coco, would you marry me and come down here to live?'

Everyone stopped and stared in their direction waiting for

Coco to say something but to their dismay Coco's mouth was opened wide, she was unable to utter a word.

'We could start our own farm. We could have all these sheep and things and you could make the fried bread. You could get lessons on how to make the fried bread from Roisin.'

Coco went into convulsions of laughter.

'Is this a proposal, Bill? Or are you just completely overwhelmed by the country air?'

Tomàs said, 'Now you had better be careful Bill, your words could be written down and used as evidence against you. You'd better think before you utter another word.'

Bill said, 'Sin Scèal eile'.

Coco closed her mouth and joined in the banter.

'Before you answer, not only are my best friends here but Roisin and Tomàs are here, there's Oisin the dog, sheep, two donkeys and chickens who are all witnesses to the words you've just uttered.'

There were a couple of moments of silence while Bill frantically tried to gather his thoughts. Everyone waited with anticipation and mouths open, staring at Bill's mouth waiting for it to utter the answer.

'Jesus, Christ almighty' said the girls together. 'We could be looking forward to another wedding, another occasion to dress up.' all the pals chimed in.

Georgia even thought she heard the donkeys saying Hee Haw, Hee Haw (Yes, yes) and the chickens saying chuck, chuck, chuck, chuck (yes, yes, yes, yes) and the sheep baa, baaa (Oh yessssss) and Oisin the dog, barked proudly, announcing Woof Woof (Yes Yes). Once Oisin said Yes Yes, the other animals knew this was for real, after all Oisin always had the final word with his woof, woof.

Tanya wondered was Bill being taken on a huge wave of nostalgia. Was he completely deranged? Or was this the way he imagined proposing to the girl of his dreams, in the country that he longed to visit all his life and with the girl he now realised he'd been looking for forever? Had he finally found her in Dublin's fair city and realised that this was the exact place, in this beautiful countryside of Ireland, to propose to the girl he had been dreaming of since the first time he heard his mother singing, *In Dublin's Fair City, where the girls are so pretty*? Was acting on impulse maybe the best way to propose? After all, nowadays sometimes lovers wait too long and forever lose the moment.

Roisin and Tomás looked on, Oisin the dog, the donkeys (Neddy and Una) looked on almost holding hooves, the sheep looked on, the chickens looked on, the pals looked on... Bill fell down on one knee. (Tanya wondered did he feel the pain with his knee hitting the rough stones on the grass) He held up a buttercup and asked Coco once again:

'Will you be my bride as soon as possible, because this is it for me? I'm not deranged or intoxicated by the country air. Since the first moment I met you I've wanted to marry you. It's everything I've ever imagined and you are the someone I've imagined it with. So will you please answer me Coco, my poor knee is killing me and I'm getting soaking wet from the dew on this damp grass, so early in the morning?'

'Well' said Coco 'I'm not standing up here looking like an Irish Colleen in a state of chassis, sure I'll join you on the grass and YES! YES! YES! you mad Irish man, I will marry you. I may regret saying this in the future but right now all my senses are saying this was meant to be. Now I have to say one thing to you while I have you down here. I think my friends were hoping for a big American wedding and something tells me you'd like an Irish wedding down here in the bog, in the heart of it all.'

'Ah sure' said Bill 'I've waited long enough for this moment so to keep everyone happy we'll have two celebrations, one in The Grand Canyon (you could hear the friends absolutely screaming with excitement) and then one right down here, if Roisin and Tomás would let us have it, in a big marquee set up on their grounds.'

'Yes and it has to be summer time so the field is surrounded in buttercups and then I'll have two rings, my engagement ring and my wedding ring. It will be magical, Bill.'

'I'd better start saving' said Bill, laughing heartily.

'Wow' said Roisin and Tomás. 'If you're having it down here in the wild, you will have to have a very big strong marquee to withstand the breezes in this part of the world but if you batten it down well, sure you can have your wedding here among the donkeys, sheep, chickens and Oisin the dog and make your dream your reality.'

Bill had no ring, let's face it until that very moment he had no intentions of proposing to anyone but it's funny what love can do. (A song came into his head, *What a difference a day makes, 24 little hours*) Now he was an engaged man with only a buttercup to wrap around Coco's finger but what a pretty flower and what a beautiful shade of yellow, strong and whipped perfectly into the prettiest shape.

Coco nodded yes and her smile said it all.

'Oh please Georgia, I wonder if we could have the pleasure of Juliet as our flower girl, when we get married down here in the wild countryside, hopefully in a meadow of buttercups?'

Now Bill was swinging Coco around in delight.

'Our wedding preparations are getting better by the minute' said Bill 'I just can't wait, can it be today?'

Georgia and Nellie jumped up and down with excitement, thrilled with the prospect, they were already imagining Juliet in a little lemon dress, maybe even lemon and lilac, Oh my God what a wedding this was going to be.

The farm animals were all forgotten as the happy contingent drifted on up through the fields to the farm house where Tomás opened a bottle of Irish Whiskey and a few cans of Guinness and for those who didn't drink, a glass of orange juice to celebrate this momentous occasion on their little farm. Little did anyone realise on their way to Westport, this wouldn't be just a normal weekend away, no this was miles away from normal, this was romantic, embracing and the happiest weekend they'd all had together for a long time.

Of course, there was a morning's work ahead for Tomás. Bill asked if it would be fitting for him to accompany Tomás and see what a day on a country farm in Ireland was like. Tomás nodded his head and seemed very pleased to have someone to talk to as he carried out his daily work. Bill had dreamt of living in Ireland all his life, maybe on a farm, he wanted it to be his forever home because in his heart he always felt it was. Now that he had this amazing opportunity to make his dreams come true he had every intention of doing just that. In fairness he was so lucky he had met Coco, who just loved him to the moon and back and wanted him to have his dream.

As Bill vanished along with Tomás out through the heavy wooden half door the girls set to work cleaning up the remains from the breakfast. As there was no dishwasher (this was a shock to the Dublin Jackeens') it was time for the tea towels and the sudsy water in the big sink, but with lots of enthusiasm and everyone mucking in, this chore was soon just a memory.

CHAPTER 78

Plans in place

It had been a lovely morning, Georgia had enjoyed every moment and now it was time to slow things down and take the rest of the morning at a slower pace. When you have a toddler sometimes they need a little nap to keep them from getting cranky, so as Nellie, Roisin and the rest of the girls set out for a drive into town to take a look at some craft shops and maybe buy a thing or two, Georgia set about making food for Juliette and taking the time to let her eat at her own pace. Poor little thing was worn out from all the traveling, all the chatter, all the different friendly people lifting her up and carrying her. She needed to just lie down, quietly rest her weary body and fall asleep without any distractions.

Georgia would have loved to accompany her mum and friends to town but Juliet had to come before her wants and needs. Her life would have been so different if Cameron was here... the two of them caring for Juliet but he wasn't, she was all alone. It was at times like this the awful reality of her being left alone without his support really hit her. Georgia knew all she had to do was ask Nellie to stay back with Juliet and in a heartbeat Nellie would have lifted Juliet up into her arms and the two of them would have waved Georgia goodbye as she headed off with her friends, laughing and happy to do girly things, but that was not the right thing to do so she stayed back and enjoyed her time with her little girl.

With Juliet fast asleep and the large country house quiet except for the odd barking of a dog, the clucking of a chicken or the quacking of a duck, Georgia felt alone. There was one thing on her mind when she came down here, if I get quiet time, I'll do this. She brought the letters with her just in case she had the courage and the time to complete the task she had set for herself. Yes, it was to read Cameron's fourth letter. She needed to read it, she wanted to read it but was now the right time to read it?

Very quietly she stood up from the chair at the side of the bed and tip-toed over to her bag, unzipped it very carefully and with perfect precision removed the big envelope with the woolly bow from the bag. The time was right, after all the whole time they'd been here and even on the journey down and in the Hodson Bay Hotel and sitting by the fire, no one, not even one friend mentioned Cameron. In her heart she had felt lonely, she felt she needed so much support in fact she knew she did, she had to take her mum Nellie with her to help look after Juliet because Cameron wasn't there to help her. She felt in her heart alone and sad. How could she be enjoying herself when all she wanted to do was scream in the loudest voice, I want Cameron here, I need Cameron here, how could he be just gone. She began to breathe slowly, in a very deep breath, out slowly, she couldn't leave the room and so she opened the window and used that as her escape to air. That went on for about ten minutes, she felt cold, the room was getting colder, not good for a little girl so as usual she did the right thing, closed the window and stood clutching the big envelope with the woolly string around it in her hand.

She sat down on the chair by the dressing table and opened the big envelope. Out they came all six letters, the one she was about to read sat there facing up at her, letter number four. This was such a poignant moment... knowing he had closed it himself, stuck the envelope and then wrote her name on the front of it. Every move she made was slow and meaningful, out came the letter, the pages still felt crisp, she began to read:

FOURTH LETTER:

To my beautiful Georgia

I can't believe how much my life has changed. Last month I wrote a letter to you. I had just spoken to my mentor. He helped me come to my final decision to leave the monastery completely. Now the monastery is in my past, my future's looking bright. But right now I'm here in Harlow, London, working on a building site to earn extra money to buy our forever home. I can't wait until you come over, just to share time together, eat in restaurants. Then to have a night at the theatre with you but most of all I am really looking forward to holding your hand as we stroll across LONDON BRIDGE. That's my dream Georgia to just share time together and make lots of memories. I'm living for the moment when our eyes meet again my love.

All of my love I send to you

Cameron

As Georgia put the letter back into the envelope and tied them with the woolly ribbon into a bow, she thanked God for all the memories she had to hold onto. The special one, when she looked into his eyes as the sun shone on the two lovers parading across London Bridge looking as smitten as kittens, so in love. That one memory alone had warmed her heart on even the bitterest, coldest nights when she was all alone and feeling sad. All the memories she had held and would always hold locked securely forever in her heart. They would be kept there until the next time she needed to feel him close to her, to reassure a very lonely young woman that her life wasn't a waste. Cameron's love would always suffice and make her feel whole, when she felt half.

Juliet lay sleeping peacefully, Georgia just sat there crying the saddest tears she had ever cried. It was just as if everything hit her with a bang, how everybody's life just continued while hers felt stagnant, stopped still, gone. She must have cried for ages, her eyes felt red raw and her skin burned from the salty tears but thank God there was one thing she had, peace, everyone gone out of the house, not a sound except for the water she threw up on her face and the deep breaths she took to control her feelings and panic. Then for the ritual of re-applying the makeup, foundation cream, great covering makeup, lip liner, lipstick and a bit of blusher on her cheeks and then of course, mascara the finishing touch, everything to cover a multitude of pain and then Georgia, the smiling, ever patient, ever loving, great listener was back to continue the charade she must continue. It was with all these things in tow Georgia met and welcomed back all the friends and Roisin.

CHAPTER 79

The big chinwag

The girls settled in for a big, big chinwag. They'd so much to cover and so many stories to tell about their time in town. On went the big heavy kettle, full to the brim with water from the well. Straight onto the turf burning range (cooker). The kettle boiled and all they could think about were the big mugs they were now hurriedly placing on the big brown table. They couldn't wait to taste the muffins and brown bread they'd brought home from town. Georgia loved that real country butter encased in that yellow butter bowl and the homemade jams, both strawberry and blackcurrant that had taken their rightful, proud places on the table. The chatty group sat down, Roisin brewed the tea and placed her biggest red teapot, slap bang in the middle of the table, right beside the large bowl of sugar and the big jug of milk. So there they sat and didn't feel the time pass as they poured out their stories from town. Heidi announced

'I was honestly surprised at how good those little stores were. There's not a small store in Dublin that would have as much variety as they have, the cakes, scones, jams, etc. etc. The country people are so enterprising, we should take a leaf out of their books and talking of books there was a bookstore with so many fabulous books I just had to buy a few. Do you know Georgia, you really missed the jewellery store. Down at the very back they sold the prettiest shoes and at the front they sold jewellery, silver jewellery, gold jewellery, plastic jewellery. The designs were amazing and all designed by local jewellers. They also sold scarves. Outside the shop was painted pink and there was a little park bench to sit on. I'm really learning a lot about country life and I'm liking it.'

'What's not to like?" said Coco. 'I saw a magnificent engagement ring in a vintage jewellery shop and can I say girls, I'm very drawn to it. I was thinking Mr Bill and myself might take a walk in that direction. I could stop by the window of the jewellery shop, gaze in and let his eyes stop on the ring and take me in there. Sure we might have a country engagement ring as well as a country wedding.'

'We did miss you, Georgia.' said Roisin 'You would have added that extra flavour to the morning.'

'Ah well' said Georgia 'I'm a mother now and my little girl needed some quiet time. Do you know everyone, I didn't feel left out. I felt happy to spend time with Juliet. It was all worthwhile, just look at her sitting over there playing with Oisin the dog. She's full of life now and not tired and cranky. Things turned out the way they should have, I did what I had to do and all of you had a lovely time. In other words a perfect morning was had by all.'

The conversation turned to Coco regarding her forthcoming wedding which in fairness to all of them, including Coco, was a huge big surprise. Everything was discussed from, was it feasible to have that big tent Bill visualised or would it be better to book a hotel? Their decision was final, pick a day, slap bang in the middle of the summer when hopefully the sun would be splitting the trees and Bill would see his dreams continue to unfold.

'Sure, that would only be fair, wouldn't it?'

Coco asked Roisin since all of this had happened in her neck of the woods on her land if Bill was true to his word and they did have two weddings, would she and Tomás please, please, please make her dream come true and come to the wedding in

America. Straight away Roisin said in a very, very nervous tone:

'I don't think we can go to your wedding in the America, Coco. You see it's only the two of us looking after the farm here and we have no one to step in but we'll be thinking of you on that day and we'll be there in spirit.'

'That's a terrible pity' said Coco.

'Speaking for Tomas, girls, I know he would love time away from milking cows and all the other things the poor man has to do from five in the morning but I'm sorry, it's just not possible. Do you know, sometimes we both feel as if we're chained to this farm. Girls, I was really bad up to a while ago, I couldn't sleep and I was getting panic attacks until one night when Tomas had had enough, he sat me down and said Roisin, you're lost. I love the old you, the one I fell in love with, you don't have to kill yourself trying to impress me with this cooking and cutting and stewing. I'm used to plain food and cooking for myself. From now on, he said, can I please help you prepare the food, at least let me try to make things easier for you. Then he said, and this was the part that really got to me, girls, I hate saying this Roisin, but I feel you're like someone wound up on a spring and if you let go it will all unravel, you'll end up leaving the farm and me, so before it goes any further let's compromise, you be you and I'll be me and together I pray we'll get through this. I'm selfish, I want you to stay down here with me and the only way for you to do that is to start living a life outside these four walls. You can turn it around, Roisin, and make a life for yourself down here. I'll help you, remember it takes two to tango and it's a while since we tangoed.

Girls, when I realised what I had been doing I took my hands out of the baking bowl, put down the sharp knives, sat on the farmhouse chair and thought, cop on or you won't stick this life, it's everything you never wanted. Coco, remember me I always loved city life going to clubs after work, dolling up and going for evening meals, never wanting to go home and then here I was, the new me doing all these things that even Tomás didn't expect and possibly didn't want.'

'Hooray for Tomás' shouted the girls. Everyone was clapping, they realised Tomas had put everything into perspective in just a few sentences.

'In that moment, he made me see the light and realise you can't be all things to all people.'

'That's true' said Coco 'the one person you have to be brutally honest with is always yourself.'

Georgia said 'When you think of it, Roisin, putting one of us Dublin Jackeens down here is like putting a square peg in a round hole.'

Tanya said 'Just imagine turning the coin the other way, those country girls coming to Dublin it must be some shock, freedom, clubs, pubs and grubs.' (A different kind of shock)

'Can I be honest friends?' said Roisin. 'I have to let you into a little secret, I haven't been doing a lot of anything lately. I've been buying the brown bread from a friend down the road, me poor fingers were fecked from kneading that dough, as for the stews, I've been buying all the vegetables pre-peeled and cut, from one of the local farms that prepare food for shops around the country. Sure, they're selling to all the local women and if the husbands know, they're certainly casting a blind eye.'

'Good for you girl' she heard her friends say.

'There was one thing though girls, that happened to me while I was kneading the dough and before I stopped kneading the dough.' Roisin said the next few words in a quiet whisper. Her friends moved in to listen to Roisin's every word. 'I remember the moment, it was one of those times in your life when everything seemed so still. I'm sure if there was a camera focussed on my hands that day everything would have been in slow motion. There I was, hands in the flour watching the white dust rise and I felt as if I was doing it against my will. Yes, I do love Tomás but it was me who had given up my life to be with him. He had to make little or no change in his life.

To be honest I found it quite boring in the beginning and then, with my imagination being one that every now and then seems to soar to great heights, I had this idea. What if I gathered all the recipes handed down from my Granny and her Granny before her and somehow documented them and turned them into a story book with recipes and illustrations? I have a friend, Marcey and she's a brilliant illustrator. I know if anyone could make someone in the Emerald Isle's mouth water from gazing at a picture they had produced and then reading my recipe, it was Marcey. With a bit of luck even the Americans will clamour to buy my book, try out the recipes, look at the pictures and enjoy the stories.'

'Roisin, you know that book dream you have in your head?' said Coco, 'Maybe Bill's mother and father might take a hand in its distribution when it's completed. Leave it with me, I'll chat to Bill when we get back to Dublin and I'll let you know the outcome.'

'Hopefully this Dublin Jackeen who ventured down to this neck of the woods not so long ago, could put this beautiful part of Ireland on the map and make it even more popular than it already is. I could see my book selling and selling and as it sells and sells my fan base will become something to be proud of. Friends, what if I turned my dream into a business.'

A little burst of applause ensued.

'Honestly friends, I could see in that moment my cookery school, (a bit like Ballymaloe) enticing so many people down here for weekends. Do you know I've joined the Irish Country Women's Association. It's the best thing I ever did, and they've taught me a thing or two about country life. The first thing I had to come to terms with was, I'm a city slicker straight from the heart of Dublin, so I must have patience with myself as I navigate my way into the country life.'

'Roisin, please tell me what is it like to be a farmer's wife when all your life you never imagined yourself living a country life?' Georgia asked.

'Well, Georgia, to be honest I really love it. Tomás is the nicest person I could ever have hoped to meet and I knew I'd be giving up a lot to come and live down here but when you fall in love, it's give and take. He could hardly leave the farm and I was free as a breeze to go anywhere my heart desired, so together we decided we'd give it a go and see where it would take us. I had to adjust myself and I'm still working on that. It wasn't as simple as jumping on the bus and heading into town or running next door to my neighbour because my neighbour is actually half a mile away. But, as they say love conquers all and I'm living it the best way I can. Tomás knows and understands if in the end it isn't working for me, he's prepared to let me commute between the two or he will sell the farm and move to Dublin with me but for now it's status quo, I'm content and happy here.'

'So' said Georgia 'you have found a way to make it work and I suppose that's the way it is, whether you live in Singapore or Westport.'

'Yes, I suppose that's the way it is. I needed to put my own slant on the way it should be for me down here. So I began to embrace the country life, to enjoy summer time and the arrival of the students coming to help on the farm. They help with the chores, collecting fruit, digging potatoes and planting seeds and in return we give them food and lodgings. They're happy to share rooms and they make everything just fun. They made me realise the amount of fun I could have down here in Westport. I began to join in with all the farmers' wives to make summer time so special. We have summer festivals and farmers' markets where we sell things we don't want, and buy things from farmers that they don't want.

By the time autumn arrives and the last student has left the farm, all the heavy chores are completed in time for the arrival of winter. Country life is not that hard at all and it's my life now. I need to make it as simple as possible and here and now I can officially announce to all my friends sitting around the table with me, country life is a great life but please, once every now and then salvage me, drag me to Dublin and make me tread the boards.'

'I don't think we'll ever have to drag you, just get yourself on the nearest train any time you want to. Our houses are open to you and Tomás, anytime day or night.' Coco assured her.

Roisin graciously took a bow. There was silence for a moment or two only broken by Juliet's laugh and her wobbly walk to her mum, Georgia, and then a round of applause from all her friends.

Tanya said with a smile '*Women (sisters) are doing it for themselves, standing on their own two feet and ringing those bells.*' (words from a song sung by Annie Lennox and the Eurythmics)

The rest of the girls joined in and began to dance around the flags (tiles) on the kitchen floor. What better way to spend an afternoon than with another big pot of tea, made with boiling water and plenty of tea leaves, a good strong cup fit for a farmer. But of course, sitting down calls for another chat and so a question is thrown at Roisin from Heidi.

'Now a not so in-depth question from me' said Heidi. All the girls turned in Heidi's direction. 'Firstly, Tanya, did you sleep all night in that fantastic bed in that fantastic bedroom and was the shower perfect this morning? Did the sun shine through that little window, in other words was everything just perfect for our Tanya?'

'From beginning to end friends, everything was perfect, the bed was springy, the shower was at a perfect temperature and the sun shone brilliantly through that pretty window, all in all perfection.' Tanya looked over in Roisin's direction and said with a smile on her face 'Thank you, Roisin, I had a perfect night's sleep.'

'This question is directed at you, Coco, and this is from all of us.' Woo woo could be heard from the rest of the girls. 'I'm sure we all heard the two of you laughing out loud last night.' All eyes were on Coco. 'The laughing was so loud the neighbours must have heard it, a half a mile away. What was all that about? Can you share?'

'Well I can tell you, Heidi, we were both in shock. Bill for the fact that he'd actually proposed when he had no intentions of doing that and for me, accepting. I was asking myself in my mind, could I seriously settle for one man when I love the adoration of quite a few?'

'So what was the conclusion, Coco?'

'Bill in his own words, likes to do things spontaneously. He gets a feeling, he knows it's right and he just does it. He says there's an A, B, C to everything he does. (A) The feeling! (B) The knowing! and (C) The doing!'

The girls liked what they heard and there was a nod of approval going round the table while they put lashings of butter and big helpings of blackcurrant jam on the brown bread. Sure they'd be fat as fools if this wedding ever came off. Still this weekend was a special weekend and getting more special with every moment.

'When we were alone' said Coco 'I began to get this giddiness, I think it was my nerves. I started to laugh for no reason at all and Bill joined in. That's what you heard, the two of us laughing out loud. We were hugging and kissing and thinking how romantic it all was.

Like all of you, I imagined how it would be when the man of my dreams proposed to me but never in my wildest thoughts did I dream I would be in a field, surrounded by Oisin the dog, two donkeys, numerous sheep, chickens and the best friends in the world. What a surreal moment but shared by everyone I would ever wish to be there and for some reason it was just right, I knew it in my heart and in my soul. Funnily enough that buttercup just sealed it all and made it feel the most romantic few minutes of my life.

We talked for hours and eventually fell asleep, so no, the bed didn't break, it wasn't a night of mad passion, it was more a night of realising how dreams can become a reality and if our lives continue like this, all we can say is wow! bring it on.'

'Good answer, Coco, I think you deserve a round of applause from everyone at the table.'

The friends lifted their cups in a toast to Coco, her new American dude, her engagement (they could celebrate again once the engagement ring was purchased) and of course a big toast to the forthcoming wedding.

CHAPTER 80

The last lunch in Westport

'Christ Almighty, look at the time' exclaimed Roisin. 'Tomás and Bill will be back in a few minutes and the table is not even cleared, all we've done is talk.' Everyone laughed.

'Well, we all needed a good long chat.'

The girls got up from the table holding their cups, saucers and side plates and scurried away. All you could hear was the squeak of the wooden chairs being pulled back from the table. Roisin stood at the sink filling the large basin with Fairy Liquid and very warm water. It was Roisin washing, Coco rinsing, Tanya drying, Georgia putting the dishes back into the press and Heidi sweeping the floor, it happened with military precision. In ten minutes the kitchen was ship shape, strawberry and blackcurrant jam back in the press, brown bread wrapped tightly to keep it fresh, country butter and milk back in the fridge. All that was left to do was give the table a quick rub, empty the basin, hang up the tea towels, then everyone scurried back to their rooms for a quick freshen up and then they were back like soldiers ready for the Lieutenants to return.

Now was the right time to take a walk out on the lovely lawn that was separated from the fields by a wooden gate. The breeze blew ever so gently and the tiny flowers looked as if they were dancing back and forth. There on the grass sat, all tucked in, warm and cosy in the soil, buttercups in abundance. Out came the cameras and snap, snap, snap could be heard in the quietness of the countryside. Plenty of photographs were taken of Coco standing, sitting and pointing towards those flowers that were now closest to her heart. These photos would no doubt be part of Coco and Bill's story for ever and ever. She made sure to include her friends in these pictures, after all that's what they always did, make memories.

What a lovely sight to see coming up towards the white gates, walking very slowly as they came into view, the two little donkeys and there, fenced in, in the corner of the garden sat the hen house. The hens ran around on their own patch of grass with Juliet in hot pursuit throwing little pieces of bread and grain on the ground for them. What a lovely day to have a little girl out in the fresh air, with the light breeze blowing. Everyone including Nellie and Juliet were very happy. There were only a few hours left for the happy group to enjoy in this beautiful part of Ireland.

They knew the time was drawing near for their farewells as they saw their two men coming into view. They kicked off their boots as they arrived in the lovely homely farm house. It was funny to see all the friends gathering around the men as if it was like times gone by, when the men did all the foraging for food and the women stayed at home looking after the home and children, longing for their return. Yes, they were enjoying the moment. They'd already had a great oul chinwag in the warm and cosy kitchen and it wasn't long 'til more tea was pouring, gorgeous meaty sandwiches were being made and placed so nicely on the table and of course another chinwag, this time all about the men's morning escapades, as they enjoyed more scones, (bought from one of the other farmers, {shh no one must know}).

'Those scones are just delicious, Roisin, I don't know how you find the time to bake them.' remarked Bill.

The friends giggled, winked, smiled and kicked each other under the table, after all, *all for one and one for all* was always their motto. All these little carefree moments helped to seal the deal of friendship. They all shared Roisin's little secret, she wasn't baking scones. It was nice to have a little secret, in fact they shared not one but two little secrets. Instead of baking scones Roisin was collecting cookery recipes, the ones passed down from her granny to her mammy and then to the third generation, Roisin.

Bill, Coco, Heidi and Tanya gave €50 to the Roisin and Tomas fan club, Georgia put in €100 for herself and Nellie. All the notes were placed in an envelope accompanied by a card, signed individually by each person. It was interesting to see the written word on paper. Coco and Bill's words were,

'Being with you made the impossible possible. When we set our date please make sure to check the date on your calendar and keep it free.'

Tanya's words were 'Love the scones Roisin and Tomás. Someday I hope to come back for more.'

Georgia wrote. 'This was just what the doctor ordered, a few days away from the big smoke for Nellie, myself and Juliet. It's given me time to gather my thoughts together. I've realised that some dreams can come true. So thank you so much from the bottom of my heart on behalf of all of us.'

'Thank you for the lovely time.' wrote Heidi. 'It did all of us friends the world of good to come together for this weekend.'

Bill waited for his moment, when it came he placed the envelope under Roisin's pillow, then he sneaked back out of the room and just as he was about to join his partners in crime, he heard Georgia's voice in the bedroom, in he went.

'You're doing a great job with your little girl' he said. Georgia smiled.

'It must get very lonely for you, sometimes, when you see

everyone happy and you're feeling sad.'

Georgia was delighted to have someone say exactly what she was feeling, to her.

'Yes, Bill, I'm very, very sad. I keep on saying to myself, why did this happen to Cameron, such a good person with such a lovely future to look forward to. I just cry when I look at Juliet, when I think that all her life she will be missing her lovely daddy. But to change the mood slightly, Bill, so everyone doesn't see me drying my eyes full of tears, I'll fill you in on a few things Coco tried to organise today.'

'OK' said Bill as he sat down on the bed with his arm around Juliet and listened attentively.

'Coco invited all of us and also Roisin and Tomas to your wedding. She knew you'd approve but unfortunately it seems Roisin and Tomas won't be able to attend, they've too much to do down here and to be honest I don't think they can afford the journey.'

'Well' said Bill 'Roisin and Tomas are coming, I can tell you that now, especially if it's to do with money.' He continued with that American drawl 'Sure look what they've done for us here and look what they're going to do for us for our Irish wedding here. When we go abroad and I want you to tell your friends this, we're not going without you, Tanya and Heidi and we're certainly not leaving Roisin and Tomas behind. I will be paying for everyone to come if we have a wedding in America but please don't breathe a word to my future wife, Coco. I want all of this to be a surprise, we'll conjure it all up together and surprise her on the day. Before I go back to join the wolf pack will you promise to work with me to make all of it happen, then you can keep your friends up-to-date on everything that's happening for our American wedding.'

'I'm flattered, Bill,' said Georgia 'and I'm thrilled to have something to keep me busy during these hard days.'

Back in the kitchen with Juliet all dressed up and ready to go, Georgia had a happy smile on her face dreaming of conspiring with Bill to give Coco a second wedding day that she would never forget.

Coco said 'Maybe with the money we've left under the pillow they'll buy a little girlfriend for Oisin, another pig or sheep or little donkey and they could call it after us.'

Georgia said 'Then we'd have culchie relations' (be they animals).

When every last morsel of food was eaten and their bags were packed it was time to say their final farewells, to Westport in the county of Mayo. Before each one of Roisin and Tomas's visitors climbed back up into the Defender, they hugged the happy friends who had welcomed them into their country home with so much love and waved them goodbye until the big jeep was out of sight. The Defender began its journey back to the big smoke.

The journey home took longer than it did on the way down. Thank God Bill the driver stayed awake as everyone else, with the exception of Georgia and Juliet, fell asleep and sure would you blame them, it had been a long but lovely few days away from the big smoke. There had been a lot of excitement in Mayo and now they were back on the road, all exhausted and worn out.

Georgia could hear the little group quietly breathing, she looked out through the window and decided, as soon as I get back I'll ring RTE and see if they can locate the footage of the St. Patrick's Day parade. There is nothing Bill would like more than having his mum and dad here to see him getting married and then as a big surprise (and a present from Georgia) a big huge screen hanging from somewhere and that video of Bill being interviewed with his mum and dad on St. Patrick's Day in Dublin all those years ago.

When this wedding comes to pass I will make sure everything is sorted for the big reveal of Bill and his parents, so if that's the only thing I do for a wedding present, I will have done a good job. Just imagine how they would feel as they look back on photographs of Bill in the army in America and the latest photographs of him down in the country milking cows, playing with the sheep dog, cleaning up the donkeys and chasing the chickens. I can just imagine everyone in the room with Bill's parents chuckling away to themselves, enjoying the moment, then the room quietens, the lights dim and then the screen, up high, will light up and there will stand Bill, a little tiny tot, chatting up to his mum and dad, enjoying the parade. Sure it's every parent's dream, especially when they are Irish parents who had emigrated to America all those years ago. I'm sure they will recall that parade with their little son. Just imagine them seeing it for real, for the first time up there on the screen. Georgia just had to make that dream become a reality for them. She would definitely need Dorothy's red, glittery shoes from the Wizard of Oz to make Bill and Coco's wedding a complete success.

CHAPTER 81

What a day

The four girls in Dublin and Roisin in Westport organised the wedding and not one man, not even the groom was involved. It was all Bill's fault, he had said

'I'll tell you what I want, what I really, really want. I want to get married in Ireland, I want to have an Irish theme all the way through my wedding. In the evening at the reception I want Ceili Music, I want everyone to wear green, white or orange, you can squeeze a bit of gold in with that too to represent the gold in the Leprechaun's pot of gold, so those are the colours. If Coco's in agreement and the priest is happy to marry us, we want to be married in the little church down the road with a sea view. The day has to be a very special one. I picture the wedding reception under a starry sky surrounded by lanterns and candles and everyone I love.' He said all this with such enthusiasm and without taking a breath.

Coco said 'Girls, I know it's usually the girl's dream that's fulfilled for the wedding day, but I don't care, I just love him, every little bit of Bill I just love. I love his enthusiasm, his charisma, his build. Oh! I could go on and on but instead I just want to explain to anyone who's wondering am I a pushover, I am not a pushover. I live here in Ireland, Bill was born in Ireland, he emigrated along with his family when he was very young. All his life he dreamt of returning to and living again in Ireland. He has lived it in his head, he has dreamt of it, now he has to have the reality he has dreamt of since he was born all those years ago in Ireland. If Bill gets the wedding of his dreams, I will have the wedding of my dreams, that's just the way it is. We both have to be happy on our big day.'

So with the enthusiasm of a Sumo wrestler, the speed of a gazelle and the invaluable help of Roisin and the locals down in Westport, the girls organised the wedding for the 17th March making sure to include all of Bill's wishes. A Celtic band and Irish dancers from Westport had offered their services for the evening, as their day was taken up with the local St. Patrick's Day parade. So from five o'clock onwards they would join the wedding party and bring fun and laughter to an already fun and laughter wedding. The tricolours would fly, an Irish stew would be on the menu and green Guinness, not forgetting all the guests dressed in snippets of the tricolours, green, white and orange and a little helping of gold. Now what more could anyone ask for? The wedding date couldn't be any more Irish, the 17th March, St. Patrick's Day. The wedding reception would of course be in Westport on Roisin and Tomas's farm. The only thing they couldn't plan for was the weather so they put out the Child of Prague the night before and all prayed to St. Patrick.

'Please St. Patrick we beseech you, the weather has to be fabulous, in other words, go hána mhaith for our friend's wedding'.

Bill's mum and dad would arrive a few days before the big day and Bill wondered would they ever get used to drinking from jam jars, yes jam jars? The wedding was organised as fast as a leprechaun could hide and guess what, with the help of all the local farmers and their wives the wedding was sure to be a success. Of course the food would be sourced locally. All local animals were invited. Bill's best man would have to be Tomas and Roisin's donkey, Una. She would have a ribbon around her neck with a small box attached, with the wedding rings inside.

All the locals were combining their efforts to make a huge

stew for the wedding and provide big dishes to eat from, soup spoons and ladles to serve the guests. After that rustic wedding dinner it would have to be followed by a real old Irish dessert dish, of freshly cooked apple, with lashings of caster sugar and creamy custard from the surrounding dairies. The fun would really begin with all the dancers dancing, all the singers singing, tenors sounding like John McCormack (to keep Bill's mum and dad happy) and a Ceili band belting out songs like *Hail glorious St. Patrick, dear saint of our isle.*

All guests would no doubt be hungry again as midnight approached and as they say empty vessels make the most noise, in the Irish language that would be *Soithí folamh is mò torann*, so at 12 midnight, to stop the hungry horace's getting cranky, there would be fish and chips delivered by the local fish and chip shop on wheels. Sure everything would be *go h'alainn*. There'd be a lot of *scèal agus craic.*

CHAPTER 82

A trip back in time

On one of her very dark days an unexpected phone call came from Ross. 'Hello Georgia. I was just wondering how you are keeping these days.'

Georgia's cue – (Answer) 'To be honest with you, I'm just taking my life a moment at a time.'

(She found herself opening up to Ross, he was the only one she could be completely honest with, she tried to shield everyone else around her from the fact she was not sleeping.)

'Sometimes I find it difficult even looking after Juliet, because when I get panic attacks and find it hard to breathe I have to open windows so I don't feel like I'm drowning and that can be cold for Juliet.'

Ross – Question 'Would you like to meet up for maybe a walk on the beach? It might do you the world of good, Georgia.'

Answer – 'Why not?'

Ross – Question – 'Where?'

Georgia – Answer – 'Killiney beach.'

Time settled at 1pm Sunday.

It must be at least four weeks since I chatted to Ross, Georgia thought. She was quite looking forward to the meeting, after all they shared history together that no one could take away. She would have loved to take Juliet with her so she could meet Ross again and maybe they'd even buy a bucket and spade and they could make sandcastles and play on the beach. The idea was tempting but the reality was, absolutely not going to happen, it would seem as if she was rushing things. The meeting last time just didn't work so how could she expect this one to be a success? Nellie would mind Juliet, that was the decision. She could put Juliet into her car and take her into town for an ice cream and if Nellie was agreeable Juliet could stay overnight – Nellie agreed. Now Georgia had a whole day and a whole night off, all to herself. Yes, Sunday 1pm was a date on her calendar not to be missed.

When the day arrived she dressed up in her runners, jeans and warm top, all comfy. Of course, Georgia would have loved to dress in something pretty but with all those big stones in abundance on the strand in Killiney, she opted for the comfortable option, just in case she fell and cut her knee. Then she sat into her beautiful little mini car and headed out to the coast. This was one of the good things about Dublin, it never took too long to get close to sea water, all in all only 40 minutes. She drove into the public car park, pulled on the hand brake and sat there for a minute or so until she regained her composure and felt ready for her next conquest.

There were quite a few people walking along, she wondered if he was among them. It was a bit chilly, not a time to stand around waiting, so she started to walk towards the strand down past the public toilets, under the tunnel and onto the silvery, stony sand. She looked around trying to locate Ross, there he was sitting on a rock and looking out to sea. Her heart skipped a beat as she made her way to where he sat. There was no big hug, just quiet smiles to mark the occasion.

The couple strolled along listening to the waves as the tide made its way closer and closer to the shore. Ross didn't seem aware of the situation, Georgia knew him well, his body language said it all, he was nervous. He walked closer and closer towards the waves. Georgia wanted to warn him but knew it would be best to leave him alone and make sure she kept a safe distance between herself and the water and with a bit of luck he might follow, but he didn't. Although it was a bit chilly and there wasn't a breeze, still one couple had their kite out. They tried to encourage it to rise towards the sky but unfortunately there was one vital component missing, a strong breeze, needed to prevent the couple feeling foolish. Ross hadn't the patience to watch so instead walked closer to the edge of the shore. Georgia looked on wondering if indeed he would take his shoes off and have a little paddle? He had no intention of doing that, no, instead he just wanted to embrace the fast approaching tide or maybe he just wasn't aware of it. Then for a moment he just stood there contemplating, while the tide came in with a vengeance.

Ross became aware of the situation too late. From her perfect position and they say position is everything, Georgia had to admit this was a very amusing sight to see. As he retreated backwards poor Ross stumbled. His shoes became embedded in the sand, he fell down into a sitting position with water all around him. Now, in fairness he no sooner fell down than he was up and running back to safety. Georgia ran to his side just to make sure he was OK. There he was with two circular wet patches right on his ass. Georgia felt embarrassed for him when she realised not only was his ass wet but his shoes and stockings were also soaking, uncomfortable and full of sand.

She wrestled with her facial muscles in an effort to keep a straight face but lost the battle as she watched him stagger along looking forlorn. It was a long, long time since he had wet pants. He clearly wasn't a happy man, especially as he watched his estranged wife fold up with laughter, still at some level it was the little incident needed to defrost the tension between them and sure enough Ross began to see the funny side, even if the joke was on him.

She noticed the other couple walking hand in hand clutching the limp kite that today had not lived up to their expectations, through no fault of its own. They smiled as they passed. Maybe the kite for them was like the fall for Ross and they saw the funny side when the wind in Killiney just didn't perform. Ross also saw the funny side of his situation as he walked along like a cowboy who just dismounted his horse after days sitting in the saddle, riding the range. Georgia held on to his hand.

Since he hadn't taken his car to Killiney, instead travelled by train, it was Georgia's greatest pleasure to do the driving, a task she loved especially as her little red mini with the white roof, was a joy to drive. Georgia found a white towel in the boot which she strategically placed on the passenger seat where Ross would park his ass, after all, the car was only relatively new and Georgia wouldn't let a stain appear on those immaculate seats.

Ross began to really relax in Georgia's company, he began to tell how his heart had been broken when first she walked out on him. She could hardly believe it when he told of his very sad moments, and nights when he just pined for her. This was Georgia's opportunity to make a move.

'I'm sorry I made you so sad.'

She rubbed the sand from his trousers but sand on a wet article doesn't come off. Maybe Georgia just wanted to have some physical contact with someone who had always been there for her. Ross put his hand down on her hand. Georgia didn't know if he was going to stop her being affectionate but no, he was encouraging.

One thing led to another and Georgia thanked God there was no one around. This love making was far more dynamic than it had been, when Ross and Georgia were a married couple. Unlike the romp under the sheets with Cameron that was wild and erotic, this was gentle, passionate and beautiful. It had history, it had knowledge and most of all it had love. Georgia was amazed how a car that looked so small from the outside could be so large on the inside and the square shape made for perfect moments. It was no wonder the mini was so popular in the sixties when the sex revolution and flower power took hold. Admittedly there were no flowers around this mini but there was certainly a lot of power.

There was no awkwardness after the event, only the fogged up windows and there was a real reason for them! Georgia turned the engine on and sat back waiting for the heater to clear the fog from the windows and make the mini safe to drive. It only took seconds, now the outside world was clearer and inside the mini Georgia and Ross continued to open their hearts and minds to each other and everything became clearer. Ross told Georgia of the loneliness and the pure despair he had felt. Georgia felt awful as the whole thing began to sink in. She felt especially bad when he told her about the night he found himself standing by her wardrobe, opening it up and holding one of her dresses in his hands, just to smell it, just to find her scent.

'And did you?' she asked 'Did you find me there?'

'I did find you there in that red dress, it still had your scent on it. I even remember the night you wore it, it was about a week before our wedding. I remember feeling so proud of you as I looked on and watched you chatting away to your mum. I couldn't believe you were going to be my wife forever and ever.'

Feebly Georgia said 'I remember that night too, Ross. I was so happy.'

Ross had an angry look on his face 'Georgia, you burst my bubble, you left me feeling numb. I kept asking myself, where did I go wrong to end up losing you.'

'It wasn't you Ross, it was me. You did everything right. It was me who did everything wrong.'

'Don't worry Georgia, I don't torture myself asking myself questions like that anymore, because constantly there were no answers. I've stopped blaming myself now. I know there was nothing I could have done, it wasn't me.'

'No Ross, I walked away, it was me.'

Georgia could still see the anger in his eyes.

'I've forgiven you, I'm trying to move on but what's just happened will make it much harder. Would you believe, Georgia, I thought I was moving on, I even went on a date for the first time.' He blurted out and laughed nervously.

Georgia didn't ask who the lucky girl was but Ross said,

'She was a girl from work.'

'It usually is, that shoulder to lie on, that's what you needed, Ross' said Georgia.

'But Georgia I felt nothing. I think I'm afraid to trust! I'm praying that will change for me but every time I go back to that night at your wardrobe, I realise how low a human being can sink. I think the lowest point was when one of those wedding dresses of yours, seemed to appear from the wardrobe. I touched it, trying to remember which one it was, the first one or the second one.'

'Ross, was it the one with all the lace or the one with all the tulle?'

'I don't even know what tulle is, Georgia.'

'Yes but you do know what lace is, Ross. So was it lace or was it flimsical?'

'It was lace, Georgia. Now I remember, it was the first one you wore.'

'You're right Ross. It was the flimsical one I wore later on in the day, it was soft and flowy. Ross don't you remember how happy we were?'

Ross didn't answer that question, he continued:

'Georgia, you'll have to take those wedding dresses away. I just can't be reminded anymore' he said with mad anger flashing in his eyes for a moment. 'If they stay there I'll burn them. I won't mention it again but please promise you'll take them away.'

Georgia nodded her head in agreement 'I will Ross, I will.'

Georgia was very honest with herself, she felt the lowest of the low, how could she be so cruel to such a good man? She hadn't given a thought to how he was doing all on his own, but now she felt horrible. His eyes had a look, hard to describe, you'd really need to see it for yourself to understand, you know that vacant look coming right from the soul. In his eyes there was anger and darkness, even though they'd made love earlier and Ross had put to the back of his mind the hurt he still felt, he was overtaken by the passion he felt. He was now right back to hurting inside and that darkness that seemed to surround him still surrounded him.

Georgia could feel the tears clouding her eyes, she blinked trying to eliminate her clouded vision, it worked releasing the tears onto her cheeks. She felt stupid, silent. A strange feeling came right over her body, it was as if something was happening inside, she saw the reality, all the hurt she'd inflicted on a decent, young man and it was only now she realised how much he loved her, he'd never feel that way again. She looked at the expression on his face, it was pitiful and the look in his beautiful eyes was devastating, so dark, so helpless, so not really there, afraid that even the slightest touch would take him right back there. He couldn't bear to go back there to a place where he lost all sense of himself.

She knew he was thinking why have I let her seduce me again? She felt ashamed, a fallen woman and so sorry she had tempted him back to where he fought so hard to get away from. Yes, he'd fought a good fight, he had begun to come around but maybe next time he might not be able to fight his way back. A song crossed her mind, her mum used to play that song, *I know I'll never love this way again but I still keep holding on until all the hurt is gone.* Georgia knew once you break trust there's really no going back. Maybe they could have a different relationship, maybe they could learn to make more time for the things that mattered. It could even be exciting. At least for now they were able to talk to each other (make love). Georgia began to feel some peace within herself.

It seemed years since the night she left. She hadn't even passed by the front door of their house and in all honesty during that time, she hadn't really missed it and there was no need until now. They drove along quietly and as they drove Georgia wondered if Ross was remembering the time they spent together. He never asked if she was taking him right to their front door and she never said, instead Georgia just drove, it seemed like the right thing to do. Her heart skipped a beat as she indicated and pulled in. Ross held her hand for a moment, kissed her gently and in a moment he was gone, no long goodbyes just a smile then nothing, no date, no promise to phone, no offers of lunch, nothing, nada, zilch.

Alone once more Georgia felt stuck to the spot, she just sat there gazing at the empty space where Ross had sat just minutes earlier and the white towel still with the marks of his wet ass, embedded. That loneliness hit her again or was it emptiness. *How could she have left him?* She asked herself as she picked up the damp white towel from the passenger seat where Ross sat and held it to her heart. It made the saying clear to her that love is a drug. She didn't want to leave, she wanted to run into the house, open the door with the key she still held in her bag and let him hold her in his strong arms once more. But instead, she held back, turned on the car's engine and began driving back down the road towards home half blinded by the tears that just wouldn't go away.

Without giving it much thought she put her foot hard down on the brake and stopped the car. With the impact she almost went flying through the window. She could feel her head sore from the wallop as her forehead connected with the glass, luckily the glass didn't break. She didn't allow herself time to think, she turned the car right back around. Lucky for her it was a quiet road and there she was parked again right outside her old house. She could hear her heart beating, tears were still flowing down her face, all the time she'd taken to make herself look together, calm and beautiful for Ross was definitely wasted, gone up in smoke. She knew she must look terrible but she didn't care. Now she was standing outside the door, she didn't reach for the keys in her bag, instead she pounded on the door. Bang, Bang, Bang. The door almost rattled and then he was there, standing looking mesmerised, amazed, concerned.

'What's wrong Georgia, did you crash the car? Oh my God what's wrong with you I never saw you looking so…'

He didn't get a chance to finish the sentence. Georgia rushed into his arms, lay her head on his warm chest and cried hysterically for what seemed like ages. Ross just didn't know what to do, so he did what he thought was best for Georgia, carried her to the sitting room and sat her down.

'Calm down, I never know what to do when you cry, Georgia, especially when I don't know why you're crying.'

Out came the words, hard to make any sense of but they came out anyway.

'You've been so nice to me, Ross, even after all I did on you. I didn't deserve you, I don't deserve you.'

'Look, we all make mistakes, that's life, that's how we learn to move on with things, to understand' then he paused and pondered on the words he was just going to say, 'to forgive, Georgia.'

'I'm such a mess, as I drove down the road I didn't want to go home, I wanted to come back to you and then I started thinking how selfish I was. Even leaving those dresses there, it was mean of me. I never considered how difficult it must have been for you to see them every time you opened that wardrobe, all I thought about was me not you and even today I was thinking about me. I'm sorry, I'm sorry, I'm so, so sorry.' She was still crying hysterically. 'I came back for two reasons. (Sob, sob). 1. To tell you how much I still love you and 2. I'm taking those dresses with me tonight. (going up an octave) I've got to give you some closure.'

'There's no need, Georgia, no need. Take them when you feel more relaxed. Just use your key, come in, get them, take them.'

(She's on high doh now, almost sounding like a soprano)

'No. I've made up my mind they're coming with me tonight. Nothing will stop me. In fact, if I could make a bonfire of them, I'd do it right now.'

'You can't do that.' He laughed. 'You'd either burn down the house or ruin my vegetable patch. Neither one sounds like a good idea, Georgia. Just sit there and let me make you a cup of tea. Here's some tissues, dry your eyes and I'd strongly advise you to take that black stuff from around your eyes. You look like a panda bear.'

For the first time in what seemed like years, Georgia could

feel herself honestly smiling. It was a good feeling. When she eventually looked in the mirror she couldn't believe what she saw. She looked like someone who'd been pulled through a hedge backwards. Not a pretty sight. On went some Vaseline. It felt cool on her red and black eyes. Eventually after a couple of wipes, all evidence was removed.

'Ross.' She shouted towards the kitchen. She could hear him stirring the tea.

'I'm going upstairs, I'll be down in a moment, this needs to be done now.'

Up the stairs she bounded with the speed of a gazelle and returned down the stairs moments later pulling two big dresses in their half zipped up bags behind her, holding two pairs of bridal shoes, one long veil and a tiara. She continued to drag them behind her into the sitting room. They now lay on the floor. Ross stood there holding two cups of tea. He looked even more mesmerised than when he saw her at the front door.

'I told you there was no need to put all this strain on yourself, Georgia.'

'But now is the only time to do it. (sob) I just know it, Ross. Now is the right time to get rid of the past and start looking into the future.'

She took a deep gulp of air into her lungs and almost knocked herself out. Holding onto her head she continued.

'I'm so emotional, (sniff) I don't think I've ever been this emotional before in my life. I feel like something inside is changing.'

'Just sit down, Georgia, take a few deep breaths, you're in a terrible state. Don't say another word, just sip that tea, I'll keep a close eye on you, I think I need to.'

Georgia just sat down in a heap on the chair, surrounded by

her wedding dresses, shoes and accessories. By now she was absolutely exhausted from all the crying, sobbing, sniffling, the guilt and then dragging those dresses down the stairs, not forgetting bounding up the stairs in the first place. As for all the time she'd taken over her make up earlier, she had to admit it was wasted.

'Can I drive you home, Georgia? Just leave your car here, I'll drive you home. You did enough driving for one day and you're in no fit state to drive.'

'No. I'll be OK. I've had my tea, I'm feeling better now. I think I needed to let go all my pent up feelings and for once come to terms with the enormity of everything I've done to you and everything that's happened in my life since then and up to now. If you'd help me put the dresses in the car, I'll be eternally grateful and you'll never see them again. (sniffle and sob)'

Ross did exactly what was asked of him. He was some man for one man. She could only imagine the wonderful life she would have had if she hadn't broken his trust.

That night had to be the loneliest night of her life Georgia thought, as she tossed and turned in bed not able to sleep, her eyes burning from exhaustion. She thanked God Nellie had Juliet for an overnight stay, she just wouldn't have been able to mind her with the state she was in. She didn't want to imagine how bad her body would feel in the morning, she would have to deal with it then. In the meantime maybe counting sheep would do the trick, all she needed was a brilliant imagination in order to visualise the sheep walking procession like back to their pen. I'll give it a go, she thought. She couldn't even visualise the numbers, let alone the sheep, 1, 2, 3, 5, 7 feck the sheep.

With that she sat bolt upright in her bed and grabbed her new diary from her bedside locker. She liked this little diary even though it wasn't her favourite, she'd left her favourite five year diary behind her in the house that Ross now only occupied. She began to write. Her mind wandered again, should I just drive back there, pound on the door and when he opens it refuse to leave? Nothing made sense, words didn't matter tonight, it was all about thoughts and her thoughts were racing. Her mind refused to relax and let her fall asleep, so when all else failed she threw her diary, it didn't land on the locker, it landed on the floor. Feck that too, she said as she put her hand up to the light switch, not even looking at it she rummaged around until she felt the switch, turned the light off and lay there motionless in her empty bed. Maybe I'll buy a single bed tomorrow, she thought or join a nunnery, she hated both of those options. But there was something she hated even more, someone else in Ross's life, but at the same time could she imagine herself being back there with him?

In Georgia's brain she could hear this girl's voice, the new girl in his life, it was squeaky and high pitched, almost like a cartoon character… she was saying the words *I love being with you Ross. I can't wait to see into our future. I hope you'll be there with me.* Somebody loved him, why was she jealous?

CHAPTER 83

Christmas

Georgia was happy to keep very busy as she planned for Christmas. A time she was both looking forward to and also dreading. This year herself and Juliet wouldn't spend Christmas in their beautiful bungalow, instead Georgia had chosen to spend Christmas with her mum. It would be too sad and unbearable to even allow herself to imagine how wonderful and magical Christmas would have been with Cameron, Juliet and her mum Nellie, in their beautiful bungalow, if Cameron was here with her on planet Earth.

Instead she would meet all her friends on Christmas Eve, at 6 o'clock Mass in Clarendon Street. They'd bring their presents with them to the church and distribute them after the beautiful Mass and singing of the choir. Georgia knew she would feel very at home in the church surrounded by the hymns and music that Cameron loved. She knew she would feel he was so close to her.

Once they'd exchanged the Christmas presents, the girls would take a little walk over to the crib, of course the baby Jesus wouldn't be there and would not arrive until after the next Mass. Warm hugs and kisses were always one of the big highlights of Christmas Eve. Then everyone would go home, happy to have Mass and presents all done and dusted, only then would their Christmas festivities at home begin. They would all meet up again on the 27th of December in Georgia's beautiful bungalow.

Everything went to plan, Mass, singing, exchanging presents, warm hugs and embraces. Georgia was still feeling the warmth of her friends' hugs smiles and greetings surrounding her as she drove Juliet to her mum's house. She wondered how it was possible to have this amount of clothes and presents on board? Of course, firstly there were Juliet's and Georgia's clothes and then there were presents for themselves and Georgia's mum.

Now they were inside sitting by the warm fire and enjoying the comforts of Nellie's home. Isn't it amazing how being in your old home with your family is the nicest feeling ever, it's as if the whole house gives you the warmest embrace. Georgia was happy to be there, she always felt the pressure lift from her shoulders the moment she stepped inside her mum's magic hall door. Christmas was nice, it just glided over, she did speak of Cameron quite a lot and made sure to have photographs of him strategically placed all around her mum's house and one on the side table where herself and Juliet would sleep. Juliet could see her dad smiling back at her. Inside, Georgia's heart was broken but outwardly she was smiling. Life has to go on and from the day you're born, you know that people will come and go throughout your life, people you just love with all your heart, but you still have to trudge onwards until your life levels off again.

Nellie was a real dreamer, she never lost contact with Ross, maybe she believed and hoped someday Georgia and Ross would find their way back to each other. Sometimes when you are looking in on a relationship you view it in a different way. From the first day she met him they had built up a really strong bond between them, from the moment she was introduced to him she just knew he was an honest good man. In her bid to get them back together again she had invited him over for Christmas dinner. He was so grateful and happy for the invitation, he said before Nellie's invitation to Christmas dinner he had felt lonely and just didn't want to spend this Christmas alone. He was aware that by being there it could make things awkward for

Georgia and Juliet but having talked things through with Nellie he said 'I've got to face my fears, put on my big boy pants and take a chance. If it pays off great, if it doesn't at least we tried. Isn't that right Nellie?'

It wasn't awkward, in fact it was quite natural having him there, it was as it was supposed to be. They enjoyed watching the old Christmas movies on TV and playing games with Juliet.

St. Stephen's Day was more relaxed with Cameron's mum and dad coming to visit. They arrived looking sad and forlorn but having had an early lunch, a few glasses of gin and seeing Juliet they left feeling still very sad inside but happy to have Juliet because looking at Juliet was just like looking at a mirror image of Cameron. Georgia noticed Cameron's dad was wearing his watch. The two of them caught the moment, he was looking down at the watch and Georgia was looking over at the watch, their eyes met for a moment. Words weren't needed as in their minds eye they could see happy Cameron, proudly wearing that watch. The biggest hurdle was jumped. Christmas was over and New Year resolutions were made.

Looking Forward, not looking back and would you believe Nellie's cruise, now just a memory. Photographs, videos and a tan to prove she had cruised around the south of France. Let's not forget the captain's table and Nellie perched right beside him in that fabulous photograph. She already had it enlarged to 8 x 10, now it was sitting in pride of place on the big wall in her sitting room, in a gold frame looking ever so posh. Nellie was all the better for that cruise, she was already looking forward to the one she was hoping to go on with Georgia and Juliet next year but right now she was getting ready for the wedding in Westport. It was all systems go as the year moved on like the fast and the furious.

CHAPTER 84

The enchanted wedding

Georgia's mum had really turned out to be a jewel in the crown, everywhere Georgia went, Georgia's mum accompanied her helping out with her little girl but not interfering in any way. It was really a perfect combination. Georgia was happy to have her mum around. OK it was a little bit selfish but 99 per cent of Georgia's time was lived around Juliet and that 1per cent that Nellie gave her back was the icing on the cake, she never had to say no to an invitation. It was Georgia's mum Nellie, who always got the first call. She never complained, in fact she just loved being the chosen one, nothing ever seemed too much for her, she just slotted into place like a perfectly fitting glove.

'OK Nellie, the time has come we're off to Westport for Coco's wedding on Sunday morning, get yourself packed, bring a few really good rig outs, after all there might be a few banquets we will have to attend. See you in the morning.'

Seven o'clock sharp next morning, there stood Nellie with her little case packed. She was wearing her comfy shoes and her high heels were sticking out of the bag. They were off again on another adventure.

The sun shone all day and the moon came out at night. If they had been able to order the day and night it couldn't have been any better, it was just perfect. An old song came to Georgia's mind, *We've got the sun in the morning and the moon at night*. A song her Grandad always loved singing to her when she was a little toddler. Georgia couldn't believe how carefree the whole thing was, how unorganised it looked but how organised it really was. Bill's mother and father absolutely beamed all day with pride and gratitude, love of their son and the realisation that they achieved what they set out to achieve. They had returned to the Emerald Isle and what better thing to return for than their son's wedding.

Coco bought her dress online, cream lace and a magical veil edged with tiny diamonds and an absolutely beautiful tiara that glittered and gleamed as she walked up the aisle of the tiny church overlooking the ocean. Coco was holding a bouquet of yellow roses as she glided up the aisle accompanied by Tomas who was standing in for her father, who had passed away years before. Georgia, Heidi and Tanya, the very important brides-maids, held small posies of yellow roses.

To their surprise just as they were taking their places, already decided, three very, very handsome American soldiers all dressed in their pristine American army uniforms, walked up to the top of the church and stood one, two, three behind Bill, all soldier like. What were the girls to do but rethink their strategy fast and place themselves one, two, three behind each other. The organist began to play the wedding march, Coco and Tomas walked to the top of the aisle where Coco joined Bill. Now the girls were looking straight across at these gorgeous hunks of junk who were smiling over at them. The girls smiled back and tried to close their mouths. Coco and Bill turned around and said in unison:

'Do you like our surprise, girls? Our photographer is in on this. He's snapping away there taking photos of you all with your mouths open. The photos will be shown at a later date in the Trocadero.'

It's hard to believe but these three American soldiers taking their places beside the bridesmaids at this fabulous wedding, changed everything in a moment. Guests in the church began to clap and cheer. There was never a wedding like this in this church before, where guests cheered, clapped and someone even gave a wolf whistle. All of a sudden this was not just a wedding, this was a show, a performance, it was magical.

Guess who arrived a little late, the unannounced Ross. Georgia didn't know he was invited to the wedding. Her friends had kept the secret close to their chests. She also didn't know until this moment that apart from missing Cameron and wishing he was there, her heart was longing for Ross to be there at the wedding. She knew if Ross was around she wouldn't feel alone, she also realised he still meant the world to her.

When she saw Ross walking into the church, from her pivotal position as bridesmaid, her heart had skipped a beat. He had smiled at her nervously, as he walked to his seat. She just looked on and took everything in, his white tie and his deep green suit, just as well he was tall otherwise he might have been mistaken for a leprechaun. She prayed he might be her tall leprechaun again one day. Just about time for the penny to drop but as the old saying says better late than never.

Coco's hair was beautiful, all curly and wavy, it swayed as she turned to Bill and said the words, *I do*. There must have been no better feeling for her, than marrying the man of her dreams, Bill, and being surrounded by her friends, his army friends in uniform and family. She felt like an Irish Càilìn back in the day all pure and innocent as she gazed up lovingly at her new husband Bill, who was dressed in tweeds with a yellow rose in his lapel, looking quite dapper. Outside, after the glorious ceremony, Bill put his càibìn (cap) on his head. He was absolutely delighted when guests told him he looked like John Wayne in the film *The Quiet Man*. All the ladies wore fantastic plastic, buttercup earrings, buttercup bracelets, and buttercup necklaces, especially made just for them and ordered on-line. After all, memories bring back memories. Even Maisie Coyne wore the whole ensemble from London and Fr. Fergus Breen wore a yellow rose in his lapel.

The bridesmaids' dresses were the most beautiful warm tone of gold with creamy white sashes. Their bouquets were made with green natural foliage taken from the farm, with some yellow roses added. Juliet wore a pretty creamy white soft dress with the same gold fabric in her sash. Her posy was made of yellow rose buds with sprayed gold leaves around the edges. The dresses just fell like a dream almost to the ground. The shade of gold was definitely a winner, even Juliet loved them, she loved putting the fabric through her fingers, she loved the feel of the organza and the satin underskirts. She loved the buttercup baby slides in their hair, the little girl was mesmerised by the beautiful colours and she was so happy with her granny Nellie minding her for the day. Tomàs wore a tweed suit and a càibìn although he took it off in the church, after all that's manners.

Bill's mum wore a gold suit but a much deeper shade than the bridesmaids' dresses so they didn't clash. Her blouse and her shoes were a fabulous shade of pale green. Bill's dad wore a white suit, an orange tie and a yellow handkerchief tucked down into his breast pocket. He was a slim and tall man and although the colours were different they fell in with the green, white and orange and just somehow worked. There was a combination of the tricolour or Irish flag scattered throughout the guests, everyone tried to be mindful of Bill and his mum's wishes, they all did their best to comply one way or another, including the soldiers who had a yellow rose pinned onto their hats. All in all it was a kaleidoscope of colour.

As the wedding guests arrived into Roisin and Thomas's field and made their way to the tables where they would dine, their eyes were dazzled by the evening sun. It showed off the sparkling cream tablecloths and the beautiful yellow, white and green flower arrangements on the tables. In the corner of the field, beside the wedding table another farmhouse table stood and on it were three large skillets full to the brim with Irish stew gently simmering. The aroma was amazing, it sent the guests taste buds crazy. Roisin's friends from the Irish Countrywomen's Association and neighbours from near and far had offered their services free of charge. There was only one condition, they could eat and drink as much as they liked once everyone else was served. By the end of the night everyone would, no doubt, be fluthered, paralytic, (drunk as skunks).

The icing on the cake

The icing on the cake was yet to come.

The bride Coco and the groom Bill, plus Georgia, Heidi, Tanya, Juliet and Nellie took their rightful places with Thomàs, the best men and Roisin at the wedding table. They also included Ross because after all, he was such a big part of all their lives. Their meal was served to them by the waiter who lived a field or two down the winding road. He was so kind to take a day's holiday from his job as a waiter in a hotel in the centre of town.

Everyone, including the soldiers helped themselves to the stew, they even had second helpings and drank from the tumblers. They held on to the glasses so they could re-fill them continuously with the green Guinness that was there in abundance. The host was the local Seanachai, Seamus, he did a great job of telling Irish folklore stories and introducing the various guest singers, harpist, Irish tenors and later on the Irish dancers, step dancers and anyone else that wanted to join in the wedding hooley. He explained to the guests how a lot of these artists had come home especially for this weekend to perform and bring these green fields to life.

'As all of you know there is no money involved, the comedians, the singers, the dancers and everyone else here performing are giving their services free. But maybe, before the night really gets started and most of you get drunk and disorderly, we could do...' There was a pause, then he continued in a half joking whole in earnest tone of voice, 'a whip around. You guests,' he looked straight into the crowd, 'might be generous enough to part with a little bit of your cash as a thank you and give the performers a few bob to take home with them.' Everyone clapped and danced.

Then a few of the locals took off their caibins, caps, and around the guests they went, shaking them in time with the rhythm of the Celtic music that filled the air. Not one of the performers would go home empty handed, because the great response to the comperes request was like the Irish people, generous.

The last few hours had been full-on with so much to be fitted in. It was only now that Ross and Georgia could really say hello properly to each other. Because the American soldiers had just left the table to dance and get to know the bridesmaids, they now had a few minutes alone with the bride and groom. First and most importantly Ross spoke to Coco the bride and Bill the groom. Georgia could hear him saying:

'Coco you look absolutely magnificent and Bill the only thing I can say to you is you look real Irish. I know that will make you happy.'

Bill was more than happy to be told he looked Irish.

'My wish for both of you' said Ross 'is that every day your relationship gets stronger and stronger and most importantly that you share all your adventures together and stay strong.'

Georgia could hear that quiver in his voice, she knew he was wishing for them, everything he and Georgia had not shared, but now that they were a little wiser, maybe if they were together all of these wishes he wished for Coco and Bill, might be the reality for both of them. When he finished his little speech to the bride and groom, Ross came straight over to Georgia and whispered in her ear:

'I hope it wasn't too much of a shock to see me here but you see your three friends, Heidi, Coco and Tanya and Bill thought it might be good for both of us to meet at this big event, when we would have time to sing and dance and just be ourselves, forgetting our past and living in the moment.'

Georgia just smiled. Before she had time to comment Coco came over to her.

'Sorry Georgia, we planned all this as a little surprise for you and after all both of you are friends of mine. My wedding wouldn't have been the same without Ross being here.'

Georgia smiled again, she could think of lots of things to say but she was afraid to say them. One was, thanks a million for bringing Ross here and making my day perfect, so instead she said:

'You are all true friends, thank you so much for everything.'

Ross seemed a little emotional. He stood up and walked away to join the three soldiers and their audience and the next half hour or so was just all fun for him. Now that everyone was full to the brim with food, they needed a little rest and everything went quiet for a little while. The guests just mingled with each other, some caught up on old times with friends. Some met new friends, the bride and groom, bridesmaids, best man, Nellie, Juliet, Maisie and Fr. Fergus Breen and Ross who sat at the large table chatting. All of a sudden Seamus the Seanachai began to speak through the microphone. His voice was so loud the whole wedding party jumped and came back to earth with a thud.

'Now Folks, he said. It's time. Our harpist will play and sing an old Irish song for you. This is the last quiet piece of relaxing music you will hear for the day so sip your drinks, sit back and relax, as Saoirse plays music for your ears only, the beautiful haunting sound of An Chulainn. She will be accompanied on tin whistle by Tommy, the small red haired, curly headed guy over there'.

461

With that the small red haired, curly headed guy over there stood up and came over onto the stage and joined the harpist and soloist Saoirse. Seamus was right, the tune was haunting and made even more haunting by the combination of the tin whistle, the strings of the harp, and the beautiful sound of Saoirse's voice as it soared, hitting every note so effortlessly. She sang and gently caressed the strings of the harp, managing to bring a little something extra special to that beautiful music and song. The arrangement and the rendition were out of this world.

Some of the guests became really emotional, Georgia was one of them, as she wept she grabbed her little girl Juliet and her mum and gave them the biggest hug ever, while Ross looked on. Georgia felt this weekend was giving her a sort of closure, not that she was ever going to forget Cameron, how could she? He had been that someone who made every breath she took worthwhile. Georgia was thanking her lucky stars that now, against all the odds Ross was back in her life. God knows why? But thanks to her friends he was here with her today. Somebody in Heaven loved her, she hoped it was Cameron. Georgia didn't feel empty or lonely instead she felt this day and its outcome for her, was written in the stars.

The speeches were short and sweet like an ass's gallop, everyone thanked everyone for everything. Seamus the Seanachai introduced different performers to the stage as darkness began to fall so gracefully. By now some of the guests were more than merry, no doubt later they would be drunk as skunks, even before the night fell.

CHAPTER 86

Bill's surprise

They sat around eating more apple pie, as evening turned to dusk, then darkness. The only thing you could see, apart from the flickering candles and lanterns lighting up the darkness, was the beautiful full moon in the sky. It added that magical ingredient to the night that nothing else could. The Irish word ciunas could be heard being repeated throughout the crowd and the guests eventually fell silent.

The movie began (it wasn't really a movie, just the showing of all the pictures). It was so exciting viewing photographs of Coco when she was a little girl in kindergarten, with all her friends. There were photographs of Coco and her friends on their first Holy Communion day, photographs taken on their confirmation day and more photos taken years later at their graduation ceremony. Of course there were lots of photographs of Bill taken as he ran around the fields of Ireland when he was a little boy, at the St. Patrick's Day parade, and lots more taken of him in the army. There were many photographs taken of him with his family at various parades in America. He loved all animals so a lot of his photographs were taken on horses or beside horses, donkeys, ponies and even the odd few chickens.

Not a lot had changed for Bill, except back then he was just a boy. Now he was a Man all of 6 feet tall with big broad shoulders and beautiful blonde hair and a smile that would light up a room. It seemed Bill and his mum and dad always dreamt of this magical moment in Ireland. Georgia wondered if they came to live in Ireland would it live up to their great expectations. Then there was another sound of ciunas, Seamus, master of ceremonies for the night, stood up onto the stage and said a few words.

'First I would just like to thank Coco and Bill, Georgia, Heidi and Tanya, Juliet and of course, the best men, Chuck, Brad and Cheyanne, not forgetting Roisin and Tomas, for adding such handsome glamour to this beautiful day and now we come to the icing on the cake... Ruadhri down there, sìos san seomra, las na soilse. In other words, ladies and gentlemen I'm having the lights dimmed. Ciunas, a cairde òga, stad agus suigì sios agus gur raibh maith agut, to one and all.'

Everyone sat down. There was silence. You could almost hear a pin drop on the grass and then that short film, the one that Georgia's friend had worked so hard to retrieve from the archives in RTE, was on the screen. There he was, Bill, standing at the St Patrick's Day parade with his mum and dad being interviewed by one of Ireland's best known interviewers. At this point Bill was ecstatic, his mother was ecstatic, his father was ecstatic. It was amazing how a sixty seconds piece of film could do so much and bring back so many memories for all of them. Everyone prayed all three of them wouldn't have a heart attack from the excitement. After all three quarters of the guests were now drunk and couldn't drive a nail into a wall let alone drive the three musketeers to the nearby hospital.

When all of the wedding celebrations were over, everyone who wanted to stood up and gave that speech from the bottom of their hearts and added that piece of spice. His mother, his father, her mother, Tomas spoke on behalf of her dad who had passed away and of course the three friends added their three and four pence, in fact four because Coco had her say too.

To cap it all, the actual wedding ceremony had been filmed earlier and now it was being shown up there on the big screen, up there for all to see the two wedding rings hung around the donkey's ears swaying to and fro. Georgia imagined she saw the donkey laughing, maybe it had encountered some of the black stuff and drank a whole barrel full. This night was fantastic, one of those real happy occasions. That film of the wedding also showed the guests at their tables enjoying their stew and made everyone in the room feel part of this momentous occasion. The wedding didn't cost Coco and Bill a lot so they still had enough money for a deposit on a house if they wanted to stay in Ireland.

Just before the hooley began Seamus began to sing songs that had been requested by Coco for her new husband and his family, starting with *A Nation Once Again*, followed by other Irish songs. Bill sang along with Seamus. Everyone could see he was in his element belting out the words of all those protest and Irish romantic songs with his mum and dad, songs they had played and sang along to, since he was a boy.

CHAPTER 87

That dance

Seamus stood up on the stage. 'Now this is to everyone, I have a little gift of music for all of you, as they say there's a song for everyone in the audience. Darkness is falling, everyone is starting to wilt and slow down, well after all you all had a very early start. I apologize to everyone in advance because I'm not letting any of you fall asleep. I have a dance routine and a song that will have all of you up on your feet dancing the night away. Romance is in the air, I'm taking the tempo up a notch and with that in mind I would like to introduce to you one of the best singers in this neck of the woods. I'm proud to say the singer is also a first cousin of mine.

Before I introduce him and his band to all of you I would like to say to you, please, when the music starts,' he sang out loud 'Get up, stand up, strut your funky stuff. Come on up on the dance floor and strut your stuff. Oh yea, take a look around you and see if you can find your soul mate. If you can't, please don't worry, just pick someone from the audience who you think will make you laugh and ask him or her up to dance with you because my gift to all of you is music, dance and song. A thirty minute dance sequence that offers to all of you a wild let your hair down section, followed by a catch your hair up romantic section, then we will round up my gift to you with a change partners and dance with me, followed by the dance that says it all, the I'll take you home or on this occasion, I'll follow you to Dublin, song. Who will be Mr Lucky? So without further ado it is my pleasure to present to you Daniel and the Dudes.'

To great applause, from the back of the marquee right up through the crowds past the wedding party, ran Daniel and his Dudes followed closely by the locals plus helpers, the band's relatives and anyone else who wished to join in the celebrations. This night was becoming a Westport and family affair. In only moments Daniel and his Dudes struck up a musical note, then with a few clicks of his fingers and a great musical intro, Daniel announced:

'We, that is my band and I would like to invite the bride and groom, bridesmaids, best men, American soldiers and families to start the ball rolling to the sound of everyone's favourite song, *Rolling On A River*, a Tina Turner song guaranteed to keep everyone who is wide eyed and legless or stone cold sober up on their feet and keep this party going.'

To everyone's delight the song and the rolling went on for ages and ages. One enthusiastic guest, who was legless, jumped up on the stage with Daniel and the Dudes. Once she was up there a few more of the guests jumped up to join her, but they weren't dancing to her beat, she had taken that dance routine so seriously. Coco looked at the stage and to her horror the enthusiastic dancer pushed two of the guests off the stage because they weren't doing it right. Thank God there were no casualties. The rolling was over, the whole crowd sat down not able to move from rolling and dance exhaustion.

Lots of drinks of water were consumed and then it was time for the wedding host, Seamus, to invite Coco, the bride and Bill, the groom to have their first real romantic dance together. Bill took Coco's hand and glided her across the floor to the Elvis Presley song, *I can't help falling in love with you*. Georgia sat in a daze looking at the newly married couple with the world at their feet, thinking how lucky they were to be just married.

All of her being at that moment craved a real love, a deep and meaningful love that would last forever, just like the love she'd had with Cameron.

A shadow of someone passed in front of her and took her hand, she didn't look up, she just knew it was Ross's hand holding hers. Were her wishes being granted that quickly? Together they slowly walked onto the dance floor. He very gently pulled her close to him and sang the words of that iconic song into her ear, *Only fools rush in, but I can't help falling in love with you*, in that instant something changed inside Georgia. It was as if they were the only couple dancing on that dance floor, for that moment her world stood still. She knew she had found, once again in Ross, something very special and precious. That dance sequence turned out to be the icing on the cake. It was a humongous success, the best few minutes of the night. Just dancing, moving to the music, being at one with Ross, with absolutely no guilty feelings, just a feeling of love and pure peace in her soul.

Daniel and the Dudes finished right on time. The Celtic band and the Irish dancers had just arrived from the St. Patrick's Day Parade in the town. They brought along with them a couple of extra performers, American cheerleaders and a very loud brass band, including three drummers with very impressive large, loud drums that could be heard before they even made their grand entrance to the big marquee. The band played as they entered the marquee and the cheerleaders cheered and waved their batons as they twirled around all the way along through the marquee. Oh what a hooley this was turning out to be.

All the excitement and nostalgia of the St Patrick's Day parade seemed to sprinkle on the guests at the wedding, as the band and cheerleaders walked across the marquee and up onto the stage.

Now that the cheerleaders were on solid ground it was safe for them to perform their fabulous routine.

The Ceili band struck up, the Irish dancers began to dance a reel around the stage. Now it was official, this wedding had turned into one big hooley. Even though a lot of the guests had never gone to Irish dancing classes and didn't know how to dance like an Irish dancer, the night was saved by everyone around the town who had come to help with the country wedding and of course, Seamus, the Seanachai. Seamus with the help of his microphone encouraged everyone to dance three steps to the right and three steps to the left, then holding hands and standing in twos facing each other dance in one, two, three, the other foot and back. This night had turned out to be beyond their expectations.

No one was drunk now, they had sobered up as they danced around like Jackasses. There was nothing left to do but suigh sios (sit down) and rest. The fish and chips from the van had put the final touch of magic to the night and helped to sober everyone up.

There was only one surprise left as they sat eating their fish and chips with plastic knives and forks. The surprise was for Bill's lovely mum Kathleen. The Celtic band slowed things down, the violin player began to play the music and Bill began to sing the words *I'll take you home again Kathleen.* Oh what a song, what meaning and what truth, you could hear a pin drop and the sobs of Bill's mum and dad. She and her husband had certainly been taken home again back to their grass roots, back to the town they knew so well, for such a momentous occasion.

The good thing about all this apart from the fabulous day, brilliant weather, happy people, great food, lots of *Ceol agus Craic*, every moment had been filmed and now was being shown. The camera had taken beautiful shots of Bill singing that song with a pool of tears in his eyes, the camera had panned over to his mum and dad, who had tears running down their cheeks. Today, tonight, was a win-win situation, everyone would go away with something, even the cheerleaders might meet some Irish men and settle in Ireland, and as for those drummers they could join the Artane Boys Band and come up to slick city, Dublin. Just what the Irish like, they only understand winning, they hate losing. This whole day and night was a win-win situation, 'Oh what a day and night'… 'Go hana mhaith'.

CHAPTER 88

Ross and Georgia

The night was over, in fact a new day had almost dawned as Georgia and Ross calmly made their way to Ross's room, a nice bright room overlooking Roisin and Tomàs's garden. Georgia felt a little bit guilty or maybe it was ashamed of almost creeping into someone else's room, even if it was her ex-husband's room. It brought back memories of her love in the cloisters with Cameron. They crept in, closed the door behind them, it made a loud noise… memories. Ross hurriedly removed Georgia's clothes one by one… memories. She was a little reluctant but she wasn't showing it. should she do what her body was telling her to do, pull that shirt off him, even if he lost a few buttons on the way. Fuck it, she thought, in for a penny, in for a pound. There she was acting like a sex starved beast. Well maybe she was, that was the truth.

She had flashes of Cameron before her eyes. Georgia didn't need flashes of Cameron before her eyes when her body was in this heightened state of ecstasy. Those flashes weren't there to make her feel bad about her feelings, he was there to tell her everything was alright. In her mind she could hear him say, calm down Georgia, you're not in the right place yet but life has to go on, feelings like these have to be felt. We'll meet again someday and until then I couldn't think of any better hands you could be in than Ross's. Of course, all these thoughts Georgia was thinking were all of her thoughts they had to be. He's not in my brain telling me these things, I am alone, I need to retrace my steps back to my happy time. In her mind she said to Cameron, I've loved you, I love you forever but please help me to move on, I'm finding it so hard. In that moment her mind felt clear, she knew he was there, somewhere very close. For the first time since he evaporated from her life, she gave herself completely to the way she was feeling and made love with Ross. It was a surreal time, after the heated bodies, came the calm as they slept peacefully, quietly, in a calm state of mind, soundly, until 9am, then up. It seemed like Ross had never been out of her life when he gave her that big warm hug and kiss like he often did when they were Mr and Mrs. She felt that he felt something had changed for him too, he knew she was all his again.

At the breakfast table there were no questions asked, no one made any reference to the two of them spending the night together or that passionate dance that almost burnt up the dance floor. God bless you Seamus and your gift of the thirty minutes romantic dance sequence.

'Can I say a little thank you to everyone' said Georgia 'for plotting behind my back and inviting Ross, my ex-husband to Coco's wedding. I know this was a collaborative decision between all my friends and Bill, but it was a great decision because it's funny really, when I look back, I felt so alone even when I was surrounded by all of you. I missed everything about my past life, Cameron and Ross.

When I saw Ross walking into the church, my spirit just soared. I'm so happy that we can be friends again and here and now I'd like to make a little declaration and say I never fell out of love with you, Ross and I never will. Thanks for the invitation, you have made me understand myself more, in other words I have answered a lot of my own questions to me, while I've been here. I've decided I want a new life now and I pray, with the magic of the wedding falling like stardust all over the guests, in some way it will benefit me.'

Georgia wondered just how many guests were struck by the magic on the wedding dance floor. She glanced at Ross, he looked back at her, he had a secret smile on his face, again no one mentioned Ross or Georgia dancing together, everyone just spoke of the amazing time they had had at a wedding that surpassed all other weddings in this lovely countryside and left Ross and Georgia alone to dream. Coco concluded:

'Bill was completely right to have had our wedding down here, in this lovely tranquil countryside. My friends, myself and Bill were completely right to invite Ross to the wedding. It made our whole little group complete. You're great company, Ross.'

'Thank you.' said Ross 'Can I say a few words. Well girls, Bill and Tomas, I have to tell you my little secret, I used to pray every night for an invitation to your wedding. I wanted to spend time with you all but mostly I wanted to get to know Georgia and Juliet again. The invitation was a surprise but a must have. So thank you again for everything.'

Then, Coco said she couldn't have asked for a better wedding, or better friends to stand by her through everything or better hosts than Roisin and Tomàs. She thanked them for allowing her new husband and herself to have their dream wedding on their lovely land beside their magical country farmhouse.

Bill also thanked them for allowing his new wife and himself and their friends and Nellie and Juliet to take over their beautiful country farmhouse and also for their wedding reception extravaganza on their grounds, in that fantastic marquee. Bill admitted he had worried a little if his decision was the right one. He said he knew he had been very cheeky to expect everyone to go along with him. He could now say, he was so relieved it turned out to be such an amazing success, not just for him, but for his mum, his dad, his new bride Coco, all his friends and Nellie who did wonders minding Juliet and keeping everyone happy.

Juliet, the little flower girl, loved playing with all the farm animals, she had learned a lot about chickens and their eggs. She was mesmerized when she saw boiled eggs on the farmhouse table ready to be eaten and couldn't understand. How could the little girl understand eggs could be boiled and you could eat them?

Then Bill's dad, a quiet man, said:

'I'd like to say, we've been the ones who have been given all the attention for the last few days. We have been fed and watered by Roisin and Tomàs and we have been entertained by all of you girls, Coco our beautiful new daughter in law, Georgia, Heidi and Tanya, Nellie and last but not least, our favourite little girl who has been a pleasure to get to know, beautiful Juliet. Now I think it's time to turn our attention to Roisin and Tomàs. We're not putting the spotlight on you, but we would like you to say a little something, if you would like to.'

Tomàs seemed delighted to have this opportunity to say a few words and share a little bit of their experience regarding Coco and Bill's wedding.

'I must say folks when we were asked to host this wonderful wedding reception, to say the least we were both scared. Firstly we didn't know if our neighbours would approve of the influx of Dublin Jackeens and Americanos invading our quiet countryside. To our relief, after we had all of the neighbours up to our farmhouse and treated them to sandwiches and a couple of drinks and explained the whole goings on to them, instead of being against the wedding reception in our farmhouse and grounds, our neighbours were very supportive. They were all here for us and for all of you, to do whatever was needed to make the big wedding hooley the huge success it turned out to be. So later on this evening when all of you have left for home, we're having a night for all those lovely people. We are inviting all of our neighbours to the local pub.'

Bill jumped in there:

'I'll buy the beer in your local pub. I will pay for all of that. In fact, I will sort it out with the proprietor of the pub before we leave. They might even make some sandwiches for you. This is our way of saying a big thank you to all of your neighbours and yourselves.'

Tomàs said 'A big thank you to you from all our neighbours for your generous offer. We'll all have a great time tonight. Now all that's left for me to do is give you my blessing from our happy home. We pray you have a very happy life together and when you're old and grey, you'll remember our country farmhouse and your wedding day in Westport. Now I'm going to pass you on to Roisin, my quiet wife, who gave up the good life in Dublin to join me in this neck of the woods.'

Roisin stood up:

'I'll tell you what, everyone, you brought Dublin and America down to our neck of the woods, it was more than amazing and those American cheerleaders showed me a new way to live. One day I will wear an Irish version of a cheerleader's costume, I'll have to lose some weight first, I will just positively amaze you. Now on a serious note, I do have one thing I'd like to share with you, this will be the first time my American friends will hear of this, it's a new venture for me.'

She looked at Tomàs, he looked bewildered. 'To be honest, Tomàs has been too busy on the farm to notice the goings on inside the farmhouse. Well, Tomàs, I've been gathering up all my mother's, my grandmother's and her mother's recipes from days gone by. They are wonderful old Irish recipes, I've tried them, they do work, you're the living proof Thomas McDermot. Sure you've been congratulating me all year on the food I presented to you. You said my homemade soups, dinners, desserts and cakes were the best and the tastiest you've ever had.'

'Yes, Roisin I did say that and I meant every word I said. Every time we ate food I left the table licking my lips.'

Roisin continued 'Each and every Irish dinner extravaganza for the past year was only made possible by working from the old recipes.'

Tomàs gave a little clap and cheer for Roisin and her wonderful cooking.

'My wish' said Roisin 'is to self-publish my recipe book. I have this feeling I would like to have it in two sections, like an A and a B, one half of the book my old recipes and the other half maybe American Irish recipes. As a matter of interest, Kathleen, do you have any old recipes from way back in the day from Ireland, that we could incorporate with the American recipes you used for your tasty dishes when you emigrated?'

Roisin sat back down. Everyone at the breakfast table turned their attention to the lovely Kathleen to listen to what she had to say.

'As a matter of fact,' said Kathleen 'do you know, Roisin, I have hard-backed books packed with my Irish Grandmother's recipes and another one Dermot's mother insisted we take with us when we departed Ireland. To tell you the truth I just knew she was afraid her favourite son would starve if she didn't give us that recipe book with her mother's recipes inside.

You're not going to believe what I'm going to tell you now, but every word is true. When I moved into the house we have lived in since the day we emigrated from Ireland, the first place

I started to explore was the attic. You see, I have a thing about attics, you know spiders in attics, bodies in bags in attics and so that was my first port of call. We were so lucky because our attic was magical, full of beautiful old rolls of wallpaper, amazing old ceramic tiles and books full of stories and other books full of old American recipes, handwritten, if you don't mind, by the previous owners, and their ancestors. Of course, me being Irish and a hoarder, I think all of that goes together, I have kept everything.

When we extended the house I used some of the patterns from the old wallpaper, I had them copied and printed and now they hang on the walls of our home. Somehow incorporating the old and the new brought real life into our lives. The wallpaper is here and there on the walls throughout the house. I can't wait to entertain all of you in our happy home if you come to stay. When we return home I will gather everything up, then we can start working together on the recipes and the book. I'm so excited Roisin, I'll give you a call when I have more information and know if it's possible to get the impossible made possible and have them published.'

These two women had just found a new, amazing, exciting adventure to look forward to, at a time when Kathleen couldn't help but feel a little happy and a little sad inside. Sad because herself and Dermot were going back to America and leaving her son Bill and Ireland behind them again and the thought of leaving was opening up old wounds in Kathleen's heart. She was happy Bill had met an Irish colleen, the love of his life and that the wish she had wished for Bill for years and years had come true and because of that, her life was changing too. Now she had a new exciting future of her own to look forward to, recipe books to be published with the help of Bill, front covers to be designed, lots of excitement ahead and a reason to dress up and look even more glamorous than she already was.

The journey back to Dublin was a different journey than the one they had on the way down when they shared their time with the new bride and groom to be. They did have the same small comfortable coach, with one new passenger, Ross, who seemed to be enjoying himself with his two favourite people, Georgia and Juliet. Georgia was even happier to have Ross sitting beside her.

Bill, Coco and his mum and dad had just started their journey to Galway by train because that was the best way to travel, to take in all the beautiful scenery. Bill and Coco's honeymoon would consist of lovely family hotels, walks by the beach, the boat to the Aran Islands, staying over on Inis Mòr and a night or two in Galway. Then back to the big smoke where they would catch up with their bridesmaids and tell their stories before they returned to work and normal life.

CHAPTER 89

Roisin's cookery book

With all the excitement of trying to settle back into a routine, Roisin and Kathleen's book, it seemed, was left as they say, up in the air but how wrong would you be to think that. In the background, Roisin McDermott, Bill and his mum had been working like little beavers on publishing the cookery book in Ireland and then of course, the big thing, seeing if the Irish publishers could also have it published in America. Now, as we know Americans love the Irish and they love the idea of the stews, bacon and cabbage, potato cakes, fried bread, black and white pudding, gorgeous Irish pork sausages and gur cake.

The decision had been made to include in the book actual pictures taken at the wedding, the big pots of stew and the lanterns and candles surrounding the gorgeous greenery. Sure, what American wouldn't love the real thing? Each recipe would begin with the story of the dish and what part of Ireland it originated in. All the illustrations would be mouth-watering. The decision had been made that if they were lucky enough to have the book published, all three would travel around the country to publicise this magnificent book. The cover would be a beautiful shade of emerald green with a very trendy leprechaun sitting on a tuft of grass in the right hand corner, with a small plate on his lap and on it a nice chunky slice of apple tart and fresh cream. In the middle of the cover, would sit a big skillet with stew inside and on the front of the pot, compiled and written by Roisin and Kathleen. The cookery book would be called, 'Granny's Recipes from the Emerald Isle and the

USA'. The first part of the deal was almost done, a really good publishing house had taken on the book. The next part, having it published in America, had almost come to pass.

CHAPTER 90

Bill's mum

So there she was Coco, sitting by the big warm fire enjoying her all-alone time. For the next two weeks Bill was working away. Every time he had a minute to spare he was on the phone asking her was she all right. If she needed anything all she had to do was ask one of his friends and they would be up to help her straight away but the truth was Coco enjoyed her alone time. After all she'd been alone for quite a long time doing her own thing, enjoying flitting in and out after work to cafes and evenings out. The last thing she wanted to do was ring one of Bill's friends to come up and talk to her.

The phone rang, Bill's mum Kathleen:

'Hello Coco how are you. What's been happening over there in Ireland?'

'Well let me start at the very beginning by saying, I love doing my own thing, and you know your son Bill, he likes doing his own thing and then we do our thing. Our thing is the most exciting. Do you know Kathleen since we last spoke to you we've travelled around Ireland a lot.'

'Tell me more' said Kathleen.

'Well, as you know your Bill is so exuberant, he just loves doing exciting things, so what we have done is stick a map of Ireland up on the wall, he sticks pins in the places he wants to go to next. Places I hardly know the names of and to tell you the truth I feel so ashamed, considering I was born and bred in Ireland and I haven't been to half the places yet. Bill says this is my opportunity to get to know more about my very own country and I agree, so every weekend when we're free, we visit a certain part of Ireland and tour around.

Don't laugh, Kathleen, you won't believe it when I tell you we're travelling in a camper van that's not up to my usual standard. There's no en-suite so I'm going kicking and screaming. It got so bad that we've had to make a pact. I said, Bill have you heard the saying I'll show you mine if you show me yours. Your son assured me he understood what that saying meant.'

Kathleen laughed and Coco continued and said:

'Kathleen, your Bill is showing me all the beautiful spots around Ireland, I'm just accompanying him. It's like we're playing a game of blind man's bluff because I haven't got a clue where I'm being taken but it's great fun, Kathleen. That leads to the second part of what I'm hoping to do in the future. I told Bill in no uncertain terms, now it's his turn to show me his, all the places in America that I want to see. I can't wait for him to make all my dreams come true. You know your son, Kathleen, he always gets what he wants and what he wants is to see as much of the west of Ireland as possible. He has promised me if I accompany him to the spots in Ireland that really make his heart sing he will take me to see the Grand Canyon, Los Vegas and New York.'

'That's great news.' said Kathleen 'Would it be ok with you if Dermot and I accompany you to some of the places you've just mentioned. I really want to get to know you as much as I can now that you're my daughter-in-law.'

'Absolutely, we'd love your company and after all we want to make memories that include yourself and Dermot.'

Kathleen was so pleased with everything she'd just heard. The thoughts of sharing a week or two with her son and her new daughter-in-law made her spirits soar.

CHAPTER 91

Bill's turn to shine

Now it was his turn to complete his side of the bargain and show Coco his part of the world. He had booked everything with the help of his mum and dad. Now, all he had to do was tell Coco. He didn't have to have a special time, no big meals, no introductions, just breakfast. Bill placed the airline tickets in the middle of the table. It was just an ordinary morning, Coco was busy making two cups of coffee. Over to the table she went and put the two cups down, then she noticed the airline tickets sitting right there in front of her eyes.

'Oh My God, Bill, is this what I think it is? Tickets for our flights to America?' She couldn't take it in. 'When are we going?'

'The flights will coincide with our first wedding anniversary, three months from now, but sit down there Coco, I want to tell you some other good news. Roisin and Kathleen are close to having their cookery book published in America. 'Granny's Recipes from the Emerald Isle and the USA' will go on sale on the first of August.

Our first port of call will be to New York. We will have two nights there. It's all arranged, we don't have to do anything, just turn up.'

Coco was so happy, she had waited so long to hear those words. She was exhausted accompanying Bill all around Ireland and he had promised to take her to the one place she always wanted to go and see, The Grand Canyon. In Bill's style, he had kept his promise and here was the evidence. Coco had a few very special things to look forward to, especially their second wedding in the Grand Canyon but also a trip to the theatre to see one of the big shows and then, of course, the cookery book. She felt so happy to have something great to look forward to as even now all thoughts of their Irish wedding were just happy memories and Coco always needed something to look forward to. Coco wasn't too happy when she thought about her friends not sharing this fantastic trip with her. She would even take a loan from the Credit Union to make sure they were there but felt mean because she knew Bill wanted to make her happy and would insist on paying their fares.

Coco had never discussed money with Bill. The subject just never came up, she had her own money and he had his, so they never discussed which way things would work out once they got married. That subject had to be broached sooner rather than later. Now they were in rented accommodation paid for by the American Embassy but Coco wanted and needed her own house with a little back garden and a big kitchen. She would wait until after her second wedding or maybe in Bill's own inimitable style he would discuss money and leave her not blushing and red faced from embarrassment. It's funny how you can just go from day to day, doing the same thing as you always did, looking after yourself. Now considering having children, it was time to turn everything around, to discuss the undiscussable. The real problem was they were so in love they couldn't see past the bedroom but one day soon they would have to discuss the boring realities of life. Coco would have to just settle for and be happy with having her second wedding in the spectacular Grand Canyon without her three friends.

Everything was arranged for their second wedding. They would have two nights with Bill's parents in New York followed by one day and night in Los Vegas, in a very nice hotel that Bill had picked and the last two nights Bill had left flexible to go to the theatre, relax, walk around, embrace the atmosphere and feel the spirit of New York. Of course, Coco wanted to share all her news with her friends. She rang all three. With each and every phone call she was getting more and more excited, all the little things they would say–

'Oh My Goodness' said Tanya 'I always wanted to see the Grand Canyon, maybe someday all four of us could go, it would be such an exciting trip.'

Heidi – 'Oh My God I want to go to New York and take a ride in a horse and carriage in Central Park. Someday Coco, we'll have to be in New York together, that will make my dream come true.'

Georgia 'Oh! I always thought we'd go together, all of us sharing that experience. My dream is to walk into Macey's and be treated like a queen in that huge big store and of course, head on into Tiffany's and buy the most beautiful ring, having been pampered by all the magnificent staff. Oh and Coco, I want to have breakfast at Tiffany's. You should book it, but book it early.'

Coco was on a high as she put her phone down after speaking with her three friends. Oh! How she'd love to have them there with her to share those experiences and have more photographs and more memories to add to their already huge collection. She was very excited about the pending trip and of course, to spend that time with Bill and his parents would be just magic but not being able to share it with her three friends from kindergarten, sort of dampened her mood. She would have to go there, take all those photographs, then come back home and once again share a meal with them and the spreading of the photographs on the table, in the Trocadero, just like Georgia did when she met Cameron for the first time. That could seem very insensitive, when the time came Coco would discuss with Georgia and whatever she wanted she would do.

CHAPTER 92

New York, New York,
so good they named it twice

The first two days of the trip were just remarkable. Bill's mum and dad did everything they could to make it memorable for Coco and Bill. They had lovely meals, especially one in a restaurant that moved around really, really slowly. In that restaurant perched on top of a huge high building, they ordered steaks, chips, some onions and no starter. Oh my God, that steak was the nicest steak Coco and Bill had ever tasted. When the four steaks arrived at the table Coco just couldn't believe her eyes, every steak she'd had in Dublin, up to this point, was succulent and lovely but quite small. In fairness they were big enough for Coco but these steaks in New York, in this fabulous restaurant were bloody huge. They sizzled, they were thick and mouth-watering. Coco took one look at them and realised this was more than she could eat. Bill was a big guy, so she persuaded him to cut away half of her steak and take it all for himself as he needed a good feed. Now looking at her plate, it looked a lot better.

The place went silent as everyone concentrated on eating. The chips were home cooked and delicious, the onions were soft and juicy. The meal came with extra salad and of course, the dessert was gorgeous, hot chocolate pudding with sauce poured over. Coco wanted to wait until everything collapsed and the sauce covered the plate but she couldn't, she just delved into that dessert. It was everywhere on her face, she just couldn't stop eating it until the last morsel was gone. Then for the tea, it wasn't as good as in Dublin. Coco came to the conclusion they weren't boiling the water properly, she wanted to go into the kitchen and give them an Irish demonstration. All in all it was a really good night, very enjoyable. Coco was thrilled to bits that she got on so well with Bill's mum and dad. She felt included in everything.

They were both very tired, the jet lag had hit and as they were only starting the holiday, they both decided to have an early night. So back they went to Bill's mum and dad's house. It was one of those houses that looked like a photograph, all American with white shutters on the windows, a picket fence and a garden with little beds of flowers all around. Some of the neighbours who'd known Bill as a child, came in to see him. Coco was thinking this must have been a lovely place to grow up in, everyone seemed so friendly.

Bill's dad poured beer into big tankards for himself and his son and for Coco and Kathleen, two glasses of bubbly champagne. The neighbours enjoyed a variety of drinks. As the night went on, gradually the neighbours left in little groups and the evening came to an end naturally.

It was time for Coco and Bill to take their leave and make their way to Bill's old bedroom. As they walked up the stairs they chatted about the amazing day they'd had, Coco told Bill how great it was to be welcomed by his family. They hit the sheets and as if a magic wand had waved they fell into a deep sleep dreaming of the plans they had for the day to come.

The sun shone into the bedroom, Bill's first words were,

'This is what I miss, my bedroom where the sun woke me up every morning. I never needed an alarm clock. Once the sun hit my face I was wide awake and ready for another day.'

Showered, blow drying sorted and dressed comfortably for the day, the two of them couldn't get downstairs quick enough to have breakfast with Kathleen and Dermot. The smiles on Kathleen and Dermot's faces showed that they were equally as happy to get their arms around Bill and Coco again. Big breakfasts were the thing in America and this breakfast was no exception. It was already set out, thick waffles with honey on the side, all kinds of cereal and a big fry, with all the extras, mushrooms, beans and some fresh buns. Lots of orange juice and tea. It was very well presented but there was an awful lot there for four people.

How wrong could they have been if they thought there were only four people for breakfast, there was Bill's Auntie Mary, Uncle Joe and all their children and of course, there were some of Kathleen's relatives who had emigrated a number of years before. There was Maeve, Padraig and all their children and thrown into the mix a few of Bill's friends and neighbours from around the area. This gathering didn't happen by coincidence, this gathering had been well organised weeks ahead, it was a marvellous surprise. His relations were so nice and his friends were even nicer. Everyone there had a little bit of Irish in them. They just loved speaking to Coco with her Irish accent and they said she looked Irish, whatever that is. They asked questions, smiled at the answers, they were more interested in listening to Coco's accent than the answer to the questions. Coco felt blessed to be part of such a lovely family.

CHAPTER 93

Shopping in New York

Coco and Bill had thought they might get to the centre of New York by eleven o'clock but this clearly wasn't going to happen, in fact it was two o'clock when they arrived at Tiffany's. Coco spent quite a while looking in the window and taking it all in, then they were inside walking from counter to counter admiring all the magnificent jewellery. Of course, Coco guessed Bill was going to buy her something but he never thought Coco was going to buy him something. Just a small piece of jewellery, a token and a memory they'd always have of their Grand Canyon wedding.

Coco decided on a brooch with little diamonds and rubies, designed almost like a flower. She just had to have that. Bill picked a clip for his tie, it also had little red rubies and a few diamonds, quite small but very nice. Then the presents were boxed up and each of them got a Tiffany's bag, placed into a bigger bag to make them easier to carry. Oh My God, one of my daydreams has just been realised I've just been to Tiffany's, the happy couple felt elated. By now they were quite peckish so they slipped into a café for tea, two very large drinks of water, a croissant and a rest. New York can be very tiring. There was a small amount of water left in Coco's glass, so she poured it out onto a napkin and dabbed her face to freshen up. Then off to the ladies room to apply some makeup and be ready for Maceys.

Oh what a huge store Maceys was, it even had a bargain basement. Coco bought all her presents to take home down there. Thank God Bill carried the bags. The only bag she wanted to carry was the large bag with that unique colour that everyone would know was from Tiffany's, with the two smaller bags inside. The selection of beauty products was out of this world, Coco was blown away. She reckoned she could have the skin of a ten year old if she invested in some of those products and Bill just loved the Creed perfume. Guess what! They treated themselves to those extravagant presents. Coco's one was a Chanel cream for her delicate skin and his was Creed perfume. Talk about pampering themselves! That was the pampering part over and as they were very tired, they slipped into one of the restaurants in Maceys and had early dinner.

For the next surprise, Georgia was taken to the theatre to see *Gypsy*. Oh what a show! What performances! Bill bought and presented her with the programme, that she would cherish forever and once back home it would take its rightful place with all the memorabilia from their wedding. Now it was almost ten thirty so the happy pair hailed a taxi, in real American style, a lovely big yellow taxi (you have to get into a yellow taxi, when in America, it just has to be done) and you also have to sing that Joni Mitchell song Yellow Taxi out loud while the taxi man drives his big yellow taxi to your destination. When they arrived home, Coco could hear the door of the taxi closing and she kept repeating the words of the song, as Bill turned the key in the hall door. In true Irish style she waved at the taxi man and blew him a kiss. He drove away happy. Coco ran in to catch up with Bill.

The house was very quiet, Bill's mum and dad had already gone to bed. In one corner of the hall there were two cases, Kathleen and Dermot's cases all packed for the trip, first stopping in Las Vegas at the Venetian Hotel. She guessed all the relations had stayed on for hours after they left to go to New York. Bill's parents must have been exhausted. They needed a lot of rest because tomorrow the four of them were heading off to the Grand Canyon and the second wedding. They very quietly made tea and some toast and headed up the stairs. As usual, back into Bill's old bedroom, where again the magic fairy with that amazing wand had them sleeping like Snow White in minutes.

CHAPTER 94

The Grand Canyon

Breakfast the next morning was a smaller affair. Today there were no waffles, no friends, no neighbours, just a nice fry up to give them energy for a few hours, lots of nice brown bread and piping hot tea.

The trip to the airport went without a hitch, the flight itself was a dream, the journey to the Venetian Hotel was exciting looking at the stretch limos in all colours, lighting the way. All Coco was short of doing was sticking her head out of the limo's window to make sure she didn't miss a moment of what was taking place. Bill's mum was almost as excited as Coco on her first trip to Vegas. This was really another world and they had fallen head over heels in love with mysterious and magical Las Vegas.

Mesmerised, was the only word to describe Coco, her expression said it all, as she gazed at the slot machines, more slot machines than she ever saw in her whole life. She had heard that when people go to Vegas they mostly go to try their hand at winning huge amounts on the slot machines but Coco was completely oblivious to that part of it, it was not on her radar, however now that she was there she would dip her finger in the gambling, casino world and maybe go home a millionaire. Pray to Christ that she doesn't get addicted to the machines. They were escorted to the reception area on a different floor, by a lovely young Irish man and of course, the first thing you say is 'you're from Dublin aren't you? What part?' He answered 'Malahide'. Coco thought, isn't it funny how we put everyone into little boxes, all of a sudden she was imagining the outdoor life he would have had by the sea in Malahide. It's no wonder he looked so healthy.

The hotel was opulent and welcoming with lovely friendly staff. Bill ordered some drinks for his tired mum, dad and Coco, while he went to reception to register the little party, armed with the four passports. The hotel laid on a really nice meal for the little group. They were happy to sit down and enjoy every morsel. Then it was time to get dressed for the trip and the wedding at the Grand Canyon. For today's beautiful wedding Coco would wear a ballet length, dusty pink dress, with a cross over top and a skater skirt. All around the end of the skirt were added pieces of chiffon in pale pink encrusted with sequins. Around her shoulders she wore a short furry jacket and on her hair she wore a flower. Today her piece of new would be the beautiful brooch Bill bought for her in Tiffany's. The necklace she wore, was something old, the borrowed jacket and the blue was a garter she was wearing. Bill dressed in a simple, grey but beautifully tailored suit, with a dusty pink tie and his lovely new tie pin. Bill's mum and dad dressed so lovely. His mum was a lovely height and she looked so radiant in turquoise, a choker necklace with diamonds all the way around and a cream, small hat with a flower and a net over her eyes. She wore cream shoes and a cream bag. His dad looked so pristine with his thick silvery grey hair, a navy blue pinstripe suit, crispy white shirt, cufflinks, a plain navy tie and navy shoes. The party of four were perfect.

Coco could feel the butterflies in her tummy as the four beauties stepped into the chauffeur driven car. She hadn't really felt like that on the day of her wedding in Ireland and it was a bigger affair altogether, but back then she had her three partners in crime to support her. If only they were here now, what a difference it would make. It seemed no time until they were walking out onto the helicopter pad to take the magnificent flight to the Grand Canyon.

As the helicopter left Las Vegas, with five people inside, Bill, Coco, Kathleen and Dermot and of course, the pilot, the music playing through their ear phones was *Viva Las Vegas*. On the way the pilot filled them in on every story to do with the Grand Canyon and everything they could see below. Thank God for ear phones. The view from the helicopter was spectacular. They could see a herd of wild horses below. Coco felt she was observing an old movie as the music of The High Chaparral took over her mind, it was amazing. The party of four all had that same enthusiasm and buzz about them. They swayed to the music as they looked down in amazement at the beauty below. Coco was very nervous, she didn't like flying in a large plane, let alone a helicopter. She held onto her hubby's hand for dear life as the engines roared. Dermot and Kathleen in the back were so happy, they hadn't done this trip before, which added to their excitement. Yes for everyone this was their first time. As the Grand Canyon came into view, the little group were spellbound. The pilot was so nice, he explained everything to them as the helicopter descended down, down, down, down until it landed safely, they had arrived.

'You know exactly how much time you have here in the canyon?' Everyone nodded. 'Please arrive back here on time, there is a tight schedule for each helicopter, landing and leaving. The helicopter will be in this exact place and I will be standing here so you recognise me.'

This is what they had come to see, one of the wonders of the world, The Grand Canyon. The helicopter engines were turned off and the door was opened. They climbed out of the helicopter and walked down the steps. With precision timing Roisin and Tomàs appeared from nowhere. Coco and Bill welcomed and hugged the happy couple who had made their wedding in Westport, Co. Mayo, the happiest wedding in the world. The sun shone right into Coco's face, she could hardly see. People were running towards her but she couldn't make out who they were.

She thought it was a mirage, (after all she was in the desert). No, this was no mirage, as the dust settled she realised they were none other than her three friends Tanya, Heidi and Georgia and following in hot pursuit, surprise! surprise! surprise! her mother. She started to cry tears of joy. When she pulled herself together and looked around she realised the girls looked stunningly beautiful in Chiffon dresses, silver with a cummerbund of dusty pink and dusty pink hairbands. They held tiny bouquets in dusty pink and silver.

Coco screamed with joy when she realised under the coat Roisin was wearing, was the most beautiful chiffon dress exactly the same as the other three bridesmaids, silver chiffon with a cummerbund of dusty pink. To Coco's amazement, Roisin was placing a dusty pink hairband on her head. She was definitely going to be bridesmaid for the day. Tomàs had that sort of Farmer Giles look about him, but the cleaned up version. Out of nowhere another vision appeared and introduced herself as the wedding planner. She took them to where the wedding ceremony would take place.

The cork on the champagne bottle popped, now everyone stood holding a glass of pink champagne oozing with bubbles. For this wedding Coco's mum was a bit more flamboyant, she wore an absolutely gorgeous lilac chiffon dress with a little bolero, a silver flower in her hair and lilac shoes decorated with a silver flower. Their guide insisted on taking a photo of the group together. The only word for it was spectacular.

Coco was so excited, she almost forgot she was there for a reason, her second wedding in the Grand Canyon. She wanted to talk to her friends and ask how this was organised but Tanya insisted:

'Coco relax, there will be time enough afterwards to tell you all our devious stories. We knew we were coming here the same time you knew you were coming here. Bill was amazing, he organised everything for us.'

They looked over at Bill, his face was glowing.

'Well girls you shared the journey with us in Westport and it's only fitting you should share the journey here. It's a pity we couldn't bring the donkey and hang our wedding rings around his neck.' Everyone went 'Awwwww'.

As Coco held her mum close and gave her the best bear hug ever, she said:

'Mum, I never thought you could tell me lies and look me straight in the face while you were telling them.'

'I know Coco, I told you this would be just your honeymoon with an extra ceremony and as far as I was concerned your wedding was in Westport and nothing could surpass that beautiful day. I also said I was happy for you to have your honeymoon without your mammy but, Coco, I was sworn to secrecy because Bill wanted this to be a huge surprise for you.'

Coco just cried, her makeup was running down her face.

'Mum, I can't stop crying, I'm so happy to see you and all the girls.'

'Well,' said Heidi 'we knew this was going to happen, we knew there would be tears in the Canyon, so we came prepared. Come over here to this shady spot and we'll fix your makeup.'

Coco felt like Cinderella just before she walked into the palace. Her makeup was fresh and Heidi had brought along a little hair tongs worked by battery, so now Coco's hair was also beautiful. She was ready with her friends (Bridesmaids) and mum beside her to do it all again.

There was just time for a big romantic kiss from Coco to Bill.

'I'm feeling a bit teary eyed but through my sobs and tears, I want to thank you from the bottom of my heart for bringing everyone I love here today, for our second wedding.'

'Well,' said Bill 'they just had to be here with you today or I would have regretted not taking them to the Grand Canyon, for the rest of my life. This will be the last time we will ever get married, Coco,' said Bill 'so from here on in let's just enjoy this wonderful, magical day.'

The Ceremony was short and sweet like an asses gallop but it was lovely, so intimate, with her friends, her mother, Bill's mother and father and Roisin and Tomàs.

It was almost time to leave the Grand Canyon. Standing on the side-line, the wedding planner waited to take the wedding party back to the helicopter where they were greeted by the pilot, who had the loveliest smile on his face. Then there was a big group hug and as the wedding party walked up the steps to the helicopter, Coco waved to her three friends and her mum Theresa, as they were escorted to their helicopter by the wedding planner. Soon they would be back on terra firma in Las Vegas.

Engines on, you could hear them roar like a lion, then with great speed it took off and glided upwards on the strip, allowing the little group to take in the grandeur of the Grand Canyon. Again, it almost took their breath away. Then the Helicopter was up, soaring to the sky, on its way back to Las Vegas. Coco thought of the song, *Let's go fly a kite and send it soaring, up to the atmosphere, up where the air is clear, let's go fly a kite*. It was a magical little song. What brought it to Coco's mind was when the helicopter began to soar up, and up, she thought of that imaginary kite bobbing all over the sky. As the helicopter descended, the song that was blasted out was of course, *Viva Las Vegas*, a great song for putting everyone in holiday mode.

They landed back in Las Vegas and the friends were reunited. There in all its glory sat the magnificent, pink stretched limousine with blacked out windows and the most handsome chauffeur standing holding the door open. One by one the happy party climbed in and took their seats. The chauffeur, Chuck, introduced himself and explained to them there were bottles of champagne stored at the edge of the seats, for their enjoyment.

'So pop the corks, toast the bride and enjoy, while my limo glides its way to The Bellagio Hotel.'

That champagne was the best ever or was it just the whole idea of going back to Las Vegas and The Bellagio Hotel that added even more bubbles and excitement. Oh what splendour, what opulence, they knew all this before they entered the foyer. Outside they looked up at the water fountains that danced to music, they could feel the spray hitting their faces and they were beyond elated.

'What will the hotel itself be like when we go in? Oh My God!'

They certainly weren't disappointed, it was palatial, huge, fabulous, buzzing, all of these things and more. The girls were curious to see what the ladies room was like, they needed to go there very urgently. Wow!!! They were in awe, the standard of this fabulous lady's room, where they freshened up, re-applied their makeup and really took too long, because it was so nice they didn't want to leave. They had better places to be like the dining room where they would feast on magnificent food.

First impressions of the opulent dining room at the magnificent Bellagio Hotel were, the table was beautifully dressed, the silver was magnificent, the glasses gleaming. No one could decide what to order, there was so much choice on that menu but eventually with a little encouragement from the waiter their choices were made. Bill ordered steak, medium rare, Coco and her mum, Theresa, ordered duck a l'orange, her three friends decided on a fish dish, Roisin and Tomas went for chicken (you'd easily know they lived on a farm) and Bill's parents both ordered lamb. They ordered a vast selection of sides. Everyone just sat there, relaxed and enjoyed a meal fit for a king or queen. Lots of glasses of champagne, lots of little chats about how amazing the Grand Canyon had been and what a different experience it was to come here. Not one of them would have missed it for the world.

The evening rolled on, at about ten o'clock it was time to leave and go back to their hotel, The Venetian. Coco and Bill were really happy with the way the Bellagio had looked after them. Looking around at all the faces, they knew this was something that would be spoken about for many a year. Everyone got back into a white stretch limo.

The little group looked out in awe at the other blacked out stretch limousines on the strip. Georgia was letting her imagination go wild, maybe Britney Spears is in one of those cars. It was the mystery of the dark windows that had her imagining who was behind them. It could be anyone, Tom Cruise, Mat Damon, Arnold Schwarzenegger. Then they were back inside the hotel, Coco didn't waste time gazing at the slot machines with an open mouth, instead they went to their separate rooms to take a little rest for a while before they would meet for a gambling night. Who knows at the end of it all, they might be millionaires.

Now they were back downstairs, this time their dress was a little more casual as they had a serious job to do, win money on the roulette table. First they bought their chips (not the greasy ones) and around they went with the speed of a gazelle, being presented with glasses of bubbly as they shimmied through the crowds. At this point they were getting high on adrenaline and a bit tipsy. A little spin of the roulette wheel, so fast that Georgia almost missed it. To Georgia's surprise she actually won $500, wow, this was looking good. That roulette wheel had spun around so fast, it was mind boggling but thank God Georgia won a few bob, she could treat everyone to champagne. Bill wished they had Irish Guinness.

As the night drifted on, the wedding party were beyond exhausted from the travel and all the excitement and magical moments they packed into such a short space of time. As wonderful as this night had been, one of life's most amazing experiences, the time had come to fall into bed and sleep 'til the cows came home.

CHAPTER 95

Goodbye to Las Vegas

Early breakfast, then packing cases with just enough time left to visit the shops in the Venetian Hotel. A few little trinkets were bought but there was no time left to take a gondola on the make believe canal of Venice. That would have to wait until another time. Then collect cases and into a limo to Vegas airport. Journey to New York... collect cases... limo... Smooth as silk drive to Fitzpatrick's Hotel... deep breaths.

'We're here in New York, where dreams are made' exclaimed Bill.

'New York, New York, so good they named it twice' said Georgia.

'New York, the city that never sleeps' Heidi said.

'The city where my handsome Bill grew up' added Coco.

Tanya said 'Oh My God, look at the height of the buildings. I feel like a dot in the ocean.'

'Roisin, I want to wish you the best of luck with your cookery book, it all starts here' said Coco.

Roisin smiled both with excitement and nerves. Bill patted her on the back and gave her a nice cuddly hug and sang, 'if you can make it here you can make it anywhere.'

It seemed a good idea for Roisin and Tomàs to stay with Kathleen and Dermot, to be together for their big day, visiting the publisher and discussing the future of the cookery book. Bill and Coco gave a real Irish hug to Bill's mum and dad and Roisin and Tomàs.

'We'll only be on the end of a phone, so talk to you later. Best of luck with the publisher.'

Everyone felt this was going to be the relaxing part of their trip but before Georgia could really relax she had one very important phone call to make to her mum, the love of her life. This phone call would be all about Juliet, her little darling who she had to almost prise herself away from before she left Ireland. In one way she was looking forward to the phone call and another part of her was dreading the phone call in case she would get upset. Whether she liked it or not that phone call had to be made.

'Hello Mum, how are you?'

'Hello Georgia, Juliet is fine. It seems to me the only word she knows is Mamma, Mamma, Mamma. I'm having great fun with her and don't kill me but I've taken her for a walk. I was very careful, put on her harness and only gave her so much leeway, but she's getting very strong on her feet and I'm having a whale of a time minding her. I won't want to give her back when you come home. Georgia, just enjoy yourself, be happy, I'm looking after her very well, there's nothing to worry about. Now, put that phone down and go back and join your friends.'

'Love you Mum, see you soon. I'll bring you home a present.'

The line went silent. Georgia thought, next year if I go away without Juliet it'll be much easier. She'll be able to talk to me when I phone.

First food, change of clothes and out into a big yellow taxi. Soon they were in Macey's where the group divided up and went their separate ways, with a promise to meet at the same restaurant that Bill and Coco had been to when they first arrived in New York. That lovely restaurant that moved so slowly around, showing you all the views from up high.

It seemed all of them had bought something new. Georgia was wearing her new outfit, a pink vintage coat with large buttons and underneath a lilac dress. She just couldn't stop talking about the variety of clothes that were in that vintage shop. Tanya had also changed into something new, a pair of five inch high heels, a white dress with a slit up the back and a black belt. Heidi wore something different, a high waisted long, turquoise skirt with buttons all the way down the front and a plain white blouse with a pretty collar. Theresa wore a lovely dress, turquoise, just like the colour of Tiffany's Sign. Yes, everyone at the table looked fresh and gorgeous, it was time for that meal that they badly needed, they were like hungry Horace's.

This was to be an early night. All too tired for the theatre or anything else. Another taxi back to Fitzpatrick's Hotel, everyone tired and not feeling like a lot of chat. Bill and Coco excused themselves and left to have some time together and Theresa, Coco's mum, was so tired she decided to rest in her amazing boudoir. So the three amigos sat downstairs for a little while and discussed the last two days which had been like a whirlwind. When the three amigos were too tired and had nothing left to talk about, they went up to the room, makeup off, and into bed, all in new pyjamas. They chatted for a few minutes, then that glaze came into their eyes, Mr Sandman had arrived, everyone fell asleep, all except Georgia.

Somehow sleep wouldn't come to Georgia, she just lay there thinking back. It seemed to her that looking back was doing her absolutely no good, too much pain, too many memories and she thought of her friends as she gazed over at Heidi and looked at that contented look on her face, as if she hadn't got a care in the world. Tanya had her new boyfriend, hopefully something good would come out of their romance. Then there was Coco and Bill, they had so much to look forward to...

Georgia said to herself, I'm so happy for each and every one of my friends. When I go back to Ireland I'm going to put my heart and soul into my relationship with Ross and make it happen.

They decided not to have breakfast in the hotel but to go straight to Central Park, and grab a pretzel and some tea or coffee or maybe lash out and have a hot chocolate. It would help to build up the atmosphere, sitting down in a New York café. Their horse and carriage trip had been already booked, all they had to do was turn up on time, climb into the carriage and take in even more of the atmosphere of Central Park.

As the horses clippity clopped their way through the park, the group took in the beauty. The sights were something to remember, the day was balmy, a lovely day for the outdoors, their moods were cheery, they didn't want it to end, but end it did. The last port of call had to be Chinatown, the girls all loved Chinese food and this would be a great opportunity to try it in New York City. Into a taxi they piled and were driven straight there. Immediately they were taken into a totally different zone. Chinese lanterns lit their way, swaying to and fro in the light breeze. The colours were so vibrant, red and gold with different types of prints on each one, some with pagodas and some with Chinese letters in black, lovely to look at. Georgia wished she understood what was written on them.

CHAPTER 96

Last night in New York.

Coco had looked forward to this part of the day for so long, she felt so carefree. Bill had excelled himself yet again and booked a table in the loveliest Chinese restaurant that he had frequented regularly before going to live in Ireland. He knew the waiter and asked him to explain the different dishes on the menu. Having listened to his explanations, they ordered a meal for five, it included so many different dishes, all so interesting. Georgia's favourite dish was crispy duck with soya sauce, scallions and pancakes. She loved that crispiness, delicious.

There was a great variety of drinks, Tiger beer, red and white wine, etc. etc. Then for dessert they had apple and pineapple fritters, so warm and comforting. It was time to leave the restaurant and stroll deeper into Chinatown where they purchased lanterns and as a reminder for each of them Bill bought a little stone with their names painted on in Chinese.

Thank God for mobile phones, ring, ring. Roisin's name came up on Coco's phone. She was free to meet for a light snack later, before the theatre. The little group couldn't wait to meet her and find out all the goss. Footsore but happy they hailed a big yellow taxi and headed down to Broadway to be close to the theatre for the performance of *Miss Saigon*. Georgia had already seen it in London but really wanted to see it again in New York. They went into a nice small restaurant and lucky for all of them there was a table free. Before you could say cock robin, exactly what they had ordered sat on the table right in front of them. This restaurant wasted absolutely no time, it was a quick turnover which was really necessary if you had theatre tickets for a Broadway show.

They didn't have to ask Roisin or Bill's Mum what happened at the publishers office, the smile on their faces told the story.

'You lot keep on eating, I'm too excited to eat. I'll just nibble along with you. Bill I want to say thank you to your mum and dad, Kathleen and Dermot.'

Roisin looked over at Bill's mum and continued, 'Honestly Kathleen and Dermot if you hadn't shown us the way and taken Tomàs and myself to the publisher's offices we wouldn't have been so calm when we got there. New York is like a jungle to us after living so long in Westport. Thank you from the bottom of our hearts.'

Roisin continued, 'the publishers loved the little touch of Americana to the book. Tracey at the publisher's office explained that it was a unanimous decision at the office meeting that the two sides of the book should be there, the view from the Irish American perspective and from the Westport, Ireland perspective.'

Bill came in with 'Mum I can't believe you're going to have your recipes published.'

'You know Bill it's been a secret ambition of mine to have something published and since cooking is my passion, I'm thrilled skinny. That was the best I could hope for.'

Then Roisin said, 'now to cut a long story short, our cookery book will be on sale all over America. We had a great time, they treated us like royalty. When we got there our tummies were rumbling and I thought everyone could hear them. We needn't have worried, they had lovely sandwiches for us, biscuits and tea or coffee. Tracey, the girl who was looking after us, had our book in front of her. She'd read the cookery book from cover to cover, starting with our stories to see how they blended together. Her words were, 'I just wanted to get the flavour of your lives'. She asked me was she pronouncing my name properly, I nodded my head, yes. She was delighted that all the measures were simple and easy to understand and not having a weighing scale wasn't a problem. She had followed our recipes to the letter and each one had turned out really well. She said her colleagues also tried out some of our recipes and the verdict was, 'this is what the Americans need right now to brighten them up. An Irish lady and an Irish emigrant with a story and an amazing cookery book, easy to understand, simple to follow and the recipes themselves delicious'.

Tracey showed us a rough idea for the cover of our book and said we could decide on any changes we wanted. My story, short and concise, will be at the beginning of the book. She said Americans will be interested in a story coming from my heart as many Americans are direct descendants of Irish immigrants. Their mothers and fathers left Ireland many, many years ago to escape the potato famine and lots of them have obtained Irish passports.

Kathleen's story will be the second part of the book, the story of an Irish immigrant coming to America. She said Irish Americans will love Kathleen's story and be interested in Kathleen's background. There will be photographs of rural Ireland and especially Westport included. She said the book is remarkable with the mixture of both our lives and our recipes. She said she really loved trying out all the recipes. I wish someone had taken a photograph of our faces at that moment as I know my mouth was open like a Malahide cod.' said Roisin. 'How about your face Kathleen at that moment?'

'Mesmerised is the only word for it. I couldn't believe what I was hearing. If I'm being really honest with you all, I had begun to think my life was just going to be mundane from here on out with Bill gone and my working life behind me. All I can do is thank God for this miracle.'

Roisin stood up at the table, with her hands in the air and said,

'For our finale, Tracey's words were, Ladies your book is going to be a great success.'

'Since everybody is starting to stand up at the table and say a few words, I think I should add to the mix' said Coco. 'Roisin, when I look back on you taking that big step in your life and going to live in Westport, all because you had met the love of your life, I actually wondered if it was the right move for you. I'm sure you wondered that yourself, but now there's no doubt in my mind and I'm sure there's no doubt in your mind, that going down to Westport was what was meant to be. You joined the ICA and you began to mix with the farmers' wives and blended some of the recipes they had with some of the recipes your grandmother had. Not only did you do a great job of blending recipes but you made a great job of our wedding day on your country farmland, in your country house and we'll never forget it. By the way, Tomàs and Roisin, would you mind, if for our second anniversary we visited your farm again?'

'Well,' said Roisin 'it would be our honour to have you there. We could be celebrating two things by then.'

Coco and Bill looked up at Roisin in shock, what was she going to say?

'Your Wedding Anniversary and our second recipe book.'

Bill and Coco took a sigh of relief and relaxed.

The food vanished from the plates with the speed of a tornado. Tanya, Georgia and Heidi were tired and happy to just sit there and listen. Time was marching on and it was now time to make their way to the theatre. Bill insisted on paying for their snack as this was the last night with his mum and dad and his way of thanking the girls for taking time out of their busy lives to support himself and Coco. Bill put his arm around his mum as they walked out of the restaurant and straight into another yellow taxi. It was becoming quite the norm, now they weren't amazed at the big yellow taxis anymore. Isn't it funny how your body and mind adjust to new situations?

Miss Saigon didn't disappoint. From the moment the curtain went up to the moment the curtain came down, everyone in the theatre, including them, was completely and utterly spellbound. Show over, out of the theatre and onto the Boulevard of Dreams, they just had to walk it. Broadway was amazing by night, the lights gleamed and glistened. Georgia felt New York was taking her breath away. The words from Alisha Keys' song New York *'Concrete jungle where dreams are made of, there's nothing you can't do, now you're in New York.'* Those words said it all… what a place! It's quite funny, Georgia thought to herself, usually I feel small no matter where I go but here where there are so many skyscrapers, I've come to the conclusion that everybody is small in New York. They jumped into another big yellow taxi and headed straight to Fitzpatrick's Hotel. Bill had decided to bring his mum and dad back to the hotel as this would be his last night to see them for some time. He had already organised it with Coco but he did explain to the rest:

'If you don't mind girls, I'm going to spend a little time with my mum and dad. I just want to sit down and be Kathleen and Dermot's son with no distractions.'

Roisin and Tomàs decided they would go to the bar in the hotel and have a few drinks, it was their last night and they had a few things they wanted to talk about. As the girls were sharing a room, Coco and her mum went along with them to have their girlie chat… Everyone was happy.

CHAPTER 97

Homeward bound

When the time came, they were sad to leave New York but one thing was for sure, they had many wonderful memories and photographs to perk them up anytime they were feeling down. The photographs would bring back memories and as the song says: *Memories bring back memories, bring back you* (New York).

It was so nice to be home. To feel Juliet's little mushy face and hold her close. Georgia was only away for a few days but Juliet had grown, even when Georgia caught her cheeks, she could feel the shape of her face was changing. Juliet wasn't a baby now, Juliet was a little girl. Georgia looked at her mum and gave her the biggest hug and kiss.

'Mum, what would I do without you? You have looked after Juliet so well for me, I didn't have to worry when I was away. You are the constant force in my life, always will be that solid rock.'

Her mum blushed, that made Georgia laugh. The moment was gone, it was time to sit down, sip on a cup of Barry's tea with gorgeous creamy milk and teacakes and chat away as Juliet fell into a nice slumber.

'Mum, I'll have to take you to New York and the Grand Canyon. I'm going to start a savings plan and in two years from now we'll be there because no matter what I tell you about Vegas, New York, the Grand Canyon you have to be there to soak it all up and take it all in. Mum, just wait until you see the vastness of the canyon itself, the roulette wheel in Vegas and the bright lights of New York the city that never sleeps. This is a promise

I'm making to you, Mum and it's one I'm going to keep.'

Georgia got up from the table and grabbed the New York bag, everything inside was for her mum.

'Now here're all your presents.'

Georgia had placed every one of her mum's presents so carefully in that New York bag, and into the top of her case to present to her mother who had made these few days possible. (after they'd had the tea and cakes)

'This is the one from the Grand Canyon,'

That was just a small present, a key ring with a helicopter. Georgia started with all the small presents first, she was going to let it build up to the big crescendo, a bottle of bourbon. Georgia knew her mother never drank it before but maybe she'd have a tiny tipple. A bag full of Hershey bars, Krispy Kremes, Red Velvet and Chiffon cakes and the pieces of jewellery that Georgia had purchased in the jewellery store in the Venetian Hotel. A necklace with different coloured stones that hugged her neck, a bracelet to match and diamante clip on earrings because Nellie never had her ears pierced.

Nellie was never the carrier of bad news and Georgia loved that about her mum. She'd never tell Georgia anything that might upset her while she was away. If Juliet was bold, or misbehaved, she just dealt with it and once Georgia came into the room Nellie stood back and let mum and daughter work things out for themselves. What a mum! What an inspiration! Georgia's mum was the one constant force in her life, always was, always will be, that solid rock that allowed Georgia to have the calm normal life she really needed to help her tread life's turbulent path without Cameron. Her mum was fun but at the same time she could be serious, a woman who understood life and most of all understood her daughter's needs. When Georgia was down her mum would quietly help in whatever way she could. Most times by arriving early to Georgia's house and just saying, Georgia, I was just passing by and dropped in for a cup of tea. (Loosely translated, I'm here to see what state of mind you're in and if you're coping today without Cameron or if you need a shoulder to cry on.)

OR:

Hi Georgia. (Nellie in that moment would have sussed out Georgia's mood) Why don't you go off on your own for a few hours, maybe meet one of your friends? I'll look after Juliet, relax here and watch a bit of morning TV.

OR:

She would have Georgia already sussed. Come on Georgia, out we'll go, I'll put Juliet's coat on. We'll bring a few sweeties with us. I'll push the pram. She never took no for an answer. We'll stroll into the village and have a snack in that little café and then she'd say come on Georgia, there's no point in moping around here.

Georgia would just go with her, sometimes with her head down, not being able to look the day in the eye and yet having mingled with people in the café and enjoyed that little snack, they'd stroll back home with the weight of the world lifted from Georgia's shoulders and another day conquered.

CHAPTER 98

Juliet

Georgia watched Nellie as she walked to her car trying to look glamorous while carrying a bag full of presents. Maria, the child-minder, had been such a great help to Nellie while Georgia was away. Now that Georgia was back Maria took some time off to be with her family in France. Georgia had taken a few days off from work to get Juliet settled. That had been a good idea, it worked very well. Now they were back on track, mummy and daughter sharing things together.

The place was quiet except for the little sounds of Juliet as she played with her toys in the corner. She could amuse herself for ages playing with those wooden shapes. When she'd get fed up playing with the wooden blocks she'd move on to her little soft, cuddly dollies and teddies. This little girl loved all toys, especially colourful ones. Of course, feeding time was the next thing on the agenda. Georgia had lots of toddler conversations going on with Juliet during this time. Then walkies time, out in the air for a walk in the park. Georgia took along the stroller because although Juliet loved to walk, she couldn't walk very far and it made her very tired. The truth was she was getting too heavy to be carried, so the stroller worked out perfectly. The fresh air had Juliet zonked. Georgia let her fall asleep beside her on the settee while she watched a little television, then she carried her to the bedroom and laid her down in her cot. Juliet's cot and Georgia's bed were almost in touching distance. Georgia often lay on her bed gazing over at Juliet. She'd watch as her little girl's hand slipped from the covers and lay down by the side of the cot. Georgia would grasp Juliet's hand in hers. She loved the feel of her so, so sweet little girl skin.

Juliet was growing up so fast. As Georgia gazed at her in wonder, she thanked God for sending this beautiful child to her, a constant reminder of her father Cameron, and the happy times they had shared together. When she'd look back at his life, she could say honestly, it had purpose, he had a beautiful child to show his life had been worth living. His mum and dad and family absolutely doted on Juliet. His mum found great solace in Juliet and said 'she is the image of Cameron when he was a young boy'. Georgia made a mental note to call his mum and invite her up for Sunday lunch. She also did her best to push all negative thoughts from her mind, it was the only way she could cope with her life right now.

She kept telling herself to keep forging ahead, be like her mum, stop dwelling on the negatives, think of Cameron and his beautiful smile. Try to stop thinking that his most beautiful smile was the one he gave her on the day he left for the last time with Juliet, on that fatal walk.

Remember his brown eyes but don't dwell on his beautiful eyes on the last day of his life.

Remember his kind ways, his patience, his understanding.

Remember the way he used to say to her when she was feeling down, stay positive Georgia.

He had a way of deciphering things and showing her how insignificant some of her worries really were. Just keep positive, thank God for letting Cameron into my life. She said all these things to herself over and over again. They'd had a very short space of time together but it was wonderful. What she would do from this day forward was, thank her lucky stars and the universe for aligning their spirits, body and mind, heart and soul together and giving her such wonderful memories. Sometimes she would say to Cameron If you can see and know what I'm going through, please help me to take the next step in my life when you're not here. Please keep me wrapped up in your love always and I pray with your guidance I will find my way. She prayed she would never forget his touch, his love and his devotion. No matter how painful remembering him was right now, she knew in time it wouldn't hurt so much and every photo, every video and every memory of him would be sweet, so sweet, just like the smell of a beautiful rose in a wild garden on a summer's day. All she needed was time.

CHAPTER 99

Indecent proposal

Through the next few weeks Georgia's friends and Nellie slipped in and out of her life discreetly, just to check on her, keep her company and talk about Coco and Bill's wedding, Vegas, the Grand Canyon and New York. The bundles of photographs were left over on the writing desk to be taken out any time a friend arrived.

Time was slipping by and now Vegas seemed like a distant memory. She still hadn't seen Ross, it was as if they were avoiding each other. Georgia had received a few texts from him and if she was honest with herself that's all she wanted. She needed that time to get her thoughts straight, as she couldn't afford to get her next move wrong, this time there would be no way back. These were the things that went through her head in the evenings as she sat alone.

It was on one of those evenings as she sat deep in thought, she heard a tap at the window. Georgia thought she was imagining things. Nobody ever taps on the window, except her mum an odd time. Her curiosity got the better of her and she had to investigate. There he was, Ross, looking at her with an expression that said should I be here at all? He'd obviously been out for a run, he was wearing shorts and a pure white T Shirt. She smiled a weak smile and beckoned for him to go to the door. Then he was in the sitting room, shuffling from one foot to the other, not really knowing what to do and feeling very uncomfortable.

'Ross you need a shower after running, so off with you and while you're having that shower, I'll pop on the kettle and we can have a cup of tea. There are towels in the hot-press just beside the bathroom and there's a dressing gown up on the right-hand side of the hot-press. It's large so it should fit you, the only one it doesn't fit is me. If you would like to rinse out your clothes and put them in the tumble dryer, they will be dry for when you're leaving.'

He didn't hesitate, he was gone. She guessed he felt relieved as he closed that door and went to the bathroom, to have a little while to pull himself together. She was left alone in the kitchen filling the kettle, keeping busy setting the small table and cutting some large chunky slices of fruit cake, after all there's no point in handing a man, after a run, some Marietta biscuits. Then he was there. Oh Jesus, thought Georgia, as her blood pressure went up and her face beamed bright red. I'd forgotten how sexy Ross was with his bare feet, tousled hair and that mischievous look in his eyes, wearing that thick chunky dressing gown and underneath to her knowledge, his hot body wore no clothes.

They sat down at the table. Ross was that breath of fresh air that Georgia needed in her life. She was so comfortable in his company, they just spoke freely of everything except them. He loved the Oxford Lunch, she loved the thoughts of him being naked underneath that dressing gown. Georgia wondered if he was thinking some naughty thoughts of her too but instead of doing anything about their feelings the two of them made themselves fat eating all of the cake on the plate, courtesy of Nellie. Thank God she'd left some cakes in the press, lemon drizzle cake and Oxford Lunch. She must have known Georgia's friends would be flitting in and out to keep a check on her lovely daughter.

'Georgia, I came around here because I wanted to ask you something, so let's get down to the nitty gritty. I need a holiday and I think you need a holiday, one that would include Juliet. I wonder if you would like to come to my apartment in Spain? As you know, sometimes I have it let out but I kept it for myself this year. I'd love you to share some time with me there.'

Georgia was elated. Ross had insisted he pay for the tickets and that's all it would really cost. The food in Spain is a lot cheaper than in Ireland and Ross made it clear he wanted to foot the whole bill. When Georgia had agreed and everything was settled, Ross flew to the bathroom and came back dressed in his freshly washed, slightly creased shorts, pure white top and runners. Georgia felt Ross looked much better in the dressing gown.

'Ross, when were you thinking of going on this holiday?'

'Well, I was considering this coming Saturday.'

'Oh my God, Ross, that soon?' said Georgia.

'Georgia, I feel the less time we have to think about it the better.'

'But, Ross, I have no swimming things for Juliet or myself.'

'Don't worry too much,' said Ross. 'Over near my apartment, there're lots of lovely little shops that cater for children, you'll have no problem getting something for Juliet. So remember, Georgia, this is about relaxing, not running around shops like a mad thing. Now, I have to go' he said.

With a kiss on her cheek he disappeared out the door and up the road, running. Georgia was in the bathroom cleaning her teeth and there hanging over the bath was the dressing gown that Ross had just removed from his naked body. She couldn't resist taking it up, holding it close. She hugged the dressing gown. The scent of Ross was everywhere coupled with the lovely fresh smell of shampoo and body wash. At that moment Georgia realised these few days away were meant to happen.

As she lay in bed that night, she felt all the nerves in her tummy jumping, that nervous feeling she recognised. There were so many questions racing around in her head. Would he expect her to sleep with him? If he did, could she resist sleeping with him? Would he be able to cope with Juliet? After all he had no children to distract him from himself and what he wanted. She hoped Ross had thought this through and had come to the conclusion there would be no point in pursuing a life with Georgia and Juliet until he could accept Juliet as his own and love her as only a daddy would. All of these things were necessary if there was a hope of Georgia and Ross rekindling their love affair.

Georgia fell into an uneasy sleep with all these questions rolling around in her head. She awoke abruptly and sat up in the bed staring into space.

How can I go away with Ross when Cameron's memories are so fresh in my mind? She sat there holding her phone, not knowing what she was doing. She was almost chanting to herself, I need to see a picture of Cameron, I need to see Cameron's face. Oh My God, I remember, I have that video I took on that horrible day, of my beautiful Juliet and her daddy going for that walk. She fumbled with the phone, forgetting how to even use it. How do I go into the videos? Her brain was blank. Something inside her head said, take a breath Georgia, calm yourself down.

Then she was there scrolling through her phone, heart beating like a drum. Excited at the thought of seeing his face again and scared stiff of her reaction when she'd see it. Was she strong enough to look back? She kept scrolling and there he was staring out from the screen, smiling. She pressed the button, the video began. Juliet in her pram, waving back at her mum and then the camera scrolled up to Cameron's face. Oh My God, he was beautiful. She uncontrollably sobbed as she watched that video about twenty times, over and over again. She couldn't take her eyes off it and couldn't stop looking at it. She couldn't put the phone down. Every time she started to look at it again, she was there in the moment. She even found herself lifting up her hand and waving. Oh My God! Am I mad? The realisation that he was gone forever hit her so hard, she was back at the funeral again, broken hearted and so the tears began to spill.

Then she remembered Audian handing her the letters from Cameron. She felt compelled to read Cameron's last letter. Georgia was engulfed in sadness. The letters had kept her going through the last few months since Cameron's untimely death. She read them when she was in despair, when she was looking for answers, when she just wanted to feel him around her. The letters had the same reaction on her body every time. Once the shaking stopped she seemed to go into a different world completely relaxed and in the story as the words unfolded but this was the last letter, she would never have another letter from him again to read. She would look back on all 5 letters and read them over and over again but this was the last time she would read his written words for the first time. Georgia realised every single solitary one of them had been read at pivotal moments in her life after Cameron, and each one had slotted in wonderfully with every occasion. So, with tears streaming down her face she began to read.

The reason this letter was so important was because she had been with Ross before Cameron and now she was considering a holiday with him, AC-after Cameron. Georgia wanted and needed to read the letter when she was alone and in her own space. If Ross was around she would feel he was an intruder in Cameron's domain, so it had to be tonight. Nellie had taken

Juliet over to her house for a sleepover, for the first time. Now that Juliet could walk and talk Georgia felt it was ok to let her leave the comfort of the house at sleep time. Georgia really wanted Juliet to see the wider world, starting with moving out of her comfort zone but still being in the bubble of Nellie and Georgia. In the future Georgia hoped when Juliet gained confidence and knew she could always go back to her mum, one by one, she would be allowed to stay with Georgia's friends Tanya, Coco and Heidi.

My Georgia

I can say that now I really feel you are mine. We share everything and now you trust me to take our little Juliet out for her walks. I'm so happy to be part of this fantastic threesome. I love how you love all of your friends and look forward to the future when they come to our beautiful bungalow and hear Juliet call them auntie for the first time. Sure it'll melt their hearts. What I love even more is the way you've embraced Maisie Coyne, a friend of mine, and taken her into the fold. She was so kind and good to me when I was in the monastery, so I'm even happier for her now that she's reconnected with Fr. Fergus Breen. I hope they spend many pleasant times at shows, cinema and having nice meals together. She deserves every bit of luck and happiness she gets. She's such a wonderful woman and your mum, Nellie, I just love her, what would we do without her? She's been the catalyst in keeping everything stable. In her own unique quiet way, even on rough seas she's helped us guide our ship to shore.

I've carried the guilt of you leaving Ross from the very moment you decided to leave him. I knew it was me who was breaking up your marriage and all the dreams Ross and yourself had for your future together. My selfishness and love for you got the better of me.

When you finally said you were leaving him I never tried to stop you. I knew I should have but the absolute desire I had to be with you blocked my mind from doing the right thing. Now time has moved on and I've accepted my faults and my part in what we both did to such a lovely man but if I had the same choices to make over and over again I'd still choose being with you at all costs. You're amazing, you're my dream come true,

Forever Yours
Cameron

She cried so much her eyes burned from the tears. At one point she thought she couldn't stop weeping. Some of those tears were for her, for the huge loss she had endured and was still enduring. Could she really go away with Ross for a few days' holidays feeling like this? The little voice of reason in her head spoke to her again. When she really thought about it she knew in her heart if there was anyone Cameron would have wanted her to be with, it would be Ross. So she just lay down on her bed, hugged her pillow and slept. When she woke the next morning, the pillow was wet from the tears and looking in the mirror she realised she'd need a lot of cold tea bags on her eyes to soothe them. Oddly enough she now had clarity, yes, she could calmly see Cameron would have wanted and urged her to go away with Ross for the few days. Ross was the safe haven she needed and whether she'd sleep with him or just have dinner with him, whether the few days would turn into a lifetime of love or just remain a pleasant memory, she would just have to wait and see. She still had Juliet to nurture and rear and she still had whatever time God would give her on this earth. There had to be a reason for all of this, only time would tell. She was resigned and very, very happy to take baby steps with Ross and see what would unfold.

In Ross's quiet, empty house, he also lay in bed that night thinking to himself, Jesus, I hope I'm doing the right thing, but since I lost Georgia to Cameron I've never really recovered. People have said to me we know you love her but what about your pride? I answer that question to myself with, I've got to put my pride under my feet. This holiday will be as much about discovering can I find it in my heart to forgive and forget the past for the sake of a love I just cannot forget and move on from. With that thought on his mind he slept.

CHAPTER 100

Spain - no expectations

Georgia's Mum had barely entered the front door of the beautiful bungalow with Juliet when Georgia proclaimed 'Mum, guess what? I'm going away for a holiday.'

'With whom?' said Nellie.

'Just hold on a minute Nellie Brown. First I want to give my bundle of joy a big kiss and a hug. Did you have a nice sleep in Nellie's house, Juliet?'

Juliet nodded her head and said:

'Yes, Mama. I played with dollies and teddies and Nellie's doggie, Mabel.'

While Juliet was having some food, Nellie and Georgia drank tea and ate the cream cakes Nellie had brought. Georgia began to explain everything to her mum.

'The answer to your question, Nellie, who am I going on holidays with, is Juliet and Ross.' There was silence. 'He has invited me to his apartment in Spain. All the time I was married to him I was never there. Remember Mum it was always let out,'

In a flash, Nellie put her sensible hat on.

'Georgia, I think that is a great idea. I think you were always great with Ross and it would really be worth your while and his, to see where a few days away can lead.' Silence. Nellie continued 'Georgia I feel a weight being lifted from my shoulders hearing you say those words. I wouldn't trust anyone else with you, only Ross, while you're in this state of bereavement. I'm sorry I used that word Georgia but it's an appropriate word and the right word for what you're going through. I have been walking on eggshells, trying to protect you and always trying to say the right thing at the right time. It's taken its toll on me as well as you because I had to look at you knowing your heart is broken. If there is one person who can help you through this, truly I believe it's Ross.

I know when you were marrying him some years ago I was against it. It was never because I didn't like Ross, it was because I felt you were too young to take on such a big commitment. Your present circumstances have made you grow up and here you are now, left alone with little Juliet to look after at such a young age. In my heart I have always felt you were truly in love with Ross but when I met Cameron I could see how he changed you and if it was at all possible, you were more in love with him than Ross.

I feel it is not impossible to fall in love with two people. After all, we all have different things to offer, we are a combination of so many elements but you were just searching, as we all do, for perfection. You came as close as you could to perfection with Cameron. He just made you shine. Sorry Georgia I haven't given you space to say anything but I have bottled up all my feelings for all this time. Now I feel free to say to you what I feel when your blue skies are starting to re-appear.'

'Oh Mum, what can I say, it must have been torture for you trying to get my ship to shore. Now I feel as if I've docked, so to speak, I am beginning to see a future for myself and Juliet. In the last week everything has been sorted out with the bungalow. We had such a great insurance policy that it's all mine Mum, so I don't have to work too many days to pay the bills and when Juliet goes to school I can work my day around her. Thank you for caring Mum. Even in my darkest moments I knew you were always there, my beacon of light.'

Early morning all chores completed Georgia called her three friends to tell them her good news. Unanimously, they agreed and said what her mum said, that it would do them both the world of good to spend some time together, just the three for them.

At this stage Heidi was only days away from giving birth to her twin babies. Tanya had learned to compromise with her English boyfriend. He had decided to come and live in Ireland but it would be six months before all that could happen. First, he would need a job transfer from London to Dublin. It would be just a matter of time as he was transferring with one of his colleagues in Dublin who wanted to go back to London, six months to be exact. Of course Coco and Bill were as happy as larks and had no big news to tell yet. Tanya being the funny one said:

'Georgia if we're going to be bridesmaids for you again, which way should we dress?' She was only being funny.

In a high pitched voice Georgia could hear herself say:

'I don't even know if I'm divorced, we might still be married and I might not need bridesmaids. But being honest with you girls, even if we didn't need to get married and our romance was flourishing, I would like to discuss with Ross maybe taking our vows all over again. If he was happy, I know I'd be more than happy, so watch this space. Anyway if you're going to be bridesmaids again for me, it would be a very small affair. Just all of you, my family and his and Juliet would be flower girl. In fairness, we have a long way to go before we consider a romantic reunion. So girls, you keep giving me excitement as I don't think there will be much happening on my side of the fence for now.'

Georgia put the phone down and thought to herself, Christ! Since we were last together, Ross and I have both grown and changed. What worked then, might not work now. There are so many hurdles to jump, I'm not thinking that far ahead, my brain won't allow me.

The day before the trip, on the table in Georgia's house sat her diary packed with things to do. Nellie had taken Juliet for the day and Georgia was now free to complete all the chores written in that diary. Well that's what she thought... then the phone rang. Johnnie (Sugar Daddy) was on the phone.

'Georgia, would you do something for me and ring your friends? Your best friend and Sugar Daddy (me) have just had twins, a boy and a girl. I'm so excited I can hardly talk. Can you believe it, Georgia, I'm a daddy? Will you do that for me, just ring around and tell anyone who needs to know? I'm just staring at the babies, I don't want to do anything else.'

Sugar Daddy was gone. What was Georgia to do? There was no option, leave her chores and ring her friends, Tanya and Coco, to tell them the great news. The best time for them to visit Heidi was evening time. Georgia would accompany them and that still left her free to go and buy the bits and bobs, the swimming togs, underwear, sandals, short stockings, sun hat and of course bath towels especially for Juliet and Georgia. It was going to be a much fuller day than Georgia had anticipated, but like the real trooper she was she got working on everything. She even found the time to bring the newly bought items home, take off the tags and put them into the case. Juliet was with mammy Nellie, so Georgia could pick up her two friends and head off to the hospital.

Oh! The babies were beautiful, the boy and the girl, Damien and Darcy, two of the loveliest bundles of joy anyone could wish for. Georgia realised she hadn't actually seen Johnnie's teeth before but now that's all you could see. He smiled that huge big open smile that said it all. As for poor Heidi, she was exhausted but putting on the best show of her life. She looked like the happiest new mother in Ireland. Georgia's guess was she was so traumatised after the birth that the new babies hadn't even registered yet.

Each of the girls had a present for Heidi, not for the babies, this was Heidi's moment. A big bouquet of roses, a box of Leonidas chocolates and a huge box filled with all the things Heidi needed, face mask, moisturisers, make up, all especially chosen because each one was Heidi's favourite. The girls had put the money together to buy the lovely presents. Between them they also gave Heidi a present of money to buy whatever she wanted to buy for her two lovely babies. They didn't stay long, she was just too out of this world. The best present they could give her was to leave her alone and hope to God one of the nurses would give her some sleeping pills, take the babies away and give her that one night's rest she so needed. Next time they would visit individually, Georgia was hoping she could have a nice in-depth conversation with Heidi and discover how she was really feeling, when she returned from her few days' holiday. Big kisses and hugs to Sugar Daddy before they left. He wasn't even listening to the congratulations, he was on cloud ninety-nine, complete with ice cream and chocolate flake.

Georgia was home again putting the finishing touches to her packing and luckily for her Nellie was going to stay overnight in Georgia's bungalow to take care of Juliet and ensure the journey started off perfect. Georgia's tummy was nervous and jittery and she understood why. This little holiday had an unspoken undercurrent. It was really a trial on both their parts to see how they would blend as a family of three for the future.

CHAPTER 101

Trial period

6.00 am on the dot there was a tap, tap, tap on the window. Nellie opened the door, it was Ross. He had taken to tapping on the window rather than ringing the doorbell in case he would disturb Juliet. Georgia caught his glance and they both smiled, immediately recognising the nervous look on each other's faces. Nellie was quiet, she could always read situations correctly, so instead of saying a word she kept herself busy helping to dress Juliet. When that task was completed she continued to keep busy helping Georgia with her precious hand luggage as they struggled to find room for it in the boot of the car.

She tried to hide the little tears in her eyes as she kissed them goodbye and waved them off. As the car disappeared down the road on its journey to the airport, she wondered if Georgia had any idea how much she would miss the pair of them. After all Nellie had almost single handedly cared for them, worried about them and had done her best to help her daughter, Georgia, cope after that tragic accident had upended her happy life and left her alone with a child to look after and Cameron gone forever from her life.

Unknown to Georgia, Nellie had felt that loss too. Firstly she had to cope with the breakup of Georgia and Ross's marriage followed by the big Cameron affair. Then when her beautiful daughter seemed like the happiest girl in the world, living in their happy bungalow with her lovely daughter and the man of her dreams Cameron, her charismatic partner, everything was taken away from her as fast as the blink of an eye. Yet through all that time Nellie had kept quiet about her feelings, always putting Georgia first before her needs but now as she watched the car disappear from view Nellie's anxieties began to reappear and raise their ugly head. All she could do was pray Georgia's life would get a lot better in the coming weeks, months and years. Once Georgia stayed strong Nellie knew she would return to her happy self and not feel that feeling of total isolation. Because Nellie was a happy go-lucky lady, no one thought of Nellie being on her own, her wonderful husband had been taken away from her when they were both still young and she had to cope alone. Nellie did not want her daughter to spend the rest of her life like her mum, alone.

Hardly a word had been spoken between Georgia and Ross on the journey to Dublin airport, in fact the only sounds were that of Juliet as she munched on an apple and chatted away to Ross and Georgia. She was such a good little girl, not a pick of trouble. Ross parked the car in the car park and the happy threesome, complete with cases and hand luggage made their way to departures. Ross lined up the cases all ready to go on board the plane while Georgia held onto their hand luggage.

The little group were happy and calm, that was, until just like a Greyhound racing off from the starting line, Juliet took off running like a wild little puppy away from them. To say they were taken by surprise was an understatement. She had been so quiet up until that very moment that neither of them was prepared for what happened next. It was as if her brain just clicked on and she went with it. Everything was left where it was and as Georgia and Ross began to run after the little darling, all they could see was her dark curly hair bobbing up and down. Her little short legs were certainly well able to gallop along and it seemed nobody was trying to stop her, instead everyone just looked on, as mesmerized as them. Luckily a quick-thinking man stopped toddler Juliet in her tracks. She stood there circled by Georgia, Ross, the stop man and onlookers, smiling and as happy as a lark holding her teddy, little realising this holiday could have ended even before it began.

The time had come to use the harness Georgia had brought to guide Juliet around Spain. Georgia realized it was really needed now to keep her toddler safe in Dublin airport. Juliet didn't know what was happening as her freedom came to an abrupt end. Believe it or not the whole incident worked to make them laugh. It seemed that was what they needed, something to take their minds off themselves and to relax them. Their moods changed, they were back to the carefree Georgia, Ross and happy go lucky Juliet. Georgia's heart was telling her to just go with the flow and not to worry, things would take care of themselves. As the old song says, *whatever will be, will be,* you just have to trust in the stars. She looked at Ross and felt he was thinking exactly the same as her. They were off to a great start in sunny Spain.

Thank God Ross had hired a car and picked it up at the airport, it's amazing how easy life can be by just being organised. Twenty minutes is all it took to arrive in the lovely village, very close to the sea with a lovely pool and low-rise apartments in a half moon shape. Ross's apartment was a three-bed apartment, right in the centre looking straight out onto the sea. During the time they had been married Ross had never really spoken about the apartment. He had it rented out and Georgia had never enquired, so this was a lovely surprise. Not only was it a three-bed apartment, it was a penthouse apartment, so far from being little it was actually quite spacious.

From then on it was holiday time, sitting by the pool, driving down to the beautiful beach with silvery sand and really blue, blue sea and a fabulous café where you could order a Pina

Colada, bottle of water or whatever you fancied. Georgia insisted on paying for some of the drinks in a bid to keep her independence. Ross protested in the beginning, he was an old fashioned guy and liked to pay for everything for Georgia. When they got tired of being by the beach and when it was too warm to lie by the sea, they took little walks in the cool breeze with Juliet in her stroller either eating, sleeping or laughing.

Georgia shared her room and an ensuite with Juliet. There was no pressure from Ross, he chose to enjoy their company and let things take their course. They all had a glorious day in the sunshine, a stroll along the promenade, an ice cream while they sat on deck chairs and an evening meal consisting of Paella and wine. The three amigos were absolutely zonked from all the fresh air, walking, playing and eating. It seemed everyone was happy to get a good night's sleep. After happy little pecks on the cheek from Ross, cleaning her teeth and changing into her light jammies, Georgia lay in her bed beside Juliet. Once Juliet was bathed, fed and dressed for bed, she was very happy to cuddle her teddy bear while she lay on her own little pillow, that she'd taken with her from home and slept like a real dreamer. Georgia grabbed a glass of water and felt happy as she lay in bed, thinking how her life had taken a complete 360 in the last few weeks. Yes, we're here on a holiday with my ex-husband Ross, how strange is that? And no, she wasn't sleeping with him! Was she happy with that? Her answer to herself was Yes. If things were going to happen with Ross it would have to be his choice and good timing or the whole thing could implode and be a complete disaster.

In his bedroom Ross lay wide awake. Sleep wasn't coming to him. His mind was racing and he began to think about how things were between him and Georgia. When he had made the decision and asked Georgia to come away with him for a holiday for a few days, he could honestly say, it wasn't on an impulse. When she'd been away in New York he had hatched this plan. For the years they'd been apart, he had dated other people and even lived with someone for a while but deep in his heart all he wanted was Georgia but she had fallen in love with someone else and left him alone, feeling deserted and disappointed with his life.

Things were different now, she was alone again searching for her future and there was a little girl to consider who needed the love and attention of a daddy, not the resentment of an ex-husband. These were the things he had to work out in his mind. He thought that if he wrote down the questions, as he had many a time since they'd rekindled a nice comfortable relationship, he had to admit that again in his heart and in his head and mind and in his body and soul, he knew Georgia was the elusive love missing from his life. If this holiday turned out to be a defining time in their lives, there were three things he really would have to fully accept:

1. That Georgia had fallen in love with someone else while still married to me. Cameron, it's hard to even say that name.

2. She now had a beautiful little toddler, Juliet.

3. He would have to accept Juliet as his own child and absolutely never resent her for something she had no control over.

Now that Georgia's here with me in Spain on this lovely night, it's real. I have to be honest with myself before we move forward. This time away is going to be taken at a hedgehog's pace. There might be lots of prickly moments but the amount of love, caring, understanding and the need to feel whole again would have to be for him bigger than life, death and his ego.'

CHAPTER 102

Finding Georgia

The way your life changes when you have a little one to consider. Standing in the baby pool trying to teach your little girl to swim, blowing up her arm bands and constantly making sure she doesn't become dehydrated. Then, of course, there was that disaster in the pool all because Georgia kept Juliet's normal nappy underneath her swim suit bottoms, which turned out to be a disaster when bits of the nappy ended up in the pool. Then there was the sun screen cream Georgia applied to Juliet's baby skin to protect her from being burned by the scalding hot sun. The tiles on the balcony were also a danger to Juliet because she refused to wear sandals or slippers on her sensitive feet. She didn't realise how dangerous it would be to put even one toe down on the scalding ground, this became a constant battle.

The truth was, for Georgia all the girly things she used to do on holidays in her previous life, like lying on a sunbed and soaking up the sun were now definitely a thing of the past. The reality was buying ice creams to keep Juliet cool and making sure to keep all bottles of water in the fridge or in the cooler bag to keep them cold for Juliet. To keep her little body cool Georgia showered her at least twice a day. Georgia was beginning to feel the strain.

At one point she looked over at Ross, he looked absolutely bored sitting there, she began to wonder when this holiday with Ross was over would they be over too? After all, most fathers have time to adjust to a new baby over the nine months when their wife is pregnant and expecting their baby. Then when the baby is born they gradually get used to having it around. Ross had absolutely no time to adjust at all, this holiday had happened so fast he was thrown into the deep end without a safety net. Georgia wondered could their new romance survive this getting-to-know-you-all-over-again holiday. Panic began to take her over, it was time to do something fast.

'Ross, I have an idea.' she said 'Starting right now I want you to take a stroll on the beach every morning while I'm washing and feeding Juliet. You know it takes time to do all the mundane things and there is nothing you can do to help. You need some time alone, then when you return Juliet will be fast asleep and we will have some time together.'

He didn't waste a moment. She watched as he put on his nice fresh shorts and T Shirt and a pair of comfy runners. He immediately began to relax and without a word he kissed her on the forehead and disappeared into the distance. She wondered was playing family man working for him. She also realised whatever the verdict was she just had to accept it. So the days drifted on, they now had a pattern… in the early morning Ross took a swim with Juliet. He enjoyed her splashing in the pool and holding her hand as he glided her along with a big smile on her face, thinking she was swimming. During this time Georgia would shower and blow dry her hair and put a little sunscreen on to protect herself from the sun, then Ross would leave and have some alone time.

When he returned Juliet was always asleep and so there was time for celebrating on the balcony of his lovely apartment. They drank champagne, ate fresh fruit and chatted away as they both navigated the road to re-union. Their evenings consisted of first feeding Juliet, then dressing her, walking with her and then popping her in her stroller. Once the evening air hit Juliet she fell fast asleep in seconds and then it was their turn, yet again, to sit outside a café and dream. Three days had passed, No sleeping together, No sex, No I love you. If the truth was known they were both scared because for them once those words were uttered, that was another stage ticked in the box of the saga of 'The Reuniting of Ross and Georgia.'

This morning was a little different. As he dried Juliet after her playful time in the swimming pool, Ross announced that he would love to take Juliet for a little walk and give Georgia some time for herself. So, all dressed up in a little pretty hat and dress, lots of sun cream and let's not forget teddy, they were gone. Georgia had to admit it looked funny watching Ross pushing the stroller but if he felt uncomfortable he wasn't showing it. This is just like heaven Georgia said to herself. Since they'd arrived Georgia hadn't rang anyone at home, this was her time to just lie on a sun bed, be like ET and call home. First call was of course, to her mum Nellie.

'Nellie I miss you. If this works out with Ross and if you agree, you can come on all our holidays with us.'

'That's a great plan Georgia. Now Georgia, I know what's behind this big invitation, you're looking for a babysitter. You know I always meet Mr Lucky when I'm away on holiday, I'd have to have some me time as well.'

'Well in that case Juliet would be a great asset for you Mum. I'd have her looking so pretty men would be coming over to ask if she was your daughter. She could be your new chat-up line.'

'Oh, Georgia I'm really sorry, I'm going out to meet someone for lunch and I'm late. Can I talk to you later?'

'No problem, Nellie, I want to ring my friends and I want to be free when my two beauties arrive back from their walk. Love you Mum. Chat soon.'

Georgia was really in luck, she rang Coco first as she would normally do and guess what, her other two friends were there with her. They were having a charity coffee morning for the local hospice. Their voices were up two octaves with excitement, pouring tea, putting out fairy cakes and chatting with their guests. It was a short conversation on speaker. Each asking a different question.

Coco: 'How are you getting on with Ross?'

Heidi: 'Is Juliet settling in?'

And of course the one question they all wanted to ask, you could hear a pin drop.

Tanya: 'Georgia, we're all dying to know, but I'm the only one with the courage to ask. Have you had a passionate night with him yet?'

Georgia could picture the scene at home. One holding a large teapot, one holding a large jug of milk and the other with a big plate of biscuits but with one thing in common, all stuck to the spot waiting for her reply. She could have told a fairy story, she could have bumped it all up and made it sound really good, but she didn't.

'Nothing much has happened.' In that moment she stopped still. 'Christ girls, is it ever going to happen?'

The question was left hanging, the girls had nothing to say. Georgia couldn't go on with the conversation. The truth was she felt a little teary, as the reality hit home. She felt anxious not knowing where she stood.

'I'll ring you later on in the week girls, or text you. When I get home I'll give you some money for the charity, I hope you collect lots more. Ciao for now.'

Then the phone went dead. Georgia sat there surrounded by the chatter of happy people sitting beside the pool. But instead of feeling happy she felt a sadness she had never felt before. Her past came back to haunt her and hit her like a brick. It fell down on her slender shoulders. Panic just engulfed her being and dragged her right back to the moment she had lost Cameron forever. The feeling overwhelmed her. Georgia didn't know how she would survive the next few hours without her mum Nellie with her to protect her, to quell all the awful madness going on inside her head. She was never so frightened, she had to take control of herself.

This was one of those defining moments, with her life flashing before her eyes and Cameron's face, his sparkling brown eyes, beautiful smile and sallow skin began to take her over. She couldn't stop the tears streaming down her face and she couldn't stop the shaking of her body. If he was here right now, in this instant she knew she would never have returned to Ross. Ross had been the steadiest, most reliable force she'd had in her life but Cameron had made her heart sing and her body feel alive with just a touch. What was she doing here? Why was she trying to relive the past? She hadn't recovered from the devastation of Cameron's untimely death.

In this moment she realised all she had done since the day of that horrific accident and losing the love of her life, Cameron, was sweep all her feelings under the carpet. First just trying to stay strong because everyone told her she was strong and she had to live up to their expectations. She tried to crawl her way through it and of course, she had every reason to get through it, in one word, Juliet, her daughter. Then for Nellie, her mother and to keep Cameron's mum and dad and his family's spirits up as they were also pining for their Cameron. The strong front she was putting up was too hard to maintain. She'd been keeping in touch with Cameron's mum and dad. She'd even gone as far as telling them she was going away with Ross for a holiday. Yes, she'd been up front with everyone, that was everyone but herself, to herself she had told lies. You're strong, you can cope, you are coping, yes but at what cost?

All she really wanted to do now was disappear to the end of the swimming pool and hear nothing. She jumped into the water and began to swim one lap after the other, only lifting her head from the water to take a breath. She didn't know how many laps she did that day but she didn't stop until her whole body was exhausted. She had to hold on tight to the ladder as she struggled to climb out from the water. She grabbed a big towel, threw it around her, almost jumped onto the sunbed and cried for what seemed like ages.

She prayed that nobody was looking at her, if they were they'd have her certified. She cried while the sun shone and the water glistened from its rays. The waiter handed out cocktails for the adults and soft drinks for the children who jumped around, played and swam or lay on the sunbeds resting. She felt nothing, nada. She lay there for a while and fell into a slumber, when she woke it was to the tap, tap, tap of her little girl's hands on her face:

'Dirty Mama.'

Ross quickly butted in. 'It must have been the sun while you were asleep Georgia, you're mascara is all over your face and your lipstick is all over your mouth. I've got some baby wipes here, sit up there and I'll clean your face.'

Georgia sat there and let it happen. Ross cleaned off all the makeup from her face, he was so gentle and so kind.

She didn't know if he had guessed she was upset, after all he did know his ex-wife very well. For whatever reason, with every stroke of his hand on her skin, she could feel her heartbeat returning to normal, her body returning to normal, the madness subsiding and that ferocious panic slowly leaving her. In its place was a calmness she hadn't felt since before Cameron's death. She heard a little voice in her head saying, you'll be ok Georgia, in time everything will be alright. This was definitely a new phase in the healing process, in the moving on process, of not forgetting Cameron but of trying to grab happiness in a way that she knew now was possible and not panicking if this holiday didn't turn out right. With that thought going through her mind, she concluded this time away in sunny Spain was a huge success.

Now she knew no matter how this holiday turned out she would go home feeling happier and healthier in the knowledge that from now on she would refuse to blame herself for falling in love with Cameron and leaving Ross. Love is something that is too hard to say no to, she hadn't gone looking for someone else, love had just found her. She had to get rid of that guilty feeling and stop putting on this front, pretending she was able to cope, trying to convince herself she was getting over Cameron.

Georgia would now be ready when friends or family asked her in the future, how she was feeling. She knew if she was having a bad day she could now be truthful and honestly say I'm having a bad day. I wonder if you would come to my happy bungalow and please sit with me for a while, or, please mum could you stay overnight, I don't want to be alone tonight, I hate being alone and I hate the dark. She realised that sometimes in life the one person you have to be honest with is yourself. With this new calmness and realisation Georgia was all set for a great finish to her holiday. If she felt like giving Ross a peck on the cheek she would just do it, if she felt like holding his hand she would just do it.

From there on in the day was perfect. With one hand holding the pram, the other holding Ross's hand, and feeling that between them, at last they had found the perfect balance. The happy couple walked down along the promenade, breathing in the beautiful sea air and just chatting away to each other, like they used to when they were Ross and Georgia. At a café on the promenade Ross had a glass of beer, Georgia had a toasted cheese and tomato sandwich and a glass of cold water, while Juliet enjoyed a little prepared snack and some ice cream. It was so nice strolling back, this time with Georgia and Ross holding Juliet's hands, one each and saying whoosha as they swung her up into the air to her giggling. They continued the nice stroll back, now with Juliet strolling beside them on her little reins held by Ross. She seemed to love him. As they walked along she turned to Georgia,

'Mama look.'

Her little chubby finger pointed towards the ground and there was a lizard. Georgia tried to look happy even though she hated lizards. Juliet bent down and tried to catch it, she had no fear. Ross grabbed her in his arms and lifted her in the air to take her out of danger.

She said 'Dada down.'

Georgia and Ross stood still. He looked at her and she looked at him, she laughed, she made light of the situation with Ross and now felt strong enough to say:

'How does that make you feel Ross?'

Then she waited to see what his answer would be.

'It's strange, Georgia. I don't want to get my hopes up and have them all blown away to oblivion. To tell you the truth, I'm afraid to love her too much just in case things don't work out and all my dreams are shattered again.'

All this they talked about as they walked back to their apartment. 'Tired Dada.'

Ross lifted Juliet back into the stroller and gave her a bottle with orange juice and a rusk to chew on.

'Look Ross,' said Georgia 'let's sit down here on this little bench outside this café. Juliet is quiet and asleep. If it's ok with you, I'd love to have a little chat.'

Ross nodded his head in agreement. The two very warm holidaymakers sat down and ordered two glasses of cool lemonade. There was silence for a minute or two and then Georgia began to speak.

'Ross, I have no intentions of taking Juliet away from you. I would go as far as to say if things worked out between us and you want to, I would be so happy if you adopted Juliet as your own daughter. I'd love to be with you. Oh, Jesus Ross, have I said too much? I'm just trying to put you at ease and let you know how strongly I feel about us, but there's no pressure from me at all. You're right to tread softly, Ross.'

He seemed to relax. Georgia's mind began to drift for a moment, she always knew Ross liked to see things clearly and liked things to be explained to him. He was very black and white. He also liked to see the written word on paper, as in their divorce. Georgia felt she had been very honest with him and she needed to be if they were to have any future ahead of them. She could see in his eyes he was visualising his future now. Juliet was such a good little girl, it seemed every time they needed to have a serious conversation, she fell asleep. Thank God for the fresh air in Spain. They walked back to the apartment hand in hand with a few more boxes ticked.

CHAPTER 103

I can see clearly now, the pain is gone

Their evenings were restricted, what can you do when you have a young toddler with you? So they dined in a local café where they had some chicken in hot sauce and a bottle of wine. Juliet had always had regular sleeping hours. She was used to going to bed at seven in the evening and that worked out very well on this holiday. Into the stroller she'd sit and as she fell asleep they'd walk in the opposite direction from the beach and look at the shops. Georgia and Ross were still getting to know each other all over again, they were beginning to let their guard down and letting each other in.

Now they could see the dream and work on the relationship, build up the love, respect and trust in each other. It could take a week, it could take a year or it might never happen, after all this was all a learning curve. When you're younger, you just fall in love and go for it and that's exactly what Georgia and Ross had done in the past. That's ok if it's the first time with this person but when it's the second time you're more aware of their feelings and yours, never venturing over the line in case you break their heart again. That night they kissed a little more, they hugged a little more, Ross played some of the songs he liked and then inevitably, Georgia went to her room with Juliet, Ross went into his room alone.

That night as Georgia lay in bed she understood one thing for sure, if this romance was to move forward she would have to make the first move. She knew Ross wouldn't push anything, (he was frightened) after all she had finished with him, it was up to her to show him she wanted his love more than anything else in the world. With that thought in mind, she sat up and stretched her hand over to the locker at the side of her bed. There lay a card she had brought with her to write a little thank you to Ross for taking her on the holiday, but now she felt she had a lot more to say. She rummaged in the drawer and found a notebook. Her decision was to say thank you for the lovely holiday on the card but her letter would need a lot more paper and would have to be written on the pages of the notebook. She fluffed up the pillows, put them behind her back, took a book, leant the notebook on it and began to write.

Dearest Ross,

I want to say from the bottom of my heart a huge big thank you for having the courage to take both Juliet and myself away for a few days. I never needed a holiday as much as I needed this one and would you believe, it has sorted out my mind and put me back on the straight and narrow. I know Ross you're saying right now, how could a few days away in Spain do all that? Well I can tell you, Ross, it made me realise I've always loved you and I'll never stop loving you. I know I need to make the first move when it comes to you because I was the one who broke your heart. This holiday has shown me how much Juliet loves you and even though I haven't said it to you I still love you. I'm going to say what's on my mind, Ross. Here goes, I'm willing and would love to continue to build on our relationship if you are willing to try. Sometimes in life our roads take us in different directions but I feel it's time to forget the past and move forward. Now I know Ross, it's easy for me to say that. I left you for Cameron and with that horrible tragedy his life was taken away from him. Now I'm alone again but this time with a difference, I have Juliet. If you can't forgive me then we can't move on and you need to tell me the truth, Ross. Then I as well as you can see a future for us. As the first move has to be made by me, that last move has got to be made by you. Whatever way our road takes us I want to tell you this collision was exactly the one I wanted and I'm hoping it's the one you wanted too. Oh! And there's one other thing Ross, if you decide to take Juliet and myself on, as I said earlier, I'd like you to know I would be so happy to let you adopt Juliet and be her real dadda. I truly believe Cameron would be very happy if we were both together because he was always sorry for the pain he caused you. Giving you Juliet would be his way of saying sorry. You are a man of integrity and strength and I know you would be her guiding light as she grows. There! I've said it all Ross, I've given lots of thought to what I've written and I've broken the rule that my mother always held sacred, never put it in writing. My hope is that you feel the same way but if the answer is no, I will be very sad but I will completely understand how you feel. If our stars are not meant to be aligned, my hope would be that we could, at least, remain friends.

Here's to the future whatever it holds.

Georgia

Georgia didn't remember falling asleep. When she awoke she checked the time on her phone, it was 2 AM. Juliet began to toss and turn then she settled back down into her nice relaxed toddler sleep, out cold, arms, legs, all over her cot. Georgia didn't have to think what her next move was, she crept out of her bedroom into Ross's room, holding the envelope containing the card and the letter that said everything her heart felt, knowing if she thought about what she was going to do, she wouldn't do it. She placed the envelope on the locker beside his bed, pulled back the covers a little and slid into the lovely comfy bed. Somehow she didn't feel awkward. Ross with just pure instinct put his arms around her and kissed her gently. They slept comfortably and happily together.

Georgia was delighted when she awoke, outside the sky looked bright and beautiful, she could hear Juliet calling 'Mama, Dadda'. Quietly she slipped out of the bed and into her little girl's room. From that moment on it was all systems go, feeding and washing Juliet, Georgia showering time.

Ross hadn't emerged from the bedroom. Was he asleep or was he afraid to come out? If he'd read her letter she would understand why he didn't want to come out. Georgia sat at the table having breakfast and while she looked out at the pool with the sunbeds all round and happy holiday makers already swimming, chatting and laughing. She noticed Ross walking back towards the apartment, he must have slipped out while she was bathing Juliet. Juliet loved morning time. She would point out the different people as she looked down from the balcony. Georgia wondered if Ross enjoyed his walk alone on the beach, she also wondered if he had read the letter she wrote to him. If he had she couldn't tell, his expression wasn't giving away any secrets. What she saw was Ross arriving back into the sitting room full of the joys of spring and giving Juliet a little peck on the cheek.

'Dadda up.'

His response was kind and gentle. They both avoided eye contact and did not refer to Juliet's words (Dadda up). Ross lifted Juliet up into his arms, into the air and danced around the kitchen with her to a song on the radio. When the song had finished Ross very gently put Juliet's two feet down on the ground. Straight away she ran out to the balcony to look down on the holiday makers and as usual pointed out all the colourful chairs, etc. etc.

The morning was flying by. Ross still hadn't acknowledged that letter. Georgia was beginning to lose hope and wondered would it ever happen. To make sense of it all she had to remember that time at the swimming pool when she awoke, the feeling she had about staying calm, being calm and letting it happen (or not). If only Nellie was here, she could babysit at night and they could go for a meal and have some romantic time together under the beautiful Spanish night sky, but Nellie wasn't here.

'Why don't you go off to the shops for a while, Georgia? I'll stay here with Juliet and I'll make her some lunch. If it's ok with you we could eat in tonight.'

'Sounds good to me' Georgia heard herself say. Maybe he did read my letter, she thought.

Georgia picked up her bag and off she went to the shops for some retail therapy. Oh! The freedom, not pushing the stroller. It's lovely being a mammy but it's lovely for a little while to have some time to yourself. Oh! The dresses in the shops were beautiful. Georgia was on a high as she walked out of Zara clutching a bag with a few pretty dresses inside. On the way back to Ross's apartment, she went into a patisserie, bought some fancy cakes and some special biscuits that her darling Juliet would like and another sun hat to save Juliet's skin from the sun.

The aroma of the beautifully scented Jo Malone candle that glistened on the sitting room table set the mood. Georgia could feel her senses heightening, she was slowly becoming aware of everything around her. The mouth-watering aroma of the food Ross had just cooked and even the smell of the fresh warm air surrounding her. She felt in her heart her time was coming, she just had to be patient. Of course, Juliet's feeding time came first, but Ross had already covered that, she was fed, washed, in her jammies and ready for bed. What a genius of a man, he was born to be a father.

As Juliet fell into a deep sleep as usual, brought on by the fresh air in Spain, Ross and Georgia sat down and ate every morsel of the dish Ross had prepared, drank a lot of wine but not too much, after all everyone must stay sober for Juliet. Then they had some ice cream, strawberries and chocolate, followed by dancing around the sitting room, with Georgia dressed in her lovely lilac, slim fitting dress from Zara and her sexy five inch heels, feeling on top of the World on this lovely summer evening. It seemed as if they'd never left each other as they laughed and joked about their friends, Georgia's mum, Ross's mum and the funny things they'd say and the great support they'd been to both of them through the years.

Georgia checked on Juliet. she was fast asleep. They both enjoyed the very slow, soft, seductive, romantic songs playing on the radio, on this lovely summer's evening, with the balcony windows completely open bringing the outside inside. The still blue skies played their part in making the night perfect. With the balcony windows opened, the humming sounds of the chatting holidaymakers drifted up to Ross's apartment, putting the finishing touches to a perfect evening and yes they almost did make love. Georgia was giving up hope, she had to remind herself, there was still time. As she lay in Ross's arms with all the panic she felt earlier gone, she realised the time was right. She just knew, Ross will talk to me, I just have to wait until the stars are in line.

CHAPTER 104

The end and the beginning

The holiday was almost over, Georgia didn't want it to end and she hoped Ross felt the same. This holiday had been a great idea, in fact Georgia felt they couldn't have moved anyway forward without it. Now they were into a routine, in the mornings Georgia did all the necessary things for Juliet, had her shower, then into the kitchen to start the breakfast but this morning was different, before he went for his walk Ross had set the table, everything was prepared. When he returned back from his walk, Georgia and Juliet were already sitting at the table.

He had bought fresh croissants, pain au chocolate, tiny butters. Juliet loved the croissants, she couldn't get enough.

'More Mama, more Dadda.'

It seemed they also had a routine that once Juliet said dadda to Ross they looked in opposite directions, still avoiding eye contact, as if trying to ignore what they just heard. Georgia didn't want him to think she was trying to nab him as dadda and Ross didn't want Georgia to know that he really loved being called dadda and secretly wanted not to take Cameron's place but to be there for Juliet. They both continued to look in different directions, not a word was spoken.

The day passed by with lots of sun bathing and that little walk on her own, in the afternoon. This time Georgia didn't bother with the clothes shops but she did visit a few gift shops and finished her alone time sitting outside a little café drinking a glass of fresh orange juice. Ross loved jelly sweets and Georgia found by accident, the perfect box of jellies just for him and one rose, his favourite colour – yellow. She felt happy as she walked back and happier when she got to the apartment and saw the two loves of her life together. She hid the jellies and the rose in her bedroom. They would be presented to Ross later.

The apartment was quiet. Georgia stayed with Juliet until she fell asleep. Then she popped into her en-suite bathroom, applied fresh makeup, changed her dress, sprayed her favourite perfume all over her body and of course for the finishing touch, put on her five inch white high heels. When Georgia emerged back out into the dining room dressed to perfection, holding that one rose and the box of sweets, it looked like a different place altogether. All the untidy bits and pieces of strewn clothes, bags, etc. were gone, the lights were dimmed, Ross had the large balcony window opened as far as possible and out on the balcony he had set the table with everything their hearts desired. There were plates of salad, coleslaw, tomatoes, ham and cheese, strawberries, melons, pineapple slices, peach segments, crackers and Pringles. He handed her the sweetest and most delicious cocktail she had ever tasted.

How could she have ever forgotten these wonderful things that he always did. When she'd moved on and focussed on Cameron's great assets, her mind must have blocked out that other person, Ross, who was really one hell of a guy. The song drifting through the air was *The way we were*.

'Ross, I hope you like this one yellow rose, it's your favourite colour, it smells delicious and of course, I had to get you your favourite jellies.'

'You look lovely tonight, Georgia.' He said with a gleam in his eye.

They sat down, there was silence only broken by the sound of knives, forks and the songs on the radio and the lifting and placing of the variety of delicacies from the table onto their plates. It seemed as if there was an elephant in the room, they both knew it was the letter. Georgia had stated in that letter, she had made the first move, it was up to Ross to make the second move. As she ate the gorgeous salad adding segments of peaches and in between the odd strawberry, calmness came over her. Now she knew she could do absolutely nothing, it was all up to Ross. She would have to have the grace to allow him to say what he needed to say.

She excused herself from the table to go and check on Juliet, but it was really time she needed to compose herself. She looked in at Juliet, she was fast asleep. Brace yourself, Georgia, he might not mention the letter. If that was the outcome she was resigned to live with that. Tonight she would walk away from the table with her head held high knowing it was not meant to be, Ross and Georgia.

Inside the bathroom her eyes drifted down to the basin as she turned on the water to wash her hands. Right there in front of her sat a large pink envelope with her name beautifully inscribed – Georgia. She picked it up with shaky hands and sat on the side of the bath. As she began to open the envelope she thought to herself, well this is it Georgia Brown. Ross is straight to the point, he's just going to tell you exactly how he feels. She didn't want to read the letter. In that very moment she fully understood what this trip was really all about. What she had hoped to get from it. Of course it was complete forgiveness from Ross for the trauma and sadness she had caused him. She just knew he wasn't going back to her and she felt it would be no to taking on Juliet, he'd never forgive her and she didn't blame him. We are over for good. She would just have to face up to it, she would have to live her life without him.

She forced herself to open the letter and began to read it. It was short and to the point.

Beautiful Georgia

We've had a great time here. I've enjoyed every moment I've spent with you and I think when I look at you, you feel the same way and just to take you out of your misery I have read your letter. In fact I've read it over and over again. I really wanted to make the right choice for both of us. I realise if we are together, we could be the incredible threesome and have amazing times as we watch Juliet grow. I was very pleased when I read, even though you'd already told me verbally, it was nice to see it in writing, that you would be happy for me to adopt Juliet, if we moved forward with our relationship. I've given it a lot of thought. I hope we can discuss it this evening.

Love

Ross

Georgia had a hard time getting her thoughts together in that bathroom, she kept going over the last words Ross wrote, which were, 'you would be happy for me to adopt Juliet', but he had given no answers in that letter. She was going back to the table not knowing what the outcome of the getting to know you again holiday would be. Then she was there sitting down facing Ross. She didn't know what came over her but she felt strong, she was sitting there not just representing herself but representing Juliet. This whole thing had to be right, her little girl needed a stable and happy life and if it wasn't to be with Ross, she would just have to face that fact. Her body was straight, her hands were folded and she was calm. Ross began to spill out his words:

'Georgia if you don't mind I want to ask you to say those words to me, that you would be happy if I adopted Juliet, if we were an item.'

'OK' said Georgia, she took in a very deep breath and began 'Ross, I would be very happy if we were a threesome, if you would adopt Juliet and be her dadda, as she already calls you that. But you would have to be very happy and very sure you want to do that. I completely understand either way. I would love if you would adopt Juliet.'

'I just want to say, I would love to do that, adopt Juliet, it would make me the happiest man in the world. In a way we're lucky because she's so young and didn't have time to get to know Cameron, so to her I'd always be dadda but I just want to add Georgia, I'll always make sure Juliet knows who her biological father was and welcome her questions regarding Cameron.'

This time they didn't avoid looking at each other, they held a gaze. Georgia felt like jumping up and down with happiness but somehow she knew Ross had more to say.

'Georgia I have been trying to work on accepting that you left me for Cameron and in the back of my mind wondering would you have ever returned to me if he was still here.'

Georgia knew the answer to that question. She had already made peace with herself regarding that question and that answer. The answer only she would ever know.

He continued 'I know I have to work on that, I'm slowly accepting it but I don't want it to come between us, so if you can accept that I'm still working on that part myself, I will be very happy for two to become one. First I have a little confession to make Georgia. Remember that night you signed all the papers for me in the restaurant, when I left you I was determined to go to the solicitors the very next day. I had already made that appointment and I did turn up and divorce proceedings were put into motion.'

'I know' said Georgia, 'I signed all the papers.'

'Yes I know you did. I also got a letter and that's when I had a change of heart. I asked my bewildered solicitor to hold on everything for a while so our divorce still hasn't been finalised. If you want to proceed, when we go back home would be a good time. But right now I have a question I want to ask you.'

Now Georgia was completely thrown. She wondered what the next thing he was going to say was and she dreaded the words just about to spill from his lips.

'Will you marry me for the second time?'

'But you've just said we're still married' said Georgia.

'You're right, Georgia, we're still married on paper, but a lot of water has gone under the bridge since then, so what I was thinking was, we could take our vows all over again and say all the I do's and I love you forever, in the church where we were first married. If you agree, Georgia, we could invite everyone who is precious to us and be surrounded by all our friends. It will be a small celebration surrounded by so much love, a whole new chapter in our lives for both of us.'

Now Georgia couldn't contain herself any longer but she didn't want to waken Juliet so she jumped up and down, kissed and hugged Ross, trying her best not to make any noise, that was difficult. There was no question about it, love was definitely in the air.

'I'm so happy' said Georgia 'I feel love like I never felt before. The first time we married we were so young and really didn't know what love was all about but now it's on a different level, Ross. We're on a different level. I know this is the right thing.'

'Georgia, do you realise I asked you to marry me, take our marriage vows again. I haven't heard your answer.'

'Of course I'll marry you and take our marriage vows again, Ross. It can't happen soon enough. Ross, there's something strange.'

'What's strange?' said Ross, looking a little baffled, knowing she had already said yes.

'At times like this, normally, the first thing I want to do is ring my mum Nellie and my three best friends. The strange thing is, this time I feel my mum and my friends can wait. As the song says *Heaven can wait*, this time it's just about the three of us, you Ross, me Georgia and our little girl Juliet. As another song says *when three (two) become one.*'

Juliet slept quietly. Georgia was happy with the peace that came from Juliet's room and she was even happier to be lying beside Ross having enjoyed making mad, passionate love. Georgia felt something had really happened at that moment. Was she pregnant again? Only time would tell.

On this lovely starry, starry night in Spain, Georgia felt her spirit soar, she was so lucky to have the two people she loved most in her life close to her, to bring her comfort through the calm and rough seas of life. She felt Cameron was close by, sprinkling star dust on the three of them. It was honestly the happiest moment of her new life. Yes! The time was right, the stars had aligned and life would be good.

THE END

ACKNOWLEDGEMENTS

James Essinger MA, Conrad Press, for working alongside me, editing and publishing my novel, *Love in the Cloisters*.

The Irish Writers' Union, who were there to support me through my journey.

A big thank you to Marie for her dedication.

ABOUT THE AUTHOR

Irene Devereux lives in Dublin, Ireland with her family. She is a Master Hairstylist. Irene enjoys listening to the stories she hears from the many interesting characters she meets in her hairdressing world. She has styled hair on *The Tudors, Vikings* and *Penny Dreadful*, these were her magic moments. Irene has greatly enjoyed writing *Love in the Cloisters* and has plans for writing many more romantic novels.